Sky above and earth below. Where was she? Other than fucked.

The last thing she remembered was collapsing in a heap against the wall, her head too fuzzed to think straight. She hadn't been that drunk.

She rocked, trying to tilt onto her side, but the ropes that bound her were held up by something else. All she got for the effort was a wrenched shoulder.

"How are we feeling?" A woman's voice? Speaking accented Balladairan.

Touraine tried not to give away her surprise, but her heart beat faster. "Good," she grunted in Shālan. It was one of a handful of words she remembered from Tibeau.

The stranger laughed, harsh and barking. "Didn't hear that," she said. Then she repeated the word, smoothing out Touraine's rough pronunciation. Her boot pulled back in slow motion, and Touraine braced herself. When she kicked Touraine in the stomach, Touraine groaned through her teeth. Curled in on herself by reflex, only to strain her shoulders in their sockets.

"All right, Balladairan dog." The woman crouched in front of Touraine. She wore dark trousers tucked into heavy boots, and one of those Qazāli vests, with the hood up and the dark veil pulled over her nose and mouth. Lantern light reflected on dark, dark brown eyes shaded by angry eyebrows and outlined in crow's-feet.

She'd been taken captive by rebels. She was double fucked.

THE
UNBROKEN

MAGIC OF THE LOST: BOOK ONE

C. L. CLARK

orbitbooks.net

Copyright © 2021 by Cherae Clark
Excerpt from *The Jasmine Throne* copyright © 2021 by Natasha Suri
Excerpt from *Son of the Storm* copyright © 2021 by Suyi Davies Okungbowa

Cover design by Lauren Panepinto
Cover illustration by Tommy Arnold
Cover copyright © 2021 by Hachette Book Group, Inc.
Map illustration by Tim Paul
Author photograph by Jovita McCleod

Orbit
Hachette Book Group
1290 Avenue of the Americas
New York, NY 10104
orbitbooks.net

First Edition: March 2021
Simultaneously published in Great Britain by Orbit

Orbit is an imprint of Hachette Book Group.
The Orbit name and logo are trademarks of Little, Brown Book Group Limited.

The publisher is not responsible for websites (or their content) that are not owned by the publisher.

The Hachette Speakers Bureau provides a wide range of authors for speaking events. To find out more, go to www.hachettespeakersbureau.com or call (866) 376-6591.

Library of Congress Cataloging-in-Publication Data
Names: Clark, C. L. (Cherae L.), author.
Title: The unbroken / C.L. Clark.
Description: First edition. | New York : Orbit, 2021. | Series: Magic of the lost; book one
Identifiers: LCCN 2020027495 | ISBN 9780316542753 (trade paperback) |
    ISBN 9780316542692 (ebook)
Subjects: GSAFD: Fantasy fiction.
Classification: LCC PS3603.L356626 U53 2021 | DDC 813/.6—dc23
LC record available at https://lccn.loc.gov/2020027495

ISBNs: 978-0-316-54275-3 (trade paperback), 978-0-316-54267-8 (ebook)

Printed in the United States of America

LSC-C

Printing 1, 2021

In Memoriam
Samira Sayeh: Le soutien, l'inspiration, et la sagesse
Clarence Lewis "C. L." Clark: The O.G.

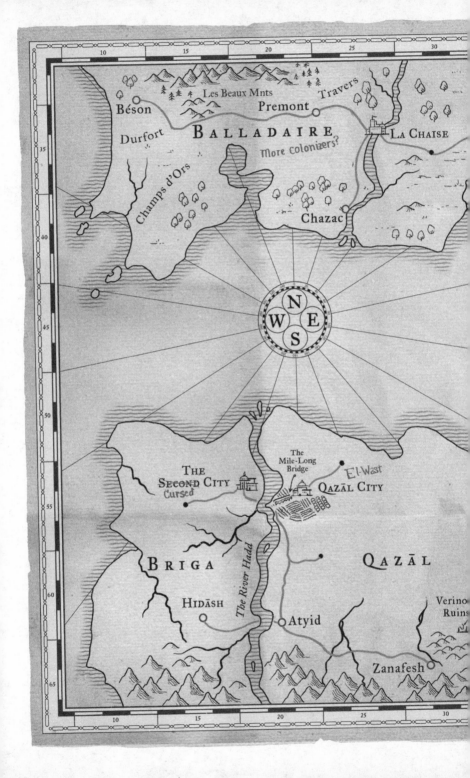

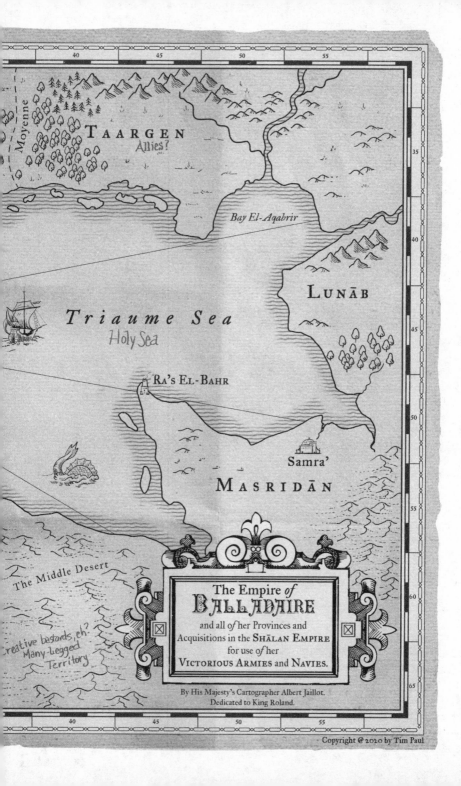

The Empire of
BALLADAIRE
and all of her Provinces and
Acquisitions in the SHĀLAN EMPIRE
for use of her
VICTORIOUS ARMIES and NAVIES.

By His Majesty's Cartographer Albert Jaillot.
Dedicated to King Roland.

Copyright @ 2020 by Tim Paul

THE
UNBROKEN

PART 1
SOLDIERS

CHAPTER 1

CHANGE

A sandstorm brewed dark and menacing against the Qazāli horizon as Lieutenant Touraine and the rest of the Balladairan Colonial Brigade sailed into El-Wast, capital city of Qazāl, foremost of Balladaire's southern colonies.

El-Wast. City of marble and sandstone, of olives and clay. City of the golden sun and fruits Touraine couldn't remember tasting. City of rebellious, uncivilized god-worshippers. The city where Touraine was born.

At a sudden gust, Touraine pulled her black military coat tighter about her body and hunched small over the railing of the ship as it approached land. Even from this distance, in the early-morning dark, she could see a black Balladairan standard flapping above the docks. Its rearing golden horse danced to life, sparked by the reflection of the night lanterns. Around her, pale Balladairan-born sailors scrambled across the ship to bring it safely to harbor.

El-Wast, for the first time in some twenty-odd years. It took the air from the lieutenant's chest. Her white-knuckle grip on the rail was only partly due to the nausea that had rocked her on the water.

"It's beautiful, isn't it?" Tibeau, Touraine's second sergeant and best friend, settled against the rail next to her. The wooden rail shifted under his bulk. He spoke quietly, but Touraine could hear the awe and longing in the soft rumble of his voice.

Beautiful wasn't the first thing Touraine thought as their ship sailed up the mouth of the River Hadd and gave them a view of El-Wast. The city was surprisingly big. Surprisingly bright. It was surprisingly… civilized. A proper city, not some scattering of tents and sand. Not what she had expected at all, given how Balladairans described the desert colonies. From this angle, it didn't even look like a desert.

The docks stretched along the river like a small town, short buildings nestled alongside what were probably warehouses and workers' tenements. Just beyond them, a massive bridge arced over shadowed farmland with some crop growing in neat rows, connecting the docks to the curve of a crumbling wall that surrounded the city. The Mile-Long Bridge. The great bridge was lined with the shadows of palm trees and lit up all along with the fuzzy dots of lanterns. In the morning darkness, you could easily have mistaken the lanterns for stars.

She shrugged. "It's impressive, I guess."

Tibeau nudged her shoulder and held his arms out wide to take it all in. "You guess? This is your home. We're finally back. You're going to love it." His eyes shone in the reflection of the lanterns guiding the Balladairan ship into Crocodile Harbor, named for the monstrous lizards that had supposedly lived in the river centuries ago.

Home. Touraine frowned. "Love it? Beau, we're not on leave." She dug half-moons into the soft, weather-worn wood of the railing and grumbled, "We have a job to do."

Tibeau scoffed. "To police our own people."

The thunk of approaching boots on the deck behind them stopped Touraine from saying something that would keep Tibeau from speaking to her for the rest of the day. Something like *These aren't my people.* How could they be? Touraine had barely been toddling in the dust when Balladaire took her.

"You two better not be talking about what I think you're talking about," Sergeant Pruett said, coming up behind them with her arms crossed.

"Of course not," Touraine said. She and Pruett let their knuckles brush in the cover of darkness.

"Good. Because I'd hate to have to throw you bearfuckers overboard."

Pruett. The sensible one to Tibeau's impetuousness, the scowl to his smile. The only thing they agreed on was hating Balladaire for what it had done to them, but unlike Tibeau, who was only biding his time before some imaginary revolution, Pruett was resigned to the conscripts' fate and thought it better to keep their heads down and hate Balladaire in private.

Pruett shoved her way between the two of them and propped her elbows on the railing. Her teeth chattered. "It's cold as a bastard here. I thought the deserts were supposed to be hot."

Tibeau sighed wistfully, staring with longing at some point beyond the city. "Only during the day. In the real desert, you can freeze your balls off if you forget a blanket."

"You sound...oddly excited about that." Pruett looked askance at him.

Tibeau grinned.

Home was a sharp topic for every soldier in the Balladairan Colonial Brigade. There were those like Tibeau and Pruett, who had been taken from countries throughout the broken Shālan Empire when they were old enough to already have memories of family or the lack thereof, and then there were those like Touraine, who had been too young to remember anything but Balladaire's green fields and thick forests.

No matter where in the Shālan Empire the conscripts were originally from, they all speculated on the purpose of their new post. There was excitement on the wind, and Touraine felt it, too. The chance to prove herself. The chance to show the Balladairan officers that she deserved to be a captain. Change was coming.

Even the Balladairan princess had come with the fleet. Pruett had heard from another conscript who had it from a sailor that the princess was visiting her southern colonies for the first time, and so the conscripts took turns trying to spot the young royal on her ship.

The order came to disembark, carried by shouts on the wind. Discipline temporarily disappeared as the conscripts and their Balladairan officers hoisted their packs and tramped down to Crocodile Harbor's thronged streets.

People shouted in Balladairan and Shālan as they loaded and

unloaded ships, animals in cages and animals on leads squawked and bellowed, and Touraine walked through it all in a daze, trying to take it in. Qazāl's dirt and grit crunched beneath her army-issued boots. Maybe she *did* feel a spark of awe and curiosity. And maybe that frightened her just a little.

With a wumph, Touraine walked right into an odd tan horse with a massive hump in the middle of its back. She spat and dusted coarse fur off her face. The animal glared at her with large, affronted brown eyes and a bubble of spit forming at the corner of its mouth.

The animal's master flicked his long gray-streaked hair back off his smiling face and spoke to Touraine in Shālan.

Touraine hadn't spoken Shālan since she was small. It wasn't allowed when they were children in Balladaire, and now it sounded as foreign as the camel's groan. She shook her head.

"Camel. He spit," the man warned, this time in Balladairan. The camel continued to size her up. It didn't look like it was coming to any good conclusion.

Touraine grimaced in disgust, but beside her, Pruett snorted. The other woman said something short to the man in Shālan before turning Touraine toward the ships.

"What did you say?" Touraine asked, looking over her shoulder at the glaring camel and the older man.

" 'Please excuse my idiot friend.' "

Touraine rolled her eyes and hefted her pack higher onto her shoulders.

"Rose Company, Gold Squad, form up on me!" She tried in vain to gather her soldiers in some kind of order, but the noise swallowed her voice. She looked warily for Captain Rogan. If Touraine didn't get the rest of her squad in line, that bastard would take it out on all of them. "Gold Squad, form up!"

Pruett nudged Touraine in the ribs. She pointed, and Touraine saw what kept her soldiers clumped in whispering groups, out of formation.

A young woman descended the gangway of another ship with the support of a cane. She wore black trousers, a black coat, and a short black cloak lined with cloth of gold. Her blond hair, pinned in a bun behind her head, sparked like a beacon in the night. Three stone-faced royal guards accompanied her in a protective triangle, their short gold cloaks blown taut behind them. Each of them had a sword on one hip and a pistol on the other.

Touraine looked from the princess to the chaos on the ground, and a growing sense of unease raised the short hairs on the back of her neck. Suddenly, the crowd felt more claustrophobic than industrious.

The man with the camel still stood nearby, watching with interest like the other dockworkers. His warm smile deepened the lines in his face, and he guided the animal's nose to her, as if she wanted to pat it. The camel looked as unenthusiastic at the prospect as Touraine felt.

"No." Touraine shook her head at him again. "Move, sir. Give us this space, if you please."

He didn't move. Probably didn't understand proper Balladairan. She shooed him with her hands. Instead of reacting with annoyance or confusion, he glanced fearfully over her shoulder.

She followed his gaze. Nothing there but the press of the crowd, her own soldiers either watching the princess or drowsily taking in their new surroundings in the early-morning light. Then she saw it: a young Qazāli woman weaving through the crowd, gaze fixed on one blond point.

The camel man grabbed Touraine's arm, and she jerked away.

Touraine was a good soldier, and a good soldier would do her duty. She didn't let herself imagine what the consequences would be if she was wrong.

"Attack!" she bellowed, fit for a battlefield. "To the princess!"

The Qazāli man muttered something in Shālan, probably a curse, before he shouted, too. A warning to his fellow. To more of them, maybe. Something glinted in his hands.

Touraine spared only half a glance toward the princess. That was what the royal guard was for. Instead, she launched toward the camel man, dropping her pack instead of swinging it at him. *Stupid, stupid.* Instinct alone saved her life. She lifted her arms just in time to get a slice across her left forearm instead of her throat.

She drew her baton to counterattack, but instead of running in the scant moment he had, the old man hesitated, squinting at her.

"Wait," he said. "You look familiar." His Balladairan was suddenly more than adequate.

Touraine shook off his words, knocked the knife from his hand, and tripped him to the ground. He struggled against her with wiry strength until she pinned the baton against his throat. That kept him from saying anything else. She held him there, her teeth bared and his eyes wide while he strained for breath. Behind her, the camel man's companions clashed with the other soldiers. A young woman's high-pitched cry. *The princess or the assassin?*

The old man rasped against the pressure of the baton. "Wait," he started, but Touraine pressed harder until he lost the words.

Then the docks went silent. The rest of the attackers had been taken down, dead or apprehended. The man beneath her realized it, too, and all the fight sagged out of him.

When they relieved her, she stood to find herself surrounded. The three royal guards, alert, swords drawn; a handful of fancy-looking if spooked civilians; the general—*her* general. General Cantic. And, of course, the princess.

Heat rose to her face. Touraine knew that some part of her should be afraid of overstepping; she'd just shat on all the rules and decorum that had been drilled into the conscripts for two decades. But the highest duty was to the throne of Balladaire, and not everyone could say they had stopped an assassination. Even if Touraine was a conscript, she couldn't be punished for that. She hoped. She settled into the strength of her broad shoulders and bowed deeply to the princess.

"I'm sorry to disturb you, Your Highness," Touraine said, her voice smooth and low.

The princess quirked an eyebrow. "Thank you"—the princess looked to the double wheat-stalk pins on Touraine's collar—"Lieutenant...?"

"Lieutenant Touraine, Your Highness." Touraine bowed again. She peeked at the general out of the corner of her eye, but the older woman's lined face was unreadable.

"Thank you, Lieutenant Touraine, for your quick thinking."

A small shuffling to the side admitted a horse-faced man with a dark brown tail of hair under his bicorne hat. Captain Rogan sneered over Touraine before bowing to the princess.

"Your Highness, I apologize if this Sand has inconvenienced you." Before the princess could respond, Rogan turned to Touraine and spat, "Get back to your squad. Form them up like they should have been."

So much for taking her chance to rise. So much for duty. Touraine sucked her teeth and saluted. "Yes, sir."

She tightened her sleeve against the bleeding cut on her left arm and went back to her squad, who stood in a tight clump a few yards away from the old man's camel. The beast huffed with a sound like a bubbling kettle, and a disdainful glob of foamy spittle dripped from its slack lips. Safe enough to say she had made an impression on the locals.

And the others? Touraine looked back for another glimpse at the princess and found the other woman meeting her gaze. Touraine tugged the bill of her field cap and nodded before turning away, attempting to appear as unruffled as she could.

When Touraine returned to her squad, Pruett looked uncertain as Rogan handed the older man off to another officer, who led him and the young woman away. "I told you to be careful about attracting attention."

Touraine smiled, even though her arm stung and blood leaked into her palm. "Attention's not bad if you're the hero."

That did make Pruett laugh. "Ha! Hero. A Sand? I guess you think the princess wants to wear my shit for perfume, too."

Touraine laughed back, and it was tinged with the same frustration and bitterness that talk of their place in the world always was.

This time, when she called for her squad to form up, they did. Gold Squad and the others pulled down their field caps and drew close their coats. The wind was picking up. The sun was rising. The Qazāli dockworkers bent their backs into their work again, but occasionally they glanced—nervous, scared, suspicious, hateful—at the conscripts. At Rogan's order, she and the conscripts marched to their new posts.

Change was coming. Touraine aimed to be on the right side of it.

CHAPTER 2

A HOMECOMING

A flea storm, the Balladairans in Qazāl called it, because grains of sand lodged in every improbable place on a body, climbing into buttoned jackets and nestling into cropped hair, whistling itchy fury into every home and guardhouse, no matter how tight the curtains were shut or how low a soldier tugged their field cap. It cast everything in brown shadow.

Touraine pulled her cap lower as the storm yanked at her black uniform coat while she and the other Balladairan Colonial conscripts stood at attention in the bazaar. Their faces were neutral, but Sergeant Pruett scanned the crowd. Sergeant Tibeau kept his eyes locked obediently forward, but he was probably contemplating every anti-Balladairan feeling he'd ever had. When the order had come for Touraine's squad to muster in the city's largest bazaar, a plaza lined with merchant stalls, the storm had become more than just a dark imagining on the edge of the horizon.

Sand skittered like dry rain against the wooden gallows in the center of the square. It flayed the Qazāli prisoners Touraine and Pruett had caught just this morning, ripping into their bare chests while they stood parched and peeling in the sun. It taunted Touraine and her squad, just like the Balladairans who called the desert-born conscripts "Sands."

Within the square of a horse-mounted guard, the Balladairan

princess shifted uncomfortably on horseback, eyes darting between the prisoners and the Qazāli civilians in the crowd. She didn't look nearly as confident as she had after the thwarted assassination this morning.

Only the Qazāli took the sand with equanimity, their bright hoods raised and sand veils or scarves wrapped to protect against the dust's assault.

As the Balladairan captain of Touraine's company strutted toward her, Touraine willed the scowl off her face, if only for the sake of the general at his side. Captain Rogan kept his bicorne hat low on his head to keep the wind at bay, preening and bowing toward anyone of higher rank. The general only ducked her head a little under the wind.

"Lieutenant Touraine. You've done well for yourself since I last saw you." General Cantic smiled, and Touraine's mouth went dry. "We have you to thank for this." The general nodded toward the prisoners awaiting their fates.

"General Cantic is giving you the hanging. I trust you won't botch it?" Rogan slipped in, trying to undermine Touraine immediately. His clipped, aristocratic accent curled Touraine's lip by reflex. His blue eyes were cold and his nose short and sharp, good for looking down. He thrust the prisoners' chain at her.

The wind blew hard enough to snap the nooses like whips.

"Of course, sir." Touraine chose to speak directly to the general.

"Excellent," Cantic said. "Move along. The weather's turning."

Touraine glanced at the sky and regretted it as stray granules of dust lodged in her eyes. She had been relieved to scuff dry land under her boots this morning, had never wanted to see another ship again. Now she wanted to get back on that wooden catastrophe and vomit her way back to Balladaire. So what if she had been born in this sand-fucked city? It was too long ago for her to remember, and she could see why she'd never missed it.

Still. The Qazāli rebels drew Touraine's eyes like a lodestone, and they squinted and scowled right back. The woman she had noticed, the old camel man, and three others. Five Qazāli prisoners, standing in loose dark trousers, stripped of the hoods and vests so many

Qazāli wore, and chained together. Their curly hair clumped with dried sweat. The brown skin of their bare chests reddened and peeled. Brown skin, like hers, like most of the Sands'. Touraine's nose burned at the smell of their piss. The prisoners must have stood there all day, maybe since their capture. If they hadn't been questioned first. The sun rose slowly, peeking over the buildings to the other side of the river, the ruins of an old city, out of the storm's reach. The chain was heavy and warm in Touraine's hand.

The pale Balladairan soldiers stood poised at attention, their musket butts digging into the earth. They formed another buffer between the princess on her horse and the restless Qazāli in the square. Touraine's attention, however, was primarily with the general. Ultimately, only General Cantic had the power to promote her, but maybe the princess would be grateful enough to commend her.

Cantic and a squat, official-looking woman walked up the wooden stairs, and Touraine followed, leading the prisoners by the chain. She gestured for Pruett to follow. From the new vantage point, she could see the tops of the clay buildings whose walls formed the edges of the bazaar, outlined against the approaching storm. Fine, maybe Tibeau was right. It was a little breathtaking.

Sergeant Pruett yanked each prisoner into position behind a noose. She nodded to Touraine, her eyes half-lidded, looking more sullen than usual. The russet-brown curls poking from her field cap were plastered darkly to the sides of her skull with sweat. Then she stepped back to wait next to the lever that would drop the rebels to their deaths. Touraine waited for her own cue on the other end of the platform.

The kick of Cantic's boots on the gallows platform killed the rumble of conversation. Time had made her even more severe. Her hair, which had grown more white than blond since Touraine had last seen her, was pulled back into a tight tail under her tricorne. Her hand rested on the pommel of her saber, and her broad shoulders were bonier but straight, despite the approaching wall of sand.

A woman worth studying, worth pleasing, worth staying close to. Touraine had been thrilled to learn she would be stationed at Cantic's base. Supposedly, the general had been expanding and protecting the desert colonies for years.

The other woman was less severe, but she cocked her head at Touraine and the other Sands in curiosity. She wasn't in an officer's uniform, which meant she had to be a government official. The governor. Touraine returned her focus to the general, like everyone else in the square.

In a commanding voice that echoed across the square, General Cantic said something in Shālan, the language of the broken southern empire. The words sounded like rocks rattling in a cup, and they caught everyone's attention. Touraine didn't know what they meant. Like everything else Touraine had taken from Qazāl when she was a kid, the language had been culled out of her.

Cantic continued in Balladairan. "Citizens, today we celebrate. Though the occasion is grim, justice has won a decisive victory." She gestured to the prisoners behind her with an open palm. "These rebels are guilty of attempted murder."

Touraine's eyes drifted back to the princess. She'd dismounted. Smart not to provide a raised target for more rebel assassins. The people who weren't looking at the condemned snuck glances at Her Highness. The heir to the Balladairan throne seemed small and fragile on the ground, surrounded for her own protection.

"With the help of the Qazāli magistrate, we have spoken with the prisoners"—there was no doubt what *spoken with* meant—"and we will find the other rebels involved. Anyone found aiding them or feeding them or sheltering them will die with them. However." General Cantic softened her tone marginally. "What is justice if it is not upheld by the law and the people? If you have any information about the rebel leaders, come to us. You will receive amnesty, a handsome reward, and gratitude for your dedication to our alliance."

The spectators craned their necks to see them: Touraine and Pruett, the general, the prisoners. Touraine and the Sands were an unspoken lecture: she was born Qazāli, but Balladaire had educated her, trained her to fight, fed her, kept her healthy. She had grown up civilized. The Qazāli could do much worse than cooperate.

General Cantic gave Touraine an encouraging nod.

The first of the condemned was a dark man with salt-crusted black hair that curled around his ears and a thick, close beard covering his chin. She hadn't seen him this morning, and he refused to make Touraine's job easier. She stood on tiptoes to loop the noose over his neck. The second person was the young woman, less bullish, delicate even. The fight in her was gone. She watched Touraine calmly and ducked into the noose, murmuring under her breath.

The woman was praying. Touraine had studiously ignored Sergeant Tibeau's praying in the barracks long enough to recognize the rhythms. Nearby, Cantic cleared her throat. Touraine shuddered and cinched the rope quickly, reciting to herself from the Tailleurist lessons: *There are no gods, only superstitions. No superstition can harm you.* And yet when their skin touched, Touraine felt a tingling sensation across her body.

She got through the others as quickly as she could, trying to forget the feeling. Instead, she felt only the pressure of everyone's eyes on her, and the tickle of her own sweat down her coat. The older man was the last one. He tried gamely to stand up straight. His shaggy gray hair hung in his face. It seemed like he'd aged decades since she'd met him at the docks, smiling warmly with his camel. *It wasn't real,* she told herself. He'd been a distraction, a pair of eyes. She pulled the noose around his sagging neck. As she tightened the rope, his eyes narrowed at her, then popped wide.

"You look just like—" the man rasped, working around his dry tongue. Louder, he rushed to get the words out. "You're Jaghotai's daughter, aren't you?"

Touraine startled and looked to Pruett, who held the drop lever. *Do it now!* Touraine said with her eyes.

"You're Hanan?" The old man's voice croaked from his throat.

Touraine staggered back at the sound of her old name. Her heart dropped into her gut like the gallows floor, and the air caught in her lungs.

The old man dangled.

Except for a few desperate kicks, the prisoners hanged in silence. Touraine saluted to Cantic and jogged down to stand in front of her soldiers as if nothing had happened. As if her heart wasn't rattled in its cage. Her men and women formed a tight square, five by five. Sergeant Tibeau caught her eye. He didn't need words to send a cold drip of guilt sliding between her shoulder blades.

The world felt muffled and slow. Beyond Captain Rogan, General Cantic had descended and left, leading the princess down one spoke of road. The true-born Balladairan soldiers had already marched to the Balladairan compound under their own captain's orders.

For the first time in over twenty years, Touraine was back in Qazāl. She looked at the swinging bodies. The old man jerked, and Touraine watched until he stilled.

How did he know who I am?

Rogan glanced at Touraine's platoon and then over to the sand-storm with a satisfied smirk. "Welcome home, Sands."

Touraine and her squad followed Rogan and the other soldiers north and east through the city to the compound, away from the storm. It would have been a long march even without the wind and dust that managed to thread through the winding roads. Still, the storm couldn't stop her from gaping now that there was light enough to see by and the city was coming alive.

Everything spiraling out from the bazaar square was clearly the older part of the city. The buildings were yellowed clay lined with cracks, and the roads had once been fitted with stones but were now mostly dirt with rugged juts to trip over. Qazāli workers prodded donkeys and goats—and once, even another camel—through the narrow passages but yanked the animals aside as the Sands marched by. The Qazāli's faces were swaddled in scarves and shawls against the stray dust. Piles of shit drew flies, and down one road, two filthy children shoveled the driest clumps into baskets.

Like at the bazaar, the shopkeepers here were mostly Qazāli, and so were the shoppers. Touraine wondered where all the Balladairans were. There'd been enough of them at the hanging.

You're Jaghotai's daughter.

Touraine wasn't the only one observing the city in proper daylight.

"This is sick, what they're doing to this place." Tibeau covered his face with a thick forearm.

"Huh." Pruett grunted. "Why? What's different?"

"Everything. Can't you tell?" Tibeau looked at Touraine for support.

Touraine shrugged. "I was barely five years old. It all looks the same to me."

All Touraine could see in her memory were vague senses of buildings, from a very low vantage point. Maybe the buildings were yellow brown, like the ones here, but she didn't recognize any sounds or people. For all she knew, her memories were just taking the images in front of her and throwing them back at her as if she'd had them all along.

"They're making us live on the scraps of the city. The Old Medina used to be beautiful. Look at this."

They passed through a massive, crumbling wall like the ones that surrounded the city, all carved with the curling shapes of Shālan script. Swirls and slashes and stylized squares, and how they amounted to words, Touraine would never know. The ceiling of the archway had been painted blue several times. The most recent layer had chipped to show a different shade of blue in some places, bare yellow stone in others.

"The New Medina used to be ours, too. Now it's their shops, their cafés, their homes."

He shot a dirty look at the pristine neighborhood they were passing through. Here—where the stone pavers were carefully placed and there was barely a whiff of animal or human shit, where the buildings were freshly sealed and sturdy—were the Balladairans. They poked their heads out from wooden shutters to check the progress of the storm.

"It's not just Balladairans, though." Touraine nodded toward brown faces over doublets, hair short and styled with Balladairan sleekness. "They don't look hungry."

"Because they've sold themselves to Balladaire."

"You don't know that. You don't know anything about—"

"Children, please." Pruett cut in, glaring meaningfully up ahead. Rogan walked with one of his men, but they were too close for loud, philosophical bickering.

Touraine and Tibeau slowed to match Pruett's pace. When Pruett spoke again, her voice was low and probing.

"So—did you recognize him?"

"What?" Tibeau looked between them. "Who?"

"On the gallows. The old man—he called her Hanan."

The look that Tibeau gave her was jealous and livid all at once. "So? Did you?"

The question caught Touraine off guard, though she'd expected it. She hadn't been able to let go of the memory of the man's face the entire walk. Or the way the woman had caught Touraine with her songlike prayer. A seed of doubt, trying to root.

She yanked it out like she always did. She was safer, stronger with Balladaire than without it. It looked like the Qazāli in this section of the city had learned that, too, and that was why they lived more happily than any other Qazāli in El-Wast.

"Do you remember Mallorie?" Touraine asked instead of answering Tibeau's question.

Tibeau and Pruett both flinched. Of course they remembered. Every Sand did. Mallorie, who'd been of an age with Tibeau and Pruett, had run away when she was fourteen, just a few years after they'd been brought to Balladaire. Cantic—a captain then—had Mallorie whipped, doctored in the infirmary, and kept under watch for months. Every Sand breathed a sigh of relief, even Touraine, who was only nine years old. The moment the Balladairans eased the leash, she ran again. Five Balladairan soldiers were in the firing squad that executed her when they caught her again.

"Do you remember what she looked like?"

Silence. Tibeau and Pruett were both taller than her, but they shrank for just a moment.

"Because I don't."

Pruett sucked her teeth. "Fair point. How do you know your memory's so sharp, anylight, Beau? It's been two sky-falling decades. Looks like the usual I-have-some-and-I-have-none split to me. Doubt it was nice and even when it was just Qazāli here."

Tibeau glared at them both. "You two can both go fuck off." He walked beside them in silence for a little while longer before falling back. His lover Émeline had already gone ahead to the compound. If she'd been here, she might have mediated better.

Once he'd left, Pruett ducked her head to look Touraine in the face. "Tour. Love. You're not all right."

"Course I am." Touraine forced herself to meet Pruett's gray-blue eyes.

"You just killed someone who knew you from before. Who knew you as Hanan. You aren't bothered?"

It was only the dust in the air that dried her mouth, that made it difficult to tell the truth. "I'm curious, I guess, but I don't know who Hanan is any more than you do. And that man didn't know me."

What would Cantic do to her if she thought that Touraine would run to the other side?

A smile quirked across Pruett's lips. "You forget—I did know Hanan. She was a stubborn clod of shit. She punched the biggest kid in the balls when she was six, and she's been insufferable ever since."

Touraine snorted. She did remember her first practice fight with Tibeau. She shook her head. "I was already Touraine by then. That's me, Pru."

You're Jaghotai's... No, she wasn't. She didn't know Jaghotai. She didn't want to.

They marched through the city, covered in dust, shielding their eyes with their arms and field caps, the perfect picture of Balladairan military might. They passed from the New Medina through another massive archway etched with stylized script in the shape of what might have been the sun. From there to the north, small town houses were clustered together like sheep. Directly east from the city gate loomed the yellow-gray walls of the Balladairan compound, constructed some fifty years or so ago.

It made Touraine thirsty just to look at it. Or maybe that was just the long city march. Her legs ached; she'd kept up with her exercises on the ship, but nothing quite prepared a person for a couple hours of marching like a couple hours of marching.

The only similarity to her old compound in Balladaire was the layout. Nothing green grew inside these walls, and the roads were trampled yellow dirt. Instead of thick gray stone blocks sealed with mortar, the walls were gritty chunks of sandstone wedged together. The yellow-brown buildings on the right were all the same—great square blocks. The barracks. The buildings on the left curved away from the street, making a small, dusty courtyard. The biggest building of the lot would be the administrators' building and their quarters. That would include General Cantic.

Balladairan guards stood up straight when Rogan approached the gate. One sneered as Touraine and the other Sands followed. His eyes were wide, incredulous, as if he were watching trained dogs marching in parade. She stared him down as they passed.

Touraine trudged to the mess hall. She wanted food and a chair and to take off her boots and maybe even drown herself in water. Before she could find shelter under the cool stone, though, a Balladairan boy ran up to her. He was sunburned across his cheeks, probably a few years her junior.

"You Touraine, then? I have a message from General Cantic." His voice was pitched to crack. Several years her junior, then. His black uniform was plain, no pins on his collar or rank stripes on his shoulders.

"Lieutenant Touraine." She folded her arms. Beside her, Pruett tensed. Touraine had gotten into more than one fight over her rank. She wouldn't this time, though. Not with Cantic so close, not with the chance for promotion at her fingertips. Her record was—mostly, minus some temper here or there—exemplary. "One of several," she growled. "What's the message?"

"There's several of you made it to lieutenant?" He threw his head back, laughing.

If you kill him, you definitely won't get promoted. Sky above, it would feel amazing, though.

Touraine felt Pruett's silent warning behind her. She snatched the paper from him. "At least we earn our ranks."

She shoved past him without looking back. She didn't know what else to expect in this new country, but some things would clearly stay the same.

"What's our dear old instructor want with you?" Pruett asked, close on Touraine's heels. "Think that she-wolf still loves whippings?" Her amusement was tinged with bitterness.

West of the compound, the sandstorm rolled north through the city and into the sea. Touraine held one hand across her face and flicked the note open with the other. Nothing but a summons and an ink stamp.

You're Jaghotai's daughter. Cantic had heard the man.

She forced a smile. "If she were going to kill me for some kind of treason, she wouldn't send a messenger first."

The logic managed to comfort her, until Pruett said, "If she were going to kill you, she'd do it when it suited her and not a second before."

Touraine snorted. "A kiss for luck, then?"

A shadow passed across Pruett's face. Touraine could tell she was scanning the compound, watching Balladairan blackcoats and Sands alike—watching them watch her and Touraine. A constant habit. While fraternizing within the brigade wasn't forbidden—in fact, it was the only fraternization allowed—Sands couldn't afford the weakness of public affection. You never knew if it might be used against you.

Touraine leaned in a hair. "If they see us as citizens," she murmured, "as more than bodies to throw in front of Taargen cannons, maybe we could be more than just this one day."

Pruett shook her head, her expression shuttered. "We have this. Please." She locked eyes with Touraine. "Don't say or do anything stupid. Kiss her ass like you used to. Lieutenant." She flicked a salute, and then she was gone, pushing away against the wind and into the canteen.

Touraine had thought about the general often since the woman had stopped being the Sands' instructor. Touraine had been thirteen and devastated when Cantic told them all she was going back to the field. She had been wearing a formal dress uniform with a lieutenant colonel's golden shoulder stripes.

The only people the Sands gossiped about more than each other were the instructors, and after Cantic left, rumors about her spread like a plague. She had been disgraced once, and teaching them had been her punishment; now she was forgiven. No, she had fucked her way up the ranks until she got to the duke—that was how she got a promotion so quick. No, Cantic was lying entirely, and it was just an excuse to retire without looking weak. Touraine had believed none of it and fiercely wished to be an officer under the woman one day. But after Cantic had left, Touraine had never thought she'd see the general again.

Now, after all that time, all those hopes to impress, here she was, summoned when she was sweaty with heat. Though she had changed her uniform and washed from a basin before the hanging, she imagined she still smelled like body odor and seaweed and fish gone bad. Her stomach looped itself in knots, and she hadn't wanted to be sick like this since the first week at sea. Yes, Touraine had stopped an attempt on the princess's life, but she'd also been recognized by one of the perpetrators. Would that condemn her, too, somehow?

He had called her out by name. The thought still made her shudder with—what? Revulsion wasn't right, and neither was fear. It was the sense that she had been walking a broad path along a cliff only to find it was a bayonet's edge. She was just waiting to be pushed.

And how she'd stumbled with the praying woman. If Cantic

thought Touraine had sympathized with the woman, this could be a different meeting entirely. One that ended with her own neck at the end of a rope. Touraine was long past the age when they were only whipped for sneaking prayers and hiding holy beads.

The administrative building was guarded by a sergeant at attention, rifle at her side. The sergeant was trying and failing to pretend the wind didn't bother her. Even though the storm was blowing north through the city, the wind here ran wild.

"Lieutenant Touraine to see General Cantic."

The soldier scanned Touraine up and down, lip curled. The effect was ruined by her flinching squint. "Address your betters appropriately, Sand."

"*Lieutenant* Touraine to see *General* Cantic, *Sergeant*." She leaned heavily on the subordinate title and left it at that. Irritation in the back of her throat threatened to bubble into temper as Touraine passed, but she swallowed it down.

She walked through the small hallway and up the stairs, dropping her eyes whenever another Balladairan passed her. They were all high-ranking military administrators or aides-de-camp. Here were officers in black and gold.

They made her feel small, even more conscious of the sand falling from the folds of her uniform to scatter across the floor. One day, she wouldn't tiptoe through compound halls. She would belong there. Her soldiers wouldn't be at the mercy of horse-faced bastards like Rogan. She'd have the certainty and safety that came with rank.

One day, even farther away, people would look at her like they looked at Cantic. She would command the same level of respect.

After passing door after plain door, Touraine knew instantly when she arrived. She knocked three times on the ornate wood.

The general's door was smooth with age and nicked by travel, but well cared for. Touraine smelled the polish. Carved rabbits chased each other along the bottom panels, and birds flew at the top. The middle panels were taken by smooth deer, two fawns and a buck grazing while the doe looked warily around for a threat.

Another rumor: before Cantic became the Sands' instructor, she was a captain in the field, instrumental in expanding the empire under King Roland. When her husband and two children died in the last Withering plague, the grief broke her. She couldn't fight anymore. The army brought her home to teach and recover.

Touraine reached to brush her fingertips across the buck's antlers.

The door swung open under her hand.

General Cantic stood in the doorway, looking sour. Not a good start.

"Are you deaf, soldier? I said come in."

"Apologies, General." Touraine saluted. "Your door. It's beautiful."

The general's eyes might have softened. Then the moment was gone, and her eyes were the blue ice chips Touraine remembered from her childhood.

Cantic had taken off her black coat with its golden arm, and her tucked shirt hung loose on her wiry frame. Her skin had leathered and freckled with sun and age more than Touraine had realized on the gallows. She still wore a thick grief ring on her right middle finger and a small one on each little finger.

Cantic finally cracked a smile. "Touraine. Lieutenant Touraine. I am glad to see you well. I always knew you'd advance. This morning was very well done."

Touraine smiled back, flush with pride and hope. "I think of your lessons regularly, General. It's good to see you again, sir."

"Good." Cantic sat behind a desk carved with as much artistry as the door. Her face sharpened from impressed teacher to inquisitor. The familiar eyes searching for missteps. "Now, first. Who was that man to you? The one at the gallows."

"No one, General."

"No one?"

"No one I know, sir."

The truth, no matter who asked.

"You know me better than he does," she added. "I've spent my entire life in Balladaire. My commanding officers are Balladairan. My teachers are Balladairan." She nodded at the general. "Sir."

Cantic nodded slowly, her face a bit too pinched for Touraine to think the general would dismiss this entirely. She shuffled the papers on her desk in silence, as if she were looking for a particular topic she wanted to discuss, and Touraine's heart crawled up her throat while she waited for the silence to break.

"I'm glad to hear it. Here, have a seat. Would you like some water?"

The sudden turn made her body lock in suspicion even as her stomach flipped with giddiness.

Cantic flicked her hand impatiently and poured water from the pitcher on a small side table. "Sit. You just marched through the whole sky-falling city, and you look drier than old balls." She caught herself and smirked. "I suppose you've heard worse by now."

Touraine took the cup out of reflex and sat slowly—an order was an order—but she wanted to look over her shoulder, just in case. This wasn't turning out to be the moment Touraine had dreamed of for months, of going from lieutenant to captain, of ousting Rogan. She didn't know what it was, but it was dangerous.

"You fought the Taargens. How was it?"

Touraine took a drink to delay. The water was lukewarm, but it felt like bliss on her dry throat, rinsing away the dust. Somehow, the question was a test.

What are you asking?

Yet another rumor: Cantic's loyalties were suspect; she hailed from Moyenne, the disputed region between Balladaire and its neighbor Taargen to the east; the spelling of her family name smacked too much of Taargen influence. Training the Sands had been penance and loyalty test, both. Touraine always cut down whoever brought this up. Cantic's loyalty was no more suspect than her own.

"We won many of our engagements. They weren't equal to our training, sir."

Their one notable loss was caused by an anti-Shālan captain of a Balladairan company who refused to send his men to help a "den of sand rats."

"No, of course not. God-loving bastards. They'll stay on their side of Moyenne for now. Tell me about your time behind their line."

Touraine's mouth went dry again, and there was not enough water in the world to wet it.

"As you said, sir. They're uncivilized."

Uncivilized. It meant they kept a god close. Touraine had never believed in magic. It was the sort of crutch the Tailleurist books urged the Sands away from. Gods were myths, and holding them close was the sign of a weak mind. Touraine had honed her mind against them.

"The Qazāli and all the other Shālans are just as uncivilized." Cantic leaned her elbows on the desk and stared at her. As if she could read the fear in the shape of Touraine's grip on the cup.

"You'll be stationed in the main guardhouse in the city, off rue de la Petière. Captain Rogan will rely on your leadership to set steady patrols in the city. The buildings are close together, so you'll want to watch the rooftops. And beware any proselytizing. Too many damned dissidents trying to stir up trouble."

Cantic gestured at a parchment on her desk, and Touraine realized it was a map of El-Wast. Smaller maps detailed the various quarters and medinas, but they all oriented themselves by the River Hadd flowing west of the city.

Touraine had never seen a map so beautiful—or, probably, so expensive. The Hadd's thick blue line flowed south from the sea, separating Qazāl from Briga and El-Wast from the abandoned Brigāni capital drawn in a faded gray. Small green flourishes denoted the rich farmland between the docks and the city; more elaborate ones indicated the Mile-Long Bridge that arched above that land (that wasn't an exaggeration; the walk from the docks to the city had felt like an age after the voyage). From the bridge, the Old Medina wall circled what Touraine understood as the oldest part of the city, including the Grand Bazaar. The New Medina wall made an additional circle around the city, a thin ring of shops and houses marked with bolder ink. And then there were the Balladairan additions, the military compound and the Quartier, where many of the Balladairan civilians lived.

Touraine sat back and exhaled. "Yes, sir."

"What I really need to know, Lieutenant, is the status of your men and women. This is an abrupt change. It might be troubling for some. We think that your presence—the colonial brigade—will have a positive effect on the citizens. To show that they can have power of their own if they're cooperative. When we open the ranks to Qazāli, I'll need experienced officers I can trust."

A recruitment initiative. The idea sent a thrill up Touraine's back. So far, Touraine's cohort of Sands was the only one. Maybe Balladaire was trying a different tactic, one that brought in Qazāli soldiers voluntarily. If the Qazāli could see how the Sands benefited from Balladairan employment, they wouldn't want to rebel. And if others were recruited, it meant being a conscript would become a job, not a life they were bound to. A choice. With rewards. And her, a captain over her own squad of Qazāli. She could make them a company to be reckoned with.

"You can count on me, of course."

And yet as she said it, Touraine thought of Tibeau's anger at the rich Balladairans in the New Medina. Cantic wasn't warning idly. She wouldn't be the only eyes the general picked to keep the Sands from straying. Eyes would be watching her, too. The test would continue.

She twisted the half-full cup of water in her hand. It was warm and brackish, but it was water. You'd die without it, especially in the desert.

"Is there anything else I can do, sir?"

Cantic's lips were pursed, thoughtful. "You've been invited to dine with Lord Governor Cheminade this evening."

"Sir?" Touraine's stomach lurched, even though she didn't understand the implications of the invitation. She didn't want to ask who that was and risk looking like a fool. "The colonial brigade?"

"No," Cantic said, as if she were just as baffled. "The invitation was for you personally. I believe she was impressed with your actions early this morning at the docks. I explained to her how irregular this would be, yet she insists. That means you don't have much time to prepare." Her voice went sharp, the confusion falling away. "Treat it as a military ceremony. Speak to no one unless spoken to, and when you are spoken to, know that you speak with my reputation at stake. Do you understand, Lieutenant?"

"Sir. Yes, sir." Already Touraine's stomach tied itself in knots over the nerves. And the excitement. No Sand had ever been in this position before. Their status *could* change, if they were noticed by the right people.

The general eased back. As if she could read Touraine's thoughts, she said, "No colonial soldier has ever been in such company. Perhaps you can further prove yourself. A carriage will retrieve you from the guardhouse at sunset after you've settled your troops. Perhaps time will see you in charge of a guardhouse yourself." General Cantic smiled warmly again, like she was oblivious to any threat in her words. "Dismissed."

The guardhouse where Cantic had stationed Touraine and her squad had once been a home, "borrowed" from a "generous" Qazāli merchant and repurposed by the Balladairans. A small sign nearby read, "rue de la Petière." It was in the Ibn Shattath district in the Old Medina, near the Grand Bazaar square. The gallows square.

The sandstorm had finally blown itself out, and the sun emerged from behind the nearest building, like a soldier leaving cover. Touraine ducked her head down to catch the glare on the brim of her cap. In less than an hour, it would be gone, and she'd be cast back into cool shadow.

Across the narrow street were more of the old city's crumbling clay-brick buildings. The whole city had no distinct shape to it. Buildings crammed themselves along the streets, not caring how much space there was: if there was no room, the building shoved itself in anylight, leaving barely enough room for a couple to walk arm in arm. The streets themselves were a labyrinth. How could anyone know where they were going in this city? As far as Touraine could see, though, all the main roads wide enough for multiple carts and livestock led to the Grand Bazaar. On the walk back into the city, they'd passed a couple of the smaller bazaars, where people were doing business as if the storm had never come through.

The narrow streets would make a good defense for a smaller force, and whoever had the rooftops would have the advantage.

The entire building had been claimed by the Balladairan military, and because of the winding, attached-at-the-rooftops nature of Qazāli architecture, that included almost the entire street. Within, Touraine's platoon could live under the close watch of their Balladairan handlers, with Captain Rogan's horse-ass face in charge of it all.

The Qazāli natives who passed them on the street stared at Touraine and her soldiers like they were animals on display in a menagerie.

Touraine scowled. She wasn't the one who looked like a bird, bright clothes flapping in the wind.

"This our shithole, then, sir?" The jaunty voice belonged to Aimée, a decent fighter who was strong in formation. She had a mouth worse than Pruett's and a sour sense of humor, but it was still a sense of humor.

"It's not a shithole, Aimée. Go in and get comfortable."

Touraine didn't like the way the Qazāli kept looking at them, and she really didn't like the way some of her soldiers were looking back. A few soldiers wore hostile sneers and a couple looked curious, but most of them were uneasy, and jumpy soldiers didn't make an easy peace.

Touraine plucked Pruett's sleeve and spoke to her in a low voice. "Get a couple of soldiers on patrol around the building and someone out here. Everyone else, inside."

Thirty soldiers filed past her, but Tibeau held back. He stared back at the civilians, searching faces. "Sergeant?" Touraine said softly.

"Do you think anyone will recognize us? The rest of us, I mean." His voice was barely audible over the city's noise. There was a longing in his voice that made her heart beat faster.

"No." The word came out sharper than she'd meant. "And in case you haven't noticed, most would rather stab us than share dinner."

A gang of kids ran by, slowing to stare at Touraine and her squad, the Shālans in Balladairan uniforms. Did the children find them strange? Being so close to the main commercial section of the city, Ibn Shattath was a mix of the lowest and the highest and everyone in between, from Qazāli merchants in Balladairan clothes to Balladairan servants running errands. With the spectacle of soldiers gone, most moved on quickly.

Touraine chanced a look at Tibeau's face. The smile she found was grimmer than she was used to, more like Pruett's. "Someone recognized you," he said.

It felt like a shove. A friendly sparring match turned cruel. She met him stare for stare as he tested her, asking her to bend.

"I was ten when I was taken," he added. "I'd already had time to grow into my delicate features." He batted his lashes over brown eyes full of desperate hope. He tried to hold on to the joke, but his voice cracked. "I should be even more recognizable, shouldn't I?"

Touraine forced a chuckle despite the growing tension between them. Tibeau wasn't what someone would call a pretty man. Like her, he was crossed by scars from growing up with the instructors and pocked by even more from going to war for Balladaire. When Touraine first met him, she'd just learned what a bear was from a lesson book. With his short dark hair, furry arms speckled with moles, and taut belly, he'd looked like a cub. Now he was full-grown. She still sparred with him for practice, but she beat him only four out of ten times, maybe. It hurt, now, to watch the tentative slump of his shoulders.

A scrawny man wearing only loose trousers ran a rickshaw past them, barefooted. He avoided colliding with them, but his cargo still shouted at him. A soft, blond Balladairan man, the lace from his clothes dripping from the cab. She felt Tibeau's anger pulling taut like a bowstring.

She gripped the back of one of Tibeau's thick arms. "Don't bring trouble on us, Beau."

"And you'd know all about that, wouldn't you?"

"I'm not as stupid as I used to be." It had been almost ten years since

Touraine had gotten her friends whipped for fighting with Rogan, before he was their captain.

She tugged him toward the guardhouse with one last look around the emptying street.

The entryway to the home had a clever partition that denied large groups a quick entrance. If anyone tried to attack, they would have to enter one or two at a time; and using muskets would be impossible. Probably not the original intent of the design.

The building rose in a square surrounding a courtyard with a gurgling fountain. It was the wettest sound since the ocean, and the air within had a clean smell. Touraine felt more comfortable already, with everyone outside cut away. Immediately, everything was simple again.

She divided everyone into rooms on the first and second stories, four or five to a room. To the left of the entrance was an office, already set up with papers. That would be Rogan's domain, then, and the biggest room would be his. Probably at the far end, opposite the entrance. To the right, there was a room with a couple of low tables and pillows to make a rough common room.

Touraine nodded, satisfied. It was already better than any of their other postings. She squeezed Tibeau's shoulder. "Be easy, Beau. Find Émeline. Let's have a drink."

"Easy." He grunted. "Right. So easy."

He and Émeline joined Pruett and the other Sands in the common room for games of tarot and cups of nutty-flavored beer. Touraine beckoned Pruett with a look. Her sergeant followed her out of the common room and back into the open courtyard.

It might have been a beautiful place before. Back when water flowed from the pale stone petals of the fountain and the planting troughs were full of living flowers instead of dried husks on their way to decomposing. The ground was scattered with dirt and dead leaves and animal shit, bird and otherwise. Someone would go on cleaning duty.

Pruett sidled in close. "What'd you do this time, Lieutenant?" When Touraine didn't smile back, Pruett dropped the wryness. "Did Cantic say something?"

"I've been invited to a dinner," Touraine whispered. "Tonight. With the governor."

"What the sky-falling fuck?"

"Shh. I don't want everyone to know—wait, should I tell them?" Touraine glanced over her shoulder. "Everything is so tight. It feels like one wrong move and—"

"Like someone's got a flame hovering over a fuse, and all you'd have to do is spook them at the wrong moment. I know." Pruett nodded gravely. She took Touraine's hand briefly and squeezed it before dropping it again.

Underneath it all, the unspoken hung. She felt it in the other Sands' glances at her, some covert, some frank and curious. They were home, and she had been recognized. They were home, and allegiances were up in the air. Only, they weren't. She'd have to address it before she left for the governor's dinner. Leaving her soldiers like this, on edge, in the middle of such a mess, was a bad idea.

"It feels like I have a chance, Pru." Touraine searched Pruett's eyes for any hint of validation. "Like maybe they're starting to take us seriously for once."

Her sergeant raked her hands through her short hair, dried stiff and at odd angles from sweat. "Sky above. The governor." Pruett gave her a quick kiss on the mouth. "Just don't—"

"Get us into any trouble. I know." Touraine rolled her eyes, and Pruett's mouth quirked up at the corners.

Touraine was considering the words she would say to her squad, when a soldier on guard shouted angrily from the street.

In seconds, the other Sands were outside, just in time to see the barrage of rotten food pelting the guardhouse walls. An egg sailed past Touraine's face, and she ducked. The sulfur smell cracked open behind her, but she tracked its trajectory to a Qazāli man in a glaring yellow hooded vest.

The handful of Qazāli scattered, except him. He jogged backward, trying to get in one last shot with his eggs. How he didn't expect Touraine's fist in his jaw, she didn't know. She was proud of the punch;

it echoed all the way through her chest to her hips. For a second, he hung suspended in the air. For a second, some idiot part of her brain thought she'd made a mistake. The only Qazāli she'd ever punched before were other Sands, and you didn't hit your soldiers like she hit him.

That idiot part of her brain was small compared to her well-trained instincts. She got him down with a knee in his back and locked his wrists in her hands. Passersby watched from a distance.

Let them look. Let them see what they can be a part of if they have any sense. They wouldn't beat the Sands with rotten eggs and cabbages. Her hands clenched tight around the man's wrists, her nails digging into his skin.

It was almost sunset. Her carriage would come soon. She couldn't afford to get bloody. Behind her, Pruett and the others waited for orders, batons ready. She dragged the half-conscious man to his feet. "Take him in. Cézanne, you're out here with Philippe, now. Patrols are three men on."

Anger welled up in her, hot and defensive, as Tibeau approached. She gave him a sharp look. He misinterpreted it. "We could let this one go," he said close to her ear. "With a warning. Show them we're open—"

"We are not open, Sergeant. And if you think we are," she continued through gritted teeth, "we should have a chat about your fitness for this position. Do you understand?"

"Sir." He straightened with a snap, his face so blank Touraine knew he was as pissed as she was.

Good. He needed to know she wasn't fucking around. She wouldn't give Cantic a reason to question her loyalty, and that meant he couldn't, either.

The Qazāli man would be bound and thrown into a room for holding. Rogan could arrange for his transport to the jail in the compound.

Back in the common room, the mood was brittle. Touraine didn't like the taste of the beer, but she drank a cup anyway. It busied her hands and cooled her off. She kept glancing anxiously toward the exit.

She had cleaned up, put on a fresh uniform. Even stolen a bit of the cologne Aimée had splurged on with their meager salaries.

Tibeau slouched in the corner against the wall, arms crossed over his chest, Émeline beside him with a hand around his waist. Aimée leaned on one of the tables, tapping her fingers noisily and looking from Touraine to the other Sands. That troublemaker was just barely holding in a smile at the tension.

Pruett sat beside Touraine, a cigarette pinched between her lips. *Now?* Touraine asked with her eyes. Pruett nodded.

Sighing, Touraine pushed herself up to her feet. "All right, everyone. Let's talk about this. Some of us are home now, yes?"

Several nods, but some of the Sands had been taken from other nations in the Shālan Empire, like Masridān or Lunāb farther east.

"And even if Qazāl isn't where you came from, you're closer to home than you've ever been, right?" More nods.

"You're feeling frustrated and confused. I was, too. The things that are confusing you aren't real, though. If you're torn between your post and some idealized past, stop and think a minute." Touraine jerked her thumb toward the street beyond the guardhouse wall, where Philippe and Cézanne kept watch. "The people you imagine welcoming you? That's them."

Thierry shifted his shoulders, glancing at Tibeau, as if for a cue. Thierry was Qazāli, too—she remembered that much.

It had been so long since any of them had talked about where they were from that Touraine wasn't even sure whom she should keep the closest eye on. In Balladaire, she had been on the outside of the warm circles when the older children talked about home and how they'd go back one day and what they missed most. If the instructors heard them talking about Qazāl or the other colonies, they were beaten, and the memory-spinning grew more and more hushed until the only thing left was silence around all they'd left behind.

"I know some of you think this is our chance." Touraine avoided glaring at Tibeau like she wanted to and leveled her gaze at each soldier. "And it is." A shock rippled around the room, and she put her hands up.

"Not to leave. To rise. I've spoken to Cantic. About a promotion. No more Rogan." She held her hands out to encompass the guardhouse. "This building would be ours. I've even been invited to a dinner with the governor-general tonight. I'll be representing our interests."

Everyone sat upright or held their drinks or cards still in shock. Touraine nodded hopefully.

"So while we wait, we watch our people get crushed under Balladairan boots?" Tibeau said softly. "Until we get to do it ourselves."

Sky-falling fuck.

She matched his softness, her voice carrying through the quiet room. "The best way to help them is to show them what they gain if they stop fighting."

"We shouldn't have to remind you what happens if you desert." Pruett's voice was sharp. "Remember Mallorie."

Everyone looked down at their boots or their drinks at that. Better for them not to delude themselves. Aimée's amusement disappeared as she nodded thoughtfully.

Touraine felt a stab of jealousy. Her soldiers were split on two sides, to stay or to go, but they weren't looking to her for guidance. Even though she was their lieutenant, they respected Tibeau and Pruett. But Touraine knew Balladaire. She knew its systems, and she knew how to be what it needed.

"It'll take getting used to," Touraine said finally. "I'm not asking anyone to be perfect. Rest up tonight."

A chorus of "Yes, sirs" followed her out.

"Good luck," Pruett murmured, squeezing Touraine's forearm.

On reflex, Touraine winced at the touch. The cut she'd gotten this morning had been clean and shallow, but long enough to feel inconvenient whenever she flexed her skin tight. It hadn't even bled through the last bandage she'd put on, so she hadn't bothered to change it when she bathed. Odd thing was, though, it didn't hurt at all when Pruett grabbed it.

Though Touraine didn't think Cantic the type to pull a prank, she was still surprised to see the one-horse carriage waiting for her outside the guardhouse in the early twilight. The Balladairan driver just nodded for her to get in the cab. She'd barely closed the door before he set the horse off, and she jostled on the hard seat. A rough start.

Touraine tried not to think about what her soldiers were saying about her in the guardhouse. She had to give them space to work out their feelings without her oversight, and trust Pruett to report any changes in the temperature.

Instead, she turned her thoughts forward. She was exhausted. She'd gone from the ship, to the hanging, to Cantic, to her soldiers' teetering loyalties, and now to this. Excitement kept her alert. Maybe Pruett was right to be nervous, but Touraine had a good feeling.

Tonight would change everything. She was going to become someone.

Touraine remembered her arm as the carriage trundled through the Quartier to the governor's home. In the darkness of the cab, she pulled her left arm out of its sleeve. Blood hadn't seeped through the bandage. Gingerly, she tugged it off.

Before panic could seize her, the carriage stopped.

"Shit." Touraine stuffed her arm back in her coat and hid the bandage in her pocket just as a footman opened the door. She tried to pull herself together. If she fucked up this chance to catch the Balladairans' attention, she wouldn't get another one.

But even as the footman—a footman!—led her from the carriage to the governor's house, the back of her mind spun in a panic over this new secret.

There'd been nothing but a thin line of blood on the wrap, and a thin silver scar across her skin.

It had already healed.

CHAPTER 3

THE GOVERNOR-GENERAL

"Princess Luca! It is my absolute pleasure to welcome you to my home and to Qazāl."

At the sound of her name, Luca Ancier startled in her carriage. The door had been thrown open, and a pale, round Balladairan woman with gray-streaked chestnut hair grinned at her from the ground. Luca had arrived, then, at Lord Governor Cheminade's home.

It was a short trip from Luca's town house in the Balladairan Quartier to the governor-general's, but it felt even shorter.

Luca had been thinking of the hanging. How hot the sun had been. How the sky had darkened in the distance as clouds of sand threatened to engulf the city. How the old man had cried out at the last and the young woman had twitched for long seconds after—Luca didn't know how long, because she hadn't the stomach to watch.

Like the heat, the old man's voice had followed her into her own town house and up to her study as she unpacked her books and placed them on the empty shelves that were waiting for her.

They were the rebels she had come to stop. Them, and men and women like them, perhaps hidden in the crowd. And when she stopped the rebellion and eased the unrest in the colony's capital city, she could show her uncle that she had the skill to rule. She would claim the throne that was her right.

The governor-general herself handed Luca down from the carriage. Luca saw the woman glance at her leg, but it seemed less boorish curiosity and more careful concern. Luca warmed slightly toward the woman.

When Luca had both feet and her cane on sturdy ground, Lord Governor Cheminade bowed deeply. "Your Highness. It is a pleasure to meet you. Your father always spoke proudly of you when you were a child. You've grown into a striking young woman. My household is at your service, as am I."

At first, Luca was put off by the effusiveness, preparing to fend off the first sycophant. At the mention of her father, she checked the impulse. Of course Cheminade would have known her father. She'd been the governor-general of the Shālan colonies for almost fifty years, as long as Balladaire had called the broken Shālan Empire her colonies. Cheminade would have spoken to her father regularly, surely. Something like jealousy bred with hopeful longing in her chest.

Most importantly, that might make Cheminade an ally as Luca worked to challenge her uncle Nicolas for her throne. First, however, she would calm the unrest in the colony.

"Thank you, Lord Governor. It's likewise a pleasure." Luca bowed her head in return.

The governor's smile reached into full cheeks, plump and still touched pink by the sun. Her eyes crinkled with pleasure. "Come, come. You must be famished. I know a thing or two about ship food. That's why I haven't gone back home all these years." She wrinkled her nose distastefully, then laughed.

She beckoned Luca to follow her into the house, and Gillett, the captain of the royal guard, fell in behind Cheminade. Luca's two other guards brought up the rear. Her constant shadows.

Cheminade kept talking as she led the princess into the town house, but Luca lost the conversation entirely as she gaped around the woman's home.

Luca was not a person to be surprised by finery, but Cheminade's home was cluttered with the bounty of a life of exploration. A massive lion pelt nailed to the sitting room wall greeted her first. The maned head was still attached, the darker ruff sticking out stiffly at all angles, its eye sockets empty and mouth gaping to show yellowed teeth almost as long as her fingers. Shelves lined the walls, and they were crammed with trinkets of gold and silver: creatures that looked human aside from an abundance of limbs or the rears of beasts, long-spouted oil lamps, intricately patterned cups and plates—and even a small skull that Luca hoped had belonged to a monkey.

She reached out a hand to stroke the lion pelt as they passed it, and Cheminade paused the stream of her chatter.

The governor ruffled the lion's mane casually, but her smile held the tilt of pride. "A gift from the wild tribes that roam the desert. They're sovereign, never did bow to the Shālan emperors. They wouldn't abandon their god, as one of their leaders explained to me. Call themselves the Many-Legged, for the animals they worship, you see."

"A gift?" Luca tentatively stroked the mane, too. The fur was coarse, the strands thick. The empty face sent a chill up her spine.

Before Cheminade could respond, another guest entered the sitting room from the foyer. He wore a thin woolen tailcoat over broad shoulders and a body that looked like strength only just softening in his middle. His knee-length breeches showed thick calves.

Casimir LeRoche, comte de Beau-Sang, a small region in southern Balladaire. His eyes were bright when he saw Luca, and he immediately dipped into an elaborate bow.

"Your Highness," he murmured to the ground. "A pleasure to see you on this side of the empire." He allowed himself to be led into the dining room by a servant, but not without one brief smile. Where Cheminade's grin was open and enthusiastic, Beau-Sang's smile was sharp, his lips thin. Luca watched his broad back as he departed. Beau-Sang owned the quarries, which meant anyone who needed sandstone or quartz had to pay him for the pleasure.

Which meant he was one of the most powerful men in the colony, even if he didn't have the highest rank.

At the door to the dining room, a Qazāli footman in a simple gray tailcoat and blue knee breeches bowed and announced Luca to the room. Inside, a host of Qazāl's most established Balladairans waited while a string quartet played in the background. Some she recognized—nobles who had come south to explore new ventures; others she did not—likely merchants, or possibly friends of Cheminade's. Even, to her greatest surprise, the Sand from the hanging, the one the old man had yelled at, was there, wearing a crisp black uniform. Luca realized she was holding her breath and had clenched her cane in her fist. With effort, she released the air and her grip and followed the footman to her seat.

Then she saw that the three tables in the room were all low, in the Qazāli style. Her heart sped up. She couldn't afford to show any signs of weakness here, not yet.

Her host recognized the hesitation. Cheminade's mouth went round, a perfect O of realization. Before Cheminade could make any embarrassing efforts to accommodate her, Luca smiled tightly.

"It's fine."

"I only wanted to give you a sense of Qazāl's traditions and culture, Your Highness. I'm so sorry."

"Truly, Lord Governor. I'll be all right."

She wasn't, not really. Though Gil helped her down with a steady arm, they were all expected to sit cross-legged. After a quarter of an hour, the pain had her shifting as imperceptibly as she could. Others, at least, were having similar difficulties. Down the table, the dowager marquise de Durfort was complaining loudly about the arrangements—"The indecency of sitting like barbarians!" Luca smiled privately, thinking of Sabine de Durfort and how, after one of their nights together, the new marquise contemplated where, exactly, to send her mother to get the old woman out of the way. Apparently, Qazāl was not far enough.

To distract herself from the pain, Luca turned to the food instead, including a Qazāli dish composed of beans that Cheminade called "chickpeas" and various vegetables. Round loaves of bread were stacked at intervals along the table, as were small roasted chickens, seasoned with a smoky red spice.

To Luca's right, Cheminade dug into the meal, explaining the dishes to Luca as she went. Somehow, the comte de Beau-Sang had gotten himself placed directly across from Luca, so that they were sharing the same pile of bread, along with another figure Luca had not expected to see so soon and in such social circumstances. General Cantic, in a fresh black uniform with a general's golden sleeve, sat to Beau-Sang's left, across from Cheminade. Cantic wielded her knife and fork surgically, taking small efficient bites and staring intently at her food— except for whenever she glanced at the Sand, who sat beside her. The Sand who had helped stop the assassination attempt.

Luca had never met one of the conscripts before. The woman wore a lieutenant's double wheat stalks on her collar—not near high enough to accompany Cantic to a meal with the elite Balladairans of the city under normal circumstances. Was she Cantic's protégé? The Sand sat quietly, observing the flow of conversation. She had steady, dark eyes, a sharp jaw, and black hair cut close to the scalp. She easily imitated Cheminade's unique way of eating the Qazāli food, folding the bread and scooping the chickpeas with tidy efficiency. She seemed completely unflustered by her return to her home country, the almost assassination, and the hanging.

Luca realized Beau-Sang had asked her a question and was waiting for an answer. His focus was entirely on her. He reminded Luca of an overturned fruit basket: his straw-colored hair, eyes like ripe blueberries, ruddy apple cheeks, and squashed strawberry of a nose.

"I'm sorry, what was that, monsieur?"

He smiled. "Is Qazāl everything you expected?" His look took in the food, the tables, and Cheminade's dining room, which was as full of trophies as the sitting room.

Luca was still grappling with that question herself. Whenever she had thought of her father's addition to the Balladairan Empire, she had imagined something more beautiful. More adventurous. More benevolent. The hanging alone was a sharp contrast to those visions, as were the dirty, disheveled masses of people her carriage had navigated through to get here.

"There were some surprises. How often are there hangings like today's?" she asked, rubbing her thigh beneath the table. A dull ache throbbed wherever the bones had broken and mended poorly—which was everywhere.

Beau-Sang's face went grim. "The rebels have been getting bolder, but this is the first attempt on someone's life, Your Highness. I'd say their numbers are growing. They need a firmer hand, or we'll all lose our livelihoods. You, above all, shouldn't be put at risk." He looked pointedly at the governor.

Luca glanced at Cantic. The general clenched and unclenched her fist around her knife before stabbing another vegetable. They had done their best to keep knowledge of the attack to those who had been there and those who needed to know: Luca, Cantic, Cheminade. They couldn't stop gossip that the soldiers and dockworkers spread, though.

Cheminade arched an eyebrow back. "Actually, Your Highness, our execution rates have remained consistent with the last five years or so. There was an increase in rebel activities, but that's why we've asked our dear general to step in. Her experience with the Brigāni and the Masridāni will be invaluable, I'm sure." Despite Cheminade's warm tone of voice, there was a bite to her smile that made Luca suspect this wasn't a compliment.

On Cheminade's other side, someone struggled to suppress a cough. Luca craned around and saw the only other non-Balladairan guest. The Qazāli man clutched his napkin to his face while Cheminade stroked his back intimately and pushed a cup of wine at him. He waved her away. Across from him, the Sand soldier was surprised at their intimacy, too—though she didn't have the grace to hide her expression, eyes wide, mouth half-open. The general whispered something sharply to her, and the Sand mastered herself.

"My soldiers' comportment has been exemplary," Cantic responded coldly. She nodded at the soldier beside her. "As you've noticed. The lieutenant and her troops will continue to do what must be done."

Luca had never known Cantic intimately, only by reputation as one of the bloodiest, most effective generals in the Balladairan military. Little was based on fact, however; the original primary reports were mysteriously unavailable, even to Luca—she'd looked. One text credited Cantic only with "Masridān's expedient surrender." Whispers spoke of massacre.

Yet Cantic was one of Guard Captain Gillett's close friends. She belonged to a minor noble house that came from the oft disputed and currently Balladairan region of Moyenne, and many suspected future treachery, but her service record was—almost—impeccable. Luca found it difficult to believe that Gil, with his distaste for so many nobles, would stomach someone so brutal, no matter how effective.

Luca turned the subject slightly. "Which colonial teaching method did you use, then, General? Droitist, I take it?"

Cantic looked surprised at first, then she frowned in disgust and shook her head. "No. The Droitists are cruel. They have no idea what it takes to run an army, let alone foster loyalty."

"So you're a Tailleurist?" Luca asked her.

The older woman stroked her chin with a thumb, and Luca wondered if she had looked like this planning the Sands' lessons years ago, rubbing her face and concentrating on the theories of leadership like Luca had. Luca also wondered if Cantic realized her dear uncle regent was behind the Droitist theories she thought were so ineffective.

"I suppose you could say so. They're the closest thing. The Tailleurists like their ideas of pruning and encouraging. I developed a suitable combination of the two, I think. Cut off the most undesirable traits and encourage them in other ways. Look at the orphan schools run by the Droitists in the empire—there's one in southern Qazāl, if you ever visit. The children are miserable wretches. Half-starved for the slightest infraction. If the children had a chance to escape or kill their masters, they'd have no reason not to take it."

Beau-Sang chuckled heartily enough that his barrel of a torso jostled the table. "General, I never pegged you for a sentimentalist."

The general's lips went tight. "Destroy your soldiers and you make them useless."

"Nonsense. Look at my boy here. Richard. Strong Balladairan name." Beau-Sang snapped once, and his personal lackey knelt by his side with a pitcher of wine.

The lackey was a young Qazāli boy, not more than ten years old, with somber brown eyes. As he refilled Beau-Sang's wine, Luca noticed he was missing two of his fingers. The knuckles were covered in thick scarring.

"He was at one of the Tailleurist charity schools. They're too soft there. You don't want them to be useless. If he'd stayed there, he'd finish and still be fit for nothing but begging."

The young conscript stiffened beside Cantic, arrested midbite, and Luca wondered what the soldier thought of her own education. She didn't look half-starved, but the quick, furtive glance she gave Cantic didn't seem so far from the looks the boy with the missing fingers gave Beau-Sang.

"He certainly appears eager to please." Luca tilted her head in acknowledgment; she couldn't bring herself to smile.

Beau-Sang saw where Luca's eyes lingered. "You wouldn't tolerate disobedience from a hound, would you? His Grace the duke regent has the right of it there. We should be grateful for his ideas."

Cheminade was murmuring to the Qazāli man beside her. Though Luca couldn't see his face, she saw the tender hand Cheminade placed on top of his darker one, the gentle squeeze.

Luca tapped her fingers idly on her utensils. "We have the perfect example of the two schools of thought. Why not let the lieutenant speak for herself?" She opened her hand to the conscript. Frankly, she had always thought her uncle's theories a little *too* stringent, but she'd never had the chance to speak to someone on the practical end of them.

At first, the lieutenant looked startled. Her voice cracked. "I am grateful, Your Highness." She cleared her throat and tried again. "For the general's steady hand. Military training, reading and writing.

History. It's an education as good as anyone else's in Balladaire, and we're better soldiers for it. We—the colonials—almost single-handedly held the Taargens out of Moyenne." The soldier straightened her shoulders and, for once, met everyone's eye.

Beau-Sang smiled patronizingly at her. "That's nonsense. Balladaire's regular regiments were there to support the colonial brigade every step of the way."

"With respect, sir," the lieutenant said, leaning forward so that she could see him on Cantic's other side, "the regular regiments were often unfortunately days, sometimes months late with their support. We fought the Taargens and their priests—"

The general cleared her throat and glared the conscript into silence. Luca was impressed, though. Whatever the general's strategy had been training the Sands, it seemed to have worked. The lieutenant was articulate, competent, and restrained. Not the most diplomatic, but soldiers weren't known for their tact.

"I always did say they were trainable," came a reedy voice from down the table. The dowager de Durfort. "Dogs, just begging for a master."

It was crude, and typical of her, but Luca didn't have a chance to react. Cheminade slapped the table sharply. Heads turned and people jumped, causing a wave to ripple across the room.

"Enough," the governor-general said. "I won't welcome you into my home and be treated like this." The look Cheminade gave Beau-Sang was quelling, and the other tables went silent. "An insult to my family is an insult to me."

"Surely you understand we're not referring to you, Nasir." Beau-Sang smiled benignly and dismissed Richard with a wave of his hand. "There are differences in ... quality."

Luca accidentally met the Sand's gaze. A flare of anger flashed across the other woman's face before the Sand lowered her gaze back to her plate and popped the knuckles on one hand, one finger at a time. That brief burst of confidence that had allowed her to speak had vanished. Luca felt a pang of sympathy.

Trying to head off the murderous look in Cheminade's eyes, Luca stepped in delicately again. "I've also been curious about the stories of Shālan magic. I'd like to read more of the histories."

Another dismissive wave of Beau-Sang's large hand. "The time for chasing their so-called magic died with the king."

Luca's lips thinned in anger, but an embarrassing flush crept up her cheeks. "I was actually referring to the Second City. I want to see the libraries."

Cantic chuckled, wiping her face with her napkin. "Not likely, Your Highness. The bridges and docks to Briga and the Second City were destroyed long before we got here. They call it the Cursed City now. The one time we went through the trouble of sending soldiers, they came back empty handed. Nothing but dust." As if it was an afterthought, Cantic gestured vaguely toward the world beyond the walls of Cheminade's home. "We confiscated books from the temple, and there were some in the buildings we converted into guardhouses. One of the aides can show you at your leisure."

"I see." Luca was filled with sinking disappointment. Until, surreptitiously, Cheminade caught her eye and winked.

With the practiced grace of a diplomat, Cheminade turned the subject to less consequential matters, like the food and the heat, and Luca let them go on without her. She found herself seeking the boy Richard in the shadows, where he waited with the other lackeys, Balladairan and Qazāli alike. She tried to catch a better glimpse of Cheminade's companion at the table, too, but all she could see of him was a thick, dark, curling beard from the front, and a bald head and narrow shoulders from the back. The Sand never spoke another word unless spoken to, as if she had been ordered to silence.

After dinner, all the guests retired to the sitting room to mingle. Cheminade deftly encouraged Beau-Sang to find someone else to talk to, while she led Luca and Cantic to a quiet corner. She foisted small silver cups of something dark into their hands. Coffee, a Shālan drink that was already becoming a prized export.

"He's certainly enthusiastic." Luca held her steaming cup of coffee, the dark liquid bitter. It cut through the lingering tastes of the meal.

Cheminade snorted. Her face had gone sour during dinner and hadn't turned cheerful again. "He's enthusiastic about his economic fears," she said. Luca hadn't thought the governor capable of the quiet discretion with which she spoke now. "Nas—Nasir, my husband—hates him. As I'm sure you saw."

Luca bit her cheek to keep her surprise from her face. Husband. The governor-general of the Shālan colonies had married a Qazāli.

"Beau-Sang is right to worry. The city isn't safe. While I work with the governor to make it safe, Your Highness, I recommend you stay in the Quartier or the compound," said Cantic.

Her tone was one used to obedience, and Luca bristled.

"How do you plan to 'make it safe,' General? Have you located the rebel leaders?"

Cantic frowned, cradling her cup of coffee in strong, leathery hands. "I apologize, Your Highness. That's confidential between my officers. Our intelligence must be kept close. We've been compromised. The attack was proof. The rebels shouldn't have known you were coming."

"Do you think I'm going to have myself killed? Or worse, sabotage my empire? I came to help stop the rebellion, General, not sunbathe." Luca frowned. "Did you get anything useful from the prisoners before they were executed, at least?"

The general's jaw flexed with her gritted teeth. "Not particularly. Only a few noms de guerre." She scoffed. "So we put them outside to bake before they hung."

"Noms de guerre actually sound very useful, General. We'll talk further soon."

This morning's attack had startled and, yes, if she had to admit it, frightened her. She wasn't going to tell General Cantic, though, and she certainly wasn't going to let it stop her from fixing the Qazāli situation. Or stop her research.

Cheminade smiled conspiratorially, looking almost eager to countermand the general. "I'd also be happy to speak with you anytime. I'll get my books in order, have legible copies made. I look forward to your thoughts on the colonial theorists and your ideas on the situation."

Cantic scowled and tossed back the last of her drink. Luca caught the general's glance to Gillett behind her.

"One last thing, and then I'll excuse myself." The general beckoned sharply with one hand, and the Sand who had been clinging desperately, awkwardly to the walls of the sitting room strode over. "Your Highness, allow me to present Lieutenant Touraine of the Balladairan Colonial Brigade, Rose Company, Gold Squad."

The lieutenant was a little shorter than Luca but broader. Handsome, with a hard jawline and striking, dark brown eyes. She bowed deeply.

"Your Highness, I'm at your service." Softer spoken now.

"Lieutenant." Luca returned the bow with a gracious nod. "I owe you a debt of gratitude. If there is a boon I can grant you, please ask."

"Always appear generous," Jean Yverte wrote in his aptly titled *The Rule of Rule*. Small gifts could breed great loyalty.

The soldier bowed again. "It's honor enough to serve the crown, Your Highness."

The general bowed stiffly to Luca and barely bent her neck to Cheminade. "Your Highness. Lord Governor. We thank you for your hospitality."

Cheminade watched the two soldiers walk away, intrigue playing in her eyes.

"What is it?" Luca asked.

"Oh, nothing." Cheminade smiled mischievously at Luca. "I was just thinking about how useful it would be to have a conscript we could send as an envoy of sorts to the rebels. The general doesn't like to relinquish control of her troops, but we are just as much a part of the empire as she is."

Luca smiled back. She was beginning to like this woman's mischievous eccentricity. It was looser than the rigid Balladairan court. "Isn't that what ambassadors are for?"

"Indeed. I just find that the Qazāli don't trust people who look like us as much. Too many like a certain comte. Plus, she's a trained soldier." Cheminade shrugged. "Anylight, plenty of time to talk about that later. Please, Your Highness. Make yourself at home."

For the rest of the evening, nobles and merchants presented themselves to her. Though she waited all night for the chance to meet Cheminade's husband, she only received Cheminade's apology.

"Nas is…distressed, Your Highness." The other woman looked away, up toward the bedrooms. Concern was plain on her open face. "Perhaps another time. A more private dinner. It would be my honor to host you again, for dinner or for any questions. Nothing is too silly or uncivilized for me. I'm also looking forward to your welcome ball."

A surprising warmth spread through her, and not just because Cheminade had hinted that she was interested in talking about Shālan magic. She finally had a peer. Someone with the same curiosities, who wouldn't make Luca feel ashamed of them, or herself.

Less than one full day in Qazāl, and she had an ally.

By the time she returned to her own sitting room, however, she had already begun second-guessing her interpretations.

"Gil. Do they all think I'm a fool?" Luca asked over her shoulder.

She stood at the wide window that overlooked the streets of the Quartier. The town houses in the Balladairan district were small, and hers was no exception. It was made of stone from Beau-Sang's quarry, with a door of imported lumber. There was little to recommend it from the outside. No garden, no escape from the sky-falling heat, not even an awning or umbrella. It sat, instead, in a patch of colorless dirt; it was shuttered tight against the warmth. It was a young construction, though, barely a decade old, compared to homes built by the first Balladairans to delve roots into the colony. It had all the modern flourishes one could expect so far from home.

Still, she found it cozy rather than cramped. She kept a small, trusted staff and had a room for her office with a desk and most of her books. That was all she really needed.

That, and the confidence of the local ministers.

Luca didn't have to turn around to see Gil's flat stare of disapproval.

"Take Cheminade. Is she just humoring me? Playing on my enthusiasms? What does she want?"

The captain of her guard, her chief advisor, her second father joined her at the window. His boots were quiet on the thick carpet. He clasped his hands behind his back under his gold cloak. Gil had been King Roland's guard captain and lover until the Withering Death took the king and queen. Gil hadn't left her side since.

A smile broke his weathered face into even more lines. "I think Governor Cheminade is smitten with you. I'm sure it's been a while since she had another scholar of her caliber to talk to."

"You know her?"

"Not well. Mostly I remember Roland muttering arguments as they wrote back and forth about the colonies."

"And Cantic? I know she's your friend. I saw that look she gave you." Her voice went sharp, and she side-eyed Gil. The general's "recommendations" for her safety still needled her.

"She's one of the crown's most loyal and competent officers, Luca. And sky above, she's not wrong. The rebels tried to kill you today. You need to stay safe."

"Which crown is she loyal to?" Luca turned to meet Gil's eyes.

He huffed into his thick gray mustache. "There's only one crown."

Luca shook her head, sighing heavily. "Not right now. There's the legal, inherited claim, and there's the one sitting on the actual seat. Right now, we're all pretending it's all right and that we'll reconcile the two into one, but—be honest, Gil.

"If I don't solve the problem here, do you think Nicolas will be so eager to move his ass? If I don't fix Qazāl, we'll have a succession trial at best. I know how that will go. We're not the first royal family to have a contested succession. Not even the first Anciers." Luca snorted and gestured out the window. "And all of that assumes I'm not murdered here."

Gil clasped an arm around her shoulder and pulled her into his side. "I'll never let that happen."

The hug comforted Luca and made her feel too small at the same time. She straightened out of it and pulled her frustration closer instead.

"I feel like the general wants to push me out of the way, like I'm too stupid to know what I'm doing—or to learn."

And why wouldn't the general assume that? An untested queen—no, a princess, who hadn't governed anything unrulier than a library and a pen to anyone else's knowledge. That's why her uncle, the regent, had sent her to this sun-scorched desert in the first place. "To gain experience," Uncle Nicolas had said, "before taking the crown." Despite his words, however, they both knew there was the possibility that she would fail. That she would make an utter mess of it and he could make a case to the nobles that she wasn't fit to rule. It wouldn't be the first time one Ancier had disposed of another for incompetence.

"I have to be the one to fix this," Luca murmured as she looked out the window.

The Quartier was only a brief strip of desert away from where the soldiers lived and one cog of her empire turned. Beyond that, she could imagine the night noise of the city far in the distance. Just beyond the city flowed the River Hadd, and beyond the Hadd were the ruins of the Second City. Somewhere in the Second City was the Scorpion Library. The First Library.

And maybe the secrets of the Shālan magic that could help her rule one day. The magic that her father had never managed to claim. The magic that might have saved his life.

Luca ran a finger along the stone sill of the window. It was cool to the touch. "I'm twenty-eight years old, Gillett. I should have been crowned this year. The only reason I agreed to this *test* of his is so we don't end up mired in another ten-year civil war. You know I have as strong a grasp of strategy and economics as Nicolas. I've read everything there is to read. I've been tutored in Shālan since before I could walk." She turned to him, her voice low and bitter. "He's too excited to test his Droitist this or Droitist that. Every corner of the empire will be like this if he's not careful." She gestured back to the city, as if she could point directly at the gallows and the hanged rebels.

"I know, Luca." He tried to soothe her with his murmurs, his rough hands rubbing her shoulders. "You're going to need people to do this, though. The right people."

Luca made a delicate, peeved sound in her throat. "The right people?"

"Like Cheminade. Cantic. Even Beau-Sang. Never overlook a good weapon."

Luca grunted and rolled her eyes. Later, however, her thoughts drifted to the handsome conscript. Perhaps she would make a good weapon, too.

CHAPTER 4

CAPTIVES

A live.
Her mother was alive.

Touraine reeled silently in the lonely dark of the carriage cab. She wished, not for the first time that night, that Pruett or Tibeau could have come with her.

After the meal, Touraine spent the evening standing awkwardly to the side just like the body servants, except for when Cantic introduced her to the princess. She'd thought this dinner would be the peak of her success, that she'd show everyone that the Sands could belong just as much as anyone else. That hadn't lasted long at all, between the comte de Beau-Sang and whoever that old noblewoman was. So it was a relief, at first, when Cheminade approached her.

"Lieutenant Touraine." The governor-general handed her a drink. Lord Governor Cheminade had a surprisingly tender air for a politician. The wrinkles in her face spread as she smiled.

Touraine bowed, more out of uncertainty than anything else. The drink was sweet and fragrant and delicious.

"I wanted to apologize personally for the comte de Beau-Sang's behavior," Cheminade said, peering into Touraine's eyes like she was searching for some kind of reaction.

Touraine looked into her cup instead. It was cut crystal. Cool to the touch and dazzling to the eye. The governor lived in a completely different world. The fine food, the beautiful home—Touraine could never imagine living in a place like this. And yet Cheminade was the first Balladairan she'd met to suggest that Balladairans treated the Sands...less well than they deserved.

"It's nothing, Lord Governor," she said into her cup. "We're used to it."

"Yes, well. That's the problem, isn't it?"

Touraine looked up, startled. "I don't understand?"

"I've been curious about Cantic's project for a long time now." Cheminade regarded the room casually, taking in but not lingering on the general. Cantic was trapped in a scowling conversation with the comte de Beau-Sang. "About what they taught you, what they plan for you when all of the fighting is done." She waved her hand as if gesturing to battles gone by. "Do you know you're the first conscript I've ever met?"

"As far as I know, this is the first time the colonial brigade has been used in the colonies, my lady."

The older woman smiled tightly. "Indeed. Imagine my surprise when I heard that one of you had already distinguished yourself by saving the princess's life."

Touraine raised an eyebrow. Even she could tell the flattery was thick. Still, she ducked her head in appreciation. "As I said, I'm happy to do my duty."

The same tight smile. "I'm sure. Do the conscripts remember much about their pasts?"

Touraine's alarm must have shown on her face. Cheminade laughed and put her empty hand on Touraine's arm.

"Don't worry. I'll be honest," Cheminade said, lowering her voice and smiling conspiratorially. "I did hear the man on the gallows. I can't say I know his connection to Jaghotai—sky above knows the general will sniff it out—but I do know the woman. An overseer in the quarries. Excellent liaison between the city and the laborers."

In a matter of seconds, Touraine felt as if she'd been stripped naked. She even clutched her left arm closer, wondering if Cheminade knew about her newly healed wound, too.

"I could arrange a meeting, if you'd like."

And just for a second, Touraine hesitated. What *would* it be like to have a mother again? What was this stranger like? Then the curiosity passed, leaving horror in its wake.

"No. Of course not." Touraine shook her head hard, eyes shifting nervously to General Cantic. She lifted her cup to her lips only to find it was already empty. "I mean, thank you. But I think we should all keep our distance from the uncivilized."

Cheminade grimaced, but when she followed Touraine's glance, the expression softened. It wasn't tender, but it looked like pity, and that put Touraine off even more.

"I understand," the governor said. "I don't mean to make you uncomfortable, so I'll excuse myself. If you do change your mind, however, just let me know."

And before Touraine could gather herself again, Cantic swooped in and made their goodbyes, dragging Touraine to her carriage.

Now, bumbling through the dark streets, she was sure it had been a test, and she knew she'd given the right answers. So why did it feel like she'd failed?

The carriage jolted to a halt, and the driver thumped roughly on the wood of the cab. Touraine fumbled the door open to see what was the matter. She didn't usually feel so clumsy, but then, she wasn't usually plied with wine fit for royalty and no rationing chit.

"What's going on?" she asked, stepping out.

"This is far enough, friend." The cabbie spoke in a way that implied they weren't friends at all. He looked down at her from his perch while the horse stamped impatiently.

Touraine blinked stupidly at him. "The general said you're to take me to the guardhouse."

"Not the general that paid me." He shrugged and spat and flicked the reins.

Touraine dived desperately for the door but found herself stumbling through air while the wheels clattered away into the night.

"Sky-falling shit." She kicked the dirt.

Where even was she?

Above her, the sky stretched inky black, starless. She turned down one of the wheel-spoke roads to take her deeper into the city, away from the clean, wide boulevards of the New Medina, occasionally taking other turns and noting landmarks. The farther she went, the more she hated it. Give her back the wide roads of the Balladairan countryside, the march through Moyenne, not this cramped misery. The disorganized layout of the city made it difficult to make a mental map.

Two dogs sprinted from an alley, a spotted one chasing a mangy gold one. Touraine jumped back, heart hammering. Her head spun.

Hounds.

That bastard at the party had called them hounds. And the things that old hag had said...

And that poor kid. There were Balladairans like Cantic and even Cheminade, then there were Balladairans like the comte de Beau-Sang. When Touraine saw what the comte had done to the boy's fingers, she'd felt the kind of anger she'd reserved just for Rogan.

Some Balladairans would never see the Sands as true citizens. Those people didn't matter. Or they wouldn't if the law would protect the Sands as citizens. And it didn't. Which meant Beau-Sang and Rogan were dangerous. Which meant she had to keep knuckling her forehead at them, keeping her eyes and her voice down whenever they said shit like this.

It was so unfair that the anger pulled tears from Touraine's eyes. There had to be something better than this. *Look at Cheminade*, she told herself. Married to a Qazāli! If that was possible, why not a promotion? Why not a Qazāli-born captain? General, even? It was hard to convince Tibeau of it, though, when there were a dozen moments like the one she'd had with the shit cabbie. A dozen chances for him to say he'd told her so.

And what would he say if he knew her mother was alive?

Her mother was alive—or no, Touraine thought, maybe not. No one had said with certainty that the woman was her mother, just someone she resembled a little. It was hard to convince herself. The old man *knew her name.* The name of that woman's daughter. That woman was alive.

Alive.

Cheminade was kind, sure. But she was Balladairan. She didn't understand the lines a Sand had to dance between. Even if Touraine *wanted* to meet Jaghotai, it would be impossible to open the doors to her past *and* keep her vision of a golden future in Balladaire's army. And that was what she'd always wanted.

Cut off the most undesirable traits.

Was family an undesirable trait?

Touraine's head was thick and woolly. All she wanted to do was lie down and sleep. She took a shuddering breath and tried to get her bearings.

She was lost.

From what she could tell, the Grand Temple and the Grand Bazaar were the social center of the city, closest to the river but still outside the floodplain. The Mile-Long Bridge stretched from the dock quarter over the floodland and into the city. She could see none of that from the ground where she walked; the clay buildings were too tall. Only occasionally did she glimpse a temple spire. She angled herself toward them. If she could find the temple, the bazaar and Ibn Shattath couldn't be too far off.

The sickly sweet smell of refuse grew as Touraine walked on. A woman with a cart trundled behind Touraine. Beggars lay against walls, some maimed, some drunk. A small family, a mother and two children, slept under a single tattered blanket. Touraine shivered and walked faster. The desert night was chilly.

Those children should have been in a charity school. Balladaire made provisions for children. What kind of mother would keep her children from those benefits?

Dizzying anxiety seized in Touraine's chest, competing with the fog in her mind. She stepped into a narrow lane to lean against a wall. Just to have something at her back until this all passed. Just to stop spinning. She hunkered down on her heels, pressed her palms into her eyes, and tried to pull herself into the moment with the techniques the instructors had taught her.

What could she see? Dirt, yellow brown like everything else here. Her boots, worn, polished leather, well trusted. The clay wall of the building opposite her, just two paces away. Another cart woman, dark skinned with braids, out on the street, pushing whatever remained of the day's wares. But Touraine's vision blurred and her eyes crossed.

She could hear the wheels squeaking away. They sounded familiar, as if the sound of cart wheels in the city streets were a constant. The night sounds of a city, so loud but so easily lost to the background, like the buzz of insects. She'd never lived in a city. Then the buzz faded, as if her ears had been stuffed with wax. Then her blurry vision went dark.

Touraine woke on her stomach, ankles tied to wrists behind her. The ropes dug into her flesh, and she tried to stay as still as possible. A muscle cramped along her lower back. With her face pressed into the floor, every breath tasted like dirt. Sand gritted in her teeth.

Sky above and earth below. Where was she? Other than fucked. The last thing she remembered was collapsing in a heap against the wall, her head too fuzzed to think straight. She hadn't been that drunk.

She rocked, trying to tilt onto her side, but the ropes that bound her were held up by something else. All she got for the effort was a wrenched shoulder.

"How are we feeling?" A woman's voice? Speaking accented Balladairan.

Touraine tried not to give away her surprise, but her heart beat faster. "Good," she grunted in Shālan. It was one of a handful of words she remembered from Tibeau.

The stranger laughed, harsh and barking. "Didn't hear that," she said. Then she repeated the word, smoothing out Touraine's rough pronunciation. Her boot pulled back in slow motion, and Touraine braced herself. When she kicked Touraine in the stomach, Touraine groaned through her teeth. Curled in on herself by reflex, only to strain her shoulders in their sockets.

"All right, Balladairan dog." The woman crouched in front of Touraine. She wore dark trousers tucked into heavy boots, and one of those Qazāli vests, with the hood up and the dark veil pulled over her nose and mouth. Lantern light reflected on dark, dark brown eyes shaded by angry eyebrows and outlined in crow's-feet.

She'd been taken captive by rebels. She was double fucked.

"We don't really want to hurt you," the woman said, giving no sign that this was true. "We should be on the same side. You and the other dogs—you're slaves, too."

Touraine's laugh scraped her throat. "You're sky-falling crazy."

The Balladairans could—would—flay them all alive. Or whip them just as near. It baffled her, how stupid the rebels were about the balance of power: the Qazāli had nothing. Balladaire had numbers, equipment, supplies—they were winning, had been winning for decades. Some of the Sands might miss their families, their pasts, but it would be better to stay on the Balladairan side of the conflict. She'd kept that in the back of her head even as she'd wanted to strangle Rogan in the past.

"You want food, you talk to me. Let's start small—where are your guns?"

"Can't talk," Touraine whispered into the dirt.

The next kick to her side cracked something. Sky above, she was going to look like a lavender field the next time she took her clothes off.

When she caught her breath again, she said, "We don't have guns. You like my baton? You can have it. We keep them on our belts." The familiar rod dug into her hip. It was almost a relief when the woman tilted Touraine over casually and unhooked the baton from her belt. Almost.

The woman flipped it through the air to catch it several times, as if she already knew its weight intimately.

"You're soldiers without guns?" she asked.

Touraine imagined the disdain and suspicion on the woman's face. It probably matched hers when she learned she wouldn't have a gun.

"Ridiculous, I know." Years of training, to find out the gun was hers only before an engagement or in active war, to be returned immediately after. Any soldiers who refused were to be shot.

"I'm not an idiot. Where are your guns? Or tell me how your shipments come in. Or your guard rotations." The boot swung back again.

"I'm not lying!" Touraine said harshly, watching the boot. The kick wouldn't break her mind, but it could break something else, and sky above, she hurt. She couldn't help thinking about the cut on her arm, which now seemed like the one place she didn't hurt. "I'm a Sand. They don't tell us shit."

"So tell me what they do tell you," the woman hissed. Her dark eyes were almost black in the dim room.

"Fine." Touraine relaxed a hair. "I set guard ro—"

The final kick ripped a scream out of her, and it broke down into a dry sob.

Sharp words outside the door in Shālan made the woman growl, irked. She stalked out.

A thick, metallic paste of blood and dirt coated Touraine's tongue.

The door opened again. She had a brief glimpse of light from the courtyard before a shadow blocked it out.

"Let me help you." A new, calmer voice came from behind her in crisp Balladairan. It sounded like her tutors in Balladaire and was a pleasant change from the bitch with the boots and the growl.

The relief, however, was short lived.

The world lurched as she laid Touraine on her side. She groaned gratefully at the sudden lack of tension. This captor wore a scarf that covered all but her golden eyes, which dazzled in the lamplight, emphasized by dark kohl.

Touraine's breath stopped in her chest. A Brigāni. The woman's long dark robe puddled around the floor as she knelt next to Touraine. According to the Tailleurist history books, the Brigāni were the cannibal Shālan witches from Briga, the country across the river from Qazāl. They drank their enemies' blood to kill armies, ate their hearts to destroy cities. According to the history books, they had also died out.

"Are you thirsty?"

Just the word *thirsty* dried up what little moisture Touraine had left. She shook her head.

"You're lying. I'll drink first." She drank from a clay cup and then held it to Touraine's mouth. Most of the water spilled across her lips and onto the ground, but what she tasted was delicious.

The room was small and bare, with only one lamp. The Brigāni placed a cushion in front of Touraine and sat on it, watching her. Like the Tailleurist tutors, again, who'd watched the Sands like they were fascinating animals.

"What?" Touraine's voice was a hoarse and dusty thing.

"Why are you really here?"

"You put me here."

"You're the highest-ranking soldier of the Balladairan Colonial. They made you an officer. Technically, you're a gold stripe." She scanned Touraine over, from the bristles on her scalp to her bound fists and worn boots. The slang sounded strange on her tongue. "Gold stripe" was the nickname for Balladairan officers—or really, anyone with government favor—so called because of the gold on their collars or sleeves. By contrast, grunts were called *blackcoats*. The Sands were never called blackcoats, even though their coats were just as dark. They were something apart.

"Untie me. I'll talk."

"No. It was easy to carry you when you were unconscious. I am not particularly interested in trying under fairer circumstances."

Touraine frowned. Maybe the fog in her mind hadn't been natural. The headache at the back of her skull was definitely not like any hangover she'd had. That would mean she had been drugged, though, and the throbbing pain in her head barely left room for the requisite panic, let alone the puzzle.

"How long have I been here?"

The Brigāni shrugged.

The Sands would have noticed that she hadn't come back from dinner, and Rogan, too. He'd report it to Cantic giddily. How many of them would think she deserted? Would they look for her?

"Are you going to eat me?" Touraine masked the very real fear churning in her stomach with a taunting lilt. The Brigāni legends were only legends. None of the Sands had ever met one, but they had all heard scare stories from their parents—if they had parents.

The other woman rolled her eyes. "We'd actually prefer not to hurt any of the dāyiein. We could be mutually beneficial to each other."

Touraine snorted, and the sharp breath caught on a probably broken rib. "Not feeling very benefited. What's a dayeen?" She tried to repeat the word, but it didn't fit right in her throat.

"The Lost Ones. We can…give you a place. Reunite you with family, if they live."

It echoed Cheminade's comment at the dinner so closely that it sent a shiver up Touraine's spine.

"Half of us aren't even Qazāli."

"*You* are."

That drew Touraine up short. The Brigāni rested her hands in her lap in a strange palm-up gesture.

"I also hanged five of your people," Touraine said. "This isn't personal."

The lie sounded hollow even to her own ears.

"It's always personal." A grief-stricken grimace passed over the woman's face. "They're using you. Like they used you in their latest Taargen war."

Touraine didn't answer. The Sands had started fighting for Balladaire in earnest during the second Taargen war. Five years ago, now. They were always the first to fight and the last to get relief. Of a thousand kids taken, fewer than half of them survived, a brigade winnowed down to a few companies. They'd been trained their whole lives for it. Almost a year and a half had passed since Rogan read the official cease-fire agreement to Touraine's company. The one time she hadn't wanted to shoot him.

"Balladaire and Taargen haven't been on good terms since the Balladairans started their purges to 'civilize' anyone who believes in a god. Balladaire is picking fights and throwing you in the middle."

Touraine still didn't answer. She remembered a bitter cold night following a frigid day. Blood practically congealing on the dead before they hit the ground. She opened her eyes wide against the memory, trying to fill her mind with the Brigāni, with the small room.

The Shālans are just as uncivilized.

"I've heard the Taargens eat their victims, too," the Brigāni said. A knife appeared in her hand, and she came closer.

The Taargen fire. Her captured soldiers being pulled to it one by one.

"No," Touraine finally choked out.

Touraine tried to catalog her surroundings again. Dirt. The Brigāni's robe. The knife. The walls—not things to make the growing fear ebb.

"Well. Rumors must come from somewhere." The Brigāni's voice was darkly ironic. Then it softened. "How many soldiers did you lose?"

"Enough."

The Brigāni tilted her head.

The day Touraine was captured, seventy-six soldiers died. Fifty-eight on the field. The rest of wounds and frostbite. They'd been lucky it was only a small group of the bearfuckers. Just over two years ago, now. They'd promoted her after that battle.

"Too many died in a war that's not theirs."

"Your rebellion would be another one."

"You'll have to fight for one side or the other. Why not fight for the side that gives you freedom?"

"Because I can fight for the side that's winning."

"Winning isn't everything. It's how you win that matters most." She held Touraine's gaze before looking distantly into a corner. When she spoke again, her voice cracked before steadying.

"Once upon a time, a young Brigāni girl stood poised to be the greatest healing priestess of all the tribes, probably in the whole Shālan Empire. A little vanity goes a long way, and she left her tribe to study at the Grand Temple in Qazāl across the river." She trailed her knife along Touraine's shirt, drawing a path from Touraine's neck to her collarbone.

"She enjoyed her studies, so much so that she avoided going home until caravan after caravan brought rumors—rumors that an army from the north was traveling the Holy Sea and the Brigāni were in its path. Rumors that a young Balladairan captain was making a bloody name for herself. Perhaps you know her?" She fixed Touraine's eyes with her own, the gold unnerving as she pressed the point of the knife just deep enough to draw blood.

"I don't know—" Touraine started through gritted teeth, but the woman spoke over her.

"So a foolish youth buys a camel and catches the first ferry to southern Briga to put her mind at ease. She finds embers and char when she arrives.

"How does she know this is her family? The Brigāni are nomads now—it could have been anyone. However, there are distinguishing factors. A father's belt buckle. A mother's bangles melted into each other nearby. A sister's jeweled knife. Frankincense mingling with smoke."

The silence when she finished pressed on Touraine's ears like the knife pressed on her chest, tearing through her shirt. A bloom of red spread across the cloth. She clenched her jaw until her teeth hurt.

The deep lines between the stranger's eyes deepened. "Do you want to ally yourself with people who murder indiscriminately? Or will you help me stop the Blood General?"

The Blood General. Another name for Cantic, fuel for darker rumors. After the statesmen in Masridān surrendered, she invited them to a party to cement the alliance and murdered them all. No, even worse, she drowned their children in the city baths when they refused her terms. No, it was like this—on and on, but Touraine never believed the rumors, because she knew who they came from. The Sands could get creative about the instructors they didn't like.

"Tell me about her," the Brigāni said.

It wasn't the knife that made Touraine tremble. She'd been cut before, and worse. Strips of skin gone with a bad whipping. Sky above, she'd never forgive herself if she pissed her trousers now. *You are not weak*, she chanted in her mind. *You are not uncivilized. No superstition can harm you.* But the woman had said *healing priestess*. Touraine's mind flicked back to the new scar on her arm, and she pulled it away just as fast.

The Brigāni took the blade back and stared at the line of Touraine's blood sliding down the knife. She licked her lips. Skimmed the blood off the knife with her thumb and rubbed it between thumb and forefinger. What could she do with that blood? Control her, like the Taargens, turn her into a beast? She looked away, beyond the Brigāni. Fixed her eyes on the swirls of an old tapestry on the wall, pale with dust. Anything to get away.

"I can't. I don't know anything about her—none of us do." Touraine's voice wavered. "That's not how this military works. A private is a private, and the Sands are even lower than that."

"A pity. Well, if you remember anything useful, let me know. I'll be back soon, after I've made things ready for you."

She stood and rolled Touraine back onto her belly. Her muscles cramped immediately. The lamplight vanished, and her soft boots padded away.

CHAPTER 5

THE FIRST BROADSIDE

The next day, Luca disregarded Cantic's "suggestions" and went on her first proper visit to El-Wast, to the largest bookshop in the city, run by a Balladairan man with a squint and a shining bald head. She had hoped to go with Cheminade, but the governor-general was busy with the fallout from the hanging.

She had woken this morning to a small unmarked parcel. It was a book about Shālan history. There was no name card or note, though it seemed like the sort of gift Cheminade might give. But why wouldn't the governor leave a note?

The text was simple, but not in a foppish way. More like it was an introduction to a work that could be longer with more research. She didn't recognize the author, whose name was inscribed only as PSLR. It included an intriguing discussion of a Shālan text about the last emperor of the Shālan Empire, before it shuddered under its first blow five hundred years ago—*The Last Emperor* by bn Zahel. The author had never read this elusive book, or even seen it, but said the last emperor was rumored to be a sorcerer and that it was sorcery alone that allowed her to so devastate Balladaire's coastal cities.

Luca tried to tell herself that her research itself wouldn't save or ruin her attempts in Qazāl. In the back of her mind, however, she thought about how easy it would be to rule Balladaire if she had magic on her side. If magic actually existed. How people would look at her if she managed what her father could not.

And if she failed? How would people look at her then? If they thought she was chasing down gods to worship, as uncivilized as the colonials?

She wasn't doing that, though. She had no interest in savage gods or prayers. She just wanted to learn magic. To see its proof, to use it for Balladaire. No one could fault that. They were two very different things. Magic was a tool, perhaps even a weapon. Religion was folly dressed as hope.

Luca was skimming the shelves when she heard women tittering noisily near the door. She huffed loudly and did her best to shut them out, but the shop was small. They kept on. She huffed again, louder.

Her newest guard, Lanquette, shifted uncomfortably on his feet. Luca shot him an annoyed look, then caught the women's conversation.

"She looks exactly like that, leg and all. I saw her at the hanging. I told you, I was there."

"She can't possibly be that—why, she looks like—have you seen those tall, spotted horses at my mother's menagerie back home?"

"Those giant, skinny things? A...zeeraf?"

Luca's face burned as she stepped out from the shelves and approached the entrance. The two young women stood outside, parasols raised against the sun, staring at something on the wall of the building. One had dark hair, the other fair, both in a braid that coiled about the head in the style of the colonial nobility—supposedly elegant yet cool. Luca wore her hair in its usual bun, pale wisps tucked behind her ear.

"A giraffe, exactly like them." The dark-haired one leaned into her companion and lowered her voice. "She only needs a fourth leg."

Luca cleared her throat, and when the women turned, their faces paled. Luca wanted to hurt them, to punish them, but what, realistically, could she do besides harbor a grudge against them and call the debt later? She lingered on the notion of having Lanquette shatter their legs slowly. With a blacksmith's hammer. Actually, she'd rather do it herself. Ah, but for diplomacy.

"Hello, mesdemoiselles."

The women bobbed into curtsies, but Luca pushed past them to see what had caught their attention. The single sheet of a broadside had been pasted to the clay wall. A picture took up most of the space on the page, a crude woodcut rendering of two women on puppet strings—one with a dark tricorne, a sagging, lined face, and hands dripping dark ink; the other with a tight bun, lips pursed sourly, hunching over a cane on impossibly crooked legs. The strings linked their hands to wooden handles held by sausage fingers. A large belly filled the background of the picture. She wondered if it was meant to be Duke Regent Nicolas Ancier, who was known for his belly, as Luca was known for her leg. "Puppets of the Empire's Hunger" was printed in large block letters across the top. She scowled.

It came too close to her own feelings for comfort. Her uncle had sent her here as if she were nothing more than an errand child to clean up his messes or chase his coin. The humiliation of it made her eyes sting. She ripped the broadside off the wall. Her fist convulsed around the page.

She turned to the women. She didn't recognize either of their faces, but only one woman in Balladaire—besides herself—had enough money and land to maintain a menagerie with giraffes. Lady Bel-Jadot. She could turn this to her advantage one day.

"Mademoiselle Bel-Jadot, yes?" Luca said to the dark-haired one. Lady Bel-Jadot had similar coloring.

"Yes, Your Highness." The young Bel-Jadot curtsied again, her face blushing red beneath olive-toned skin.

Lanquette had hardened into something handsome and formidable, someone who could increase the women's embarrassment. Luca was grateful. Surely it wouldn't do for so eligible a bachelor to think so ill of the two women before her. It wouldn't do for their princess to want them hanged, either, but there they were. She exhaled sharply through her nose. *You need them.*

"We apologize, Your High—"

"You may leave."

"Thank you, Your Highness." They bobbed again and vanished up the street.

Lanquette glared after them. "I'm sorry you had to see that, Your Highness. Shall I look for any more?"

"Not yet." Luca could tell he was trying to be kind and reassuring, but it irked her that her pain was so evident.

She stepped back inside the bookshop and called for the proprietor, who had been shelving his latest acquisitions in the back. He huffed his way back to his counter, mopping sweat from his face even though it stained the front of his shirt and under his arms. She wrinkled her nose at the odor.

"I'm at your service, Your Highness. All that you like is yours, of course, as I said."

"What I like is this sterling piece of art." Luca waved the broadside she clutched in her fist. "What I would like is to never see its like on this shop ever again. Especially not if you'd like me to remain a patron. Where did it come from?"

The shopkeeper flushed and stammered as he set his page to running up and down the streets to look for more of the broadsides to tear from the walls and doors of the neighborhood.

"I'm so sorry, Your Highness. I never saw it! Forgive—"

The poor man had a point. Luca hadn't seen it when she arrived, either, which meant it was probably recent.

"Do you have *The Last Emperor* by Yeshuf bn Zahel?" Luca cut in.

The man pursed his lips. "No, Your Highness. Only Balladairan books here, or approved Shālan authors. I'm afraid I don't know Yeshuf Benizel."

"Bn Zahel," Luca muttered. She cleared her throat. "Nothing else, then."

"You might try down in the Old Medina," the man said quickly, mopping his face again. "I've...heard—that is, there are some Balladairans who collect Shālan books as decorations, and I've...heard them...speaking of a place in the Puddle District. Better to send someone, though. Like him." The shopkeeper nodded to her guard and then to the sword on his belt.

Ah. *That* kind of quarter. If Cantic didn't even want Luca in the New Medina, she would be thrilled about this. Inwardly, she snickered to herself, the spark of curiosity catching in her. Outwardly, she nodded once in thanks.

"If someone ever plasters broadsides of this nature on your wall, or any other door in sight, what will you do?" Luca asked the shopkeeper.

The man paled and bobbed up and down in a bow again. His throat bobbed, as well. "I'll tear it down, of course, Your Highness. And notify you immediately."

"Wonderful. Your loyalty is commendable."

Outside the bookshop, Luca sat in her carriage with her second guard, Guérin, and wouldn't meet the woman's eyes. She realized she still clutched the broadside in her fist. She smoothed the large paper out over her thigh. The creases and smeared ink made the angles of her drawn legs look even more disfigured.

"Your Highness? What is it?" Guérin leaned closer, perhaps to comfort, perhaps to see the object of distress. Luca shook her head and tucked herself against the wall. It had felt good to intimidate the poor bookseller, but he wasn't the one she should have directed her anger toward. He was helpless against her.

"The problem's not with me. It never has been."

And yet Luca still wished after all these years that her life had turned out differently. That she had turned out differently. That her legs were fine, that her parents were alive, that no one tittered behind their hands at her limping arrivals and departures. She had tried to offer them something else—as a child, she gave them precociousness, a memory for facts and languages that astounded her tutors. When she was older, she thought to impress suitors with her musical talent, since dancing made her bones ache. Now she was trying to prove to her empire that she didn't have to ride into battle to be a worthy ruler. That her mind was weapon enough. Yes, she lacked experience, but she had maneuvered in court all her life, and she was here now. By the sky above, she wanted to be enough.

No. More than enough. She wanted to be a queen for the histories. Someone who changed Balladaire for the better. Someone who changed the world.

How to do that when this is how my people see me?

It wasn't just her, though. Whoever had made this didn't like the military or the empire—or at least, the royals. That left the nobles and the general citizens. She didn't understand why either group would object to her stopping the rebellion in Qazāl, unless the broadside was from a Qazāli source. The likelihood of Qazāli having access to a printing press, however, was slim.

A knock on the carriage. Luca wiped her eyes with a finger. She opened the door on Lanquette.

"Your Highness. Where to now?"

Luca thumbed the broadside again, her lips pursed. Bn Zahel's book would probably not be at a dockside bookstore, if it was this rare. And if it were, PSLR would likely have found it; PSLR seemed like a devoted scholar, not one to leave avenues untrodden. Neither was she.

More importantly, she needed to understand the city. *A ruler who doesn't see their city is a ruler who won't see the knife plunge into their back.* That was already too true. Luca needed to know the city to change the city, no matter what the danger was.

And yet... she swallowed against the quick rise of her heart in her throat. If that conscript hadn't caught the woman at the docks, Lanquette and Guérin would have, but that didn't make the reality of the cold steel any less sharp.

Luca slumped against the door in defeat. "Back to the Quartier," she said softly.

Lanquette's shoulders relaxed, and Luca heard Guérin exhale a sharp breath of relief. Lanquette was a few years younger than Luca herself, which said something for his skill and the trust Gillett had placed in him. Guérin had, at most, a decade on Luca, near retiring if she wanted to. She was still at least twenty years younger than Gillett.

Lanquette closed the door with a bow, and the carriage shook as he climbed on top with the driver.

The cabin was too quiet as they began moving. She wondered if Guérin judged her silently for not being the right kind of queen.

"Guérin, what do you think of the Qazāl question?" Luca asked abruptly. She flicked the curtain to peer through the window. The clay buildings passed quickly. The streets in the New Medina were clear, except for the odd Balladairan or well-dressed Qazāli shopping or conducting business.

"Not my place, Your Highness." The other woman's grimace showed something else, though.

Luca fixed her with an eye. "Shall I order you to have a frank conversation with me? You and Lanquette must talk about this when I'm not around."

Guérin bowed her head. Her words came out rushed. "I think we should pull out of the colonies and focus on the Taargens. We share a border with them and no natural defenses. No disrespect to the king, of course, Your Highness. We weren't spread so thin then as we are now."

"Even though we've signed a peace treaty with Taargen."

Guérin made a skeptical sound in her throat. "Might be best to stay prepared instead of spending the money to keep a pack of jackals in line. Instead of teaching them, we could teach our own. I know a few kids back home who'd love a decent book, or to know how to read one."

Guérin was from a town northeast of La Chaise, surrounded by mountains on three sides, known more for its sheep than its people. It was part of the Marquisate de Durfort, her friend Sabine's domain. Luca had heard more than one joke about the "simple mountain folk" in court—which meant Guérin had, too.

"You make a fair point." One that Luca had considered, of course. Still, it was hard to reconcile that with how much Balladaire's economy was fueled by *controlled* trade—which was to say, control that benefited Balladaire first and foremost—with the Shālan colonies.

"It's risky, too." Guérin hesitated before adding, "Guarding you— it's an honor I've been given, I understand that. Worked hard to earn it. But I do—uh, miss my family sometimes, Your Highness."

"You're right. You do take grave risks. Stopping the rebellion will help us, though." So would taking her uncle off the throne; she made a mental note to address literacy soon. Maybe Sabine could help her set something up now, while Luca was away.

As the carriage rolled on, Luca let herself get lost in thoughts of home—Sabine de Durfort more pleasantly, the rest of the court rather less so.

When she was young, after that horse had trampled her leg to pieces, she noticed the young nobles wearing beautiful new swords, gifts for their comings-out, and she made the mistake of saying aloud that she'd like one, someday. Later, she overheard Sabine, the lordling of Durfort, laughing at her earnestness.

The next day, she hid herself in the armory and tried sword after sword, all heavy, some ancient and broad, some newer, fashionably curved after cavalry blades but less functional.

"You'll never beat anyone with a sword you can't carry," Gil tried to tell her when he found her in tears, her arms shaking with fatigue.

With one hand on her cane, she yanked another blade from the hanging rack. She had never wanted a sword, never wanted to be a fighter, before the accident. Now she *needed* it.

The weight of the weapon surprised her, and it plummeted down. Out of poor instinct, she dropped the cane to take the weight. Her leg gave out, and she, the sword, and the cane clattered to the ground.

Gil folded his arms across his chest. "Are you ready to listen, Luca?"

She scowled, stubbornly bit her cheek to keep from crying. "Fine."

He scooped her up and helped her back onto her feet and cane. Then he went and plucked a small rapier from the most ornate swords on display. Not one of the broader blades that were stylish among the other youth, but it was beautiful.

"I can't fight anyone with that," she said sullenly.

"You can. Not like they expect you to, but you can. I'll teach you. And then you can give young Durfort a demonstration."

Six dedicated months of sweating and constantly aching muscles later, Luca challenged Sabine de Durfort to a private duel and beat her.

Now, as then, Luca couldn't face this challenge the same way as everyone else. But like her own rapier, she was flexible. She knew the value of finding other avenues of attack, and she was patient.

Cantic and Beau-Sang wanted to crush the rebels with brute Balladairan might, and King Roland would probably have done that.

But Luca wasn't them. She had never even been in battle; in that respect, she was more like her uncle. Uncle Nicolas was rigid in his own way, though—he was so sure that the Shālans were incapable of rational thought, he'd declined to meet with any Shālan representative for the last decade.

She could be different.

She could send the Qazāli rebels a negotiator who would hear their grievances. She would offer them the dignity of taking them seriously.

At best, she would end the rebellion without bloodshed and turn enemies into allies.

At worst, she would have someone close to the seat of the rebellion's power. She would have a glimpse at the rebels' plans and resources in a way Cantic clearly hadn't managed.

The right negotiator would have access to the rebels, which meant either that Luca needed a well-placed spy from Cantic's intelligence branch or that the delegate must already be well connected in Qazāli society. They would speak Shālan fluently so that no nuances escaped them and a knife in the guts couldn't be construed as a "misunderstanding." Similarly, they would have an awareness of Qazāli culture so that a knife in the guts couldn't be construed as a "redress to insults."

The perfect negotiator would be well educated, diplomatic, and courteous and would have a sense of tact. They would be loyal to Balladaire, above all else. And yet Luca couldn't ignore how often the possibility of a knife in the guts arose, so she added combat skills in the "nice-to-have" column of her mental checklist.

As she shaped the list, the image of the perfect candidate formed in her mind. Bald and bearded, not physically intimidating but with clever, insightful eyes and the ability to keep his tongue civil in front of Casimir LeRoche de Beau-Sang. That feat alone impressed Luca.

Cheminade's husband, Nasir, would do perfectly.

As if on cue, the carriage lumbered forward again.

CHAPTER 6

A FAMILY

This time, shouting jarred Touraine from fitful half sleep. Sandals slapping, bare feet or boots scuffing outside the door. She snapped herself fully awake and reached for her baton before she remembered she'd been trussed up like a pig. She strained at the cords on her wrists again. Her skin was on sky-falling fire where the ropes had rubbed it raw, but if she could just get loose—

At the crack of musket fire, she stilled, stopped breathing entirely.

Someone yelled in Balladairan close by. She flexed her hands, looking for more play in the rope. Nothing.

"I'm in here!" she shouted.

She yelled until the footsteps came to her. She braced herself. *Please don't be the desert witch.* Even the bitch with the boots would be all right. Didn't fill Touraine with the same kind of fear. The kind of fear that kept her half-awake, even though she was exhausted from travel and fighting and surprises—

It was Émeline. She held a musket, bayonet silhouetted against the light.

"They're on the run." Émeline picked Touraine's bindings apart with the bayonet. "All right, sir?"

Touraine groaned as her arms and legs sprang apart with relief, settling back into their sockets. She felt like soft candy stretched too far.

"I'll take that as a yes." Émeline let Touraine hold her arm as she stood. "Pru's going to fucking kill you, sir."

"Is she the only one?" Touraine searched her face.

Émeline cocked her head apologetically. "Tibeau might be in line, yeah."

"Excellent. Sky-falling excellent." She limped out of the room, her hips grinding back into place.

The rest of the building looked like the guardhouse. Rooms square around a courtyard in the middle. They were on the second floor, and a rotting, latticed railing clung to the stone pillars. There weren't enough lanterns in the corridor to lift the shadows, and the stars shining through the courtyard didn't offer much light. The courtyard fountain was dry.

Musket fire shattered the fountain's ornament in a spray of shards and dust, a burst of thunder followed by pattering rain. They hunched behind the rail, and Émeline dragged her down the corridor. Only slightly better protection than standing in an open field.

Another shot and someone below screamed in pain. Émeline knelt behind a pillar to fire back. Touraine dropped to the floor, hunting for the gunman. They fell into the roles so seamlessly that her blood sang with the beauty of it.

"One shot."

Émeline nodded.

Touraine poked her head up to look at the corridor on the other side. A dark figure craned around another pillar to look down into the courtyard.

She ducked back. "On your left, third pillar—"

"Got it."

One deep breath, then Émeline turned, waited, fired. The rebel fell. The women moved again, down the hallway, to the stairs.

Each breath Touraine took was a wince. She didn't hear the other footsteps. She didn't turn until she heard a sharp, surprised gasp. Touraine spun, ready to help Émeline finish off their attacker.

The bayonet of an ancient musket stuck out of Émeline's stomach. Her eyes and mouth were wide, fishlike with shock. Even the rebel looked surprised at what they had done, their eyes wide above their hooded veil. The blade glistened wetly with blood in the dim moonlight that came in through the courtyard.

Touraine was the first to recover. Without thought, she shoved the rebel toward the rail. Sharp pain, dangerous pain in her ribs where her first captor had kicked her.

Touraine registered the wet suck of the bayonet as it lurched from Émeline's body, and the other woman's yelp of pain and surprise. Then the snap of the railing. It gave almost instantly under the rebel's momentum. Finally, the sick thud as the rebel hit the stone floor below.

"Sky-falling fuck."

Though Touraine's brain hadn't caught up, her body knew the motions. She ripped off her coat and pressed it against Émeline's wound.

"Émeline?" Touraine murmured. "Émeline, you're all right. I've got you." Even though a voice in her head whispered *You aren't safe here* over and over.

Touraine's heart buzzed in her chest as she did the sums. It wasn't safe for them to stay, to get a medic to Émeline here, but running away would only run her closer to death. Émeline's blood smelled earthy and metallic—shit was mixing with her blood. The bastard rebel had gotten her in the bowels.

They were saved by the last person Touraine wanted to see as she tried to press Émeline's guts whole. Tibeau stormed up the stairs, holding his rifle across his chest as he scanned for fallen Sands. He saw them.

"Tour, you bastard." In an instant, he scooped Émeline into his arms, cradled against his chest. "We have to get her help," he growled, setting off at a lope.

"Beau, if we move her—"

Touraine let her protests drop. Here or there, now or later. What did it matter? Grief settled over her. They were too used to hope's quick flicker to spare the words for arguments or questions when each second could mean the difference between life and death, but Touraine still had one, more important than everything—

"Where's Pru?"

"Held sniper. She cleared them, so I sent her back."

"Not clear enough, Beau," she growled back.

Tibeau looked stricken, and Touraine wished she'd kept her mouth shut. He'd never forgive himself for this. She wouldn't forgive herself, either.

The night went quiet except for their desperate huffing breaths as she followed him back to rue de la Petière.

Émeline was dead before they reached the guardhouse. Tibeau had run silently with her in his arms, but Touraine knew they'd shared at least some of the same thoughts.

Don't die. Of course she'll die. Please don't die. This is my fault. Fuck the rebels. Fuck Balladaire. Fuck me. Please don't die.

It was hopeless, as she'd known it would be. Émeline and Thierry lay in the courtyard on blankets someone had sacrificed for their bodies. She didn't even know when or how Thierry had fallen.

Touraine let the cold night air cool her flushed body. Her jacket was stiff and stinking with blood and waste. She balled the collar into her fist and let the hem drag through the dirt. Her hands were bloody to the wrists. She waited for everyone to bring in a cup of beer from the Sands' common room. (Had they been there all together just a day or two ago?) Tibeau looked to the corners of the courtyard, avoiding everyone's eyes, but especially hers. Pruett stood next to him, a quiet hand on his elbow.

The night had turned cold, but some soldiers stood with their coats unbuttoned, pale undershirts spotted with sweat. Some still had them buttoned to the throat.

Touraine took her usual place at the feet of the dead, and the rest of her squad circled off her. She hated this part of battle, of course. No one but a sadist could like this. Still, it reminded her why she did fight. As long as the Sands went into battle, she would go beside them.

She imagined that some of her soldiers prayed, forbidden as it was. Touraine didn't, but she had an old Qazāli song she remembered, and

the hum of it in her throat. As she stared at the bloody hole in Émeline's stomach, Touraine thought about her promotion. They'd died
coming after her. Being their captain wouldn't stop moments like this.

A jostling at the guardhouse entrance—tipsy carousing, a bawdy
joke—interrupted the vigil. Captain Rogan and a couple of other off-
duty captains swaggered into the courtyard. Rogan might even have
been sober. He stopped at the edge of the circle. Stared right at her.

"Lieutenant!" Rogan's voice was bright and cheery. "So glad to see
you've been retrieved."

Touraine let him take in the scene behind her, the circle of friends
around their fallen.

He tsked. "Sacrifices must be made. A pity."

"Will they be burned, Captain?"

Rogan flicked his eyes to the bodies, lips pursed in false concern. "I
don't think General Cantic will spend the little wood we have. You'll
have to do with a field burial, I'm afraid."

Cantic wouldn't waste the wood on a couple of Sands is what he
really meant. Never mind that they could fire horseshit to burn the
bodies. Never mind that the desert was dry and packed so dense that a
shovel would bounce back up.

Rogan went to his rooms, his friends chortling behind him like
geese. She wanted to scream at him, but she bit her tongue on the
words, blinked away the burning fury in her eyes, and took a deep,
shuddering breath.

A finer person, like Tibeau, would feel some pure selfless grief. Or
like Pruett, a tender empathy for the grieving. She would know how to
comfort them. Touraine felt only rage.

As long as Rogan was in charge, this was their lot. Nothing but
humiliation. Tibeau's dreams of revolt were—the product of a weak
mind? Uncivilized thinking? She couldn't bring herself to blame
him, but the dreams were flimsy, in any case. The Sands, the Qazāli,
wouldn't win that battle, and no one in their right mind chose starvation over food and pay. The problem here was Rogan and his ilk, not
Balladaire.

And yet a small voice said at the back of her mind, if the Sands didn't have to be soldiers at all, they wouldn't have to die. If only they were given the choice.

Touraine raised her cup to push the thoughts away, and the other Sands followed suit. They drank as one.

Then, as if a string knotting them together had been cut loose, the Sands went their own ways, to bunks or the small infirmary. Tibeau and a few others wrapped the bodies to ready them for transport to the compound. Noé, a small man with a handsome voice, sang a sad Balladairan song they all knew as they worked.

"As it whistles through the mountains, as it tickles blades of grass, as it pulls me from my bed, again, the wind, it cries your name."

Everyone found their own dark corners to mourn in. Someone's arms, the bottom of a cup. Touraine decided on her bunk. She trudged up the stairs alone and slammed the door shut behind her—tried to. It caught on Pruett's propped boot.

"Hiding from something?" Pruett cocked her head and an eyebrow. She held two cups of beer. She didn't show any signs of wear from the night's fighting. That, at least, was a relief. She stepped inside, set the cups down on the one small table, which held a lamp. She lit the lamp before closing the door.

"Hiding? Who? Me?" Touraine limped to her bed and eased herself down with the wall's help.

"You need the infirmary, Tour. Don't be stupid."

"Nope. The infirmary needs us. Without us, the medics would be out a job."

Pruett rolled her eyes and shoved one of the cups at Touraine.

"You know I hate drinking. I'm already fucked enough as it is." Just that many words left her wanting breath. Maybe the rib was more than fractured.

"Thought you'd make an exception tonight. You were blasted for three straight days after we got you back from the Taargens."

"Exactly."

Still, Touraine swallowed against dryness, weighing the potential dizzy sleep against the last—few?—days. She took the cup, and Pruett sat down on the bed beside her.

"You gonna tell me what happened?"

"She got caught by a bayonet. I flipped the bearfucker over the railing, and he cracked like a melon. How did you find me?"

"We got a tip. Not all of the Qazāli like the rebels. Might have exchanged some money, too." Pruett put a hand on Touraine's lower back. It was warm. "Where did you go, Tour?"

"I didn't go anywhere." Touraine drank deeply. The beer was better than she remembered.

"Why'd you leave? Did you...mean to leave? Did Cantic say you wouldn't get a promotion?"

"No. She said she could see me as captain one day." That wasn't exactly what Cantic had said, but she forced more confidence into her voice. "Head of a whole sky-falling company. Sky above, I ate with the fucking princess."

Pruett slouched, elbows on her knees. "What's wrong, then? Did they do something to you?" Pruett sounded guilty, as if she were the one who had done something wrong.

"Am I on trial?" Touraine snapped.

Pruett flinched. Touraine dropped her head against the wall, letting it loll, and caught the shape of the tapestry hanging behind her. A rug with a thick layer of dust covering a swirled pattern, just like in the rebels' room.

After a silence that stretched too long, Pruett spoke in the barest whisper. "The others are worried about you."

Touraine drained her cup, then held her hand out for the other. She emptied it in one go. Filling her stomach felt good. She only just realized how hungry she was. How hungry she would be in the morning.

"I could use a few more of those," she said.

Pruett stared at her in silence for one long breath, then stood. "I'll be back."

She returned with a tray of cups. "I had to fight for these. We should get you rinsed up first."

Pruett helped Touraine pull off her undershirt. She raked her eyes up and down Touraine's torso, the black and blue of it. Pruett's hand hovered over the scabbing cut the Brigāni had given her.

"Sky above, Touraine. Sky-falling fuck—"

Touraine gave her a crooked, tired smile and tried not to slump back into the wall. Part of her wanted to point out her new scar, to ask her about it. But the urge to sleep was sudden and real, as real as wanting to keep the lamp up high, to keep looking at Pruett.

So she drank while Pruett wiped down her back and chest, going carefully over the cuts, murmuring and soothing, until Touraine didn't feel the ropes around her wrists anymore.

She startled from her doze, jumping out of the bed, sloshing beer over the bedclothes, over her trousers. The room spun, out of focus, in focus, out again. A shadowed figure in the corner, that woman with her sky-falling boots—Touraine lurched.

Pruett leapt to her, snatching the cup away with one hand and holding her close with the other arm. "Shh, shh. Tour? Stay here, okay? Here. I've been there. You don't have to go back today. Stay here."

She kissed Touraine's temple, her eyebrows, her cheekbones, finally her lips. Then she led Touraine back to her bed and propped her up with pillows. She settled on the narrow cot beside her like a spoon.

"They don't trust me like they trust you." The words spun out of Touraine like the room spun. The rug on the wall spun, too. She turned away. "They listen to me because I'm your and Tibeau's friend."

Pruett settled against her. "That's not true. We're not that fickle. You get shit done like he and I don't. You're balanced."

"I'm not clever enough. Not brave enough, not passionate for the right—"

"You keep a cool head, Tour. That's what we need. Maybe not all the time, but that's okay." She rubbed Touraine's back in broad circles. "You think before you act. More than Tibeau, anyway. And I'd probably never act for thinking if I had my way. Me and him both need you.

The Sands need you. The Balladairans listen to you. That's why you're lieutenant. That's why you'll make captain." She punctuated each sentence with a gentle kiss on Touraine's shoulder, but the sensation was distant, and exhaustion pulled Touraine toward darkness.

A pounding on the door yanked Touraine from sleep. The stabbing in her ribs clenched her up.

"Sky above and earth below," she groaned. Fully conscious, she registered pain everywhere, as if she'd been beaten in the training yard a week straight.

Pruett startled awake beside her. She jumped back into her trousers.

The banging came again. "Lieutenant Touraine, open this door immediately."

Rogan's sharp accent stopped them cold, Touraine with an arm in her sleeve, Pruett with her hands on her trouser buttons.

Justice had always been a tricky thing with the Sands, even when they were innocent. It was hard to meet the fear in Pruett's eyes. Touraine cleared her throat and gave her the steadiest smile she could. Even though standing straight made her chest ache, and her brain felt too big for her skull.

"It'll be all right," Touraine promised. She was glad Pruett let her keep the lie.

She swung the door open. The morning was beautiful. Touraine could tell from the clear sunlight shining into the courtyard and into her room. It lit up the tapestry, a dark burgundy under the gray dust. The three cots, two pushed together, one untouched. The sun sparkled on Rogan's sleek dark hair as he grinned, wrist irons in his hands.

"Lieutenant Touraine, you're under arrest for sedition and the murder of a Balladairan soldier."

CHAPTER 7

THE GOVERNOR-GENERAL, AGAIN

The morning after her visit to the bookshop, Luca didn't have time to finish composing her request for Nasir to come work for her. Instead, she was woken from a deep, self-satisfied sleep by an urgent knock.

"Luca." Gil stepped inside and closed the door. "The general's come. It's an emergency."

That snapped Luca awake. "The city." She pointed for a pair of trousers—Gil shook his head. No time even to dress? Luca splashed her face with water and then wrapped herself in her evening robe, a voluminous thing of dark silk embroidered with pale roses.

General Cantic stood when Luca entered the sitting room. She held her tricorne in one hand against her chest. She was elegant in her well-tailored black uniform, gold sleeve gleaming in the morning light. Black boots polished to a high sheen rose to her knees. She must have been sweltering, but she didn't show it.

"Lord Governor Cheminade is dead, Your Highness."

Luca stopped midstride. Her hand jumped to her throat in surprise. "Killed?"

Cantic frowned sharply and shook her head like a displeased horse. "We aren't sure. She was found in the streets of the Old Medina. There were no visible marks of struggle or murder." But there was a *but*, and Cantic hadn't let go of it. She was frustrated over the failure of her people's examination, Luca could see.

Luca tried to placate the gaping ache she felt with logic. Otherwise, the loss of her first true ally felt too large to grasp. "She wasn't young. It's possible she suffered an attack of the heart, isn't it?"

As shock relinquished her limbs, Luca made her way to her own chair near the window. She gestured to the servant standing at the edge of the room. "General. Will you have a drink?"

"Thank you, no, Your Highness." Cantic didn't even take her seat. She stood with her arms behind her back. "I have other business to attend to this morning. I just wanted to give you the news and—"

The general began to steeple her fingers to pursed lips and then aborted the gesture, gripping her hat instead. She looked uncertain. The general was not a woman to look uncertain.

"We'll need to replace her immediately, Your Highness. The city is too strategically important to be without a governor, and she was also responsible for managing the lieutenant governors in the other provinces of Qazāl. There's correspondence to monitor, complaints from citizens to address regarding tariffs..." Cantic's voice rose in frustration before she controlled herself again.

"You won't take the seat yourself? You're the highest-ranking official here—"

The general bent her neck as if to stretch out tightness. She cleared her throat. "No, Your Highness. I'm not."

Ah. No, indeed, she wasn't.

"Anylight, only despots put cities under martial law," the general added.

"So you want me to take the position."

"Only as a stand-in, Your Highness. Temporarily until we find someone suitable. I wouldn't presume to give you a job, of course. Only to let you know that there is a vacancy that must be filled as soon as possible."

Luca looked out the window, picturing the city beyond, full of people pressing and pressing against each other in the Old Medina and avoiding each other in the New Medina. She thought of Cheminade's wink and the tender hand on her husband's. An ache spread through her chest and made her eyes sting. She blinked it all away.

She said, "If I take on Cheminade's duties—the governor-general reports directly to the metropole. I am the metropole."

"With the duke regent, of course."

Luca ignored that. As governor-general, there would be no middle official to wrangle. She could change policies in Qazāl herself, without weighing them over meeting after meeting. She would rule this city, the nation, every colony in the region, and the success would be hers. It would show her uncle and the people that she was formidable and sensible. A worthy ruler. The rebellion would be hers to end.

Any failure would be hers, too. No one to hide behind, to blame decisions on, except, perhaps, for Cantic.

"As regent, he only wants to maintain King Roland's empire, Your Highness. He won't jeopardize it."

Luca had no response for this. Her uncle had come up with the Droit-ist theories, ostensibly, yes, to integrate the colonies into the empire. His attitude and the theory itself, meant to curtail children with pain and rigid rules, would never achieve it, she was sure. Even Cantic said she disapproved of the Droitist methods. She sipped the coffee that the servant brought her, then twisted the cup in her hand.

Cantic dropped her hands to her sides and set her shoulders. "Will you accept her duties, Your Highness?"

Luca gave one slow nod. "I will."

"When you're ready to begin, I can show you her notes, the records, everything you need. Her aides will fill you in on everything, I'm sure.

"That said, there's the matter of your safety, Your Highness. Cheminade's death is suspicious on its own. When I consider your—" Cantic cleared her throat. "There's already been one attack on your person."

Luca nodded briskly. "I'll keep to the Quartier and the compound unless my duties take me elsewhere."

Cantic's relief showed in the sudden straightening of her shoulders.

"Thank you, Your Highness. Cheminade's death was…unexpected. A blow. If something happened to you, the empire would reel."

Luca raised her eyebrows. The words sounded disingenuous, but Cantic looked sincere. The older woman had a serious face, sharp jawed with deep-set eyes. Surprisingly, she reminded Luca of Gillett. They were both so rigid, and it made them capable. They were like oak trees, deep rooted and unbending. The similarity made Luca want to soften toward her, but this particular trait was also Gil's most infuriating.

"Thank you for your concern. Have the streets been like this very long?" *Or is it my arrival that makes them bold?*

"As much as it pains me to say it, Beau-Sang might have been right. It seems the rebels have grown more dangerous. After you read Cheminade's notes, we can go over the details." Cantic looked agitated again, eager to be gone. "She and I had discussed mandatory documentation for Qazāli, river sanctions, a citywide curfew to start."

Luca was intrigued. It sounded like the changes could help quell rebel activities, or at least make it difficult for them to maneuver. However, the implication that all Qazāli were prisoners would end poorly, like it had with the Verinom city-state back in the ancient ages. She knew enough of history—Balladairan included—to know they would toe dangerously close to breeding further resentment.

She caught the general's quick look toward the window.

"Are you worried about something, General?"

Cantic looked down, and her lips moved in what might have been the shadow of a smile. "Your Highness. I command over one hundred thousand lives. I'm always worried. It keeps us alive. I do have an urgent meeting, however, and I'm happy to leave you to your morning." The general tried and failed to cover up the exhaustion in her voice with a short, businesslike tone.

Luca wanted to ask, Had it ever been this bad? Did she think it would get worse? They were the questions of a child in need of reassurance. Luca wasn't a child.

Instead, she asked, "Where is Nasir?"

For a moment, the general's mask of command dissolved entirely.

She closed her eyes and shook her head, lips folded in. A second later, she was stern and implacable.

"It's hard to lose a spouse. He's gone to be with family in Zanafesh."

"I see." A palpable grief hung between the two of them, though Luca wasn't sure it was Cheminade that Cantic mourned. She wasn't sure it was Cheminade *she* mourned, either. "I'll come to go through Cheminade's office later."

Cantic's visit left Luca's mind full and fogged at the same time.

As she dressed for the day, she imagined Cheminade splayed across the ground. Had she been poisoned? Had she spasmed and choked on her own tongue? Had it been sudden and painless?

Had she seen it coming?

If Luca died, Uncle Nicolas would stay on the throne. The man was a coward. He wouldn't protect the nation from another outbreak of the Withering. He had chosen to run away to the north rather than stay in the city with the king and queen, helping their people. And he had signed away a fertile region of eastern Balladaire because he was afraid of the Taargens. If he stayed on the throne, who would stand for Balladaire? Her father's legacy, their empire, *her home* would be chipped away by enemies and plague until it fell.

When Luca emerged, Gil was waiting outside her door. She put a hand on his arm. She wanted to put her head on his shoulder and find comfort in his hug, but just the thought of it made her feel too small for the role she'd set herself.

Instead, she went up to her office and sat at her desk. With so much to do, and the city hostile to her, she couldn't get to the books and the magic they offered. That was only a dream, anyway. As governor-general, she held true power in her hands, and an entire quartier hoped for influence with her or her uncle. Time to play the role, then. To gather all the pieces to her and see how she could make them move.

CHAPTER 8

THE LIEUTENANT

The murder of a Balladairan soldier?

Rogan whistled as he marched Touraine to the general's door. Dread weighed her boots down, but she refused to let Rogan drag her. He knocked sharply, regulation three times. Cantic called, and he pushed Touraine in. Rogan saluted; Touraine did not. The effect would have been ruined by the manacles around her wrists, and Touraine preferred not to call attention to them.

"Thank you, Captain. You're dismissed."

Rogan's glee flickered. "Yes, sir." A smirk still played across his mouth as he walked out.

The room was bright with sunlight, and Touraine squinted. She would kill Pruett for this hangover. She blinked hard and focused on the general.

"Explain yourself, Lieutenant." General Cantic loomed over her desk, which was covered in stacks of fresh ivory-colored paper, pristine and more expensive than Touraine could even imagine. Letters from the regent, perhaps. The lines of her face were deep with disappointment. No nostalgic fondness this time.

Touraine looked suspicious. She couldn't change that. And if she couldn't convince Cantic that she was innocent, she would die.

She spilled everything, from the carriage driver tricking her and her getting lost in the Old Medina to Émeline's death in the rescue.

Everything except that she had gotten so drunk on the governor-general's wine that she had passed out.

"You deny killing the Balladairan soldier?"

"What soldier, sir? I have no idea what you're talking about."

"We found his body in an alley, his skull bashed in and his...testicles removed and placed inside his mouth." Cantic frowned in distaste.

Touraine's mouth dropped in surprise. Despite the horror of the crime, though, she couldn't muster much sympathy. She had her own grudges against Balladairan soldiers who thought those with less power were playthings. Cantic's frown deepened.

"Whoever he pissed off, General, it wasn't me. I never even saw a blackcoat that night. I swear it."

"A bloody baton lay nearby."

Touraine stopped breathing. Her baton was gone.

"Sir, one of the rebels took my baton that night." Touraine had forgotten. Stupid. If she hadn't goaded that asshole of a woman, maybe Touraine would still have her weapon. She wouldn't be in *quite* so shitty a position. "She took my baton off my belt. They—she must have killed him. She could have left him to set me up, or—"

"If that's true, help me help you. Did you get any information from the rebels? Anything could be valuable." There was an urgency in that rusty, smoke-damaged voice. Had the damage happened because of the general's smoking habit, or in the Brigāni's fires?

"I don't have anything, sir. I'm sorry. They questioned me but they covered their faces. They never even said their names."

She started to say *There was a Brigāni who asked me to spy on you* but stopped herself. Cantic would never trust her again.

"Did they torture you?" Cantic's expression was part tenderness, part threat.

Touraine nodded slowly. "I was beaten. And cut. They threatened me with...magic. As you said, sir. They're uncivilized. Nothing worse than we were trained to tolerate, sir."

And yet. Touraine still felt the knife on her chest, still saw the

Brigāni studying her blood. As if she would make Touraine a puppet. The wound began to itch.

"Then why didn't you report to the infirmary?"

"I don't know, sir. Exhaustion was no excuse." Nor was grief. "I'll show you the damage if you want further proof."

Cantic frowned at her desk, shifted something on it. Shifted it back. Nothing hidden meant less guilt. As Cantic opened her mouth to pass judgment, Touraine said in a rush, "The second one asked about you, sir."

Cantic paused the shuffle of papers. "Who?"

The general's blue eyes dug into her, picking her clean. It sent Touraine spinning back into an insecure vulnerability she hadn't felt for a decade. She froze before she could respond one way or another, hesitated a moment too long.

Cantic misinterpreted the silence. "Enough." She threw the papers down in disgust and turned away. "We're done here."

"Sir, a Brigāni, golden eyes, I don't know what else, a robe—"

Cantic looked back sharply. "A Brigāni? A woman?"

"I don't know who. Just…" Touraine flushed. "She claims you killed her family. That you burned them all."

The general's breath caught, and something unreadable crossed her face. "Anything else?"

"No, sir." Touraine shook her head. "Except—sir, please look at my record. It's excellent. I would never betray you or Balladaire. You've given me too much."

"I understand, Lieutenant. However, it's difficult to believe under these circumstances, and you actually do have some particular altercations with other Balladairan soldiers against your record—"

"Sir, I'm not asking you to believe me. I'm asking you to trust me." Touraine's fists were clenched white-knuckle tight in front of her, as if she could hold Cantic by the coat and shake the truth into her. "Please, sir."

Cantic deflated. She kept her eyes on the desk. "This is unfortunate, Lieutenant."

"Sir?"

General Cantic held out her palm. She still didn't meet Touraine's eyes. "You are relieved of your rank as lieutenant until further review. You will not return to the barracks. For now, you'll be in custody."

Belatedly, Touraine realized the general was waiting for her lieutenant's pins, two pairs of golden wheat stalks bound together. Her hands shook, clattering the manacles as she grasped her collar.

"Now, Lieutenant."

Touraine pulled the pins' clasps and dropped the golden wheat stalks into Cantic's palm. The general finally looked up, and Touraine held her gaze as steadily as she could.

"The charges stand. You'll be tried, and your commanding officer will have a chance to speak on your behalf. We'll weigh that, along with any testimony you have to offer, against the evidence." Cantic sidestepped around her desk, ushered Touraine out of the office, and gestured to two nearby blackcoats. "Take her to the brig. Give her water and food. Send a medic."

Touraine spun around, her knees weak, hoping for a hint of the woman who had slipped her candy when she was a child. "Sir!"

The words died in her throat. The general was giving her the other look Touraine remembered from childhood. The look that said, *I don't want to do this, but you've left me no choice.* It said punishment was coming.

For murder and sedition. Sky above. Touraine was as good as dead.

The soldiers pinned her arms roughly to her sides and marched her all the way to a squat building at the far end of the compound.

Despite everything, the coolness of the rock and the windowless dark was a relief. And then the sergeant shoved her into her cell.

"Here you are, *Lieutenant*," the sergeant sneered.

They left her in the dark.

In the darkness of the jail cell, Touraine blinked and stared until the black outlines of the bars were silhouetted against the darker black of the small corridor. The jailer must keep the lamp in his office. No reason to waste a torch on a Sand prisoner.

A prisoner who would be court-martialed and likely executed in less than a week.

Touraine growled wordlessly at the empty dark.

"Shut your mouth, Sand whore!" the jailer said.

Sky above, if she could kick that asshole rebel with the boots in the teeth just once, she'd go happily to her grave. Thanks to her, Touraine wouldn't even go to a firing squad like a soldier but hunched like a beggar.

The worst thing about the darkness was that even when she opened her eyes, her mind could still project one of two pictures on a black canvas:

Pruett's fear-gray face, stormy eyes wide as Rogan locked cold iron around Touraine's wrists and led her away, or—

Cantic's face, red with anger held in check, words toneless in disappointment.

No, worse than that was not knowing which woman's face had been the greater blow. Didn't matter. As a lieutenant, she'd failed them both.

If Cantic would just listen to her, if there was a way to get the rebels, to bring them in and prove she was innocent *and* loyal—if she could make the lock open by waving her fingers over it, if she could kill Rogan just by saying his name and biting her tongue. As Aimée liked to say on campaign—and in the canteen, and in training exercises—wishes were like assholes. Full of shit.

Touraine pushed herself off the ground. Her body was tight, but her headache had eased. The food and water the jailer had brought after she'd arrived were basic but satisfying to a starving body. She hadn't eaten since that fancy dinner with the fancy governor and her fancy guests. Perhaps Lord Governor Cheminade would reach out again. Little silver threads of hope to trail after.

It helped to go slowly through her fighting forms. To give herself some occupation instead of letting the fear coil into desperate energy that would only chew at her from the inside. It ordered her thoughts. When she was moving, she was powerful. Her body rarely let her down. She knew its faults and its compensations, knew when to back away from the pain and when to dig into it, even when injured. She knew what her body could do, what she could teach it to do, and what it never would do. It was hers.

Or so she thought. The more time she had to think, the less everything made sense. It didn't seem right that she would pass out like she had that night. She hadn't had more than two cups of that wine, one with dinner and one with Cheminade. If it had been that strong, she would have felt the effects sooner. Wouldn't she?

It had felt more like she'd taken a dose of valerian, the sleeping herb the Sands took when nightmares or pain kept them awake. Or like the valerian and a kick to the head. But if Touraine had been drugged, it meant someone at the dinner had done it. Maybe even Cheminade. Why? She was just a Sand.

Probably a dead Sand, at that. She would never prove she was drugged before trial, and no one would take her word over a Balladairan's. Even if she survived, the dream of her promotion was dead. She was a compromised soldier. The best she could hope for was low camp-follower duties, like digging latrines or scrubbing dried blood out of uniforms.

At this remove, losing the dream felt like being cut adrift in the ocean and forgotten. No—not exactly. Balladairan justice was a swift shot or a short drop. So this was more like being cut adrift and then torn to pieces by a sea monster with rows of dagger teeth and—

Touraine stopped and straightened, shook the acid burn in her body away. She slumped against the bars of the cell door and let them dig deep into the tight muscles. She slid from side to side, reveling in a friendlier pain.

Until she found the cracked rib instead of the muscle.

"Ugh."

Her pain sounded bizarre in the emptiness. Had she ever been so alone before in her life? No complaints, no jokes—no hushed moans of a covert fuck in crowded barracks, no whispered arguments.

Actually, this was the worst thing, worse even than her Sands at Rogan's mercy: if she was left drying to leather on some gallows frame, the Sands would break apart. Tibeau and his band would go. They'd run to find family or to disappear in a desert of brown faces. That would leave Pruett and those sensible enough—or too afraid or too attracted to Balladaire's gifts—to take the punishment instead. Whips, docked pay, brands, hunger, more—Balladaire's gold stripes were full of creative ideas, Droitist and otherwise.

And when the blackcoats found Tibeau, they would kill him.

Touraine found herself short of breath just thinking of it. She didn't know how it could be more terrifying than leading them into battle after battle, and yet…

Balladaire was a land of gifts and punishment, honey and whips, devastating mercies.

When she was a child and new to the green country full of massive trees and covered in grass and flowers, she ate too much. Always afraid the food would be taken away—or that it would run out. Such luxury, to sit at a full board every day. One day, she ate herself sick, and a young Cantic carried Touraine in her arms like a baby to the infirmary for a miracle medicine. Perhaps she hadn't been so far from that. A baby.

Then there was the first time she'd fought with Rogan, ended up on the wrong side of a midnight brawl. If Pruett and Aimée, Tibeau and Thierry hadn't come to rescue her, Rogan would have had his way with her a long time ago. The next morning, their captain (Cantic was long gone by then) led Touraine to the infirmary. She'd scarcely believed her luck! For one delusional moment, she'd thought Rogan and his flunkies would pay. Justice was sweet enough to ease the shame of her helplessness.

The whip snaps and the screams filtered in through the infirmary's open window. She couldn't see outside, but she knew Pruett's raised voice. She knew Tibeau's yell and Thierry's shriek and Aimée's swearing growl, and Touraine had to listen to them all as she wept into her bandages.

They'd all been whipped when Mallorie "came home," too. While Mallorie watched. Before they executed her for desertion.

Harsh training, but easy to learn, to fall in. To do well and keep your doubts to yourself.

It was Balladaire where they'd celebrated the harvest season every year with the smell of baking bread and roasting vegetables wafting across the compound to mix with the wonderful rot of autumn leaves. Their mouths watering during drills. The race to bathe and get to the table for the feast.

It was the mountains and the trees she had fought for, the bread and the herbs her soldiers had died for.

It was home. And she was drifting farther and farther away from it.

Deep down, maybe she'd thought that her promotion would show the other Sands that it really was best to stay with Balladaire. That there was fairness. That loyalty really would be rewarded and there was logic to the world.

"Argh!" She slapped the wall in a burst, and the sting echoed up her forearm.

"Said shut your fucking mouth, didn't I? Or I'll come shut it for you!"

If Cantic found her guilty and executed her, she'd prove Touraine wrong. And why should the Sands stay then?

CHAPTER 9

THE COURT-MARTIAL

Two days later, or maybe three, or maybe just one, things got worse.

The jailer was speaking to someone, but she couldn't make out specific words. Only a familiar honking bray. Touraine recoiled from the bars, like she could hide somewhere in the cramped cell.

"You're looking well, Lieutenant Touraine." Rogan raked Touraine up and down with his eyes. He turned to the jailer with a smirk. "Did you manage to have any fun before the trial?"

Touraine made out the disgust on the jailer's face in the light of his lantern. The man had the single wheat stalk of a sergeant pinned to each side of his collar.

"Best not to mix with the like, Captain," he said.

Touraine was offended and comforted at the same time. Without another look at her, the jailer unlocked her door and cuffed her wrists behind her back. The skin was healing slowly from the rebels' ropes, thanks to the medic's ointments and quiet *tsks*.

Rogan led Touraine out of the jail, his fingers tight on her arm.

The sky was blindingly bright with late-morning blue; the sun warmed her immediately. Soldiers and aides and all the others who made an army run smooth marched or scurried through the compound, from barracks to mess hall, from sick bay to barracks, from training yard to sick bay. They barked orders that would be followed half-heartedly, delivered bad news, practiced drills they should have known better. It looked different here in Qazāl, all bare sandstone and clay, dirt and sand, but this was the world that made sense to her. She knew her place in it.

But it came with problems she couldn't escape on her own. When she glanced sideways at Rogan, his expression was professional, a consummate soldier following orders. His words, however, were his own.

"I haven't forgotten what I owe you," he said.

They fell in smooth step together, as soldiers do. That alone was intimate enough to make her stomach churn.

"Your trial will not go well. The general will hear your testimony, and she'll be gravely disappointed. She'll want to believe you. Until I testify. And when the court finds you guilty, I'll pay you a special visit in your cell. I'm sure the jailer will turn a blind eye despite his opinions on mixing with ... the like. How does that sound? Even Cantic won't care what I do with a condemned woman."

Her pulse beat like a frightened rabbit's, and she hated herself for it.

A blackcoat opened the door of the administrative building, and Rogan pushed Touraine through. Aides and soldiers alike stared at them as Rogan marched her inside and down to Cantic's office. He didn't say another word, but the damage was done. She couldn't possibly win.

"Touraine. You're accused of treason against the empire and murder of a Balladairan soldier. How do you plead?" General Cantic leaned forward, elbows on the long table at the front of the small audience room, her hands steepled.

Touraine. Just Touraine, the name unadorned, the way the Balladairans had handed it out to her as a child, along with her new clothes and new bed and new language. She had never disliked the sound of her name before that moment. She sat in a stiff-backed wooden chair, her arms wrapped around it and her locked wrists dangling. She was going nowhere. She wondered if the Sands had been told about her trial, or if Pruett and Tibeau had been left to wonder.

Cantic wore her formal uniform, all black except for the gold left sleeve. The four other gold stripes presiding wore their formals, too. They sat arrayed to Cantic's left and right at the long table. The room they all sat in was probably where they all came together to discuss strategies when they weren't glaring disapprovingly at soldiers, waiting for them to answer for their crimes. It lacked the usual attempts at martial decor, no mounted swords or old muskets on the walls, no war tapestries. Maybe they kept those in another room. The starker, the more frightening.

The princess was in the small room, too, waiting. The heir wouldn't come to a simple court-martial for murder. That meant Cantic was taking the charge of treason seriously. The young woman's face was stern and haughty, lips pursed. The elegant woman Touraine had met before looked cold and intimidating. The effect was enhanced by the two royal guards flanking her and the captain of the guard standing at the door. They wore black coats, but their button panels were gold and the buttons black. Their short gold cloaks hung still, as if the cloaks, too, were waiting for Touraine's answer.

Touraine had always had faith in Balladaire, or at the very least, Cantic. She hoped that faith wasn't misplaced. She took a breath, deep as her healing ribs would allow.

"I'm innocent, sir."

"Then explain yourself for the jury."

"As I said before, sir, I got lost after the driver let me off too early."

Touraine fought for another breath. The windows were shuttered tight against eavesdropping. It kept the sun out, but it kept clean air out, too. A room full of sweating men and women shouldn't be closed off from a breeze. The manacles on her wrists were already slick with sweat. One officer hadn't put on enough scent to mask his body odor; another officer had put on too much.

"As you say. What next?"

"I . . . think I was drugged, sir. At the governor-general's dinner."

Now someone did laugh. Touraine turned sharply. A muscular colonel with gray streaks in his close-cut beard smiled. "She drank too much, General, and she's trying to cover her mistakes."

Touraine ignored him. "Truly, sir." She tried to explain her logic—the strange drowsiness, the fog—but one of them was picking her nails and another was looking at Touraine like she was something he'd cleaned *out* of his nails.

"Maybe you could ask the governor," Touraine said, reaching desperately. "Maybe she noticed someone acting strange that night." Touraine wasn't going to throw her life away by accusing the governor of drugging her, no matter what reasons the woman had. Accusing a Balladairan never went well for a Sand.

Cantic laced her fingers and rested them on the desk. "Unfortunately, Lord Governor Cheminade is dead. Furthermore, whether you were drunk or drugged, it is your actions on trial, not your mental state at the time."

The news shocked Touraine's body rigid against the chair. How? Why? Was it the rebels? The questions ticked one after another, spinning in her mind so that she didn't hear Cantic at first.

"Soldier!" barked Cantic. "What happened next?"

Touraine recounted the rest: waking up in custody, the questions her captors asked. She lingered on the woman who had kicked her. Cantic asked her the same questions as she had before. The rest of the panel seemed almost bored until the questions circled back to the Brigāni.

"What did she talk about?" Cantic asked.

"You, sir."

The jury of officers took a collective breath, and Touraine rushed to continue while she had their attention. "She wants to kill you."

Cantic raised an eyebrow at the bluntness. "She can get in the queue with everyone else. For the sake of the court, did she say why?"

"You killed her family."

"Very good." Cantic's face was impassive again.

Touraine was losing her, losing all of them. She'd run out of what little good faith they had, if they'd had any. She didn't know how else to prove her loyalty.

"Sir?" she started. "The Brigāni also implied that the Shālans had magic like the Taargens, sir." Touraine shrugged apologetically.

The general narrowed her eyes. "Implied? Did she or didn't she say so?"

"She said, 'Rumors must come from somewhere.' I took that to mean there's a hint of truth even in our stories. If the stories about the Taargens had some truth, so do the ones about the Brigāni. There might be plans to use this magic against Balladaire again. Whatever it was."

Touraine thought of her arm again and felt the need to rub at it, as if she could pick it raw and learn what had happened to her. She'd bet that was Shālan magic, too, but she didn't dare show that to anyone.

For a moment, Cantic only shifted her jaw, like she was working something in her mouth. She spun the ring on her right little finger. Even the secretary's pen stopped scratching as he waited. Touraine had struck a nerve, and all that pain and fury working behind those eyes— she'd suffer the brunt of it.

The princess had lost her stern disinterest. She sat on the edge of her seat, hands balanced on her cane, right leg straight out. When they'd been briefly introduced at Cheminade's dinner, she had seemed courteous but aloof. Now Touraine saw that she had clever eyes that didn't miss much.

"This is preposterous, Cantic. Are we holding court or listening to fairy stories?" said the gray-bearded colonel. "I support due process, but this?"

The general waved him down. "Colonel Taurvide, please. Touraine, what of the other rebel?"

"Nothing important, sir. She only kicked me in an attempt at torture, but as I said, I gave her nothing."

"Anything else in your defense?"

"No, sir, only—two of my soldiers died in my rescue."

"Yes."

"They should have a funeral."

Rogan interrupted. "General, resources are precious. Sacrifices—"

"I'll pay the funerary expenses. Carry on." Princess Luca's voice was cool, matter-of-fact. It was the first she'd spoken since the trial began. Catching the princess's equally cool blue-green eyes felt like catching a sniper that had you in her sights.

"Captain Rogan," Cantic said. "Your testimony regarding the accused?"

Rogan stood at attention between Touraine and the jury, grimacing.

"Perhaps one might call Lieut—excuse me, Touraine capable. Her loyalty, however, has always been in question. She has attacked Balladairan soldiers in the past." His face was grave.

He pulled a piece of paper from his pocket and unfolded it, snapping it crisply before giving it to the general. "I also present the following examination notes on Corporal LeBlanc's body. In summary, he was attacked with a long, blunt object hard enough to fracture his skull. The…disfigurement…to his face suggests multiple strokes. The wounds are congruent with those inflicted by the conscripts' batons, sir, and Touraine was the only conscript unaccounted for at the time of his death. The baton found near his body makes it clear, as all other conscripts' batons are accounted for. I would not put collusion with intent to mutiny beyond her."

"Any evidence against her own claim? That she was taken by rebels?" Cantic asked without taking her eyes from the paper.

"Wounds can be fabricated, sir, if you're desperate enough to build a lie. Moreover," he added, his voice turning somber, haunted even, "I'll never forget the time she led her…comrades in an attack on my men and me. Late at night. Years ago, but I don't think that the seed for that kind of insurrection ever quite dies."

She saw the bait, how he dangled it in front of her. Touraine clenched her fists so tight behind her that she thought she'd cut herself and bleed all over Cantic's stone floor. It was too much.

She bit the hook. "You lying bastard!" The words burst out, even though she knew her temper would condemn her. Her pulse throbbed all the way to her fingertips. Her body burned with heat. "I ought to cut your own dick off, you raping—"

"Touraine!" Cantic slammed her palm on the table.

The general's face remained unreadable, but the other officers glowered at Touraine's outburst. She saw her guilt in each gaze and last of all Rogan's smugness. It made her want to be sick. Blood pounded behind her eyes, and she ground her teeth.

"Sirs," Touraine started again, in as measured a tone as she could manage. "I lost my baton to the rebel who kicked me, not fighting a blackcoat."

"That was careless of you," one of the jury officers said.

"More careless than killing a man and leaving my weapon in the street with his body?" she snapped. "Which makes more sense to you?" Touraine bit down on her tongue. She needed to get herself back under control, but the unfairness of it all was driving her ragged.

She turned to Cantic. "Sir, you said the soldier's balls were stuffed in his mouth—I couldn't do that. We don't have knives."

"So you threw the knife away—"

Touraine cut off the other officer. "If I would hide the knife, why wouldn't I hide my baton?" She turned back to Cantic. "Sir."

Cantic looked from Rogan to Touraine. There was disappointment, but maybe pain, too. Did the general feel guilty? Guilty enough to give her another chance?

How had Touraine gone from saving the princess and receiving the highest honor a Sand had ever received to begging for her life in front of this farce of a court-martial?

"Thank you, Captain," Cantic said, as if Touraine hadn't said a thing. "Sergeants, escort her back to the jail while we recess. Not you, Captain, stay—"

As the sergeants approached her, Touraine had a desperate thought, more desperate than the host of desperate thoughts she'd had over the last few days.

She had saved the fucking princess's life. Princess Luca owed her. She'd said so herself.

If this backfired, Touraine might be shot on the spot for her audacity. Still, it was better than waiting in jail for Rogan and *then* being shot.

"General," she said. The other officers were talking over each other in outrage. Rogan watched her, and even though his face was the picture of grim dignity, she read the smugness in the cocky set of his shoulders. The princess was watching her carefully, as if she could read Touraine's mind. As if she could read it and wasn't upset by what she saw there.

The sergeants had her by the arms. Louder: "General Cantic, sir."

The general held up her hand to stem the conversations. "Speak."

"I saved the princess—"

"Helped save. You alerted us to a threat."

Touraine pursed her lips tight. "Just so, sir. I helped save Her Highness's life." She nodded to the princess, the closest to a bow that she could manage. "Your Highness, I would ask the boon you promised me."

The princess's mouth made a round moue, her eyes just a fraction wider. At the table, the officers clamored again, but Touraine didn't look away from the princess, who didn't look away from her.

"Ask." Princess Luca's cool voice cut through the noise, silencing the officers as effectively as Cantic's hand.

Touraine swallowed, her mouth suddenly dry.

"I ask for my life," she said, as steadily as she could. It was as if saying it aloud reminded her how badly she didn't want to die just yet. Not here, not without any say in it.

General Cantic slammed her hand on the table, breaking the link between Touraine and the princess as everyone jumped.

"Touraine, you overstep. Sergeants—"

"I would like to ask her a question or two, General." The princess stepped in again. Her voice was like a dip into a cold river on an already frigid day.

The look of hesitation passed so quickly across Cantic's face that Touraine almost missed it. She sat up straighter.

"Heads of state have no sway here, Your Highness. This is strictly a military proceeding."

"She is on trial for treason against the crown, is she not?"

Cantic's lips tightened and she nodded. "Yes, Your Highness."

"And as the governor-general of the southern colonies, I'm also responsible for crimes committed in my jurisdiction, correct?"

She's the governor-general now? Touraine thought with surprise.

Cantic nodded again.

Princess Luca limped to stand in front of Touraine, slouching to favor her right leg. If Pruett's eyes were the sea in a storm, Princess Luca's were the middle of the ocean on a cloudless day, clear and blue green with nothing friendly in their depths. She was a slight woman, wearing simple but elegant clothing tailored close to her narrow frame. A golden horse head gleamed on her black cane. Her lips were pink and parted as she studied Touraine. Touraine's heartbeat sped up under her gaze.

"Lieutenant Touraine. Did you receive any letters of seduction from the rebels? A message to convince other conscripts to join them?"

"No, Your Highness."

"Have you attempted to coerce your fellow soldiers to join the Qazāli rebellion?"

"No, Your Highness."

"Have you passed sensitive information or military knowledge or weapons to the rebels?"

"I would never, Your Highness."

The princess weighed Touraine's answers with pursed lips and narrow eyes. Her tight bun made her even more severe. She had the same clipped accent as Rogan but without the condescension. To condescend, you had to be close enough to have an opinion. The princess held herself apart from everyone.

"Did you know or were you alerted to the attempt on my life in advance?"

"No, Your Highness."

"Then how did you know the attack was coming?"

"I saw a man, the old man..." Touraine trailed off. *You look familiar*, he'd said. "He kept trying to pull me into a conversation, but I caught him looking toward the girl who attacked you." The girl who had prayed on the scaffold before Touraine hanged her. "That's when I sounded the alert."

"Why would the rebels frame you for murdering a Balladairan soldier?"

Touraine looked at the princess's boots for a long moment before finally shrugging helplessly. "I don't know. I wasn't cooperative? To move suspicion somewhere else? To make a rift between the Sands and the blackcoats? They might not have been trying to frame me at all."

The princess's face was solemn. "General, other than the baton, is there evidence to prove this soldier is lying?"

The princess cocked her head at the general like an owl. Cantic bounced the gaze to Rogan, whose lips tightened.

"I have no more questions." The princess sat back down.

The silence of the room weighed on Touraine's shoulders. She kept her eyes on Cantic, who stared her down.

"We'll have a brief recess to discuss sentencing—"

"Hang her and let's be done with it," Colonel Taurvide said, already standing up. "We've all got more important things to do."

"We'll discuss sentencing." Cantic glared at Taurvide until he sat down again. Then she nodded to the waiting sergeants. "Take her back."

"Guilty!" The colonel called Taurvide yelled so adamantly that his saliva splashed Luca's face. She pulled out her handkerchief and dabbed it away.

Luca had been focused on the soldier's retreating broad, straight back, even after the door had closed. The other woman was frightened—that much was clear—but she was also bold in a rather intriguing way. It took a certain kind of strength to fight for your life when everyone around you had already decided you should die.

"I know you trained half of those sand fleas, but even you can't be thinking of keeping her in with the others. That talk will spread, and soon we'll have a whole other revolt on our hands, this time from the inside." Taurvide tried to loom over Cantic and, by all accounts, should have done a good job at it. He was a slab of muscle who hadn't formed the same administrative paunch as the other high officers had. He was bluster and heat, but she was the chill stone of a mountain face.

Other officers protested on top of each other.

"You can't possibly think she deserves anything but the noose. She's no better than a common criminal."

"The screws first, so we can get the truth out of her. Then shoot her and clean our hands of the whole business."

With separate looks, the general bade each of the officers to speak their piece on the verdict and sentencing, while she said nothing. It was a strange place for the general to have a tender spot, if Luca read the drag at the corners of Cantic's eyes correctly.

After the officers had spoken, Cantic turned weary eyes on Luca. Perhaps Luca only imagined the pleading in her expression. "You don't owe the girl anything, Your Highness."

Perhaps Luca didn't owe her. Perhaps Lanquette and Guérin would have caught the would-be assassin in time, even without the lieutenant's alert. But Luca had given her word. She wanted to be the kind of queen whose word meant something.

As if he knew what Luca was weighing, Colonel Taurvide crossed his arms over his broad chest. "You can't be worried about keeping your word to a Sand. They're like children. Promise them sweets to make them happy, then put them off until they forget." He waved a hand carelessly. "She can't come back for a sweet bun when she's dead, can she?"

He grinned at his compatriots, and all but Cantic joined him, chuckling.

The young captain Rogan was smug but had been reserved thus far. He clenched his fist in restrained triumph, and something about that felt wrong, too.

Luca had been careless with her words to the soldier at Cheminade's dinner. Her offer had been flippant; she had only expected to give the woman some money or some other royal bauble. The lieutenant *had* tried to save Luca's life, though, and that was worth something.

And, perversely, the more Colonel Taurvide and the young captain wanted Lieutenant Touraine dead, the more Luca wanted her to live.

Those were not the only reasons she wanted Touraine alive.

"To the contrary. I owe that woman my life as much as I owe my guards," Luca said from her chair. Flanked by Lanquette and Guérin, she felt more force behind her words. Still, she was in hostile territory. The military didn't look kindly on conceding military decisions to politicians. "It's one of the highest levels of loyalty. As for her crimes, the evidence is not conclusive. Even if she were guilty, we can't deny that she could be useful. She has a history of loyalty to General Cantic. She's Qazāli. She's met the rebels."

The soldier sounded educated enough, even if she wasn't a scholar. Her comportment at Cheminade's dinner was more than impressive. And she had combat skills. With Nasir gone...

"Let's send her back to the rebels. As my assistant, my negotiator."

The line in Cantic's forehead deepened as she frowned. "We're not negotiating with rebels against the empire, Your Highness."

Luca folded her hands over her cane in front of her. *Slowing down is the key to control.* A rhetorician's guide. She let herself take a breath, instead of rushing to justify herself and prove to Cantic why they should be negotiating instead of fighting. The present company would never accept it.

"General, you said yourself that you struggle to get spies into the rebels' ranks. We can try again. Let her play the origin-searching sympathizer. Even if the rebels never fully trust her, we can get trickles of information. At worst, they'll kill a soldier who's already condemned."

"If they don't trust her, why would they give her information?" It was a woman colonel, almost as solidly thick as Taurvide. The one who wanted the thumbscrews before execution.

"What makes you think torturing the soldier will get you good information?" Luca cocked her head and gave a condescending shrug. The colonel shrank back. "She'll earn their trust by feeding them fabricated leads. If they think we're willing to make concessions, they'll warm like wax. If they feed us false information, we can cross-reference it with other intelligence you gather. We'll learn just as much by what they tell us as by what they don't tell us."

Most importantly, the soldier would be in a position to ask questions. The rebels wouldn't tell her about the magic outright, not at first, but the soldier could observe. With time, maybe the answers would slip out naturally, or they could make an alliance, trading the magic...So many possibilities.

"And if she runs off to play rebel with the lot of them?" Taurvide asked. He still sat with his arms folded, fingers now tapping on biceps that strained against his coat.

Here, Luca had no other response. The woman's life was already forfeit. It couldn't be more forfeit. It was as risky as hiring a mercenary. But everyone was a mercenary, according to *The Rule of Rule*; it was only a matter of finding their price. Sometimes that price was money, but it wasn't the only—or even the most—effective payment. As Gil had said, never overlook a good weapon. It would be silly to throw out a sword because it needed sharpening.

The general stepped in. "I have every reason to believe that this soldier, if given another chance to prove herself, could be extremely loyal. It's a classic part of the punishment-reward cycle in Droitist and Tailleurist theories. She responded well to the hybrid form of teaching I used in her youth."

The mention of her uncle's theory still sent crawling ants up Luca's back, but she nodded. "I'll take her as part of the governor-general's staff." At Cantic's surprise—and Gil's stiffened back—she added, "As you said, she's not fit to return among the ranks."

For several tense, silent seconds, they all watched Cantic thinking, her steepled fingers against her lips. Finally, she folded her hands on her desk.

"Use her, Your Highness. But if you have even the hint of a suspicion—" Cantic met Gil's eyes.

Luca nodded crisply once. "As I said, General. She's already condemned."

And that was how Luca came to be visiting a condemned woman in the dimness of the compound jail, with a secret aim she hadn't discussed with the military court. An aim she'd barely thought through herself. Adapting worked like that sometimes.

She wanted that soldier. Needed her. The soldier knew about the magic. She had connections, however tenuous, however dubious, to the rebels. And she was a loose agent no longer earmarked for another task and otherwise sentenced to death. She was, in other words, dispensable. Despite what Luca had said to Cantic's face, that thought didn't sit well in Luca's chest. It made her think of Beau-Sang's boy with the cut fingers. She couldn't even remember his name.

If the soldier could play her role well enough to learn about the magic, all the risk would be worth it. Luca got a weapon; the soldier got her life. If the woman was loyal.

So I'll keep her loyal.

"Are you sure about this?" Gillett asked quietly, for her ears only. "We could think on this overnight."

"Of course I'm sure." If she waited overnight, she might lose her nerve. That and she didn't trust Colonel Taurvide to leave the soldier unmolested.

The soldier—ex-soldier now, Luca supposed—leaned against the yellow-brown stone wall of her cell. Everything was yellowed further by the lantern light, even the woman's skin. Everything that wasn't cast into dim shadow, rather.

The woman squinted up. Then she scrambled to her feet and bowed, hissing slightly at some unaccounted-for pain. "Your Highness."

Luca turned to the jailer. "You may leave, monsieur. All the way out. Close the door." He gaped, trying to find some excuse not to abandon his charge, but she held her hand out. He gave her the lantern and returned to his office in the dark.

The soldier in the officers' planning room had looked desperate, almost frantic. Until she had called Luca's debt. Here, in the half dark, the lone lamp deepened the shadows under her eyes and made her look like a starving wolf. Rangy and wary and dangerous. The steady strength from Cheminade's dinner party was buried almost too deep for Luca to see—there were still traces of it in the set of her jaw, her weary but unbowed shoulders. Again, the impulse that Luca did not want this woman to die. Not like this.

The woman wore only her uniform undershirt, which was unlaced to show collarbone and muscle. Muscle showed in her forearms, too. She had broad, scarred hands with long fingers. Luca wondered—only academically, of course—how much strength it took to bludgeon a man to death with the Sands' batons. Luca cleared her throat.

"Lieutenant Touraine," Luca said. "I'm sorry to meet you again under such circumstances."

Touraine bowed again. Luca caught the brief twist of an ironic smile. "So am I, Your Highness. How may I serve?"

Luca held the lamp higher. "I have a proposition for you," she said bluntly. "I need a well-rounded assistant. Someone martially skilled and intelligent."

Wariness shadowed Touraine's eyes and leaked into her voice. "Your Highness?"

"The general spoke well of you before this incident, and I believe she would like to give you one last chance."

"She would?" Hope inflated the other woman into something almost living. "Whatever she wants, I'll do it."

The quick agreement took Luca aback. Maybe Cantic was right, and the soldier would be obedient under—she shuddered to think of the Droitist wording—a kind master. No. The Droitists were wrong about that; the colonial subjects weren't more suited to masters.

Anyone would be more cooperative with someone who was kind to them. So she laid out the offer she thought would most entice this particular mercenary.

"Your status would increase dramatically. In addition to being in my service, you'd have my ear and perhaps my influence in certain matters." Luca raised an eyebrow pointedly. "Some might say that Balladaire owes the conscripts a great deal of thanks."

"You mean you'd help the Sands?"

Good. She could listen for the words behind the words.

Luca gave a slow nod.

"Thank you, Your Highness." The soldier bowed again. "You're generous, and I would be honored."

"You don't even know what you'll be doing."

A strange mix of emotions flickered across the other woman's face. Luca caught an initial flash of anger followed by dutiful resignation.

Inside the cell, there was a piss pot in the corner that was pungent with dehydration, and an empty tin bowl with scraps of watered grain drying to paste along its sides. Luca doubted honor had anything to do with the soldier's eagerness.

"We'll discuss it later, then. I'll get the good sergeant to assist us."

After a silent carriage ride, in which Gillett sat warily across from Touraine and the bodyguard Lanquette sat beside her, they arrived at the town house. They'd taken off the soldier's handcuffs, but she still held her wrists close together. In the daylight, she was only marginally less imposing. The look on her face, though, was one of such amazement that Luca smiled a little behind the woman's back.

"Welcome to your new home," Luca said.

CHAPTER 10

THE ASSISTANT

Welcome home, Sands.

The princess's words echoed with Rogan's scorn, and Touraine flinched, but the princess didn't seem to notice as she led Touraine inside.

Touraine had expected opulence, of course, garish displays of wealth from a woman who had never lived without in her life.

She was not prepared.

The princess's sitting room was full of books. An entire wall was covered by a shelf more than half-full of books and sheaves of paper and even a few scrolls. The table in the corner was messy with paper and writing materials, and a large book lay open on it as if the princess had been studying and called away abruptly.

There were a few minor flourishes, too, like the Shālan carpets stretched over the floor, springy beneath Touraine's boots. One of them depicted angles and rigid shapes, and the other had designs of the Shālan script, curled into shapes at the center. They showed slivers of a wooden floor, not earth. Two stuffed chairs sat beside a small table with an échecs board. A rough metal stand held spare canes near the door.

"It's rather small," Princess Luca was saying. "When they built this place, they never anticipated...esteemed guests, so I'm afraid I have no private chambers for you. The guards' room connects to mine, so you'll share with them."

Small? To get to the bedrooms, they passed a flight of stairs, the wooden handrail curling up like a cat's tail to the second floor, and then walked through a dining room. Luca's rooms were closed off, but even the guards' room was airy compared to the room she'd shared with Pruett and Tibeau in the guardhouse. And then Luca led her up the stairs—haltingly, for both of them—to a bathing room with a wheeled tub.

The princess gave Touraine the same appraising look she had in the jail. It was different in the sunlight streaming through the window—a glass window!—but Touraine still felt like a new horse getting its teeth checked.

She was suddenly self-conscious of her ragged black coat, the old spare she'd put on before Rogan arrested her. The other one was still crusted in Émeline's blood. She'd worn this coat—or one just like it—every day in her working memory. And the undershirt, stained with blood and dirt and smelling like week-old sweat.

For her part, the princess wore trousers and a black coat as well, a swallow-tailed velvet one that should have been too hot to even dream of wearing. Gold embroidery shaped like braided wheat grains crossed the torso and met at the black buttons in the middle. A shock of gold lace spilled from each cuff. It told Touraine everything she needed to know about her: stiff, formal, and very expensive.

The princess came to the same conclusion Touraine had: "You'll need new clothes. We'll have your measurements taken soon. Until then, I'll send Adile up to start your water, and something spare from Guérin. Do you know they've had Balladairan plumbing here for a few hundred years? Before it was even a colony. This is newer, obviously, but still. Isn't it marvelous?"

Touraine bowed again. Already it had become habit, like saluting. "Thank you, Your Highness."

Then she was alone, and she stood unmoving until Adile came, and even then, it took the maid's prodding to shake Touraine out of the physical stupor.

"The bath will help, sir, I promise you that. You need some help, is that it?" It was the kindness that jolted Touraine into the moment. Adile pushed a blond curl back behind her ear.

"No, thank you."

Adile tsked. "You're not so different from the other soldiers, are you? They think they can do everything alone, too. Here."

She set to work at Touraine's golden buttons and didn't grimace once at the stains or the stench. She stopped only when she saw the bandage below Touraine's collarbone. "Make sure you tell Her Highness about that if you don't want to go rancid."

Then Adile was gone and Touraine was in the bath, fighting the pressure in her chest that squeezed tighter whenever she tried to think.

The trial had been only this morning. *Squeeze.*

She wasn't going to die. At least not right now. *Squeeze.*

She'd been stripped of her rank. *Squeeze.*

Her mother might be out there, in this city. *Squeeze.*

Adile came back with her change of clothes and then led her to Princess Luca's office. Unlike every other room in the house, there were few books, and the desk was surprisingly empty. Touraine suspected that the sitting room had replaced this office, since it was downstairs and more accessible.

"Adile was worried you might drown yourself," the princess said when they were alone.

Almost alone. Her guards stood close.

Touraine didn't know how to answer that. "Your Highness, may I ask a question?"

"Yes?"

"What is today?"

"Ah. It's seventh-day. It's been a week since we arrived." Her cool voice softened just a little on the edges.

Only a week, but her body felt like it had been on campaign for a month. Her knees threatened to go soft. Émeline and Thierry had been dead for days.

"Your Highness, my soldiers—"

The princess bowed her head solemnly. "Arrangements have already been made. The pyre will be ready by sundown. Rest. I'll send some-one to collect you when it's time."

For a second, she looked like she wanted to say something else. Touraine was glad when she didn't. She dragged herself down the stairs and into her new room. A small bed rested against each of the three walls, each with crisp, clean bedclothes and pillows.

It was wonderfully, terribly empty.

Touraine stayed quiet in the carriage on the way to Émeline and Thierry's funeral. Luca let the heavy silence hang, and Touraine was grateful. Touraine had avoided thinking about her friends' deaths, let-ting the grief crouch at the edge of her mind, waiting until the shock of the last week wore off. It was unavoidable now. She hadn't even begun to contemplate what it would mean to leave her squad.

Their pyre was built out in the desert just beyond the compound. The night was deep, and Touraine would have been able to see the stars if not for the lanterns and torches.

The princess and her retinue hung back. Gracious or indifferent?

There was barely enough wood for the pyre to be ceremonial. How-ever, by chance or by choice, the scent of burning pine sap eased the smell of the fire's main fuel—thick patties of camel shit.

And the bodies.

When the fire was set, Touraine went to her soldiers.

Aimée didn't hesitate. She scooped Touraine into a great hug that made Touraine cry out. Aimée never was cautious about affection. She eased out of the embrace but supported Touraine with an arm at her back.

"Fuck me, sorry, Lieutenant. We just thought you'd be—" The sud-den flash of joy was gone.

"Good to see you, too, Aimée."

And it was. Touraine let herself be passed around her squad, to arm clasps and shoulder squeezes and tender head ruffles. She wanted to enjoy the love—and a part of her did—but she knew it wouldn't last.

After the funeral, she would be alone again, with the princess and her "small" house and her guards and servants.

This was the fairness she'd wanted. The future queen standing vigil over Sands' funerals. And Touraine's promotion wasn't a soldier's rise, but she'd never dreamed of wearing a silk shirt as a soldier. When the princess stood over her in the jail, that lantern hanging from her fist as she sized Touraine up, Touraine had calculated.

She was always good at the hard math.

Death and nothing out of it, or life and the chance to better the Sands' lots.

That wasn't even a question.

At the end of the line, her sergeants waited, and everyone else fell back. Tibeau stared into Émeline's fire with his arms crossed, and Pruett stood close beside him, arms at her sides. Tears glistened amid Tibeau's stubble. Touraine wanted to wrap him in her arms and hug him to her chest. She settled for a hand on his shoulder.

"I'm so sorry, Beau," she whispered.

"We heard the princess got a new concubine." Tibeau turned his head to look her up and down. He didn't even try to hide his distaste.

"Concubine? No." Touraine spoke to Pruett instead, searching the carefully blank look on the other woman's face. "I'm just an assistant. Cantic stripped my rank. I can't wear a uniform anymore." It sounded unbelievable, even though she'd spent half the day saying it to herself and trying to figure out where she belonged. *I'm not a soldier anymore.*

"She really did court-martial you, then," Pruett said in soft surprise.

"For treason. And murder."

Tibeau squinted. "And you're still alive? That's gonna cost."

Touraine glanced over her shoulder. Princess Luca and her guards waited patiently, for now.

"The cripple queen." Tibeau sucked his teeth.

"Princess Luca promised to help me change things for us—for the Sands." *Balladaire owes the conscripts a great deal of thanks*, the princess had said.

"Tour, you're missing the point." His wide hand slashed the air. "You've always missed the point. I want to be *free* of them. All of them. This includes their 'help' and anything else that comes with a collar."

"Like their food? Their money?"

"Starve me, then. Been close enough to it on campaign. Give me hunger on my own terms."

"You want to go die by yourself? End up some general's boy when they catch you? Or would you let Pru hang you for a traitor? You go, and you bring every other one of us down with you."

Tibeau's face purpled and he opened his mouth, but Pruett stepped in with a hand on each of their chests.

"Fucking shut it, you two," she whispered harshly. "We're not in the barracks. Don't wave your shit stains in front of the whole sky-falling army." Her breath came heavily. "We're safer together, and right now"—she moved her hand to Tibeau's face to stop his interruption—"we're safer with the Balladairans. And not because they're looking out for us. No one is looking out for us. Not them, not the Qazāli. No matter what either of you do, we only have each other."

When Pruett locked Touraine in her sights, though, her voice was bitter. "What's she offering, hein? This pretty funeral?"

Layers in the question, in the voice—measured mediation over cold iron over a tremble.

"She'll intervene for us." Touraine gestured to the fire. "She already has." She met Pruett's eyes, pleading. "I can change things. I know what to say to them. I can do what they want me to do."

Tibeau sneered. "You really are their pet monkey."

The insult cracked like the whips of their youth. Like the whips, the epithet was a memory Touraine tried to keep buried. Tibeau had been the first to call her that, and it had clung to her with every test she'd passed with high marks. The Balladairans' pet monkey, ready to dance for them. Even after the three of them became friends, he and Pruett teased her with it occasionally, but it hadn't bit like this for years.

"Beau!" Pruett rounded on him and pointed to the other Sands. "Fucking leave."

For a moment, Touraine thought he'd apologize. Instead, his face walled up and he left, shaking his head.

Touraine blinked hard and turned toward the fire. "If I don't do this, I'm dead, Pru."

"He hurts, Tour. And if you'd died, I...I'd be a pain in the ass, too." They stood so close that Touraine felt the shake of Pruett's pained chuckle. After a moment, she added, "He's right. It'll cost you."

Pruett's body heat, the heat of the fires: a fortification against the cold night. The invisible belt around Touraine's chest tightened again.

"You and her really aren't fucking?" Pruett asked.

"No. If she wanted to fuck me, she could have pulled me out for a night and sent me back." Maybe that was naive. Maybe Touraine had misinterpreted the princess's looks, her hospitality.

"What could I do if she did want me?" New fear made Touraine's voice bitter. She tasted bile, remembering that night in Balladaire, surrounded by Rogan and his men.

"Not want her back. Don't give her the satisfaction."

"I don't want her at all."

"You want what she can give you, and that's real fucking close, Tour."

"To help you? To get you paid and treated fairly? Yeah. I want that."

Pruett pinched the bridge of her nose, a muscle flexing in her jaw. "That's not all. It never has been. You want to be one of them. You're not. You never will be." Pruett slipped her warm, calloused palm into Touraine's and squeezed. "Anylight. She's waiting."

PART 2
TURNCOATS

CHAPTER 11

THE MODISTE

The morning after the funeral, Touraine presented herself promptly after breakfast, back rigid, arms stiff at her sides. Luca had thought to give her some time to adjust, but the soldier insisted, so Luca rescheduled their appointment with the modiste for that afternoon so that Touraine could get clothing befitting her new station.

In the carriage, her new assistant sat stiffly beside Guérin, her fists balled tight on her knees across from Luca. The carriage cabin felt smaller than usual. Luca shifted her small satchel on her lap; it held the mysterious book about Shālan history that had come out of nowhere.

Touraine's face was neutral, but Luca caught the lines of tension around her mouth, in the careful, awkward way she avoided looking at Luca or brushing against Guérin at all. Luca had the impression that being so still took an effort.

"Not one for carriages?" Luca asked, trying to ease her with a smile. She'd seen Gil do it with young soldiers who fumbled around him, nervous and awestruck by the dead king's champion.

"I'm fine, Your Highness." The soldier bowed from her seat.

And resumed staring at the cushion opposite her.

The cart jostled in the silence that followed, the rattle of wheels transitioning from dirt to fitted pavers. Luca steadied herself on the side door.

"You can look out, if you'd like."

"I'm fine, Your Highness." Wooden. Obedient. Nothing like the woman who shot down Beau-Sang over dinner or had the audacity to call in the future queen's debt. Unfortunately, Luca needed that fierce, independent soldier. How would her father bring out the lieutenant's fiery assertiveness? How would Gil? How would her uncle?

She didn't have her father's example. She had barely witnessed Gil's, and she didn't trust her uncle's. She had only her books and the years of study she'd spent hunting for the best way to wear her parents' crown.

She read Yverte most often, wearing the spine of *The Rule of Rule* ragged. For a leader to be respected, they must show power. Never show doubt, for a ruler does not doubt. A ruler decides. A ruler acts.

She scooted over on her bench until she was directly in front of Touraine. She snapped her fingers.

"Lieutenant. I didn't save you from the gallows just so you could stare. If I were Cantic, how would you behave right now?"

She'd seen the way the woman looked at Cantic—like she wanted to fuck the general, or be her. Or both. Cantic was respected. Cantic was decisive. Luca wanted to inspire that kind of devotion. She wished she could ask Cantic how she'd drawn Touraine in.

The soldier blinked at her slowly, as if trying to bring Luca into focus. "Thank you," she said. She looked down at her fists and flattened them to cup her knees. "Thank you for Émeline and Thierry's pyre, too."

Heaviness settled around Luca's shoulders and seeped through her chest. She couldn't bring herself to say any of the standard patriotic platitudes her uncle might have, all of that "meaningful service to Balladaire" drivel. Especially because she wasn't sure she'd have done it if she hadn't already been thinking about what the soldier—the ex-soldier—Touraine—could help her accomplish. About what the woman knew, or could learn, about the magic. And how glad Luca had been to upend that self-important young captain at the court-martial.

"I owed you a life," Luca said simply.

It was as good a moment as any for her to introduce Touraine to her new job.

"I saved you so that I could send you back to the rebels."

As usual, Guérin was perfectly unflappable, keeping an eye on Touraine and an ear to the streets, even though Lanquette was outside with the driver.

Touraine looked up, eyes wide, jaw tight. Clever enough to be patient, but it appeared the ex-soldier couldn't control her expressions, and that wouldn't do in front of the rebels or the Balladairans. Another strike against her diplomatic skills.

"You're an assistant to the governor-general of the Shālan colonies. That's me now. You'll be my envoy and represent the empire's interests while I work toward peace."

"An ambassador?" Touraine's shoulders relaxed, but her face remained tense. "And my mission? Your Highness."

"More like a negotiator. The rebels aren't a sovereign nation unto themselves. They won't get an ambassador. But the mission is peace. For the most part. To be my spy, for the other part. If the first part fails."

Touraine's brow furrowed. "They know me, though. I'll be a shit—sorry, a terrible spy, Your Highness." Then her face closed off as she realized she'd spoken out of turn, and expected chastisement.

"It's all right." Luca smiled to ease Touraine's fears. "I've heard worse. And yes, I know. We'll use that to our advantage. You're going to play both sides."

Understanding dawned on Touraine's face, followed closely by horror. Another tick against her diplomacy skills.

"You'll go to them as my negotiator. See what it would take for them to ally with me. If that doesn't work, you can pretend to betray us by giving them choice information. Locations of food deposits, things like that. First, though, we'll start with peace. Either way, you know them. They know you. Any knowledge is better than none at all."

A leader should never give more information than necessary. Better not to mention tugging out the secrets of Shālan magic just yet.

Touraine's eyebrows shot up. "As you command, Your Highness."

"Do you know how to find the rebels who held you?"

After a moment's thought, the woman shook her head.

That was disappointing. It would have sped things up tremendously. "You'll have to speak to the locals, then. Sniff around for them. We could do you up a disguise." Luca waved her hand mysteriously.

"I'll do my best, Your Highness. I don't speak Shālan, though."

Luca sat upright, feeling the sudden panic of plans disintegrating from the inside out. "You don't?" She shook her head before Touraine could even open her mouth again. "No, of course you can't—even the Tailleurists wouldn't allow that. That's shortsighted of them." Shortsighted of her, not to have thought of that.

"You said you can read Balladairan, though?"

Touraine's cheeks flared, and she looked down at her lap, hands gripping tighter on her knees. "Of course, Your Highness."

"Can you lie?"

Touraine looked startled and then flushed. "I suppose?" she stammered, showing that her lies probably wouldn't go unnoticed by any but the most oblivious party.

Sky above. "What else can you do?"

The woman sat back and crossed her arms peevishly. "I can kill people. Scout. Plan military maneuvers. Organize a hundred soldiers, wounded and well, their food, their pay, their leave. Simple soldier things."

Ah. There was the bite Luca was looking for. Whatever else Touraine lacked, Luca could work with a backbone. And above all, she was loyal. Even Cantic had vouched for her loyalty. And so here they were.

At Madame Abdelnour's shop, ready to outfit Touraine as the loyal servant of Balladaire that she was.

"Your Highness, your presence is an honor." A short woman with long curling dark hair bowed and led them in, to a small table. Luca saw the high chairs and sighed internally with relief. Two cups of steaming tea waited for them. Luca sat. Touraine didn't sit until Luca gestured to the second chair. Even so, the ex-soldier eyed Guérin and Lanquette, who stood beside Luca and by the door, respectively. It would take the woman some time before she stopped thinking of herself as a soldier.

"How may we serve you, Your Highness?"

Madame Abdelnour's back was hunched from years over a seamstress's table, and she wore spectacles, likely as a result of the same. She was elegant in a simple red robe over an orange underdress. A gold belt wrapped around her plump waist before hanging down in the middle. The colors complemented the deep brown of her skin. Luca would have looked like scraped parchment.

"I need to outfit my new assistant as befits someone of her station." Luca gestured at Touraine's current outfit. More of Guérin's off-duty clothes, well made but ill fitting. "She has a military background, and I don't mind if the clothing reflects that. I'd also like it to reflect a unity between Shālan and Balladairan sensibilities. And of course, comfort in this heat. Can you make something like that?"

Madame Abdelnour's eyebrows hung somewhere near her hairline. "Military background, you say? Unity, you say? Of course, Your Highness. It will take some time to design and test pieces, but we can make some simple ones immediately." The modiste studied Touraine as if she could size the woman right there, in her seat. She probably could. Still, she gave Touraine a small bow and beckoned with one crook of her finger. She strode to the center of the room without waiting for Touraine to follow.

At the modiste's shrill whistle, a few young women appeared from a back room. One of them had the same thick dark hair and bold nose as the modiste, plus a vivid scar on her chin. A measuring tape hung across her shoulders.

"And, madame—she'll need something formal. Appropriate for a ball."

Touraine stumbled as she walked to a stool. "A ball."

Luca drank her tea. It was light and sweet. Saturated with mint. "In two days. I know it's soon, and I'd rather we didn't have it at all, but..." She was the first of the royals to visit the colony in too long. It would have to be celebrated with the proper pomp and preening and ingratiating, and as a member of Luca's staff and household, Touraine would have to be there.

"Your Highness, I've never—"

Madame Abdelnour snatched Touraine's left arm up to run the measuring tape down from Touraine's armpit.

"I don't know—" Panic was writ clear on the other woman's face. It was the closest she'd come to outright dissent. Like each time before, she stopped herself. The fear vanished, replaced with that impassive wall again. "Of course, Your Highness."

Luca turned the cup in her hands. Her grief rings clinked against the fine clay. The gold band inset with onyx for her father, the thinner gold band with a black diamond for her mother. *Make those you would lead depend on you.* "Don't worry. I'll make sure you're ready. Can you dance?"

"No, Your Highness. It wasn't—" Touraine yelped as the modiste's daughter pushed her legs wider to measure the inseam of her trousers. She blushed and cleared her throat. "It wasn't considered a training priority for us, even by Tailleurist standards."

Luca perked up. "You study the theorists?"

That blank expression. Again. Luca was beginning to recognize the topics that sent her new assistant into stony obedience.

"I don't know if *study* is the right word for it, Your Highness."

And yet—here was a change. A hint of wryness in the other woman's voice this time.

"If not study, what would you call it?"

"Only living, Your Highness." Touraine grunted as she was pricked by a pin.

For almost an hour, Madame Abdelnour and her daughter molded Touraine up and down like one of the miniature wooden figurines that stood posed around the shop. They held bolts of cloth up to her body, discarding some and draping others across her shoulders. For almost an hour, they all looked to Luca for approval.

Make those you would lead want *you.*

As Touraine stood there, it grew easier for Luca to understand why

Touraine admired Cantic so. Touraine was a soldier. It was written in the straight lines of her, the breadth of her shoulders, the steady strength of her legs at attention. The same steel that held up Cantic and Gil—and Guérin and Lanquette, for that matter. Rigid as a rifle.

Luca, on the other hand, had a leg with a tendency to give out at inopportune moments and a cane to keep it from showing.

But Luca wasn't weak. She also had a rapier inside the cane, thin and flexible but strong.

She would pull Touraine to her, her own way. Something else from Yverte: know a person's desires, and you have leverage—give a person their desires, and you have an extension of your own will.

Touraine wanted a place. She wanted respect from Balladaire's powerful—why else chase after Cantic's approval?

Luca could give her both and much more.

CHAPTER 12

THE BALL

On the day of the ball, Luca woke up swearing, her bad leg cramped and burning.

Auspicious beginnings.

Luckily, she had spent the last two days ironing out every detail of her welcome ball so that she wouldn't have to rely on the auspices of fate. She wasn't nervous at all. She had prepared for everything.

A knock on the door.

"Come in," she said, gritting her teeth against the pain.

Touraine opened the main door, not the door connecting Luca's room to the guards' room. She bowed, eyes averted. She'd taken to the formalities of interacting with Luca easily enough. Her manners irritated Luca this morning. She'd seen the way the soldier's eyes had flicked immediately to Luca's legs and now looked studiously everywhere else.

"Your Highness, Guard Captain Gillett wants to talk about final preparations for tonight." She sounded as if she'd been a butler all her life.

Luca tossed the covers off and inched her legs off the bed. She must have slept on them wrong. Not that she knew of a right way to sleep on them after almost twenty years.

"Give me a moment." Luca went behind her dressing screen and traded her nightgown for the shirt she'd worn the day before. Sitting on her dressing stool, she tried to pull on the trousers she had discarded, too, but they tangled and twisted around her knees. She swore. The painted birds on the screen mocked her with their open beaks. The ball had flustered her. Touraine had flustered her. She took a deep breath. Yanked again, achieving an excruciating inch. She turned a near whimper into a grunt.

"Princess?" It was Gillett at the door now, concerned.

And Touraine silent. Luca could imagine the contempt. But Luca Ancier was the sky-falling princess. No one would sit in contempt of her from afar.

"Touraine?"

"Yes, Highness."

"Come here." The chill of her court voice frosted Luca's words.

There was no hesitation before obedient footsteps.

Behind the screen with Luca, Touraine bowed slightly, not looking at the princess's scarred, naked legs and the mess of trousers around her calves.

"Look at me," she said with soft menace.

Touraine raised her eyes. Luca expected the usual blank obedience. Instead, Touraine's dark eyes were steady, poring over her, seeing everything, unflinching. There may even have been anger in the cant of her eyebrows—but there was no pity.

"May I help you?" she asked, soft enough for Luca's ears alone.

Luca's heart stuttered like a flame in a storm. She swallowed and nodded.

The soldier's hands surprised her. They weren't gentle, not truly. They were efficient, however, without being rough. They didn't hesitate with disgust or uncertainty as Touraine slid the trousers up Luca's legs. She helped Luca stand, placed her arms around her neck.

"Put your weight on me."

Luca did. She clung to the woman's neck like a drowning sailor. The woman smelled heavily of sweat, and her collar was damp. She must have come from her exercises. Her breath was warm against Luca's ear.

In one final, deft movement, Touraine pulled Luca's trousers over her hips. Then she knelt until Luca was seated on her stool again.

"Will that be all?"

Luca nodded. She didn't trust her voice.

Touraine nodded and left. The door closed.

"Luca?" Gil said.

She limped back to her bed and picked up her cane. "I'm fine. A rough sleep is all."

He looked suspiciously at the door Touraine had shut rather harder than necessary.

"We've done none of that," she said, reading his look. Her face burned.

He grunted, frowning.

"Of course, it's an option," Luca said in a low voice. "She's attractive, for a Qazāli." Touraine was attractive, period. More handsome than any of her previous lovers, men or women. That wasn't something Balladaire's queen regnant came out and admitted. "However, as an ambassador in my employ, it's hardly professional."

Gil snorted. "Really? I recall a seamstress, a coachman, a chambermaid—"

"Fine! All right. That's not the reason, but for the stars' sake, it's none of your business, Gil. I'm too busy trying to quell a rebellion started by her people."

"A rebellion started by her people to protest the fact that we came and invaded in the first place. Your Highness."

Luca blinked, stunned. He bowed his head slightly but kept his eyes locked to hers.

"Do not mistake me, Luca. I'm loyal to you and the crown. As loyal to you as to your father." The old man ran his thumb absently along his own grief ring for the king. He spoke gruffly, but there was a wry tilt of an eyebrow as he said, "Maybe we should change the way we relate to them." A hint of mischief in the faint smile as he glanced back toward the door. "Just pick a less prickly one."

She met his mischief with the truth she hadn't told General Cantic when she negotiated for the soldier's life. "I really do want her to succeed with negotiations first. Spying is a last resort. We're more likely

to learn the truth about the healing magic as allies than as assholes."
That's where her approach differed from everyone else's.

He took a deep breath and regarded her silently. Finally, he said,
"Finding the magic won't bring them back."

Luca stiffened. "I know that," she snapped. "It's not because of
my parents." Probably a lie. "If I have something to offer my people,
Uncle Nicolas can't say I'm not ready." Unfortunately true. "I don't
want this to come to civil war, but Nicolas has the advantage. He does,
doesn't he?"

She opened her hands, as if she had her papers with all the figures
in front of her.

Gil nodded slowly before meeting her eyes. "Nicolas and Roland
never had the wide view Étienne did. She balanced your father well."
He paused a moment. "What is your soldier's role tonight?"

A flush crept up her neck. The tailor had sent a handsome suit fit
for a formal occasion. Since it was Touraine's first public function as
Luca's rebel "envoy," the other Balladairans would need to know how
much of Luca's favor Touraine had. Luca hoped the clothes and their
associated rank would put Touraine at ease, as well.

"Touraine?" she called through the door. "Come back."

The ex-soldier returned, stiff and striking, head tilted deferentially.

"Has Adile given you your outfit for the evening?"

"Yes, Your Highness."

"You've tried it on?"

"Not yet, Your Highness."

"Do it soon, in case we need to send to Madame Abdelnour for
alterations. You remember where you're to stand?"

"I'll mingle as necessary, Your Highness, and I'll follow you when
you wish. I'll have no more than one glass of wine and no spirits. Dancing isn't required, but if asked, I may do so. I'm to say nothing of the
rebels or my time in captivity. Is there anything else, Your Highness?"

The recitation left Luca breathless. She'd meant to press Touraine
back on her heels, to take back the power she'd lost in her naked
vulnerability.

"Just one more thing. Stars' sake, lift your chin. You're my assistant, not a slave."

Touraine's chin jerked up, her expression fierce and overall a bit too angry, but—

"Perfect. That's how you should look tonight."

This time the soldier's bow was a deep, tilted nod. She didn't break eye contact. "As you wish, Your Highness."

From her false dais, Luca surveyed the improvised ballroom with pride as the music played and her guests mingled with their hors d'oeuvres and aperitifs.

So far, no civil war.

She had wrought this.

The large sitting room, the main room of the house, had become a ballroom overnight. Luca's upstairs study was locked off, but the bedrooms became new sitting rooms, quiet places for guests to retire or smoke, away from the dancing and music.

The company was mixed: Balladairans from the Quartier—almost all of them nobles or their offshoots—and influential Qazāli, like the magistrates and the more powerful merchants. They mingled only fitfully, and rarely one to one.

And yet the tightness of the ballroom made the modest gathering feel festive, and the musicians played to that mood, though no one was dancing yet. In one corner, the pile of host gifts grew—a stack of books tended to by one of the servants. Lanquette or Guérin hovered near her at all times, and Gil had brought other guards in for the occasion. They stood at the corners of the room, scaring everyone into good behavior. Touraine stood to the right, just behind Luca's seat, the most ornate chair she had. Stiff and haughty, just as Luca had commanded.

Everyone was waiting for her word, and that thought alone filled her with a secret thrill that straightened her back and eased her grip on her cane. They were here for her.

She raised her hand and the music stopped. She took the champagne a servant offered, while other servants offered glasses to the guests.

"Citizens of Balladaire." She smiled. "Welcome to my home." A polite smattering of applause and smiles.

"My new home, I should say. Before I arrived, I'd heard Qazāl was a land where kindness flowed as wide as the Hadd, and the only thing the Qazāli value more than compassion is intellectual curiosity. I have not been disappointed. Qazāl is a gracious land full of gracious people.

"First, let us remember the late Lord Governor Cheminade, who welcomed me into her home on my first day and lived as an example of peace between Balladaire and Qazāl. It is with a heavy heart that I step into her role as acting governor. I thank you all for your patience in the meantime."

Around the room, heads nodded solemnly.

"I offer my thanks to my latest acquaintances—especially to Madame Abdelnour, by way of her daughter, Mademoiselle Malika Abdelnour, for costuming my household so elegantly."

Luca held her arms out for a flourish. She wore a Qazāli formal black tunic that stopped below her hips, stiff enough to hold the sharp lines but supple enough for comfort. The buttons were pure gold. She stepped aside and gestured toward Touraine, who took the hint and stepped forward with a bow. The soldier wore a pale cotton blouse and a black vest with a standing collar and ornate gold trim, modeled after the Qazāli's hooded vests. A gold sash streaked with black swirls and dangling with small, flat gold circles and black beads wrapped halfway around her hips like a skirt to hang down behind loose black trousers. Madame Abdelnour said the sashes were common accoutrements among the Qazāli dancers and throughout the old Shālan Empire, and Luca had to admit that Touraine looked striking in it.

Another shimmer of raised glasses while the mademoiselle curtsied. The guests clapped on cue. She scanned for the less enthusiastic. The real test was coming.

"Thank you. I confess myself a stranger here, in a conflicted land, but I hope to change that—both my strangeness and the conflict. My strangeness is my own burden, which only study and friendship can cure. The conflict, however, will require us to work together, Qazāli and Balladairan alike. Let the boundaries between us fall. Allies must be open and honest with each other, about their fears, their hopes, and their needs. They must hear when the other speaks. May every citizen here know that my ears are open.

"As proof of that, I offer the Qazāli a token of Balladaire's good-will, a hope for our unified future: at my invitation and under my own purse, fifty Qazāli children will attend the Citadel, the finest Balladai-ran school in Qazāl."

Across the room, Gil's mouth opened in surprise before he sealed his lips. It was the first gesture she would offer the Qazāli, an incentive to work with her instead of against her.

This time, Luca raised her glass high. "Enjoy yourselves together. To your health." She drained the last of her glass and lowered herself into her chair, heart racing.

The music started again, and people claimed their partners for the first dance. Instead of joining them, Luca sat while guests paid their respects, bowing over her hand and commenting on which book they'd brought for her host gift.

One of the first to approach her was LeRoche de Beau-Sang, practically pushing the previous person out of the way. He was sur-rounded by youths: two women she recognized and a young man she'd never seen. Beau-Sang bowed elegantly before eyeing Touraine and smiling as if he had won a bet. Luca fought the urge to look behind her.

"May I present to you my daughter, Aliez?" Beau-Sang guided the blond woman forward. "And her friend, Mademoiselle Bel-Jadot?"

Luca smiled tightly, acknowledging the young women as they curtsied. "We've met before. At the bookshop in the New Medina. Welcome."

She had recognized the Bel-Jadot girl, but she hadn't realized at the time that the other girl making fun of her that day was Beau-Sang's daughter. She might leverage that better in the future, as well. Not now, however. Tonight was about peace. And the pieces on the board. Luca turned to the young man in the group.

"And this is my son, Paul-Sebastien." Beau-Sang touched Paul-Sebastien's shoulder with a tender hand.

The young man wasn't as broad as his father, but he wasn't frail, either. He wore his blond hair pulled back in a queue and had to tuck loose strands behind his ears. He wore spectacles, too. His entire mien was awkward and nervous, and Luca couldn't tell if it was endearing or off-putting.

Beau-Sang's smile widened. "I also see that you've taken my advice. They're a fine investment, aren't they?" He nodded behind her.

This time, Luca allowed herself to look. Those thick dark brows. The cold glare into the middle distance. That square, clenched jaw.

"That's one of Cantic's, is that right? The lieutenant."

As if Touraine were a prize hound she'd purchased to race against his Richard.

(Had Luca not purchased Touraine? Was Touraine not useful?)

Touraine couldn't keep her mask on in the face of Beau-Sang's needling. Her nose flared in a flash of anger as she scoffed.

Beau-Sang's smile at Touraine showed teeth. "Unfortunately, it seems like her manners are not so refined as I remember."

Sky above and earth below. Luca wanted to hide her face with her palm.

Instead, she cleared her throat sharply and nodded in dismissal. "Monsieur le comte. Mesdemoiselles. Thank you."

As the others left, Paul-Sebastien hung back, nervously watching Aliez and Bel-Jadot as each sorted herself with a dancing partner. When his father gestured sharply for him to follow, Paul-Sebastien held him off with a sharp shake of the head.

"Yes?" Luca raised an eyebrow.

Paul-Sebastien came closer and bowed deeply, but he also looked past her shoulder, where Touraine stood at attention, his head cocked. To his credit, he looked slightly embarrassed for his father.

"I only wanted to ask, Your Highness—did you enjoy the book I left for you?" Paul-Sebastien's face flushed.

Both of Luca's eyebrows rose in surprise this time. The unmarked history book that had sent her chasing Yeshuf bn Zahel at the bookshop. "That was you? My thanks for the gift. It led me to interesting questions about...oh." Paul-Sebastien LeRoche. PSLR. "You wrote it."

He brightened and stood a little straighter, but he still managed to look apologetic. "I did, Your Highness. However, my father doesn't approve of the subject matter."

Of course he didn't. Luca remembered his dismissal of her own curiosity at Cheminade's dinner. To be quite honest, Luca imagined Beau-Sang was the kind of man who disdained all books, which was a black enough mark on his record.

"Then we do have a lot to talk about. You know much about this city for a Balladairan."

"I should hope so. I've lived here my whole life." He chuckled, growing a little easier with her. "By some standards, that would make me Qazāli, wouldn't it?"

It was laughable, given the contrast of his golden hair and pale, pale skin compared to the native Qazāli. There were fair Shālans in the city, from other countries in the old empire, but not very many. It made Luca wonder what new boundaries people would have to make in the future—how they would call themselves, what else they would find to separate themselves from each other. Humans tended to do that.

Luca waited until the next song began so that her words were covered by the music and the clack of dress heels on the floor. The line to greet her only grew longer. She should hurry him on and be done with this, order him to call on her another day. But she had to know.

"Have you had any luck finding bn Zahel's book?"

Paul-Sebastien shook his head hard enough that a lock of hair flopped into his eyes. "*The Last Emperor*? I wish, Your Highness."

"Not even in the First Library?"

He made a wistful sound in his throat. "No one can get there, Your Highness. Which is to say, one hears things, but one shouldn't trust them."

She laughed, and his shoulders relaxed at the ring of it. "What kinds of things?"

"Preposterous things. More than one man has approached me as I left a bookstore, offering a ride to the Second City, as if I'm a fool." He smiled. Under the fringe of hair, behind his spectacles, his blue eyes were rueful. There was nothing of Beau-Sang in him but the curling blond hair. "I'd give anything to see it, though."

"Perhaps one day. I'd like to speak more about your work another time. Expect an invitation soon."

"I would be honored." Paul-Sebastien finally tucked his hair back behind his ear, but as he bowed, the curl fell forward again. He left her with a spring in his heels. For a moment, she felt lighter, too. Then she felt Touraine's presence just behind her, and her mouth tightened. Touraine had behaved abominably. Luca only had time to chastise her with a look before the next guest stepped forward.

Mademoiselle Malika Abdelnour mounted the dais with grace that set both Luca's heart beating faster and her teeth on edge. When Malika curtsied, her gown flared. Waves of dark hair crashed over her shoulder.

"Your Highness. It is an honor to receive your invitation. My mother sends her sincerest regrets. She's unwell." Though Qazāli, she spoke in perfectly unaccented Balladairan.

"I'm sorry to hear that. I trust you're enjoying yourself?"

"Of course. Marvelous food, wonderful conversation." A crooked smile accentuated the scar on her chin, but it wasn't directed at her.

Luca refused to follow the gaze to Touraine.

"I am especially pleased to hear about your generous donation to the children."

The woman had a disarming stare, with narrow eyes lined in kohl that Luca quite thought she could lose herself in. The long scar on her chin was a sculptor's slip, but it added an edge of mystery, of danger.

Luca sipped her wine. "Are you familiar with the school?"

"Of course, Your Highness. I attended myself. It was a...peerless education." She smiled, but the words gave the expression an ironic twist. Or perhaps it was the scar.

Luca didn't know the protectorate well enough to place the woman's import among the Qazāli citizens. "And how did you find it?"

"Well...I learned much about Balladaire."

Luca's lips quirked. "I admit, that is the one fault of a Balladairan education. We can only teach so much about Qazāl. I could use a few lessons myself."

Malika raised an eyebrow and looked over at Touraine again, then back to Luca. "I only hope it fares better than past initiatives to educate Shālan children."

Luca's hand went tight on the stem of her glass.

Then quickly, smiling as if she hadn't just insulted the Tailleurists, the Droitists, and the Sands all at once, Malika turned the subject. "One hears you can read Shālan? Our host gift is a book of poetry by one of our dearest poets. My mother also sends a scarf she hopes will suit your tastes."

Her eyes trailed once more to Touraine before she bowed and returned to the crowd.

CHAPTER 13

A DANCE

Touraine had felt strong at Luca's back until Beau-Sang approached them. She'd felt elegant in her new clothing, felt pride even, at the approving nod General Cantic had given her as she passed by.

During the two days between the modiste and the ball, Touraine had scrambled to find her place in this new world. Exercising gently in the morning with Lanquette and Guérin was the easiest bit to adjust to, because it was the moment that felt most like home. The two guards weren't Tibeau or Pruett or Aimée, but they respected her skill even if they never laughed or wrestled just for fun. (Touraine secretly thought that Guérin had never had fun in her life.)

When Touraine hadn't been training or stacking papers, Luca had drilled her in courtly etiquette.

Touraine had thought she knew how to deal with dignitaries and nobles. Say "yes, sir" or "madame" or "Your Highness." Bow enough, salute as necessary, and let them overlook you.

"That's all wonderful for a soldier, I'm sure," Luca had told her in the beginning, "but you're not a soldier anymore. You represent me personally, not the empire. People will ask you things to get to me. Stop making that face."

Dread had tugged Touraine's face down. She fixed it back into the polite, formal, but pleasant expression Luca had been coaching her in.

"You can hate this as much as you'd like, but I shouldn't know it."

Luca pushed Touraine's hand away from her belt—where the baton used to rest. Luca's hand was cool and dry. "And sky above, stop trying to reach for a weapon."

The rest of the house hadn't been spared preparations for the ball. The town house felt like an army camp getting ready to march. Furniture was packed away like tents. Luca barked orders like Cantic, swinging a pen instead of a sword, spattering ink instead of blood. Clerks scribbled majestic invitations to colonial nobility on paper that cost more than a month of a Sand's allowance, and messengers ran them from house to house throughout the city like couriers between companies.

Touraine felt the same deep-belly dread as she did before marching, too.

Guard Captain Gillett took the two other guards aside several times to talk about the house's defenses. He only grudgingly brought Touraine into the discussions when he realized Luca was going to keep her close.

Three days before the ball, Touraine hadn't thought she'd be alive in three days. Now she stood at the princess's side, with the high-society types she used to make fun of with her friends.

And then, in a single sky-falling second, the bastard comte had stripped all of that comfort and her growing confidence away, and Touraine had become just a Sand again.

Just a Sand. She had never been ashamed of that before.

And she had stumbled. She'd done worse than show her hand. She couldn't help it. She wouldn't forget his comments at Cheminade's dinner anytime soon. Seeing him only made the anger from that first night bubble back up all over again. At least Touraine had kept her mouth shut. Add to it the princess—Luca was even more furious with Touraine than she had been this morning. She could see it in the sharp set of the princess's shoulders and the way she refused to look Touraine's way.

And if Luca hated her, she was royally fucked.

Touraine recognized the young modiste when she approached the dais, but this time, she kept her head forward. In her peripheral vision, though, she saw the woman watching her.

When the modiste insulted the Sands' education, she was ready. She ignored it.

Still, the all-too-familiar bitterness in it caught her attention, and when the woman retreated, Touraine stepped up beside Luca. "May I be excused a moment, Your Highness?"

"Go." Luca didn't even bother to face Touraine as she waved the next supplicant forward.

Touraine used her own anger to add authority to the strike of her boot heels upon the floor. A small thing, but it made her feel better. She'd seen Malika Abdelnour gliding toward the food that was spread almost obscenely along buffet tables. She wondered what the Qazāli woman thought about all that wealth disguised as lamb and lemons, mint and olives, poultry dripping with honeyed sauces. What of the heaping bowls of Balladairan and Qazāli grains alike, nestled beside baguettes and tart cheese?

This would have been a legendary feast for the Sands. And she suspected something similar was going through Malika's head.

Malika wasn't a Sand, but maybe she'd gone through some of the same things—and yet she'd risen enough to be at the princess's ball freely. Touraine saw in Malika someone with the same ambitions and frustrations. Ambition and frustration made for a suspicious combination, one worth exploring.

The music swelled around her like a wave. She turned, hunting, but the crowd pressed in around her.

Instead of Malika Abdelnour, she made eye contact with General Cantic. The general raised her wineglass and approached.

"Lieutenant Touraine. It looks like you're doing better for yourself already." She appraised Touraine's new outfit, making Touraine self-conscious all over again.

"General. Sir. Thank you." Touraine didn't know what to say to Cantic or how to act. She held her hands clenched awkwardly at her sides and wished desperately for a drink to hold.

"I'm glad Her Highness was able to find a use for you." Cantic tilted her glass toward the princess on her dais. "I would also like to offer my thanks. Because of you, we've been on the hunt for Brigāni in the city. It's a good start to settling the rebel situation. Surprisingly few here, but those nightmarish gold eyes are a dead tell. I'm dying for a smoke. Did you never pick up the habit? I started back when I came in as a lieutenant." She took a deep drink of her wine.

Touraine hadn't picked up smoking. Pruett had, though. She'd been particular about keeping her tobacco and papers dry in the little tin she carried around. Something was slightly off about Cantic this evening. Her eyes were too bright and her words too fast, too casual. Touraine started to excuse herself, and Cantic grabbed her by the arm and stepped closer.

"I let her save you for a reason. You're in a position to do great things for Balladaire." Cantic lowered her mouth to Touraine's ear to be better heard over the music. "Don't let me down. You know where to find me." And then Cantic pulled back, smiling the smile of proud confidence that she had turned on Touraine at the hanging, before everything had gone to shit. Touraine couldn't help it: it triggered in her the same desire to please that it always had.

At least, it did until Captain Rogan sidled up beside them with two glasses of wine in hand. He wasn't in uniform. He'd taken the opportunity to show off his noble blood and nobler purse.

Sky a-fucking-bove. Touraine should have realized that he would be counted among the socially required invitees.

"General Cantic, sir." Rogan saluted the general with one glass and then bowed over the second glass as he handed it to Touraine. "Lieu— ah, excuse me. Touraine."

Despite the oozing charm, Rogan's voice snapped into Touraine like a whip. She flinched and hated herself for it.

"Forgive me for interrupting, sir," Rogan said to Cantic. "I wanted to take the opportunity to apologize for any misunderstandings between me and the former lieutenant." A grin split his long face, showing bright white teeth. "Then, perhaps, she would help me show a united front by honoring me with a dance."

"That sounds like a good idea, Captain." Cantic nodded over her own glass. "I'm sure there's already gossip spreading about the trial."

He grabbed Touraine's empty hand with his before she could snatch it away. His grip stuck like a bayonet wedged in bone.

Touraine weighed her options. Fight him off her and break half of Luca's fine ornaments in the process. Embarrass Luca and Cantic in the same blow. Or do nothing and accept the humiliating touch. Touraine met Cantic's eyes again and saw in them the same words: *Don't let me down.* This time, they were a warning, not encouragement.

Grinding her teeth, Touraine let him lead her to the floor. They gave their wineglasses to a milling servant. Her skin crawled where he touched her wrist and under her jacket where his hand rested on her waist.

"I don't even know how to dance," she hissed. "Aren't you worried I'll make you look like even more of an idiot?"

She expected any expression but the smile he gave her. If it had met his eyes, it would have been tender. "Some sacrifices must be made."

He spun her around the floor with effortless grace. She had no choice but to follow his lead. She cast glances around the room even as Rogan dragged and pushed her footsteps. Malika was dancing now, and Luca—she was across the room, and Touraine desperately attempted to make eye contact, but the steps carried her away again.

Touraine didn't know how long the song would last. Her hand was a sweaty claw in Rogan's, and his cologne burned her nose. Fury clawed up her throat. It tasted like bile. She couldn't do this anymore. In the middle of a complicated turn, she yanked her hand away. Rogan grabbed it back. She pushed him off, but he held her fast. Others stopped to watch them and whisper, and the whole dancing formation ground to a halt.

"Everyone here knows what kind of meat your new master prefers, now that she's parading you so openly. I'm not the one who looks the fool tonight," he said.

"Are you entirely certain?" Luca said. She had come up behind them when their scuffle broke the flow of the dance. And her voice was even colder than usual as she almost whispered to Rogan.

Touraine's world shrank to that voice and the desire to break out of Rogan's grip.

"You will release her, Captain."

He didn't. He held on tighter, forcing a grunt out of Touraine as he pressed her against him. Warm. Hard muscle and breastbone, soft cotton. "Your Highness, surely there's nothing wrong—"

"Release her, Captain, or Guard Lanquette will release your testicles from your body."

Lanquette and Guérin flanked Rogan, and Gil stood just beyond.

Rogan's grip slackened slowly. He puffed his chest forward, bowed sharply to Luca, and brushed through the guards.

Touraine stood rigid, her whole body hot with humiliation and fury.

"I'm sorry," she murmured to Luca, her voice tight. Her fists shook at her sides. She resisted the urge to wipe her hands on her trousers.

The princess put a hand briefly on Touraine's shoulder. "No, I apologize. I should have rescinded his invitation after the trial." The ice had melted—a bit.

"Take your place at the dais." Luca's voice remained just audible. "I don't advise a retreat on your part. It wouldn't look good for either of us."

Touraine was torn. She would be damned if Rogan ever made her retreat. And yet—"And if I hound your heels? If he's right and everyone does think you...a fool?" She uttered the last words barely audibly, afraid even to say them aloud.

"I would never send one of my guards to her room like a child." Cold again, and her eyes left no room for argument.

It was the middle of the night when the last guests left. Luca still sat in her fine chair on the dais. Touraine's legs were as stiff as if she'd been standing on the parade grounds a full day. The house felt too empty now, even with the extra servants on hand for cleaning up. Lanquette and Guérin were securing the house. Silence pressed on Touraine's ears. It was wonderful.

The reprieve was brief.

"Lieutenant," the princess said sharply.

Touraine snapped to attention out of habit before rounding Luca's chair to stand in front of her.

"What did I say about embarrassing me?" Luca let her head loll forward, then side to side before her eyes pierced Touraine's. She inhaled sharply through her nose, as if she were dragging her temper back from the edge of a cliff.

The retorts ran through Touraine's head.

Rogan grabbed my *arm.* He *made me dance with him.* He *insulted you. I didn't ask to be here, paraded at your right hand, dressed like a prize. I don't want to be your pet.*

She bit her tongue on every sky-falling one. She hadn't forgotten the warning in the cramped dark of that sky-falling jail. And she *had* asked for Luca to save her from that darkness. It was this or the sharp nothingness of half a dozen rifles.

She wasn't sure if living was worth it. She rubbed her wrist. Her legs and feet ached from standing all night. She'd told Pruett she would help the Sands. That she would rise, and here she was already. Dressed like a noble, with a princess whose eyes searched her openly.

Luca was as much a jailer as she was a safe bunker.

Touraine bowed low. "Have I done something wrong, Your Highness? Forgive me."

The other woman's narrow jaw was clenched, and Touraine understood why. After just a couple of days in Luca's household, Touraine already recognized the way the princess needed everything to be propped just so, and everyone under her orders. Luca thought she knew people, and expected them to do as she thought. Or she would make them do as she thought.

Luca hadn't expected Rogan, and what an oversight that was. Now she would have to reconsider her plans for everyone who had seen Touraine dragged across the dance floor until Luca came to her rescue. Touraine didn't know the intricate webs of Balladairan noble ties, but she knew gossip. Luca's reputation might not be ruined, but tonight was a blow.

No wonder Luca's knuckles were clenched white on the arms of her chair.

To Touraine's own surprise, the fingers eased up, one by one.

Finally, the princess exhaled sharply through her nose. "An insult to my staff is an insult to me. As such, I will seek redress. Your job is to act with the dignity and self-control as befits someone of my staff. Do you understand me perfectly?"

Touraine stiffened at the rebuke. "Yes, Your Highness."

"Good. You're dismissed for the night."

Luca closed her eyes and leaned back again with a sigh.

Touraine hesitated, caught between the two prongs of Balladairan obedience: avoiding wrongdoing and doing good work. It was the delicate dance she'd been doing her whole life.

"Was there something else?" Luca asked.

"The modiste girl. I wondered if she might be a rebel."

Luca opened one eye. "What makes you say that?"

Touraine shrugged. "The things she said. She didn't sound impressed by us."

Luca sniffed and closed her eye. "I half expect any Qazāli with money to have some deal with the rebels. She did speak as if she was on their side."

Touraine looked wistfully around for a chair, but none were close enough for debriefing. That, and Luca had not invited her to sit.

A tense silence. "Excellent. Maybe the rebels will use your indiscretion against me as well." Could acid freeze? If so, that was how she sounded. She cleared her throat. "Help me up."

Luca half pushed herself out of the chair, strain clear on her face.

Touraine went over, arms out. Luca shooed her back.

"Don't be stupid. Get the chair. Corner of my room."

Touraine retrieved the chair. It was normal for Luca to be angry. A plan had fallen through; her weapon had misfired. Touraine wasn't above being afraid of where that anger might turn. No matter how unfair it was, she couldn't let Luca see her as a liability. Right now, Touraine was definitely that. She needed to give Luca something in return. She'd learned young that fairness and Sands rarely went together.

As she wheeled Luca across the threshold of the bedroom, her face warmed with the memory of this morning. The way Luca had looked at her as Touraine helped her dress. The husky whisper of Luca's voice.

Touraine could help Luca out of the sleek trousers now. She could make the rumors true, and Luca probably wouldn't mind as much as she seemed to.

It's the truest rumors you deny the hardest.

It was one thing to dodge Rogan in the compounds or the field. It was another impossibility entirely to deny the Balladairan heir. Even she wasn't that stupid.

And Luca had already given her so much. What gifts would she give to a lover?

Touraine stopped beside the bed and stood in front of her. Luca's mouth was twisted with her mood. She raised a pale eyebrow.

Touraine bent over the wheeled chair and kissed Luca on the mouth. No small satisfaction knowing it would catch the scholar off her guard.

It did. Luca tensed but relaxed into it almost instantly. As if it were a matter of course that Touraine would give her this.

And then Luca's hands were pushing against Touraine's chest, pushing her off, even as she held on to Touraine's vest. The princess's face was bright pink.

"You want this?" she asked, shrill with surprise.

Fear kept Touraine frozen in place. Her mouth worked, but she couldn't get the words to come out. *Say yes. Say yes. Make your life easy for once, you sky-falling idiot.*

"I didn't think so." Luca let go of the vest and sank back into her wheeled chair with a huff. "That's got to be the worst kiss I've ever had. If you're going to pretend to want me, you'll need to pretend harder."

Touraine let out a strangled cry, caught somewhere between insulted and flabbergasted.

"Well, no offense to you. I'm sure you can do better under other circumstances." Luca shrugged and sighed, shaking her head. The corners of her lips twitched, the only warning before she exploded into laughter and Touraine followed her, chuckling nervously.

It was like the venting on a meat pie, and the tension steamed out—just a bit. Enough so that when Adile knocked on the door and offered to bring tea, Luca invited Touraine to stay for a cup—and she said yes.

To leave that new space so soon would have made Touraine's relief feel false. And maybe it was. Maybe in the morning it would be gone, and regret would crash in. Right now, it felt real, and right now she was lonely.

While they waited on the tea, Luca began to lever herself out of her wheeled chair and into the bed.

Touraine reached to help. "Your Highness, do you—"

An impatient wave. After a series of grunts and winces, Luca sat in her bed, legs stretched out. She sucked air through her teeth as she kneaded the muscles in her right leg. Slowly, the lines of pain in her face softened.

Touraine pulled the chair from the small writing desk and sat at the side of Luca's bed, facing her.

"Does it hurt often?" Touraine found she was rubbing her own leg in sympathy and stopped.

"Yes. It's why I hate these stupid parties."

Adile came in and set the tea on Luca's bedside table.

The warmth of the cup was a comfort in Touraine's hand. "You fight, though." When Luca raised a questioning eyebrow, Touraine added, "You stand like a duelist."

"And it's awful," Luca said after a sip. "However, being able to fight could be the difference between life and death. Knowing the latest dances, not so much."

The same logic ruled the Sands' training.

"It happened on my birthday. A beautiful autumn afternoon." The word *beautiful* came out more like "sky-falling." "Red leaves on the trees, even more rotting underfoot, the smell of two hundred horses' shit, and about fifty trumpeters who kept blowing triumphant even after I'd fallen."

"You mean the autumn parade?"

Luca nodded.

Touraine laughed softly. "I just thought it was a national holiday. Your birthday. Same thing, I guess."

At a sore spot on her leg, Luca hissed. "Yes. I was lamed on my birthday because of a shoddy saddle buckle."

Touraine raised an eyebrow. "A saddle buckle? That's a bit obvious, isn't it?"

She thought of the stories where dark villains from the south allied with Balladairan princes and betrayed them, only to fall to the righteous heroes. They'd inspired her own fantasies—and experiments—of rigging Rogan's saddle. In her head, she had been the Balladairan hero, despite all physical evidence to the contrary.

Luca cocked her head. A trail of blond hair escaped to fall across her face, and she pushed it back. "How do you mean?"

"It's the oldest trick, isn't it? Makes it all look like an accident."

"Ha! If my uncle had wanted to kill me, there are a million equally subtle and more guaranteed ways to make it happen. That only barely works, even in the stories."

Touraine's face warmed in embarrassment.

"If I'm honest," Luca added, grimly, "I think he'll try to discredit me first. Less messy."

"Over the rebellion."

Luca nodded, doing that dismissive wave again. "I don't want to think about him. You like the old adventures, then? Did you ever read 'The Journeys of the Chevalier des Pommes'?"

Touraine grinned and nodded. The Chevalier des Pommes was a knight of lore who walked a thousand leagues, and every time he slept, an apple tree grew. "What about it?"

"When I was quite small, I tried to fall asleep in the palace gardens so there would be trees when I woke up." Luca's smile slid sideways. "No, now that I think about it—my father was so angry at me, and I don't even know why. It was my mother, I think—when I fell asleep that night, she tucked an apple in my bed."

They talked through the entire pot of tea, about stories and their youths, though Touraine kept only to innocent misadventures and Luca avoided further mention of her parents. The pot was down to the dregs when Luca drained her cup and then peered somberly over the rim at her.

"Is Captain Rogan one of the Balladairans from your old compound, then?"

"Aye."

"Has he always been like…that?" Luca waved thin fingers in the direction of the dance floor, which was a sitting room again.

"You mean a rapey son of a bearfucker? Yeah." Darkness crowded back into Touraine's thoughts.

Luca's face went open in alarm. "He—"

"Tried to."

The memory of that night closed hard around her. She'd been on her way to visit Pruett's bunk for a night's tryst.

There were things she still remembered when she didn't want to. The sound of boots behind her in the dark. The feel of a brick wall, cold through the back of her shirt, the fabric snagging. Pruett and the Sands who'd saved her, screaming at the whipping post.

Luca's mouth went into a thin line. She looked down at her lap, one hand playing with the bedclothes, the other still around her empty teacup. "I'm sorry I invited him. He's a captain and represents an important house. If I had realized the full extent of his behavior, I would have happily snubbed him. I apologize for putting you in that position."

"Thank you for standing for me." Touraine tilted her head.

"If I could, I'd have him killed." The princess spoke it as a matter of fact, and it was more frightening for it. It wouldn't take much effort at all, Touraine supposed. A word to Guérin or Lanquette or Gil—and Luca would be held blameless. Touraine wondered what mistakes she would have to make to turn Luca's whim against her.

Luca continued to muse, "It might be difficult if he's one of Cantic's favorites. She doesn't like to believe ill of her favorites." She gave Touraine an arch look with her lips pursed.

And then she was Luca the woman again, gazing away at her window, where they could see the black of night turning into deep blue. "Sky above, it's late. Early. Sleep in tomorrow. Rest. Don't think about that bastard. You're safe with me." She punctuated her words with a yawn.

Touraine's own jaws cracked in echo as she stretched. "Thank you."

Before Touraine made it to the door, Luca called her back. "And—I spoke to you as a friend tonight. Don't betray that trust. Please. I'll do the same."

Lines of uncertainty shot across the princess's forehead, her eyes just a little frightened.

Touraine ducked her head. "Of course."

She left lighter in her step. Whatever she'd done to make the princess so angry, she had corrected it, that was certain. But Luca's affections were just another edge to walk.

CHAPTER 14

THE BOOKSELLER

B reak fast with me." Princess Luca pointed to the table with a long, just barely ink-stained finger. The late night showed in the hollows of her eyes, but she smiled warmly. Over a breakfast of a crusty baguette and soft eggs flavored with pepper and herbs and tart, soft cheese, Touraine got her first mission.

Touraine wanted to love the food. When Adile brought in two small cups on a tray and poured the coffee, it smelled like fresh earth, churned by boots on the march. She was breaking fast at a princess's table. She also wanted to love the idea of her new clothing from the modiste's. Her narrow victory over Rogan still felt unreal.

It should have been easy to be grateful, especially after their conversation last night.

It should have been easy to answer the princess's questions. Easy to show an interest.

This morning, though, Touraine had woken up uneasy.

Yes, deep, deep down, Touraine was curious. She wanted to know what Princess Luca wanted and how she thought. But the truth was it didn't matter what the princess thought, because Touraine would obey anyway. Tibeau was right. She was their pet. And she'd be a well-dressed one, but she'd dance all the same.

Touraine mimicked the princess's small bites instead of scooping the eggs with a fork and bread like she would've with her squad. Her mouth was full when the princess set her knife and fork down and wiped her lips delicately with her napkin.

Today, the princess wore a deep-green coat open over a cream shirt and brown trousers. Green vines twined up the coat. Her blond hair was pulled back, and her spectacles perched on a lightly freckled nose. She radiated control.

"Today," she said, "I need you to go down to the Puddle District, near the docks."

Touraine swallowed and put her own knife and fork in the same position, on her own plate. "Yes, Your Highness."

"There should be a bookstore run by a Qazāli. I'm looking for a book called *The Last Emperor* by Yeshuf bn Zahel."

"Yeshuf bn Zahel." Touraine repeated the name to get the feel for the syllables. They felt awkward and familiar at the same time, like picking up a toy you outgrew years ago.

"I'll write it down for you. You're done already? Would you like some more?" She nodded to Touraine's empty coffee cup.

Luca tended to ramble. Still, she had a sharp eye.

"Yes, please." The taste was growing on Touraine, like a callus.

Instead of the coffee, Adile returned with a package, smiling at Touraine. "Your new clothes, it feels like."

Princess Luca gestured for her to go try them on and followed. Malika and her mother had rushed to complete the order for the ball first. Touraine had been wearing Guérin's plainclothes during the days.

Touraine tossed the wrapping paper onto her new bed and shook out the clothing. A black sleeveless vest with a hood, like the Qazāli wore, only made of finer fabric than Touraine had ever touched in her life, smooth against the hair of her body, embroidered with black thorns that shone just a little in the sunlight. The trousers were black, too.

The princess leaned against the door, and when Touraine was dressed in the vest and trousers, she made an appreciative sound in her throat and smirked. "It's a crime to keep those arms of yours hidden away in an army coat."

Touraine blushed. The vest did give her greater freedom of movement, and it was light. The trousers were loose enough to be cool, but not so baggy they'd trip her up with useless fabric. And the ensemble did suit her.

What she heard as she turned about, though, was Pruett's voice. *You want what she can give you.*

"It all fits well, Your Highness," she finally managed, smiling. "Thank you."

"Yes, it does." Luca's voice held a touch of humor.

Touraine pushed at that humor, tried to give the princess some of what she wanted. A gamble toward impudence, but—"If you outfitted the rest of the conscripts like this, you'd have the most loyal army in the world."

"And the most expensive." A crooked smirk. "There's also a heavier set for evenings, shirts. New boots will come later, and we'll go to the armory soon and see what we can do about..." She waved her hand in Touraine's general direction as she limped to the door that separated her quarters from the guards' room. "You need to be properly armed if you're going to traipse through the city."

Touraine's heart leapt. A weapon of her own, to keep. That alone would be worth the position and whatever duties it came with. She'd been feeling naked without her baton at her hip.

"In the meantime, here's this. Basic but serviceable." She disappeared into her room and came back with a belt and a long knife. Given so casually and secondhand, but it was finer than an officer's sword, its silver handle etched with leaves. "I never wear it, but it's in good repair."

Touraine stood speechless over the pile in front of her. She had never imagined owning anything of this quality before. A series of extravagant gifts. Balladaire never gave gifts freely.

And you couldn't own anything if you were owned yourself.

That thought strangled Touraine's excitement.

"Thank you, Your Highness. Very much." No jokes this time. "Shall I go for your book now, then?"

"Yes. Come with me."

Touraine followed her back to the desk in the sitting room, where Luca scrawled something on a piece of paper. Then she pulled a small pouch from a lockbox and handed it to Touraine, along with the pieces of paper. The pouch clinked with a few coins and crunched with paper.

"I don't know how much he'll ask for." For a second, the princess looked troubled. "If he has it, pay whatever he wants."

"As you say, Your Highness."

The Puddle District smelled like a puddle of piss, for sure. The pass Luca had given Touraine had gotten her a carriage that had taken her from the Quartier all the way across the Mile-Long Bridge arching over the rich farmland and the irrigation ditches that spread from the river's banks. Along with the piss, she could smell the fresh fishy smell of the river, the stale fishy smell of fish carcasses in the garbage, and the cooked fishy smell of fish soups and fish pies and fish fry. Qazāli fishing boats and shipping vessels from Balladaire creaked, and their masters shouted. After the carriage left her—intentionally, this time—at the entrance to the warren of the dock district, Touraine wandered on foot.

She squelched through the winding street and glared at anyone who sized her up. The glare, plus the bare muscles of her arms and the knife at her belt, was a good deterrent.

She stopped at the address written on Luca's note. An open door showed a man sitting on a pillow, leaning over a book on a low table. A stack of books rose messily beside him. The small shop looked a lot like the princess's sitting room, but the extra books were in crates, not on shelves. Not to mention the books were water stained and ragged, swollen with moisture or wrinkled from drying out. A waste.

He welcomed her in Shālan when she stepped in, a waterfall of incomprehensible syllables. Then, after he'd actually looked up from his book: "Shāl take my eyes. You really do look like her."

Touraine stopped in her tracks. She didn't have to ask whom. She'd spent too long trying to forget the sound of the woman's name. She'd spent the last week trying to forget about the woman everyone seemed to think was her mother.

"Are you here to see Jagh—"

"Do you have this book?" She thrust out the paper Luca had scrawled on in Shālan. The ink was smeared a little from sweat but still legible—if you could read Shālan. It was nothing but swirls and dots and slashes to her.

He grunted. "Act like her, too." His excitement turned to an ironic smile that put Touraine even more on edge. She had never liked people assuming they knew her.

He stood to take the paper. He was a big man and looked like he belonged in a wrestling circle. He didn't move like a fighter, though. Too slow. Tibeau would beat him a hundred times over.

He read the note, studied her from under his thick eyebrows, then shook his head. "Why do you want this? Can you even read it?"

"I'm here to buy it if you have it. I'll go if you don't."

"Tell your princess I don't have it."

Touraine's mouth dropped open. "How—"

"Not hard to see if you think." He grinned. "You look very nice. Madame Abdelnour does excellent work. Expensive work."

Touraine huffed. "Is there anything like it she might want?"

"No. If she wants this, she's serious. A real scholar. Haven't seen her like in years. If it's not sold, it's across the river."

"Across the river?"

"In Briga. The Cursed City. The library?"

Touraine shook her head each time.

"Did they teach you anything over there?" he muttered.

"They taught us plenty." Her hand moved toward her belt, and she was surprised to find the knife instead of the baton.

He held his palms up. "Sorry, sister. Nothing against you, just—it's not right."

"I can decide what's right for me, thanks." She turned toward the door. "Stars and sky and all that."

Her frustration warred with the depths of her mission. If Luca wanted an inroad with the rebels, the best way would be to ask. And here was a man who seemed more than happy to pull her into Qazāl. She didn't know if he was connected with the rebels or not.

And to ask meant to expose the dangerous questions she'd buried since the old man had recognized her—where had she come from? *Whom* had she come from? Even Lord Governor Cheminade had offered, at dinner, to help Touraine reach out to her mother. Was her mother a rebel?

She kept telling herself that she didn't care about her past. That she cared about the rebels only because the princess cared about the rebels. That she cared about the rebels because they'd killed two of her friends. No more than that. And yet...

She put her hand on the edge of the clay doorframe. Dragged her boots to a stop. Turned back.

"Who was he? The man—who recognized me," she asked, looking at the table. She couldn't bring herself to meet the bookseller full on. Not when she was seeing the old man's eyes bulge and the vain struggle of his tongue to make sound or find air. Looking at her. Calling her out. She didn't want to see that same accusation in the bookseller's face.

"Not who is *she*?"

"No—never mind." Touraine rolled her eyes and spun for the door.

"Ya, wait." He shifted some crates as if he knew what was in each stack by heart, and came back with a worn book.

Touraine took it skeptically.

"It's a reading primer. For Shālan. You can teach yourself. Ask your, uh, friend to help."

Suddenly, it felt like holding a live scorpion. When they were kids, Tibeau and Pruett had tried to talk to her in Shālan. She'd refused, to please the instructors, and she'd never regretted it.

Suddenly, she missed the two of them so fiercely it caught in her throat. The idea of a peace offering to them felt like a good idea. "Do you have something—nice to read?" she asked. "Something to enjoy, but not too hard?"

The man's face split in a smile. "Do you like poetry?"

She didn't. Pruett had a penchant for quoting Balladairan poetry when she was in a good mood, though. She'd even written Touraine a romantic verse or two. *Who needs a god of oceans when I could drown inside your eyes? Who needs a god of grain when I could feast between your thighs?* Touraine smiled. Frowned. Maybe Pruett would like Shālan poetry. She and Tibeau could share it.

He came back with a small book, slimmer than her little finger. "A personal favorite. Words are easy enough, but you can chew on them for days. Come back when you can read one. Tell me what you think."

She handed him a couple of silver sovereigns, well more than the books were worth.

"I know this isn't yours, so I'll take it." The silver glinted in his palm. He wouldn't stop smiling. "My name is Saïd. The dāyiein are welcome here."

The Shālan word reminded her too much of the Brigāni and the woman with the boots for her to accept the welcome with more than a terse nod and quick thanks.

"Idris Yassir was his name. Jaghotai's brother."

It felt like a kick out the door, and Touraine stumbled into the street.

The dāyiein. The Lost Ones. She was halfway up the street, skirting the curious glances of the Qazāli, when she remembered what, exactly, the word meant.

She'd never considered herself lost before, but every day since she'd stepped into this sky-falling city, the path she'd expected to walk crumbled beneath her boots.

Idris Yassir. A mother. An uncle. A whole language.

She didn't want any of it.

She paged through the poetry book as she walked. Nothing she could read. She shouldn't have bothered. She'd tell the princess it was to gain his confidence, but what if she considered it as good as treason?

"Ya, sister!"

She slowed at the bookseller's deep voice behind her. He beckoned for her to come back.

"I was just closing my shop to meet some friends. Would you like to come?"

The big man spoke softly, not as if he intended to go carousing. Not as if he intended to extend a welcoming hand to a lonely stranger. It was one conspirator to another, and his face was deathly serious.

Touraine thought of Luca in her study, planning. Luca in her bedroom, laughing over apples and tea.

"All right."

CHAPTER 15

REBELLIONS

S aïd the bookseller blindfolded her and banished any lingering ideas that he was taking Touraine to an elaborate drinking party. Saïd guided her with a hand on the small of her back on a dizzying, circuitous walk. Finally, he untied the scarf.

They were in a different building than she remembered from her captivity. No crumbling railing, no bloodstained corridor.

"We also rotate locations," Saïd said. A warning: if you look to betray us, you will not find us here.

"If you're so worried, why did you bring me?"

"Hope," he said simply. "But I'm not naive."

He led her upstairs, following the sounds of heated voices. They went silent as Touraine and Saïd grew closer. He knocked once and said a short phrase in Shālan. The door opened.

Touraine recognized the woman at the door immediately, even with the frayed deep-red scarf around her face. More accurately, she recognized the boots. The woman had escaped the Sands' attack, then.

Touraine's hand went to the knife at her side. She heard the echo of Luca's warnings—how a Balladairan representative conducts herself and all—but this wasn't Luca's realm. Her grip tightened on the handle. Touraine would bet her teeth that this was the woman who had framed her for killing a blackcoat, too. She'd ruined Touraine's life in more ways than one.

But this wasn't Touraine's realm, either. She was used to rank and file, the open sky above, and clear enemies. Not mazes of close buildings and secret alliances.

"What in Shāl's name is she doing here, Saïd?" the woman asked.

Saïd used his bulk to usher Touraine through the door so he could close it. Trapping her in.

"Easy, Jackal. Today, she's a friend."

"A friend my ass. She's one of their tools. You just compromised all of us for your stupid dream of reconciliation. It's not going to happen, Saïd."

Touraine was inclined to agree and started to say so when Saïd held his hands up and stood between Touraine and the woman he'd called Jackal.

"She's here now," he said. "Give her a chance."

Touraine scowled at them both as they talked over her. "Give me a chance to what?"

Saïd smiled back at her. "We've all had bad first impressions. Let's start over." He turned back to the Jackal. "She has the foreign princess's ear."

The Jackal glared at Touraine, her snarl baring teeth. Touraine thought the woman would stab her rather than let her stay, but finally she stepped aside. Saïd ushered Touraine forward.

Princess Luca wanted to open peace talks with these people.

The room was cozy, with five people sitting in a circle on poufs or boxes with cushions. Sunlight streaming in through the windows lit their veiled or scarf-covered faces. A beaten metal plate held half a circle of bread and a bowl of oil. In the back, a small altar held a stub of incense. The room smelled sweet with its smoke. Touraine spotted the Brigāni woman immediately, her golden eyes like a falcon's.

"Ah, dāyie. Welcome." The woman smiled, though it didn't reach her eyes. "Sit. Eat."

Touraine thought through the forms of address Luca had drilled into her, then settled on a simple half bow. "Thank you."

The bitch with the boots, the Jackal, dropped onto a pillow next to the Brigāni witch and rolled her eyes. "Yes, welcome, Mulāzim. Careful not to spill any oil on your new clothes." Her left arm ended in a painful-looking twist of flesh halfway down her forearm.

Touraine tried to ignore her, tearing a chunk of bread off the round, swiping it almost carelessly through the oil. The oil was sweet but sprinkled with salt that dissolved against her tongue.

"You don't look like a conscript anymore," the Brigāni said, leaning forward. She sat with a blanket over her lap. Her face was tight at the eyes and lips. Strained.

Touraine took her time chewing and swallowing her bread.

"No. I'm not. One of you framed me for killing a blackcoat. I was supposed to be executed. I lost everything."

The Brigāni witch gave the Jackal a questioning look, and the dark-eyed woman shrugged innocently.

"Now I'm the queen's assistant."

Saying it out loud felt strange, as if she were stretching out a pair of tight trousers and feeling them loosen until they fit. This was what she was now. What she would learn to be. Which meant she had to put aside what she wanted and think about what Luca wanted. Presumably, that didn't include killing rebel leaders. Not yet, anyway. She glared at the Jackal. What a shame.

A curvy rebel sitting with legs crossed and palms on knees laughed a tinkling, self-assured laugh and said, "Balladaire has no queen." That voice was familiar. Touraine's suspicions had been right.

"Mademoiselle Abdelnour." Touraine saluted her with a piece of bread. "Princess Luca will be queen soon enough."

The young woman only laughed again. She wore a gray scarf that, at first glance, was nondescript. On a closer look, though, it was woven with a delicate pattern and made with almost the same quality as Touraine's own clothes.

"A dog with a fancy collar is still a dog, Mulāzim." The Jackal chuckled at her own joke, crossing her legs to prop one bastard boot on a bent knee while she slouched back on her hand.

It wasn't even a funny joke. Touraine chewed her lip until the flare of her anger dimmed again. "Why do you keep calling me that?"

"It just means *lieutenant*," Malika said. "Not an insult, for once." She pointed at Touraine, then the ass of a woman, and then the Brigāni witch. "Mulāzim. The Jackal. The Apostate."

Noms de guerre.

The Jackal snorted. Fitting.

Touraine looked sideways at Malika and Saïd. "So who are you?"

"Uh-uh. One name's enough." Saïd crossed his arms across his chest. He looked to the Jackal and the Brigāni witch—the Apostate. "Let her take a message back to the princess for us."

At first, Touraine felt indignant. She wasn't their courier. But Luca wanted to set up negotiations with the rebels, and Touraine knew for a fact that Luca didn't know how to initiate those talks, or she would have set Touraine to it already. So Touraine swallowed her pride and did her job. That's what she was good at, after all.

She bowed her head. "What do you want me to say?"

"We want peace over—"

"No one agreed to this, brother," the Jackal interrupted. "Why should we trust the foreign girl any more than the rest of them?" Then she looked at Touraine with so much scorn, Touraine thought she would spit. "And I wouldn't trust one of these bootlicking traitors to help. Tell him, Apostate."

Saïd and the Jackal both looked at the Brigāni woman for backup, but it was Malika who spoke.

"The princess did donate the slots for Qazāli children at the Citadel." She shrugged prettily, holding one edge of her scarf so that it didn't fall off her shoulder. "I checked with the school this morning. We can at least send her a few demands, see how much of this is just her putting a dress on a goat."

Malika looked Touraine up and down, and Touraine wondered if she was the goat.

It came again to the Apostate, but she looked pained as she studied Touraine. Out of nowhere, she winced and put a hand to her abdomen before recovering. She sat up straighter. Touraine could see the sharp jut of shoulder and elbow through the loose fabric of her robe. Even from the ground, she gave Touraine the same measuring eye the princess had used in the prison. Always, always someone weighed her. Always, someone looked for the flaw.

Finally, the Apostate said, "If your princess wants to show us she means well, she should release any prisoners arrested on suspicion of rebellion. Full amnesty."

"I'll ask." Touraine thought the likelihood was slim, though.

Her doubt must have shown in her voice. The Apostate added, "Even the so-called violent crimes. Until she and hers are locked up for the violent crimes they've committed against us, I don't think we should be locked up for retaliation." She shared a look with the bitch on the floor. "Shāl's peace or no."

"Anything else?"

"She'll also close down all of the Droitist schools in the region. No children will be taken to any of them, anywhere in Qazāl."

That took Touraine aback. "I thought you were happy about her offer for the orphans?"

"It proves she is a political animal, offering us what she thinks is valuable. That is all." The Apostate grimaced and put a hand to her body again. "Besides, do you think they treat students at a school for Balladairan children the same way they treat students at a school especially for us lowly, uncivilized colonials?"

The Jackal snorted. Saïd looked at Malika, who looked down at her hands, eyes vacant.

"It's not an easy life, either," Malika said, "being one of the few Qazāli at a Balladairan school, but it will teach the children a few things." Then she met Touraine's eyes with a dark, crooked smile that was mostly a grimace. "I'm sure you understand."

Touraine only partly understood. She was proud of her Balladairan education. It was extensive and effective. But any child who went to a Balladairan school risked coming out...like the Sands. Too

Balladairan and not Shālan enough. What would the Qazāli do when their new batch of orphans came out like Touraine?

Touraine was starting to think it was impossible to come from one land and learn to live in another and feel whole. That you would always stand on shaky, hole-ridden ground, half of your identity dug out of you and tossed away.

A sharp wheezing sound brought all eyes to the Apostate. The woman sank back into her cushions. A spasm racked her, and she grimaced in fierce pain.

The Jackal moved first, diving to cradle the woman's head in her lap as she writhed in pain. The Jackal jerked her head at Malika.

"Malika, get her out of here."

Touraine thought that Malika was going to take the Apostate to safety, but it was her own arm that the modiste's daughter grabbed.

Malika dragged Touraine down the stairs, but in her distress, she forgot to blindfold Touraine with a scarf when they were outside. The smell of baking bread and hot stone filled the air. Youths carried long trays of bread and dough up and down the streets. She caught the eyes of one, gangly and pimpled, a tray balanced on his shoulder while he smoked a cigarette against a whitewashed wall covered in a peeling broadside. The young man glared at her, even though he couldn't possibly know who she was.

And then Malika yanked her away, tugging her through the warren of the Old Medina until they were somewhere more familiar: the edge of the New Medina, at the Blue Gate, which opened onto the road to the Quartier and the compound.

"I trust you can find your way from here. I'm sure we'll talk soon." Though her face was covered again in that beautiful gray scarf, Touraine could hear the worry in her voice.

"What? How will I tell you what she says?"

"We'll contact you." Then the other woman said something in Shālan, already backing away.

"Hold on—"

"It means goodbye." And then Malika was gone.

*　　*　　*

While Touraine was gone, Luca spent the day obsessing about the last thing any decent Balladairan citizen should even be considering.

Religion.

Gods. Prayer and faith and magical beings that granted wishes, and the kinds of people who communed with so-called deities and only ended up looking like madmen.

She had begun to feel like one of those madmen.

She should have been combing through Cheminade's notes and getting the city under her feet. Merchants were complaining about raids from the desert tribes along the southern routes. She should have been *acting*.

Her eyes throbbed. She took off her spectacles and rested her forehead against the heels of her palms. That stupid little book Paul-Sebastien had given her hadn't been stupid at all. It just left her with still more questions.

She couldn't believe that Paul-Sebastien LeRoche de Beau-Sang had written it. The intricate knowledge of the Qazāli—of Shālan customs and religion—spoke of someone intimate with the culture, someone who had spent time around Shālans, if not with them. The last time scholars had done that peacefully was before the religious bans, before half the nations in the Shālan Empire became Balladairan colonies.

LeRoche posited that Shālan magic, if it existed at all, was actually connected to the religion. The theory was flimsy, though, based only on the Taargens, Balladaire's hostile neighbors to the east. The Taargens worshipped a bear god, and the bed tales to scare children spoke of magical bears ravaging the Taargens' enemies after human sacrifice.

The Taargens and their animal god. The Shālans and their god of the body. Luca had heard that far to the south in the monks' mountains, they worshipped a god of the mind. Before they'd developed their science, even Balladaire had fallen prey to its collective imagination: a god of harvests that wanted bloodletting in the fields.

It was exactly the kind of sky-falling nonsense that made Balladaire ban religion in the first place. By leaving behind religion, they were able to build an empire instead.

She wanted her people to be grateful to her for bringing magic to them. And that couldn't happen if it was tangled up in holy wish fulfillment. Would they still be grateful if the magic came wrapped in a god's trappings? Not a chance. If Shālan magic came from Shālan religion, her plan was finished. And yet…if the magic came from religion, was religion as uncivilized as they had been taught?

Even LeRoche stayed far from praising religion. Simply stating the facts, like a good scholar, and connecting them to completely separate and unlike things, claiming they were, in fact, related.

Most of the book was actually just history. The last Brigāni emperor, Djaya, her blind faith, and her overpowering greed. Somehow, she had managed to devastate swaths of Balladaire. There were rumors of magic here, too.

Somewhere, the Shālans had the magic to make Luca into the queen she wanted to be.

Before her father died, she would sit on his throne, try on his ceremonial crown, pretend to read his notes. She could feel the texture of the throne under her small bottom, the heavy weight of gold on her head supported by her father's hands. Her memories might have been fashioned more by what Gil had told her than by reality, but Luca held them close anyway.

Now, when she imagined herself on the throne as an adult, she always thought of her father. He'd brought Qazāl into the empire. She wanted to be better even than him, the king who "spread his wings and covered the earth," as a more poetic scholar wrote. She couldn't surpass him if she wasn't willing to risk her reputation.

A sharp rap on the door interrupted her thoughts. At some point, it had become late afternoon. Touraine hadn't reported back yet.

"Your Highness?" Guérin looked in. "Guard Captain Gillett is here for training."

Luca stood too quickly, and the tight muscles in her hip recoiled as she overstretched them. She hunched over, gasping. She waved Guérin away and eased up slowly. It wasn't as bad as it could have been. The tingles in her ass hadn't started up, at least. She limped down to the sitting room, where Gillett was waiting.

"I'm going to need a long warm-up today." She sighed and went for her practice steel. "Has Touraine come back? She's been gone all day."

Gil shook his head tersely. "She might be taking her leisure with it. Worth speaking to her."

Luca nodded, but deep down something felt wrong. Touraine didn't seem the type to take her leisure with an order.

Fencing lessons with Gil were always grueling, but today she performed exceedingly poorly. Gil wormed inside her guard several times with a blunt dagger, pretending to be a footpad, and once caught her by the neck in a maneuver she should have been able to roll out of. She took too long to react every time.

He released her and squared off with her side-on. "What's on your mind, Luca?"

Luca lowered her eyes. "What if she's hurt?"

Gil grunted. "You knew the risks before you sent her. That's why you sent her."

Because Touraine was disposable. She wouldn't be missed from the soldiers' ranks, and she had no necessary function elsewhere. If she vanished, Balladaire could try another method to subdue the rebellion.

Gil raised a goading eyebrow. "Is it not?"

His expression left a sour taste in her mouth. "Hmph. Again, old man."

He smirked and pressed her again. This time, she forced him back with a touch, then another. She rotated as he sidestepped, keeping him at a distance—

And faced Touraine, breathing as if she'd run all the way from the city. A bead of sweat curled around one dark eyebrow and down the gentle slope of Touraine's nose. The woman's mouth hung slack in surprise.

A moment later, Gil's blunt blade rested at her throat.

Luca blushed and stepped away from him. "Hello, Touraine." She told herself that it was just the exertion that had left her flushed.

"Your Highness." The other woman bowed.

Luca grunted and dropped into the sitting room's single chaise, stretching her legs out on it. She rolled her fist over her leg muscles, hoping to lessen the pain later. Like smoothing wrinkles out of crumpled parchment—futile. She hissed whenever she hit a tender spot. Touraine was still waiting.

Luca waved her over. "Sit, sit. Did you find the book?"

"No—but I—he took me to a meeting. With the heads of the rebellion, I think." The other woman practically vibrated in her seat.

"Is this—they met with you. They met with you!" She jumped up, heedless of the sore muscles, fists clenched in victory. This was even better than *The Last Emperor*. "This is—wait. It *was* the rebels? The bookseller is a rebel? Does he know you work with me now?"

"He does. They all do. Do you remember I mentioned Malika Abdelnour last night?"

Luca raised an eyebrow. "She leads them?"

The soldier allowed herself a small smile. "No. It looked more like a council."

"Who else was there?"

Touraine's face darkened. "The two who held me captive. The Brigāni and the bastard who broke my ribs. I think they're the ones highest in the hierarchy."

"The magic user."

"I never said I believed it. I don't, I swear—I'm not—" Touraine shook her head hard.

Luca knew that fear in her eyes. She'd felt it in her office not an hour before. The fear that someone would suspect you of thinking there was something greater in the world than logic and humanity.

"It's all right. What did they say?" It was happening, sooner than she'd expected, and effortlessly.

"They're grateful for your offer to send the children to school. They also want full amnesty for Qazāli arrested for sedition."

"What?" Luca said, incredulous.

Touraine nodded. She seemed irritated. "I know. I only said you might be interested in negotiating. I didn't promise anything."

Luca buzzed, pacing back and forth, one hand on her cane, the other in her hair.

"I overstepped. I shouldn't have said anything," Touraine said. "But I saw the opportunity. You have to take the open shots as you get them. You don't always get a second opening."

"No, yes, you're right." Luca stilled and pressed her hand to her forehead as if she were shading her eyes. "It's just—this has to be a secret, Touraine. An absolute secret. None of the nobles, the merchants, no Qazāli. Even Cantic cannot know any terms we propose until a deal is inked and signed. I...I need to have control over how and when I enact any demands. If Cantic disagrees with any of them, she'll stop negotiations. Worse, she'll bring the military down on them instead. They have to promise secrecy, or it's all null."

She looked around the room and caught everyone in her glance. Lanquette, who stood by the door. Gil. Even Adile in the corner, where she was preparing refreshments.

"Understood, Your Highness. But why—" Touraine shrugged helplessly. "Why not just arrest the ones we know? It would compromise their council—we can hunt the rest down and rout the rebellion that way."

This was the Cantic in her speaking. Touraine thought like the other soldiers. Maybe the strength of the military could crush the rebellion now. But what about later, when the next generation grew discontented? There would always be new rebellions if they didn't try peace first.

Luca stopped pacing and sat down, her leg finally reminding her of its pain.

"Because. I truly do want to work with them. Once you start making arrests, it's hard to turn back." Luca rubbed her eyes. She noticed Touraine held a parcel. "I take it that's not a copy of *The Last Emperor*?"

Touraine looked disinterested as she picked it up, but she handed it to Luca so gingerly that Luca knew the disinterest was affectation. There were two books, a worn old Shālan primer like the one Luca had used as a child—probably as old—and a slim book that, upon closer inspection, was full of poems. The first poem appeared to be about water—"We pray for rain," the first line read. A reasonable subject for a desert poet.

"But you can't read these."

"He—er, the bookseller picked it out for me. Said to read them when I learned enough." Touraine's chin dipped toward her chest.

She seemed embarrassed and nervous. Vulnerable in a way Luca hadn't expected to see her.

"Do you want to learn?" Luca asked softly.

"No, Your Highness. He just gave them to me."

Luca gave it a moment, wondering if Touraine would change her mind. When she didn't, Luca let it be and gave the books back before easing deeper into the chaise.

Touraine stood to leave. She hesitated. "Your Highness, I had one more question. Could I take a day of leave tomorrow?"

"For what?" Luca asked, surprised.

"I—"

"Never mind." Luca realized too late that her question, however innocent, wouldn't come across that way. "You don't need to account for it. You can take the day."

CHAPTER 16

ANOTHER BROADSIDE

Judging by the sun, it was late when Touraine woke the next morning. Guérin and Lanquette were already gone. Her cheeks warmed as she remembered Guérin's bleary curiosity when Touraine had stumbled into their bedroom near dawn after the ball.

She dressed and pulled the books she'd gotten from Saïd out of their hiding place and left for the city without looking to see if Luca had woken up. She'd learned the hard way not to waste a day of leave, and she suspected that the talks with the rebels were going to mean few restful days to come.

Touraine wandered the sun-bright streets leisurely, still avoiding people's eyes, Qazāli and Balladairan alike. In the daylight, it was easy to see how varied the city actually was. For every Qazāli with loose dark hair, there was another with skin Brigāni dark, even though their eyes were brown, not gold. She even saw a woman who was blond enough to be a Balladairan—Touraine thought she was, until she snapped back at a merchant in rapid-fire Shālan. It was the Sands writ large—all of them had been taken from all over the Shālan Empire, from Qazāl to Masridān to Lunāb, but not all of them looked the same.

She thought of the stormy oceans in Pruett's eyes. She needed to see if Pruett was all right.

Touraine was relieved to spot Noé standing at attention outside the guardhouse. The thought of going inside, being surrounded by other Sands, made her shoulders tense up. *This is my squad*, she tried to tell herself. *These are my people.*

Noé snapped her a salute and smiled. Then, when she got close enough, he wrapped her in a quick hug. The embrace reminded her how delicate he had always been and how surprising it was that he had made it as a soldier. Like all of them, though, he'd found his ways to survive.

"It's good to see you, Lieutenant," Noé said, his voice as sweet and clear as ever. A wave of longing almost pulled her under. She'd missed him.

"It's good to see you, too. Are Tibeau and Pruett around?"

He nodded behind him, toward the guardhouse. "Beau's inside, but Pru is out. Don't know where or how long." He shrugged apologetically.

Touraine clapped him on the shoulder and headed inside.

"Oh, and, Lieutenant?"

Touraine turned back to Noé.

"Rogan's gone for now, too."

That, at least, was a true relief. She wasn't ready to face him yet, not after the disaster at Luca's ball.

She found Tibeau in the courtyard of the riad-turned-guardhouse. Its fountain was still dry and now draped indecorously with the shirts of a couple Sands sparring on the dusty tiles. One of them was Tibeau, sweat streaming down his big hairy belly. He noticed her first. His opponent took advantage of his distraction and cramped his leg with a kick.

He roared as he fell, his injured leg curled and spasming. "Sky above, Aimée, you are such an asshole!"

Touraine chuckled. At least some things didn't change.

"And what are you doing here, oh esteemed—what are you now, exactly?" Aimée gave Tibeau a hand up, but she was talking to Touraine. They both looked curiously at her and the package in her hand.

"I brought a present. Call it a peace offering or an apology. Something like that." Touraine handed the parcel to Tibeau, keenly aware of the other off-duty Sands' eyes on her. Luckily, almost everyone was on patrol or guard duty somewhere in the city. Everyone else was just being polite. The Sands had a lot of practice politely ignoring each other for privacy.

Tibeau tore open the corners of the paper, enough to see the Shālan letters of the poetry book peek through. Sudden excitement shone bright in his eyes.

Aimée looked at it dubiously. "I was hoping for something more... edible."

Touraine slapped Aimée gently on the chest. "Can you even read it anymore?" Touraine asked Tibeau.

"Can't be too hard, can it? I knew it before." He slid the book a little farther out of its paper to better peek at the first page. He sounded out the words slowly. Something about it sounded familiar, but Touraine couldn't place it.

"What's it mean?" she asked.

"We pray to rain, maybe? I'll practice." He shrugged carelessly, but Touraine recognized that squint he got when he was frustrated. Still, he forced a smile. "Maybe I have something to show you, too." He grabbed his shirt from the fountain and mopped his face with it while he led Touraine up the stairs. "Aimée. I need your lockpick set."

"Only welcome when I'm useful, hein?" Aimée grumbled, but she sounded excited, too.

They trailed past the room Touraine had shared with Pruett and Tibeau. Where was Pruett? Would she be back before Touraine left? Would she refuse to see Touraine outright?

The door they stopped before was nondescript. It took Aimée only a moment of fiddling with the lock to open it.

Her friends ushered her in and stood back with pride. Inside the room were books. Not as many as in Luca's scattered library or Saïd's bookshop, but more than a dozen. The room was dusty and dark, clearly unused. She remembered dimly that Cantic had mentioned books in the guardhouses. Touraine hadn't had a chance to check before the guardhouse was no longer hers.

"We're not supposed to have access, and to be honest, a lot of them are in Shālan, so most of us can't read them," Aimée said, shrugging.

Tibeau waved the book of poems. "But I'll practice."

Touraine stepped over to browse the spines of the books on their shelves. The room looked like it might have been a reading room. There was no furniture, not even pillows on the ground like the rebels had, which made her think it had all been repurposed.

"Do you mind if I take a few of these?" Touraine asked.

"You can't afford your own books?" Aimée crossed her arms and shrugged, but she was still smiling.

"Luca—the princess sends me on errands sometimes."

"Luca?" Tibeau raised his eyebrow. "That familiar already."

Touraine's face warmed with something between embarrassment and shame. She rushed to talk over it. "There's a bookseller in the Puddle District."

"A bookseller sold you a book of Shālan poems. Not Balladairan, were they?"

He slid back into his teasing lilt so easily that Touraine's shoulders relaxed. He was on his best behavior, so Touraine could be, too.

Aimée, on the other hand, frowned sideways at her. "You call her by name. She lets you wander about like a stray dog. She's even giving you weapons."

Touraine followed Aimée's glance to the knife Luca had gifted her. She imagined how it looked, flaunting this new privilege. "The gold stripes were going to have me shot, Aimée. This way, I stay alive and the princess promises to help the Sands out. I don't have a choice."

Still, Touraine liked the knife. She liked the clothes and the food and the doctors.

Aimée reached over to pluck at the fabric of Touraine's new sleeveless shirt, eyed the new trousers and boots, and whistled. "I'm sure you're right. But your lack of choice looks a sight more comfortable than ours."

Touraine clenched her fists, ready to hit something. Then Aimée looked at her full on for the first time. The emotions on her face made Touraine ache.

Wry jealousy, disappointment, frustration. Even if Touraine was stuck with Luca, in her bed or playing traitor in the dead of night, it would be hard for any Sand to see her as worse off. With Luca's favor, she was effectively immune from being shat on by Balladairan officers. Rogan would never touch her again. But Touraine was alone now. The Sands had each other.

"Aimée." Tibeau put a warning arm across Aimée's chest. "Keep it up and I'll shove sand in places you didn't even know you had holes."

"All right, easy, Sergeant. Sorry, Lieutenant," Aimée said, pushing Tibeau's arm away. "Anylight. I'd stay close to her now." She glanced behind Touraine, back toward the door. "Rogan went into a shitting rage when he found out you'd be let off. If he and his friends liked you before…"

As if summoned, a shadow blotted out the light from the open door. Touraine spun around, a cold fist of fear at her throat. *It's okay*, she told herself. *You're Luca's now. He can't touch you.*

The thought was cold comfort when Touraine saw Pruett framed in the doorway instead.

"Pru. Hey." Touraine's throat was too dry for words.

"That's all you have to say?" Pruett sauntered in. Something crinkled in her fist as she crossed her arms. A broadside and her cap. She'd cut her hair, too, and her face was narrow without the frame. The bags under her eyes could've carried corpses.

"Pruett, I—" Instead of talking, Touraine held her arms open.

Pruett blinked hard and pressed her lips together. After an eternity of a breath, she pulled Touraine close. Her neck smelled like gun powder, oil, sweat.

"You smell like a fucking rosebush." Pruett held Touraine at arm's length, nose wrinkled.

"How is Rogan?" Touraine blurted. Her fear found its exit.

"Don't worry. I've held him off so far. Seems he's not that particular about who he chases, as long as she's in power and he can try to make her small."

Pruett looked her up and down, asking without asking, *How are you?*

"I'm fine."

"Figured you were." Pruett held out the broadside. It had been balled up at least once.

Touraine eased out the wrinkles. Her stomach lurched, and she couldn't tell if it was embarrassment or dread. "Sky-falling fuck."

"That supposed to be you and her?" Pruett asked. "They fucked up your face."

"Where'd you get this? How many were there?"

Pruett raised an eyebrow and crossed her arms back over her chest. "They're all over the city by now, most likely. I pulled this one off the wall of a smoking house around the corner."

"Shit. I need to go."

"I just got back." Pruett frowned. "Can't you give me a minute of your time, or what? Were you even going to bother seeing me?"

Touraine's heart thumped low in her stomach, making her nauseated. She could stay. Luca had given her leave. But even though she didn't know the full shape of Luca's plans, she knew that Luca needed to see this. It was the kind of picture that did damage, no matter what your plans were. Touraine tried and failed to ignore the bitterness and hurt on Pruett's face.

"I'm sorry, Pru. I have to go. She's going to kill someone."

She picked up an armful of books, plucking them almost at random. If it looked like a Shālan history, she took it. Luca would probably be interested. She tucked the broadside inside one of the covers. With one last look at her friends, she turned to go.

Captain Horse-Fucking Rogan stood in the railed corridor, his slicked hair even shinier in the sunlight.

"I hadn't expected the pleasure of Her Royal Highness's chambermaid so soon. And trespassing, no less."

As always, Pruett was the fastest on her feet. "Captain, sir. The former lieutenant is on an errand for Princess Luca. I was just hurrying her along."

"All of you? Quite a lot of help for a simple errand."

Aimée shrugged. "Spare key."

"Heavy lifting." Tibeau folded his arms across his thick chest.

"A spare key?" Rogan raised an eyebrow. "We don't have a spare key. Do you expect me to believe that you four aren't plotting something like treason?" His smile turned wicked. "At the very least, do you expect a jury not to believe it?"

Touraine stood straighter, let her anger fill out the breadth of her shoulders. "There'll be no jury, Captain. They're helping me on orders from Her Highness."

From her pocket, Touraine pulled out the pass that Luca had stamped with her personal seal.

"And I'll need their help to carry these books to Princess Luca's library in the Quartier."

It was a desperate ploy, and Rogan smiled.

"Unfortunately, they're all indispensable at the moment. You're more than welcome to come back, however. Or better yet, Her Highness can send some of the blackcoats. We'd be happy to oblige her."

Touraine looked over her shoulder at Tibeau, Aimée, and Pruett. They were all used to his bullying. It was etched in the weary resignation on their faces. It had always been one of the facts of life as a Sand, but this was personal. The four of them had gone up against Rogan and his friends years before and lost, badly. But Touraine knew how to play the Balladairans' game to get what her friends needed. Knew whose name to drop, whose boots to lick. It's why she'd been picked for lieutenant in the first place.

"Her Highness has a special interest in the well-being of the conscripts, Captain." Touraine puffed herself as haughtily as she could, and did her best to imitate Luca's cold demeanor. "And if she or I learn that you've been treating the conscripts poorly or with unnecessary severity, she wouldn't hesitate to remind you of Guard Lanquette's particular duty." Touraine cleared her throat. "I believe it was to separate your balls from your body? Something like that."

She shoved past him with her arms full of books. The silent rage crossed with embarrassment on his face made it worth it.

It was the best she could do for now, but somehow Touraine would fix this, if she had to kill Rogan herself.

*   *   *

Luca was reading through the list of prisoners in the compound jail, when the letters from Balladaire interrupted her. Guérin bowed over the proffered papers, uncharacteristically buoyant. Luca frowned at her uncle's name on the topmost.

"Have you received something from home, then?" Luca set the letters on top of the records and ledgers she'd taken from Cheminade's office. She'd been skimming through the prisoners to see which ones might be worth freeing and which ones might deserve a retrial based on...biased concerns. Luca might be willing to free someone who'd punched a price-gouging merchant, but she wasn't letting murderers back into the colony.

Guérin smiled with reserve, which might as well have been a grin on her usually somber face. "Aye, Your Highness. My oldest daughter's got a 'prenticeship with a carpenter in La Chaise."

That warmed Luca's heart. "I look forward to commissioning a piece from her."

At that, Guérin beamed. "She'd be honored, Your Highness, and I don't reckon you'd regret it."

There was a commotion outside the office, and Luca heard Touraine's voice. She was smiling before the urgency in the other woman's tone became clear.

"Your Highness?" Touraine knocked on the door three times, even though it was open. She wouldn't maintain eye contact with Luca.

"What have you done?" It came out sharper than Luca intended.

Touraine ducked her head. "I'm sorry, Your Highness. I found this in the city."

The broadside trembled in Touraine's hand as she held it out, carefully turning the image away from Guérin's gaze. Luca approached it like a snake. She didn't want to take it, afraid it might bite. It had been crumpled and straightened and crumpled again, and was damp with Touraine's sweat. The image, however, was clear.

Sky above and earth below. This was what she had been afraid of. Even though they had clapped for her, for her decision to help the Qazāli orphans. She wasn't naive enough to think that everyone approved of the decision, but she hadn't expected a rebuttal so swift.

The worst part was the way her cheeks flushed and she couldn't help it. She understood why Touraine wouldn't meet her eyes and why she'd hidden it from Guérin.

The…artist…had drawn the two of them locked in a dancing embrace. Luca, with the same too-severe bun as before, leering at a poor likeness of Touraine—it had gotten only the short military cut of her hair and the broad shoulders right. She was dressed in poor Qazāli clothing, a ragged hooded vest and loose trousers. No one who had seen Luca recently, which was to say, at the ball, could doubt who it was intended to be.

It was captioned in beautiful calligraphy: "Queen of the Sand Fleas."

Luca tore the paper in half, then quarters and eighths and more until they fell to shreds she would have to apologize to Adile for.

"Find them," she growled. When neither Guérin nor Touraine left, she shouted, "Go! Send a squad to rip them off the walls and burn them."

Luca swore under her breath. "Wait! Touraine." The soldier stepped back in from the hall outside, eyes lowered and body wary of threat. Luca's embarrassment was boiling into fury at her impotence. She forced herself to steady her breathing and her tone.

"Go back to the rebels. Ask them for a list of demands so that I can consider them. These aren't…official negotiations, but they can be a start."

"Your Highness?"

"What?" snapped Luca. "If you're suddenly incapable…"

Touraine flinched. "No, Your Highness. I mean, I will. I'll find them."

"Good." If Touraine didn't swear the rebels to secrecy soon, the fledgling talks would never get off the ground.

CHAPTER 17

LITTLE TALKS

Touraine spent the rest of the day looking for the rebels' location near the Qazāli baker. The only people there when she tramped up the stairs, though, were a small family scared shitless.

So on the following day, she went back to the beginning, to the shop in the Puddle District where the big man had first tried to pry into soft spots Touraine wouldn't admit existed. The shop was closed, but the first thing that caught Touraine's eye was a broadside plastered to the wall. *The* broadside. Her face went hot, and she tore it off in ragged strips.

Breathing heavily, she took note of her surroundings. Maybe it was her imagination, but the fish smelled extra rotten today. The Qazāli dockworkers pretended not to pay attention to her, but she caught them looking away from her as soon as she turned toward them.

She had her knife, though, and the princess's protection. So she squatted on her haunches in front of the bookshop and waited. And waited. Saïd didn't come. Nor did any of the other rebels she could recognize.

Eventually, the sun sloped down, and the noise of the Puddle District grew louder, more raucous. Laborers came off their shifts for meals, for drinking and fucking and fighting. They stopped turning away from her when she looked at them. Touraine thumbed the handle of her new knife and wondered just how far Luca's protection would take her.

Not far enough.

A burly woman who reminded Touraine of the Jackal, only more pleasant, said something to her handful of companions as they casually closed in on her. They were all built like oxen, broad backed, thick in the middle and the thighs from the burden of their days.

One of the smaller ones, a man with a close beard and twice-broken nose, said, "It's time you moved along, isn't it?"

With the bookshop to her back, Touraine had only so many options, and they were narrowing fast the closer these Qazāli got. Negotiation seemed like the kind of thing that went better the fewer people you killed. At least it wasn't her fault, she would tell the princess.

"I'm just leaving." Touraine held her hands up and sidled to her left, toward the side street.

"Meant that as a more permanent kind of thing," the smaller man said.

He closed that side of their semicircle, blocking Touraine's escape as they tightened in like a snake. The big woman came at Touraine from the middle, and another two closed in on Touraine's right. They were close enough for Touraine to see the gaps in their teeth and the grime in their fingernails. They stank like sour sweat and stale smoke.

Touraine drew her knife. Sky above, she wished she'd had a chance to train with it. It was light in her hand, its balance foreign, but it was sharp so it would do.

"In the name of Her Royal Highness the princess," she said, "I'm warning you."

They must have thought she was just a pampered show horse, all well-turned muscles and no skill. She saw it in their smirks as they closed in. Then she saw the disbelief in their faces as she struck at the small man. She caught him across the arm, and he screamed as she ran by him.

Touraine sprinted up the side street, trying to connect it to the way back to the Mile-Long Bridge and El-Wast proper. The laborers splashed and swore as they chased after her.

Turn here, she thought, *no, here*—she recognized that smoking den with a bright red curtain of beads over the door—she passed it and hung a hard right. She could see the bridge, its lanterns guiding her way back to the city proper.

She returned to the Quartier empty handed.

Touraine refused to be cowed. She went back to Saïd's shop the next day. This time, everyone watched her as she stood vigil in front of the closed shop. Before things got messy, however, a small child with tousled curls flying in a dark halo strutted right up to her. Their front two teeth were missing as they smiled and held out a small piece of paper.

The paper had the rough edge of a book's binding on one side and a jagged torn edge at the top. *Rue Tontenac, after sunset.*

Touraine looked at the kid, who stared at her innocently. What a ruse. The kid was just as wary, just as keyed into the mood of the passersby as Touraine was. What a life.

"Where's rue Tontenac?" Touraine asked.

The kid shot off an explanation that was so mixed with Shālan that it was hopeless. "Can you show me?" She mimed with her fingers a person walking. "Take me?"

A grubby palm shot out, waiting. *Fair enough.* Touraine fished out a half sovereign and dropped it in the kid's hand. It vanished. Then the child took off, bare brown feet slapping against the street. Touraine sprinted after.

Rue Tontenac was in the heart of the Qazāli districts. The buildings were cracked clay brick, and the road, once paved with stone, was now mostly dirt. Most of the traffic seemed to go in and out of a café or smoking den. The whole street smelled like rose smoke and the burnt bean water that Luca liked so much. There wasn't a single Balladairan. Now Touraine just had to find the right building.

She turned to the kid, but they were already gone.

Touraine weighed her options. Thinking about the youth who'd been smoking outside the baker's oven the other day, she assumed that same casual lean against one of the buildings and glared moodily at nothing, pretending to be lost in her thoughts. It was easiest to go unnoticed if you kept to your own business. She'd learned that the hard way in the Balladairan barracks.

After an hour of sweating in the midday sun, she noticed one building had so few visitors as to be odd.

The note said after sunset. That was hours away. She went in anyway.

The cool darkness almost made Touraine sink to her knees in relief. The narrow entry led to the sun and a courtyard on one side and up a narrow flight of stairs on the other. The ground floor was quiet. She poked her head around the corner just to be sure. The small courtyard was empty. She hiked up the stairs and paused outside the first door she came across.

Heated voices rose inside.

"What do you mean you can't heal her?"

That was the Jackal, deep and accusatory.

"You think I'm not trying?" An unfamiliar voice responded, full of pain and frustration. "Shāl is there, the magic is moving, but— nothing is happening *in her*."

Magic. Heal her. Touraine reached unconsciously for the scar on her forearm. She'd just started to believe she'd imagined the cut's quick healing, convinced herself that the wound was shallower than she'd thought. She suddenly felt nauseated.

Inside the room, the voices stopped abruptly. Touraine just had time to straighten when the door swung open and she faced the Jackal yet again. This time, her scarf was hastily wrapped around her head and face, leaving thick graying dreadlocks only half-wrapped.

The woman filled the doorway, and when she caught Touraine trying to glance behind her, she stepped out of the room and closed the door. Then she filled the stairwell instead, backing Touraine onto a lower step.

"Give me one good reason I shouldn't strangle you now," the Jackal growled. Touraine didn't doubt the woman could manage it, even with one hand.

Touraine stared her down. "I have a response from the princess."

"I said a good reason. Your princess can eat my shit."

"That's not what your friends said." Touraine nodded at the door. "Will she be all right?"

"Fuck off."

"Are you going to listen, or should I wait and talk to someone who actually gives a shit about making peace?"

The stairwell was lit only by a window higher up and the open doorway below. The resulting shadow made it almost impossible to see the Jackal's eyes at all.

The older woman snorted and said, "The only real peace'll come when all of those bastards are gone. If I have my way, these little talks are over." She took another few steps down the stairs, forcing Touraine back again.

The Jackal was a familiar type. Dogged and persistent, like her namesake, and she respected only force met with force. She wasn't like Luca or even like the Apostate, bent on outsmarting people with words. Touraine and the Jackal were similar in that way. They knew there was a time and a place.

Touraine stepped up a stair. The Jackal didn't move.

"I know you don't really give a shit about me or the other conscripts. I know you'd rather gut me here."

"Right on all counts—"

Touraine stepped up another stair. "I'm glad you framed me for that murder. If not for you, I wouldn't have my new position."

The words were a bluff, but even as something twisted guiltily inside her, Touraine knew it was true. This *was* a better position than dying on the front lines as a conscript. The fate she'd left to all her friends. She pushed the guilt down deeper.

"Frame you?" The Jackal chuckled. "That was a coincidence. We couldn't care less, though if they'd executed you, we might call it justice done."

The confession caught Touraine off guard, but she pushed that away, too. She climbed up one more step, putting her in reach of the Jackal's strength.

"Then go ahead. Strangle me. Get your justice. You kill me, she loses nothing, but you—you lose the friendship of the one person in all of Balladaire who doesn't want to kill the rebels outright." The only person Touraine had ever heard speak of the rebels with something other than disdain. *No, Luca* and *Cheminade*. "She's already given you an act of faith."

"Good faith, from the faithless? She doesn't even have the authority to make deals with us." The Jackal sneered.

Faithless. She said it the same way Cantic said "uncivilized."

Touraine hitched her chin up. "Even so. Faith is better placed in real people, backed up with real actions. And she's backed by the duke regent." Touraine wasn't totally sure about that particular, but the Jackal didn't need to know that.

"We have other friends. The Qazāli aren't the only ones unhappy with your masters."

Touraine stared up at the slash of black shadow where the Jackal's eyes hid just above the lower sweep of her scarf.

"The thing is, *Jackal*, if you could beat us, you already would have. These 'little talks' could save your ass and all the people you care about." If the bitch cared about anyone, which Touraine was finding harder and harder to believe.

The Jackal exhaled sharply and shook her head, as if in disbelief. "Why are you doing this? What do you get out of fighting for them and not us?"

Touraine was almost taken aback by the broken confusion in the woman's voice.

"This isn't about me," she answered.

"No?"

The Jackal loomed over Touraine. Her crossed forearms were scarred, even beyond the amputation. The Jackal was no stranger to a hard life, and for a second, Touraine thought the Jackal would call her bluff, push her down the stairs and break her neck. She braced herself to use the woman's weight against her, just in case.

"You and the other Lost Ones are in the middle of this," the older woman said. "Without you lot shoving your tongues up their assholes, they couldn't fight. With you, we win. You'd be free."

"Be free? To come die for people like you?" Touraine snorted. "That's hardly any better. The princess is your best chance."

Then the Jackal spat, right on Touraine's new leather boots. She sneered at Touraine's entire outfit, from the exquisite black scarf so smooth against her cheeks to those spit-smeared boots.

Anger erupted white hot in Touraine's belly as she stared at the white-flecked slime. She knew the reactions the bitch waited for. If Touraine fought with her, she could claim she had grounds to attack. If Touraine did nothing, she was a cringing dog.

So Touraine did what she did best. She swallowed her pride. She did her job.

"Her Highness asks for a full list of your requests. She'll consider them. I'll come back, we can talk, and I'll go back. Until we reach an agreement. The sooner she gets the list, the sooner we start working on peace."

Even as she said the words, Touraine disbelieved them. The Jackal didn't want peace, and how many other Qazāli thought just like her? But this was what Luca believed in. Maybe Saïd could convince Touraine; she already had a soft spot for him. But the Jackal made that hard to imagine.

The Jackal grunted. "This is why I don't see any good sending more of our children to be brainwashed. They're no good to us then, parroting the Balladairan 'uncivilized' gullshit at us. I don't have time for it, and I don't have time for you and your traitor friends. Tell your master we'll think about it."

Touraine grunted back and then flicked a mocking salute. "Yes, sir."

But there was a barb stuck in her chest from the Jackal's parting shot. She remembered Aimée's words from the other day. The Sands had a shit lot. They *were* stuck in the middle of this conflict, and neither side gave a shit about them besides how and where they could die in battle.

At the bottom of the stairs, Touraine turned. The Jackal stood like a spectral shadow outside the door.

"They're not traitors, you know," Touraine said. "They never had a choice."

"Then tell them to make a choice now." The Jackal opened the door to the small apartment. "Or we'll make it for them."

*   *   *

The broadside was only the first indication of Balladairan discontent in the colony. Over the next few days, as Luca continued to respond to grievances and requests in her new role as governor-general, she could practically feel the merchants' and nobles' whispers tickling the back of her neck. She suspected she wasn't imagining the dirty looks she received from other Balladairans as she took her exercise around the Quartier.

Her suspicions were confirmed when she received a request for an audience from the comte de Beau-Sang and granted it to him.

Casimir LeRoche de Beau-Sang came from one of the lesser noble houses of Balladaire's southern coast. Beau-Sang had made his family's fortune early as Balladaire stretched the reaches of its empire. He was one of the first to invest in developing Qazāl as a colony. His quarries were especially lucrative: marble shipped to Balladaire as an architectural luxury and sandstone for the colonies as an architectural necessity. (The Balladairans in the colonies didn't favor the pressed-mud style of building that was popular with the Qazāli.)

The quarries had turned him from a member of a small, rarely thought-of house to a major player in Balladaire's court intrigues, but for all that he preferred to stay in Qazāl.

So Luca wasn't surprised that he was the one who came to meet her in her office at the Balladairan compound.

Touraine opened the door at his knock and bowed him in—only enough of a bow so as to not directly insult him. *Close enough.* Close on Beau-Sang's heels was his little assistant, the young Qazāli boy. Richard.

While the door was open, Luca was surprised at how quiet the military compound's administrative building was. She had always imagined the noise of battle and unruly troops, even in a place where people were essentially doing sums and writing politely veiled threats.

What is war if not a complicated web of mathematics and charm? Luca thought.

It was time for her to use the charm.

"Good afternoon, Comte. How are you and your family?" Luca gestured for him to sit as Touraine stepped out to fetch coffee.

"Good morning, Your Highness." Beau-Sang eased his broad body into the creaky but well-upholstered chair in front of Luca's desk. "We're doing well, mostly. Paul-Sebastien asked that I send his regards. He's glad to have a true scholar nearby."

Luca accepted the flattery with a nod. When Touraine returned, she poured them both coffee before sitting at the small traveler's desk in the corner. Touraine offered the young boy a cup, as well, but Richard shook his head with a look toward Beau-Sang before taking his place standing just behind the comte.

The room was only barely large enough to accommodate Luca and Touraine both; it was still full of many of Cheminade's effects. Cheminade had decorated the office like she'd decorated her home, full of travel relics and curiosities. Beau-Sang gave the souvenirs the slightest sneer before he sipped his coffee.

"It's unfortunate business, those broadsides," Beau-Sang said. "I saw them posted throughout the city before you had them taken down. The right choice, of course."

Luca felt her face warm, but she kept her expression neutral. She did *not* look over at Touraine. "Yes, well. As you say, it's been dealt with."

"Of course, Your Highness. I suppose it's not surprising given some of the changes you've proposed as governor-general." He smiled wryly at Luca, like he'd caught on to her taking an extra turn at échecs. "I don't mind, of course. I trust your judgment fully. It's just that one hears people talk."

Luca sniffed dismissively, as if "people" were the last thing on her mind. This time, she did give Touraine a quick glance. Touraine met Luca's eyes from behind Beau-Sang's back and nodded; she was paying attention.

"People do like to talk. I find it to be their great shortcoming."

The comte smiled and shook his head indulgently. "Indeed, Your Highness, and about nothing important."

"Is that what you're here for, then? Nothing important?"

He smiled at the joke—or perhaps that was just a tic in his cheek. "The business owners are concerned about the new changes you've proposed regarding the Qazāli laborers. They think that you're bowing to rebel pressure and wonder why Cantic hasn't used the full weight of her soldiers to put them down instead. Your subjects are simply worried about their livelihoods." Then, as if the thought had just occurred to him: "Is that what her lot were brought in for?"

He tilted his head back at Touraine, and Luca was grateful he didn't turn around. The ex-soldier was glaring daggers at his back.

The concerns in question, Luca assumed, were profit losses directly related to her latest requirements: that all Balladairans who employed Qazāli staff were required to pay them an appropriate wage and to meet certain standards of treatment. The rebels hadn't sent Luca their list of terms, but Luca didn't need anyone to point out the bond of cruelty and desperation that kept Qazāli working for people like Beau-Sang. And the less desperate the Qazāli laborers felt, the less likely they would be to turn to the rebels to vent their frustration. Or so she hoped.

"The colonial brigade is here to be used at General Cantic's discretion," Luca said sharply. He was prying, and Luca couldn't tell if it was to irritate her, to goad Touraine, or to get information. Probably some combination of the three, like a proper courtier.

The problem was, it was working. Normally, Luca was adept at shrugging away negative comments about her—about her leg, about her social bearing, even about her lovers. But these critiques of her work pricked her like sewing needles forgotten in a coat. She wanted to end the rebellion, but she didn't want to fail the empire in the process.

"And how well do *they* think *their* livelihoods will survive if they maim their workers or starve them to death?" The question came out sharper than Luca intended. *Slow down.* She needed to take her time with Beau-Sang. He wasn't someone she could afford to alienate— prod, yes, but alienate? No. The Balladairans with stakes in the colonies looked to him as an example.

Luca cleared her throat and added, "Anyone with concerns about the changes can talk to me directly about their individual situations."

This was the crux of the delicate dance Luca had to perform if she wanted to end the rebellion and prove that she was truly ready for the throne. Any agreement with the rebels would require concessions on the part of not just the empire itself but the Balladairans who made money off the colony, and Beau-Sang was chief among those. If she didn't have them on board, the resolution might be a bloody one no matter what.

"Your own colonial businesses haven't suffered, my lord?" Luca asked Beau-Sang. "Surely a man like yourself doesn't need the law to treat his workers well."

"No, no, indeed not. Production will slow at the quarries; I'll be able to employ fewer laborers, and perhaps there will be an increase in disciplinary problems now, but we'll manage, of course."

"I hear you run a tight system." Luca couldn't stop the edge from returning to her voice. She glanced behind him at his young assistant, Richard. The boy stood with his hands behind his back, hiding the stumps of his pinky fingers.

"It's dangerous work," Beau-Sang said. He sipped his coffee somberly. "Strict discipline keeps everyone safe."

"Is it true that you cut off quarry workers' hands when they don't meet their quota?"

Luca had found this in the pile of Cheminade's unresolved complaints. One of the few from a Qazāli. Somehow, Luca didn't think this was just because few Qazāli had problems with their employers.

Beau-Sang froze with his cup halfway to his lips again. He set the cup back down on the saucer. The small dishes looked delicate in his large hands.

"As I said, Your Highness. It's dangerous work. The loss of a limb isn't uncommon."

"Then I expect you, as the owner, to enact proper safety protocols. I'll ask the general to send some soldiers and engineers to see what changes can be made."

Beau-Sang pursed his lips so tightly that they lost their color. Then he said, "Indeed, Your Highness."

This "indeed" was as false as all the others, but Luca smiled a falsely genuine smile in return. "I'm glad you agree, my lord. In these small ways, perhaps we can convince the Qazāli they don't need to rebel. We'll show them that the Balladairan Empire takes care of all its people. Good afternoon, my lord."

"Good afternoon, Your Highness." Beau-Sang stood and bowed. Just behind him, his servant-assistant Richard bowed, too.

Before he reached the door, however, Beau-Sang paused and bowed slightly again. "Is it true that Qazāli prisoners are being released?"

It was Luca's turn to freeze. She had taken the utmost care to release certain Qazāli prisoners privately just a couple of days ago. No fanfare, no celebrations of her generosity. She didn't want to call *more* attention to herself. She'd even gone through the releases with Cantic, framing them as mistrials. The general had been dubious, but she'd agreed. She'd also understood the need for secrecy; if word got out that the magistrate could commit such a thing as a "mistrial," the unrest would be total.

Now Beau-Sang had caught her in a bear trap. Not to mention, it meant he *did* have eyes and ears somewhere he shouldn't. *Was it Cantic?* No, the general hated him, maybe more than Luca did.

"Those who have served the appropriate sentence for their crimes," Luca finally said. She felt breathless, her heart hammering so loudly that surely Beau-Sang could hear it.

"Ah, indeed." He smiled knowingly and bowed again. Then he left, the young boy closing the door with a soft snick.

Touraine waited three long breaths before she growled, "Can I kill him, or do you want to?"

Despite the tension only just beginning to unspool from her shoulders, Luca couldn't help but smile.

"Let's take turns," she said.

CHAPTER 18

SHĀLAN LESSONS

Over the course of the next week, more complaints from the Balladairan upper crust flooded in. Rich bastards. They were upset because Luca's new rules wouldn't let them take advantage of the Qazāli workers. Touraine was ready to admit that the rebels had a few good points, even if she disagreed with those like the Jackal. It was just like she'd always told Tibeau, back when she was with the Sands: life with Balladaire wasn't perfect, but slowly, they could change it.

The rebels had sent their list of demands by a runner shortly after Luca and Touraine's meeting with Beau-Sang. It was written in Shālan, so Luca read it, occasionally scratching things out on her own paper. Soon, Touraine would take Luca's response to them, and the thought set her blood humming with fear and excitement.

Tonight, Luca was downstairs in the town house's sitting room, where she often spent the evening reading a book or treatise or whatever it was she did for fun. Touraine had started using this evening leisure time to sneak into the office. It was a peaceful place, without Luca frowning at her desk or one of her guards hovering just outside the door. She was starting to like the smell of ink and paper, and when she sat at Luca's desk, she had the perfect view of the sunset through the window.

"What are you doing?"

Touraine jumped up at Luca's voice, splattering ink from her pen all over the pieces of scrap paper she'd stolen from Luca's waste bin.

"I'm sorry, Your Highness. Nothing." She covered the papers quickly with her hands, then swore as ink smeared everywhere. "I—nothing."

The princess shuffled over, shoulders sagging, to peer around Touraine at the desk. She looked exhausted. Touraine hid her ink-stained hands in fists at her sides.

Luca picked up one of the papers and smiled tenderly, and then she pulled a book from underneath the other papers. The Shālan primer.

"This is a good start," Luca said. Then shyly she added, "My offer still stands. I could teach you."

"No, you don't need—it's not important." Touraine blushed. Furiously. She started scooping the papers into a stack, the better to stop embarrassing herself.

"No, no. Sit. It is important." She sat down in the chair next to Touraine's—the chair Touraine normally sat in—and put a hand on Touraine's arm. Still, Touraine didn't sit. "Would it help if I said you'll be more useful if you know both languages?"

Touraine sat.

Luca fanned out the scraps Touraine had been writing on and opened the primer to the first page. In Balladairan, it introduced the letters and their pronunciations. The following pages included introductory words and phrases that Touraine couldn't say and diagrams of the Shālan letters so that she could practice drawing them.

"First, take a new paper. Let's try this one." Luca pointed at the first one.

It was just a line. Touraine wrote it several times, feeling surer of herself with each stroke. She had been overwhelmed by it all as she tried to decipher it on her own. She didn't know how to begin, and the phrases she saw in the book all looked useless. *I want one apple. Where is my mother? I am happy.* They were for children. Alone, Touraine had spent half of her stolen evenings raging at Balladaire for not teaching her and the other half berating herself for even bothering.

Repeating the sounds after the heir to the empire wasn't ironic at all.

Luca made it easy, though. She might have been a bit of a know-it-all, but she wasn't a half-bad teacher. They'd gotten through half of the alphabet by the time yawns cracked their jaws.

"I should say goodnight. I have breakfast with Sonçoise de l'Ouest, and I told her that I would join her for a 'brisk cleansing of the mind' beforehand. It involves something called a sunrise." Luca scowled.

Touraine put her pen down with a smirk. "I've heard of that. Me and your guards know about 'cleansing the mind.'"

Luca's look went flat. "I know. I've heard you." She glanced over her shoulder to include Guérin, even though the guardswoman was now on the other side of the closed door. Then Luca sighed and slumped deeper into her chair, away from the desk.

"If the visits annoy you so much, why do you go?" It felt risky, this casual tone, but the office door was closed, and Luca had made a joke first. Luca had cracked the door of herself open, and Touraine had the crazy urge to pull the door wider.

No, not so crazy. Vulnerability for vulnerability. Touraine could think of nothing more vulnerable, more terrifying right now, than letting the princess of Balladaire teach her Shālan. It felt good to pry back.

"She's one of the few Balladairans who isn't completely against my new changes. I need friends like that. No." She shook her head. "*Friend* is too strong a word. Though that would be nice," she grumbled under her breath.

"Friends who might support a deal with the rebels. Push back against Beau-Sang."

Luca twisted toward Touraine sharply. "Someone's been paying attention."

Touraine raised an eyebrow. "A soldier who doesn't pay attention to her enemies is a dead soldier." She had even gone so far as to wonder if Beau-Sang hadn't been behind the sky-falling broadsides. Him, or maybe the dear uncle Luca groused about when she thought no one was listening. Touraine asked, "Have you gotten word from the duke regent?"

Luca settled again, dancing her fingers distractedly against her legs. "My uncle claims that he'll happily cede the throne upon my return. In every letter, he's preparing for my coronation, he's glad I'm getting firsthand experience, he's certain—" She glanced nervously at Touraine, as if she hadn't realized she was still there, listening. "Certain my parents would be proud of me. And yet every opportunity we've had to crown me before, he's blocked with some excuse or another. Regents have ceded the throne to the rightful heirs as early as twenty-five and as late as thirty. Outside of Balladaire, heirs have been crowned as young as thirteen!"

Luca frowned. "But it's only a matter of time before the letters include lectures because I'm somehow mishandling the Shālan colonies and am thus not ready to rule."

Sitting beside her, Touraine realized how young Luca, the queen regnant, was. Clear, sharp eyes behind her spectacles and tawny hair that might not gray for years yet. Even the lines in her face when she focused on her books or winced at her leg—they hadn't set permanently. She couldn't be that much older than Touraine.

Touraine wanted to ask, *Are you ready to rule?* Instead, she asked, "What'll you do, then?"

And as she asked the question and saw Luca open her mouth to answer without a second thought, Touraine imagined herself taking these words, all of Luca's words, and carrying them back to the rebels. Giving them ammunition, giving them tools, terrain, traps. She wondered what her life would look like if she went down that path, but she couldn't see anything worth gaining. Not compared to staying with Luca.

"What do you know about Shālan magic?" Luca met Touraine's eyes full on and lowered her voice. "What did the Brigāni woman say to you when you were captive?"

That startled Touraine into stammers. Unconsciously, she cradled her left arm in her right. "Nothing? Nothing. Just—that it's—she said it's just rumors. She told me a story about a kid priestess who was good at healing, made it sound like it was her." She realized she was backing into her seat, as if the Apostate were there in front of her, knife gleaming again. "She—did cut me. I thought she was going to do magic with my blood, but I think that was just to scare me."

Luca picked up Touraine's pen and a scrap of paper from the desk and began scribbling notes, muttering to herself.

"What about—" The princess waved her hand without looking at Touraine, trying to pluck the words from the air. "You fought the Taargens, didn't you? What do you know about their magic?"

Touraine's heart froze solid in her chest. She must have been silent for a long time, because Luca finally looked up. She put the pen down and really looked at Touraine for the first time that evening.

Touraine broke eye contact and started cataloging. The paper on the desk. Her wobbly Shālan letters beneath Luca's elegant script. The oak desk, sturdy, not a traveler's desk, not cheap. Luca's hands, one of them so close to her own clenched fist. The smell of Luca's perfume, rose and something darker, muskier. The musk was new. Touraine's own sweat. Her breath, too quick. Luca's breath, quick, too. Luca's hands, warm, tight, clasped around one of Touraine's fists. A squeeze.

Luca didn't say anything, and so Touraine let the silence pass as she tried to catch her breath, the room expanding and contracting.

It had happened after a clash with the Taargens. The autumn campaign was supposed to be over, but shitty orders and bad luck meant early blizzards caught the colonial brigade undersupplied as they covered the regular regiments' asses.

Everyone thought they'd gotten lucky when they routed a small company of Taargens. Touraine sensed something was off as they went to pick through the bodies half buried in the snow—there were too many of them. Her shoulders prickled with unease.

She locked eyes with a staring corpse, his pale blue eyes vacant over a red-brown beard. Then he smiled.

Touraine managed only one shout before he dragged her to the ground: *Run.*

"The magic comes from their god," Touraine said when she could. Her voice was hoarse, her throat drier than she realized. Luca's thumb brushed over Touraine's knuckles, comforting.

After the Taargens had taken her and a fistful of others—Valbré and Cariste, two siblings; Omarin, one of the field medics; a few others whose faces were starting to lose their edges in Touraine's memory— they took them back to the Taargen war camp and dumped them in their bonds next to a fire that was so warm Touraine was grateful and felt guilty for it.

Until a couple of Taargens in bearskin cloaks came up to the fire and started chanting over it. Touraine didn't speak the language, but she felt the change in the air on her skin.

They took Valbré first, his teeth chattering, dragged him to the fire, where a Taargen—call them a priest, sure—stood, and Touraine was so sure she was about to watch them burn Valbré alive while Cariste screamed for him, for mercy. What happened was worse.

The Taargen priest held Valbré's face close to their own and whis-pered something. As the priest's eyes rolled in rapture, Valbré's eyes rolled up, and he shook until the priest dropped him. Touraine thought he was dead as he flopped to the ground, eyes staring back at the captured Sands. But his chest still rose and fell. His mouth still opened and closed.

Then another priest used Cariste, then Omarin, both of them dis-carded just like Valbré.

"They take you—they take something out of you." Touraine's voice trembled as she related the memories to Luca. "While they're praying, I think. And use it. To..."

"The bears," Luca said softly.

Touraine nodded. The bears. She'd seen the priests' monstrous transformations into the animals they worshipped. Watched the bears run in the direction of her own soldiers. "Wolves, too. Then when they finish, you're gone. Just empty."

"Dead?"

Touraine shook her head. If only. If only. "We had to..." It had been Pruett who'd saved her that night. Again. As always. Together, they had put to rest the empty, breathing husks of their friends.

Luca didn't pick up the pen to take notes, and Touraine was grateful. Even if that did mean she was still holding Touraine's hand. Maybe because it meant she was. Touraine swallowed. If Pruett could see this now, she would regret ever saving Touraine. Still, a part of her wanted to unclench her fist and let Luca lace their fingers, pen-calloused against baton-calloused. So she pulled her hand away with the excuse of putting her head in her hands.

"I see." Luca laced her hands with each other instead. "My idea was that I could bring Balladaire something valuable. Something like magic. Something to stop the Withering, or to manage it better when it comes. Sabine—a friend of mine, one of the few—is worried that we'll be due for another plague soon. My uncle will run, like he did last time. I won't abandon my people, Touraine. But I also don't want to come to them empty handed."

So you'd steal from someone else, just to give it to Balladaire. Touraine didn't say it, though, didn't dare. Even if she would never go over to the rebellion, being with them dredged up complaints she had buried, the kinds of things Tibeau went on and on about but she put aside in favor of sanity. She could see the shape of empire in Luca's words.

"What are they like?" Luca asked. "The rebel council."

Touraine snorted. "One is an asshole who's going to wreck every overture you make. The bookseller is kind and Malika is savvy, but it's the Brigāni woman . . . She's the dangerous one."

"The Brigāni witch that Cantic is hunting."

"That's the one."

"I could use Cantic's goodwill," Luca mused. She sighed with disappointment. "Maybe we should stop. Give her their names, root them out, and be done. It would be easier than explaining *this* to the nobles. And Cantic and my uncle."

She gestured angrily at what Touraine realized must be Luca's response to the rebels' list of demands. She propped her head on one hand and glared at it.

"What do they want?"

Luca scoffed. "Arms, land. For nothing in return. I'm afraid—" She stopped herself and glanced at Touraine, like she was gauging how vulnerable to be. "I'm afraid we're risking everything to get nothing."

"What are we risking?"

Luca ticked the risks off on her fingers. "The empire, its trade. My reputation. You."

The last surprised Touraine, and it showed.

"What?" Luca asked. "You are risking yourself. If they change their minds, they could kill you."

That cheerful thought had occurred more than once to Touraine herself. Touraine was afraid, too, though. Afraid that she and the others who risked everything would get nothing. That they would suffer no matter what.

All Touraine said aloud was "It's fine. You'll make progress."

"You're lying." Luca raised a wry eyebrow. "You can be frank with me."

Touraine smiled ruefully. It was a pretty thing to say, but it just showed how little Luca understood. She could never tell Luca about all the doubts she had about Balladaire, about Qazāl, even about magic. Luca wouldn't trust her anymore. She would cut Touraine loose, and then where would Touraine go? So Touraine told just some of the truth.

"I don't think they trust you," she said hesitantly. "The Jackal—she's the asshole—she'll never be happy with anything you offer, and I don't know if the rest of the council has her under control."

As the words sank in, the princess bit her lip like she always did when she was thinking hard. Luca looked between the notes she'd taken and the list of demands.

"Do you think you could soften them for me?" Luca struck Touraine with her sharp blue-green gaze. The small line between her eyebrows deepened. "Because *if* the magic is real and *if* they'll give it to us or teach us or share—if we get access to the magic, we might actually be able to find a middle ground."

"Those are big *ifs*, Your Highness."

Very big ifs.

"We can reach an agreement—I know it." Luca's shoulders slumped. "I've only ever wanted to be a good queen."

Touraine scooted back into her seat. She had been sitting on the edge. "I only ever wanted to be Cantic."

Luca snorted. "I'm shocked." She was smiling.

Touraine chuckled, and then they were both laughing, and the vise grip around her body was loosening.

"I don't know what I can be now," Touraine added. "Anylight, I would have to survive long enough." She laughed again, but this time it rang false.

"I'll always need advisors, Touraine. Here and in Balladaire." They sat close enough that Touraine watched Luca's throat bob up and down as she swallowed hard. "I would like you to survive that long."

CHAPTER 19

HISTORY LESSONS

The next night, Touraine sought out Saïd and the rebels. Luca's response to their demands was locked in her mind. None of them could afford to have a paper like that floating around.

This time, she went with an offering. In the new meeting room, more spacious but more sparsely furnished, she spread out fresh flatbread and a bean paste that the street hawker at the food cart said originated in one of the far eastern countries in the old Shālan Empire. Dry black olives, wrinkled and a touch bitter.

The Jackal looked suspiciously at it all. "She's trying to bribe us."

It wasn't a bribe. Not exactly. And it wasn't from Luca—not exactly. Luca wanted this to work, and Touraine wanted to help. If the Jackal would let them.

"Not a bribe. Just courtesy. You fed me last time." Touraine ate the first bite, exaggerating the chewing motion.

The Jackal rolled her eyes and snatched a piece of bread. Saïd already had a chunk in his mouth and munched quietly, maybe even smiling. Malika took some of the food to the Apostate, who had taken up a similar position as before, in the back of the room among cushions.

"What did you want, then?" The Brigāni woman daintily rubbed the olive oil on her fingers into the smooth, dark skin of her hands. She had tucked the bread into her mouth without removing the scarf enough to show her face. She seemed like she was feeling better after the fit that had taken her the last time they had met, but she moved deliberately.

"Apostate." Touraine nodded respectfully. "Princess Luca wants your concrete support in an alliance and a cessation of attacks on Balladairan businesses. She released some of your people."

The Jackal plucked up another piece of bread and twirled it idly between her fingers. "Some isn't all. Also, saw you and her cronies burning up those deliciously scandalizing broadsides—seems a bit like she's ashamed of her *alliances*, if you ask me."

Touraine's face went hot. "They were crude slander."

The woman sucked air in, wincing. "The pup's a bit touchy about her lover."

Touraine closed her eyes and took a deep breath.

There were so many ways to die on a battlefield. A lead musket ball to the brain was simple, relatively quick compared to a bayonet to the guts or the lungs. A cannonball could take your stomach out, whole entire, or rip most of your leg off so you'd bleed to death. Touraine was a bayonet's edge away from wishing them all on the other woman.

The woman bent over her crossed legs, elbows resting on her knees. Her fingers dangled an inch above the dusty clay floor like rug tassels. Touraine couldn't see the smug expression behind the scarf, but she could imagine it. One day, Touraine would rip the mask from her face and get a good look before punching her square.

"Peace, Jackal." The Brigāni, who also kept her face masked, shot the woman a sharp look with those golden eyes. The eyes didn't cow her like they did Touraine.

The other woman just tilted her head from side to side and leaned back on her hands. "What else, then, Mulāzim?"

"First, she had a simple question. Do you know anything about the broadside artist?"

A single shake of the Apostate's head. "I don't. Which means they're not in this city."

Shit. That skewered Touraine's hopes of pinning it all on Rogan's anger. It meant Luca had bigger problems to deal with.

"What else?" The Brigāni—the Apostate—blinked once. "She didn't send you here to do research like that."

Touraine swallowed. "No. I have her response to the list."

It felt like everyone in the room leaned in to listen. Even the Jackal, who was so insistent that this was a waste of time, stopped picking at her nails.

"Regarding a minimum wage for all Qazāli workers under Balladairans," Touraine announced, "she accepts; she's already been working on it. She also says she's willing to require all businesses that rely on Qazāli land to be partly owned by Qazāli."

Touraine paused to catch her breath, and the Jackal pounced on her hesitation.

"But?" she growled.

"But... she won't give you guns. She won't send the soldiers back to Balladaire, but she will reduce the number of them in the city. They're still necessary since this is a base for the southern reaches of the empire. It also means the compound won't be vacated for Qazāli use."

Finally, though she didn't think it needed to be said, Touraine added, "She won't acknowledge the colony's sovereignty. Does that about cover it?"

The emotions around the room were mixed. Malika frowned like Touraine had pissed a puddle in her path. Saïd looked optimistic, as if he hadn't expected such a pleasant surprise.

The Jackal barked a loud laugh that the Apostate spoke over.

"Not even close, girl. But it's a start."

"If this is all she has," the Jackal said between dark chuckles, "we have nowhere else to go. I told you these little talks were a waste of time."

"Maybe not. The princess has read things. And heard rumors." Touraine flicked her eyes up from the olives and met the witch's eyes for just a moment before looking for safer targets instead, finding none. Malika's lips pulled tight, and even Saïd's eyes were angry under his heavy brows. Of course they knew what was coming. "About Shālan magic."

The Jackal huffed. "Such a noble heart, your master. She wants something that's not hers, just like every other Balladairan scavenger."

It echoed Touraine's earlier thoughts too much for comfort. How much would Luca be willing to take if it won her the throne in the end?

"She doesn't want to just take it," Touraine snapped back. "This is a negotiation."

"An alliance based on a rumor of magic." The Apostate's eyes crinkled above her scarf. "From everything I've heard about her, I expected her to be more intelligent."

"Rumors must come from somewhere." She tossed the witch's old words back at her.

The witch barked a laugh. "They do. So I'll tell you.

"The last Brigāni emperor fell two hundred years ago, depending on your position on her rule. Emperor Djaya. She commanded the respect of a hundred thousand troops—and their fear. They called her the warrior priestess because of her devotion."

The Brigāni twisted her own hands before her face, as if seeing them anew, wondering what power she had herself.

"The Qazāli stories call her greedy. They tell the tale of most empires—a hungry lord, not content with the land and tribute they've already taken, not content to call neighbors 'allies,' only 'subjects.' To them, the story isn't any different than what they say of the Balladairans today.

"But there's always more.

"Across the empire, the crops outside of the river floodplains were failing. The animals they kept died, and the desert crept closer to the cities all across the empire. People starved. Djaya couldn't send food from Briga's stores quickly enough, and she couldn't risk starving her own city. They say she lived on a soldier's rations and required it of everyone in her court.

"The Qazāli priests and priestess in their temples said the people's faith in Shāl was too weak. The scholars at Briga's university agreed—there were books in the Scorpion Library that showed this—droughts had been recorded in the past, whenever great comfort and technological advances dulled the need for faith. They took for granted the healing gifts of the priests and needed to be shown Shāl's power again."

The woman paused to take a drink of water. She looked as if the telling drained her, but her eyes glittered with life, sharp as a dagger beneath the ribs. The look filled Touraine with unease. She fought the instinct to lean closer. It was a betrayal, to want to know this in her own right, but she clung to every word.

"Djaya sent her army north, across the narrow strip of sea. The very first Balladairan raid. On a small town, one not likely to be missed, perhaps. The Balladairans were known for their mysterious agricultural talents. Their god of the fields was generous and their fields bountiful. Briga had traded with them before. No one knows quite why Emperor Djaya turned to violence instead of seeking aid. Perhaps she did and was denied. Perhaps it was greed after all. Either way, she broke Shāl's One Tenet—peace over all."

The Jackal cut in. "And she *kept* breaking it and breaking it until they went to war, and Balladaire started invading everyone who worshipped a god so that they'd never have to deal with screaming holy hordes." The woman lay on one elbow, picking at her fingernails again, now stretched out more like a cat than a dog. "That's what Djaya did for the Shālans she claimed to protect."

The Jackal's interruption broke Touraine out of the spell. Enough for her to be glad the Jackal treated everyone like shit, not just her. The Apostate glared at the other woman and grunted low in her throat.

"If you'd like"—the Apostate made a welcoming gesture—"you're more than welcome to finish your version."

"Gladly." The Jackal pushed herself upright and glared at Touraine. "Empress Djaya was glorious, they said. Burned their armies down in their armor. They say the blood ran so thick"—she paused and winked at the Brigāni—"that you could've drunk it from the streets."

The Apostate rolled her eyes. "They didn't fight in the streets."

The Jackal shrugged. "Just a saying."

Touraine reassessed their relationship. They bantered like old friends, however morbid the subject, however vicious the cuts. They reminded her of a crueler version of her and Tibeau and Pruett, the edges sharpened by time instead of dulled. Touraine looked harder at them. No distinguishing features but the Brigāni's eyes. Where the Brigāni moved almost like an elder now, the Jackal bounced like a cocksure new blackcoat.

"Djaya makes the other Shālans believe, though," the Jackal continued. "They hear the stories of how Shāl works through her. They believe. They pray and they heal. The food grows again; the animals are born healthy. Across the empire, people live again."

"Except for Emperor Djaya and her Brigāni." The Apostate slid in smoothly. "They abandoned the One Tenet, so Shāl banished them and cursed the city so that they couldn't return home until one hundred and one hundred years had passed. Those who trespassed would sicken mysteriously or have ill-born children. The magic that Shāl had taught the Brigāni, the blessed powers Djaya and her forebears used to create and protect the empire, were lost, never intended to be used again, unless we learned restraint."

"Some of the powers. The Qazāli priests kept the faith and held fast to the Tenet. Peace over all. And your master would take that gift from us," the Jackal growled.

Touraine had thought the two women had forgotten about her and the other rebels, but the Jackal turned on her fiercely. Touraine sat back, off her guard, lulled by the story. The history. The history Balladaire had never told her.

"So the magic is real." Touraine's voice came out shakier than she wanted it to, with fear or awe, she didn't know. Probably both—two sides of the same coin, really. And she remembered the first story the Apostate ever told her, about a young, gifted healer who had lost her family to a young Cantic. "And Balladaire has its own magic?"

The woman's golden eyes crinkled even more. "Don't be silly. No one here is uncivilized enough to believe that old nonsense. They're just fire stories we tell to deal with the systematic expunging of our culture and history. They keep us warm and make us feel grander than we actually are. That's all." She shared a look with the Jackal, head tilted. "We can't even agree on a single version of the tale."

It took a long moment for Touraine to regain her purpose. She cleared her throat. "The Second City. Across the river. That's Briga's capital? Is there anything that could help there?"

The Qazāli rebels flinched, and the Apostate shook her head sharply. "That's not a wise avenue. For many reasons. She won't find what she's looking for, and we don't control that territory or the river crossing."

This was the first Touraine had heard of any territory "controlled" by anyone other than Balladaire. "What do you mean?"

"I mean you should trust me and leave the Cursed City alone. There's nothing there."

"How do you know?"

The Apostate's golden eyes locked on Touraine's, her mouth set. "Because I've been. I used to be *curious* like your princess. Now I'm paying the price for that ambition."

The woman was deadly serious, her body still with a threat Touraine couldn't name. Despite the fit she had had last time, her voice was steady and strong. If she felt weakness or pain, she didn't show it to Touraine. The illness... Was that the price she paid? A shiver coursed up her back.

Still, Touraine said, "We need it. The magic will help the sick in Balladaire. And if Balladaire has its own magic, maybe that will help."

The Apostate leaned over her crossed legs, elbows on knees, chin propped on fingertips. It was so like General Cantic that Touraine leaned farther away. "Will it, though? She doesn't know that. I certainly don't know that. What's she willing to spend on a rumor?"

Touraine didn't know. She didn't know what someone could pay for that kind of knowledge. She didn't know why someone would.

Power like that cost—it had cost the Taargens, and they'd taken the price out of her soldiers' flesh. She didn't want to think what an emperor could do, would do with that kind of might. What a princess would do.

"What else do you want?"

"We told you. For her to get the fuck out of my Shāl-damned country," the Jackal growled. Then she nodded toward the Apostate. "And the Blood General's head for my friend here, as a bonus. That'll do for starters."

Touraine shook her head. "Any requests that won't get me laughed to the gallows."

The Jackal's laugh was another rough bark, and she leaned forward on one bent knee, hanging like a wild dog over a kill. A vicious mirror of the Apostate. The secret name was so apt that it seemed a poor choice.

"We could still use those guns." The Jackal smiled wide, baring teeth.

"Why would she arm a rebellion against her crown?"

"If we're allies, it wouldn't be a rebellion, would it?" The Apostate shrugged. "It would be an investment, to strengthen us."

"And a guarantee of her good behavior if we can shoot back for once." The Jackal laughed and laughed. "And tell her to come herself. I want her to look me in the eye while she tries to feed me gullshit."

Dread settled in the pit of Touraine's stomach. She wasn't fooled for a second that the Jackal wouldn't turn those weapons on Balladaire if given half a chance. There would still be a price then, and knowing Balladaire, they would see it paid—by someone else. Touraine knew all too well the coin that soothed Balladairan debt. Pruett and her heavy-bagged eyes. Tibeau's crushing hugs and Aimée's irreverence and Noé's perfect voice and—

Luca would spend them all. If the rebels got the guns and the general went against Luca's alliance—under her own power or the duke regent's authority—the Sands would fall first.

Unless they defected. Then they'd be shot by blackcoats instead.

Unless Touraine never let it happen—unless she found another way. The Jackal's laugh mocked Touraine all the way back to the Quartier.

Luca laughed in Touraine's face when she returned with the rebels' counteroffers. *Offers* was a strong word.

"Are they insane?" Luca asked incredulously.

They were in her office in the town house again, this time with Lanquette outside the door, no one privy to their schemes but them. The sky outside was clear and specked with stars. The fresh, cold air would calm Luca down. After.

Touraine shrugged, bemused. "Desperate, I expect."

"Well, I'm not. Not *that* desperate." She wanted to stop the rebellion peacefully, the right way, but she wouldn't sacrifice the empire to do it. She had accepted everything else on their sky-falling list of demands and stretched her relationships with the Balladairan nobles to their limits.

She huffed. "What about the magic?"

Her chief negotiator shrugged again, the gesture so casual it was infuriating. Why couldn't she see how important this was? They were on the edge of something great, if the Qazāli would only stop being stubborn.

"That's the interesting part, Your Highness."

Touraine always used Luca's title when she could tell Luca was irritated. Shame flooded her, and Luca eased her grip off the arms of her chair. She nodded for Touraine to continue, and the other woman told her a dazzling historical fantasy about gods and empresses. To some, it might have been laughable, but to Luca...

"That's not why Balladaire abandoned religion," Luca said when Touraine finished. "It was holding us back. When we focused on science and developing better tools, our crop yields increased. We had enough to feed the whole country, our armies—even other countries. The Brigāni just got greedy."

"Just saying what they told me, Your Highness. It sounds like they meant magic, though. Balladairan magic."

Luca paused. "Balladairan magic? As in our own, based in the empire?"

Touraine shook her head. She looked tired. Luca would let her go in just one minute; she just had to know—

"What do they know about it?"

"I don't know. Probably not much. And the Apostate says you shouldn't go to the library. That you won't find what you're looking for and you'll pay a heavy price."

"What kind of price?" Luca said sharply.

"I don't know. But that pretty much leaves them as the only source for…" The ex-soldier swallowed. Luca finally understood her reticence toward the idea of magic. It wasn't because she didn't believe but because she'd seen it in its awful power.

This won't be like that.

"Do they sound amenable? To a trade that involves magic?"

"No?" Touraine gave a sharp gesture to the desk. The list of Luca's offers that she'd memorized was still on the desk. "They want the guns. Or Balladaire to leave." Touraine snorted. "They also mentioned wanting Cantic's head. I'd just as soon not add my own to the chopping block."

Luca scowled down at the list, too. "Nor would I."

CHAPTER 20

FOR RESEARCH

Luca awoke the next morning still feeling irritable, so she kept to her rooms, rereading a book that was strictly fun—not research. Another volume in the saga of the Chevalier des Pommes. Slowly, the book and a cup of coffee were recalibrating her mood.

Someone knocked on the door. "Princess?" It was Gil, his voice only slightly concerned.

"Come in." Luca closed her book around her finger.

Gil stepped in. "You've had a messenger from the Beau-Sang place."

Luca's heart leapt with adrenaline. *What now?* She beckoned for the letter and tore it open before sighing in relief.

"Good news, then?" Gil sat on the edge of her bed and squeezed her shoulder. It was the closest he'd gotten to a hug in ages. She leaned briefly into the touch. She missed him.

"Possibly." Luca couldn't help the excitement creeping into her voice.

Gil raised a wry eyebrow. "Coming from that family?" He scoffed in disbelief. "You and the lieutenant were up late last night. How are things in that quarter?"

Luca wasn't sure if she imagined the suggestive teasing, but she chose to ignore it.

"The rebels are reticent, despite all of the concessions I'm willing to make. And"—she looked down and fiddled with the book in her lap—"I *am* having a hard time balancing the rebels' demands with the nobles'."

"Luca," Gil said softly, and Luca looked up to meet his eyes. The lines of his face deepened as he smiled at her. "Stay the course. You're doing the right thing. Just be patient. You can't expect to erase the pain of decades with a few gifts."

"Of course not." Luca was simultaneously warm with Gil's pride in her and annoyed by his advice. He was right; she just didn't like that she needed to be reminded. "I suppose I should get dressed. Thank you."

She squeezed his hand. It was dry and rough, still calloused by his regular exercise. He squeezed her hand back, then left her to change.

The short letter trembled in Luca's hand when she went outside to find Touraine. *I've found something*, Paul-Sebastien LeRoche had written. *I would be honored to host you for luncheon. Please bring your soldier.* Apparently, if she had alienated Beau-Sang, she hadn't alienated his son.

It was late in the morning, but Guérin was working with Touraine on more hand-to-hand and knife fighting. They were in their shirtsleeves, Guérin blond and towering over Touraine, her hair slicked back in a queue with sweat, and Touraine laughing as she darted in and out with a practice blade. As Luca watched, Touraine blocked a stab from Guérin and squirmed in close to hook a leg around Guérin's. Luca gasped, certain someone's leg would break. They both fell in a heap of awkward splits, Touraine laughing and Guérin smiling quietly.

Luca cleared her throat. "I'm sorry to interrupt the fun, you two. We've an invitation to the Beau-Sang place."

Touraine frowned as she wiped the desert dirt off well-muscled thighs.

Luca found herself blushing and had to clear her throat again. "We're visiting the son, not the father."

Even Guérin's shoulders sagged in relief.

It was at the Beau-Sang home that Luca truly began to understand life for Balladairan colonials, those who lived in—were perhaps even born in—the colonies.

The Beau-Sang town house was smaller than Luca's but only just, which said something about Beau-Sang's profit from the Qazāli quarries. Like most of the town houses, there was a small patio area shaded by canvas, a bit like a parade pavilion. Two young Balladairan women and two young Qazāli sat beneath the shade with drinks and fans. A hush fell over them as Luca alighted from the carriage.

She recognized Aliez LeRoche and the menagerie girl immediately. The Qazāli were at their ease, lounging in Balladairan trousers and unbuttoned jackets as comfortably as if they'd been born to it. Which, for all Luca knew, they might have been. And if Luca didn't know better, she would have thought Aliez LeRoche had been flirting with the dark young woman with short hair before Luca interrupted them.

From the corner of her eye, Luca saw Touraine staring, but she couldn't tell from her face what she thought of the scene. Was she thinking about the flirting couple? Or the Qazāli youth at ease?

Anylight, that wasn't why they had come. LeRoche the son greeted them at the edge of the patio. He took Luca's hands and bowed over them. "Welcome to my home, Your Highness. Guard. Lieutenant." He nodded once each to the rest of Luca's party.

"I believe you know my sister and Mademoiselle Bel-Jadot. They're entertaining some friends of ours at the moment." LeRoche waved to the two Qazāli, and they smiled back, as if they were used to the bookish man flitting back and forth as they drank their juices.

"If you'd like, Your Highness, we can have a drink with them first—or after, whatever you prefer." Even as he offered, he was already leading them inside, away from the socialites and sunshine and into the cool darkness of the house.

"I'd love to see what you found, Monsieur LeRoche."

He smiled over his shoulder, a disarming, excited look that made her just as eager as he was.

"Please, Your Highness. Call me Sebastien, or Bastien if you'd like."

Ducking into the house felt like ducking into a cave. There was a sense of adventure in it, especially since she knew she was going in to find some lost piece of knowledge.

They passed through a sitting room that was stuffed overfull with Balladaire, as if Beau-Sang were overcompensating for the desert outside. Paintings upon paintings of still forests, of stags chased by baying hounds, of orchards, of fields of wheat, of chevaliers in their armor—it was almost like a museum of Balladaire.

Bastien, looking over his shoulder again, saw her expression. "It's excessive, I know. Do you know Aliez and I have never seen any of these sights?"

"You've never been to Balladaire?"

"Not once. Father speaks as if it's the most magnificent place, of course, but..." He shrugged. "Here we are. My office."

Luca glanced at Touraine, who followed impassively behind her. Luca wondered what the other woman thought of Bastien and his sister. Their lives paralleled Touraine's own displacement, though, of course, their displacement had been by choice. And didn't risk their lives. And was more profitable on the whole.

Bastien's office was sparse compared to the rest of the house. A single desk and chair. A brazier in the back for the cold nights, far from the full but tidy bookshelf. Faintly scented candles lit the room. It smelled like smoking dens in the city.

All of Bastien's energy uncoiled as he stepped inside. He sprang toward the desk to a book, which he placed, open, in front of Luca. "Oh, sit, do sit," he added belatedly, pulling the chair out for her.

"*The Letters of Doctor Ay-yid* as annotated by Dr. Travers. It's a science text of all things, about medicine! I would never have imagined." Now that they were crammed into his office, Bastien let his ebullience pour out. "See here," he said. "Travers points out how heavily medical science in Balladaire was influenced by Qazāl ages ago, with these letters. It was an exchange."

He waved his hands at the oh-so-dismissible past as if it hadn't led to precisely this moment swelling in Luca's chest. The page delineated a medical debate. Dr. Ay-yid, a Shālan doctor, maintained that contracting certain diseases could eliminate or lessen the effect of worse diseases. The annotator, Dr. Travers, was clearly on the side of the unknown Balladairan recipient of Ay-yid's argument, who claimed that this idea was nonsense. Luca was inclined to agree.

She sat and pushed up her spectacles, searching for what had excited Bastien so. It was easy to find, triple underlined. She saw Bastien's marginalia first, tight, tidy letters that suited him: *Our own birthright, abandoned??* Her heartbeat quickened.

But Bastien had underlined none of the theory. He'd underlined a portion of Ay-yid's letter farther down, an aside: "This is true. My god has given me the gift of understanding this. If Balladaire and Briga were cursed to lose their gifts, that doesn't fall upon my head."

The room was so silent that Luca could hear the tinkle of laughter from the youths outside. She realized she was holding her breath, and yet she couldn't let it out. Beside her, Bastien was nodding hard.

"Bastien." Luca ran her fingers over the words again. Pointed to his marginalia. "You don't think—" This was historical evidence. This was more than a manipulative rebel's goading.

"I do. I do. Balladaire used to—"

"Have our own magic." *This could be true.*

A gasp from the side of the room where Guérin and Touraine stood. Touraine stood rigidly, trying and failing to keep her face neutral. Guérin, however, looked as if she was slowly, finally realizing something. Just like Luca was. Like Bastien had.

Maybe the Brigāni woman had been telling the truth. Luca recalled the tapestries in the rest of the Beau-Sang house. The fields of corn, the orchards. *A god of the fields.* She looked down at the braided-wheat embroidery on her coat.

"How can we find out more? These letters are from the end of my grandfather's reign." And Balladairans hadn't worshipped a god for centuries. She would have to go back home. The Royal Library, her mother's private collection—how had she overlooked this?

Bastien shook his head. "Here? Not in Qazāl. The First Library would have to have it, though, don't you think? It's old enough to have records—historical, political—something that could tell us—" He caught himself. "Tell you what you want to know."

Luca pulled herself away from the page, pulled the reins on her heart. "Does anyone else know about this?"

"Of course not." He flushed a pretty shade of pink. "I thought you might want to explore it on your own."

Oh, but she did. If she could figure out what had happened to Balladairan magic—she would leave more than a mark on the empire. She would shake its foundations and make Balladaire stronger than ever before.

She met Bastien's wide blue eyes. His blond hair had flopped into his face again, making him look sweet, hapless, a little lost in his books. Luca knew better. This was a calculated trade.

"Thank you, Bastien. This won't be forgotten. I'll take this, if I may." She gathered up the book. She wanted time to read through it in its entirety for context. She also wanted to keep the original on hand so that it couldn't be used against her. If she was going to dig even deeper into religiosity, she needed to keep her guard up.

In the future, perhaps she could change Balladairan perceptions of magic and gods. In the future, perhaps she would even be able to *use* magic.

That thought made her stomach churn a little. *Too far, too fast.* Small steps first.

She glanced at Touraine, whose mouth was tight, as if she already knew what was coming. No matter what the rebels said, Luca was going to the Second City. She would learn about magic without the rebels' help.

There were moments that defined empires, that determined how a reign would be remembered. Luca would look back on this day, years later, and know that this was one such moment.

A thousand years ago, the First Library, the Scorpion Library, had been built to stand. Built to protect. In fact, saying it had been built was almost a lie. It had been carved out of three massive rocks that overlooked the river. For years, careful masons carved shelves out of the stones, creating a shelter that would stay dark and dry in the hot and humid climate. They were large enough to store all the world's known knowledge, even as the world grew and grew.

It was not so hard to imagine Brigāni scholars recording what they knew of Balladaire hundreds of years ago.

Luca stood on a precipice. When she crossed the river, she would become one of the first Balladairans to enter the Scorpion Library since the city had been abandoned. Since before the mad Emperor Djaya had gone on her rampage in Balladaire. Luca could hardly imagine what else she would find.

She could barely let herself think about what she really sought.

The river stretched perhaps over a mile wide at this point, and in the distance, the massive stones of the Second City rose like teeth, biting the stars out of the sky. The River Hadd was magnificent enough to create the border for two nations, once part of a single empire. It was the largest river in the world—thus far—and reduced to nothing but a thumb-wide line on her maps. It was easy to forget how it dwarfed so much of her human world, especially when the docks were so far from the city proper and even farther from the Quartier and the compound that she rarely saw it.

Gil hovered close behind her, jaw tight and eyes sharp. Like Touraine, he did not approve of the venture.

The boat they approached was a narrow thing with a small, furled sail and a pair of paddles. A recent payment to the crown by a merchant whose taxes, Luca found, came up short in Cheminade's finance records. After double-checking against the financial officer's records, Luca had issued a polite invitation. Now she had a boat and a few strong-backed Qazāli to convey her across the Hadd.

Lanquette brought up their rear, and Guérin approached the boatmen, her shoulders broad and straight, exuding that no-nonsense confidence she had. It helped, surely, that she was taller than all the boatmen.

At Luca's other side, Touraine also stood stiff backed, if for a different reason. She had fought Luca all week to reconsider. Like Gil, she had surrendered. They had to understand. *Our own birthright.* If she restored Balladaire's own magic, she would be a hero. The rebels' offers of magic came at too steep a cost when she could find it on her own.

She grabbed Touraine's arm. "Look at it. It's so close," she whispered.

Touraine didn't flinch at her grip, but the other woman did give her a long look, her question clear: *Are you sure?* And that was brazen for the quiet, obedient woman.

Luca was certain.

"Come down, madame, come down." One of the boatmen held a hand out to lead Luca onto the dock. The boat bumped gently against it, still tethered at both ends. Luca hesitated, but Guérin took her hand instead.

"Steady," Guérin said. She left Luca's title off for disguise's sake. Luca had even left her cane at home so it wouldn't be so obvious what young, three-legged Balladairan had visited the docks.

The dock sang beneath their weight, and Luca yelped in surprise. *Sky above.* "It's all right. Just startled."

"You certain, madame? The Hadd, in it, danger. We warn you." The boatman looked skeptically between her and the water. He seemed to be the one in charge and spoke to the other men in some kind of patois that wasn't quite Shālan. His irises had a yellowish cast in the moonlight.

"Yes, I'm sure. It was just a creak." Luca's face warmed with embarrassment.

She followed his gaze. Something moved in the river, sleek and glimmering on the surface. Luca forced herself not to jump. "Sky above and earth below."

"What the sky-falling fuck?" Touraine whispered.

"Luca." Gil's voice was soft in her ear. "For the love of your parents' memories, if not your own good sense, please. Let's turn back."

He sounded like the voices in her head, the same ones she'd been debating with for over a month, since her meeting with Bastien. The dark shape swam up the river, south, undulating just below the surface until it disappeared. Gil was right, and he was wrong. Luca's father would understand; he'd chosen his risks, too. For Balladaire, she would do this.

The boatman with the yellow eyes hopped lightly from the dock into the boat and reached an arm out, beckoning for them.

"Let's go," Luca said before she could lose the nerve. "Guérin, you first. I'll follow. Touraine—"

As Guérin stepped onto the boat with the boatman, Luca reached back for Touraine. Touraine was looking still farther back at Lanquette, who was scanning the empty dock road, back the way they'd come.

Luca cleared her throat. "The sooner we finish, the sooner—" She turned back in time to see the yellow-eyed boatman shove Guérin into the river.

The guardswoman almost caught her balance. Her strong legs, her grace—her quick hands, reaching out for the boatman's shirt—but the rock and sway of the boat wasn't usual, and her boot heel caught something on the bottom of the boat. Guérin screamed and disappeared off the far side of the boat with a splash.

Luca startled so sharply that her leg gave out, and she sprawled painfully on the wood. She pushed herself up to her good knee. Behind her, Touraine, Lanquette, and Gil fought with the other boatmen on the dock—and several new shadows. The dock groaned and shuddered with the betrayal of an ambush. The yellow-eyed boatman balanced easily as his craft rocked, staring into the river. Then he turned to Luca.

"You don't belong here," he said with a heavy accent. "We don't bend like Qazāli."

Luca's blood ran cold at the threat in his words.

"Help!" she yelled. Touraine, Gil, and Lanquette each turned at the sound of her voice, but it was Touraine who broke away from the fighting on the dock. Luca pointed at the man in the boat. It took only a breath for Touraine to see the boatman and note Guérin's absence.

The boatman jumped back onto the dock and met Touraine with his bare blade. Luca's heart pounded in her ears. She felt ridiculous as she crawled to the edge of the dock, staying low, dragging herself across the moss- and mildew-covered wood. Ridiculous, but not useless.

"Guérin!" yelled Luca, searching for the other guard in the churning river.

Pale hands clutched at the near side of the boat, and Guérin pulled her head above water. Relief washed over her face as she saw Luca. The guardswoman was barely a foot away, wedged between the boat and the dock supports.

Luca slithered on her belly and reached. Guérin caught her forearms and soaked the sleeves of Luca's coat with cold water.

"Up you come."

Guérin clawed up Luca's jacket, teeth chattering, hair plastered to her pale face.

Then the guardswoman roared in pain as she was pulled backward into the water by something below. With Guérin's fingers still knotted in Luca's sleeves, Luca slid with her along the rough planks, dragged like a doll toward the water. Luca didn't have time to cry out or to tell Guérin to hold fast. Her heart seized in her chest, and she braced for her own splash.

Guérin let go of Luca's arms.

"No!" screamed Luca, lunging forward, but a yank on her collar choked her back. Touraine pulled her to the ground, her body heavy over Luca's, her breath harsh in Luca's ear, while Guérin clutched the dock support, screaming and sobbing.

A monster with a mouth longer than Luca's arm clamped itself on Guérin's leg while the guard hugged the support with her whole body.

A crocodile. With each lash of its massive tail, the guardswoman cried out. With each cry, Luca felt Touraine flinch.

A gunshot.

For a sickening moment, Luca hoped someone had shot Guérin out of her misery. But another thrash from the beast and it went still. A bloody hole leaked right in the middle of its head. It hung suspended on the surface of the river, bobbing against the boat before the river dragged it away.

Touraine caught Guérin's sleeve as the woman's eyes rolled up into her skull, slowing the woman's sinking body enough that Lanquette could help heave the guardswoman out.

Lanquette put an ear to Guérin's mouth.

"Is she alive?" Luca whimpered.

He nodded. Guérin's leg, however, was a tangle of shredded cloth and flesh and splintered bone.

Only then did Luca look back toward land. Gil put away his spent pistol and pulled the other, watching the rest of the docks, which were suddenly and suspiciously quiet. She let out a strangled sound of disbelief, a close relative to a relieved sob, at the trail of bodies her guards had fought near the dock. The boatman who had pushed Guérin lay on his back, eerie eyes staring up at the moon, with his own knife jutting from his throat.

"Are they all dead?" she asked, her throat tight.

"If they aren't, they're about to be," Lanquette growled. He jumped up and proceeded to heave the bodies into the river.

Meanwhile, Touraine unwrapped her scarf, took off her belt, and used the accessories and her sheathed knife to make a tourniquet above Guérin's knee.

"Won't you need that?" Luca asked, indicating the knife.

"I didn't." Touraine nodded back to the bodies, where Lanquette was dumping the last ones into the water. Touraine snapped at him, "Lanquette, come on. I can't carry her alone."

He came back, his face tight with fury. "I have her."

With Touraine's help, he hoisted Guérin across his shoulders with a hiss. He'd never looked particularly strong before. Luca had taken him for granted. And Guérin, too. If Guérin hadn't stepped into the boat first... Luca shivered.

Gil led the way with Touraine jogging half-backward to scan behind them. Luca wished for her cane and the sword inside. When she started to fall behind even Lanquette and his burden, Touraine caught up with her and ducked beneath Luca's arm. They weren't invisible, but they might as well have been. No Qazāli wanted to be associated with Balladairans in trouble.

"The rebels betrayed us," Luca hissed to Touraine.

The soldier shook her head. "No. They warned you. Why would they warn you and then—"

"Take advantage of me? Why not? It's what anyone would do in their position."

Touraine gave her a sidelong glance. They were too close for Luca to get a good look at her face. If Touraine turned, Luca could have even kissed her on the cheek, but that jaw was tight with effort or anger or both.

Finally, Touraine said, "It wasn't them. Remember, they said some-one else controls that territory."

Surprisingly enough, that didn't make Luca feel any better.

They finally made it across the Mile-Long Bridge, and Luca's heart sank. The coach wouldn't be expecting them so soon. It wasn't there.

Lanquette sagged under Guérin, legs trembling, but he didn't put her down. Touraine sucked her teeth as she weighed the situation.

"I'll go." She spoke to Gil, not to Luca, and waited until the guard captain nodded before lowering Luca to the ground and loping south and east, along the outer wall of the city as it curved away from the river. It wasn't the shortest journey to a carriage, but Touraine was less likely to get lost this way. Even through her sudden exhaustion, Luca wondered what that must feel like, to set yourself free like a horse galloping across a plain. That was the whole point of the Balladairan standard. Strength, majesty, endurance.

The thought put a bitter taste in her mouth. She snapped at Lanquette. "Put her down before you drop her."

He laid her down gently, checking her vitals once more before stepping back through the gate to keep watch behind them. Guérin didn't wake up. Her hands were freezing to the touch.

Luca waited for Gillett to speak to her, but he didn't. When she finally looked up from her place on the ground, he was looking south, toward the desert. Not too far away, a dark hump in the horizon indicated the edge of the slum city, full of tents and lean-tos to make a third "medina."

When he finally looked down, his gaze drifted to Guérin and then back to Luca. His frown lines were deep with night. He sighed before turning his back on her again.

"This was unworthy of you, Luca."

Luca held her head in her hands and pressed her palms to her eyes, as if she could push the tears back in.

They waited for Touraine in silence.

CHAPTER 21

GRAINS OF SAND

A battlefield after battle was never really quiet. The wounded would keep you company until you were a mile away. They screamed or begged or wept as they died or were cut or were drugged. Touraine never did the cutting. She'd never had the stomach for it. She said it took the shittiest kind of bastard to be the army chirurgeon. Pruett said only the kindest could do it. She and Pruett and Tibeau had been sewn up more than once, but they were the lucky ones.

Not like Guérin.

Luca insisted on keeping Guérin in a guest bedroom and bringing the best doctor in the colony to her. Which meant Touraine couldn't escape the sounds.

The doctor did his best.

Guérin lost her leg high above the knee. No surprise. The bite had put Touraine in mind of a cannonball wound, all splintered bone and dangling, bloody meat. Except she'd rather have the cannonball. At least it might have taken the leg clean off in one go. The teeth didn't. The saw didn't, either.

Luca paid for laudanum, and Guérin slept through the worst of it. When she was awake, she moaned like a madwoman, and Lanquette shadowed her bedside like a lover.

As she healed, Touraine thought always back to the Apostate's words and the seamless scar on her own forearm. If she told Luca what she thought—that a Qazāli had *healed* her—could Luca make them heal Guérin, too? Was something like this even healable? She told herself it wasn't. She told herself that even if it were possible, the rebels wouldn't help. Fear kept the words locked in tight.

Touraine tried to tell herself Guérin wasn't her soldier. It wasn't her duty, and it sure wasn't her sky-falling fault. She'd heaped enough guilt on her shoulders over her own platoons. She didn't need any more. They weren't even friends. They had only kept the same bunk, obeyed the same fool woman's orders, and trained together every morning for the last couple months. She paid the guard a quick visit whenever she was lucid.

Luca was the surprising one.

The princess sat by the guard as she slept, looked in on her when she woke up. A week after the doctor amputated the leg, Touraine even caught Luca dashing moisture from her eyes as she closed Guérin's door behind her.

Sky above, she was a sorry sight.

One day, as Luca was leaving the guard and Touraine was going to visit, Touraine reached to put a hand on the princess's shoulder, without thinking. Luca froze. Her splotchy face darkened.

The hand dropped like a cannonball. The air between them had chilled. They were master and assistant again—however valuable the assistant was.

Instead, Touraine said, "She might make it. I have seen people come out of worse."

She didn't insult Luca by pretending it looked likely. She'd never seen someone half eaten by a monster like that. Touraine had never heard someone scream like Guérin had, either, and men and women screamed a lot of ways when they were shot or stabbed or hacked at with saws by their own medics. She'd screamed her own share under whips and bullets.

Luca said nothing to the aborted gesture or the comment. She turned a cold shoulder and limped down the stairs to the sitting room, thunking her cane into the ground and finding things to shove out of her way. She'd ignored Touraine like this for days. Their Shālan lessons had stopped entirely.

Instead of checking in on Guérin, Touraine trailed in Luca's icy wake. Another feeling was creeping up, gradually replacing the pity. A familiar feeling, but one she'd kept shoved down around Cantic, down so deep she had let herself forget. Here she was a-sky-falling-gain. Worthy enough for her commander to give her the top jobs, the toughest jobs, but never good enough to be a...a what, exactly? Just a part of the whole, a real part. She would always be disposable.

The princess collapsed on one of the cushioned chairs in front of the échecs board and flicked her hand at the other. Touraine sat, obedient as a hound and hating it.

"Have you ever played échecs?" Luca asked. Her voice was rough.

Touraine blinked. "No. Never had the patience for it."

"That's a shame. You're going to learn it today."

"As you command."

Luca glared a dose of poison at her, but she set up the board without a word. The board folded out on hinges, revealing smaller boxes housing the carved figurines. One set was carved out of wood so dark that Touraine thought it was stone, until she picked out the telltale whorls of the grain. The other was pale, slightly yellowed, like bone that had been picked over.

"These were my father's." Luca held one of the bone-colored camels, stroked it with a finger. "Someone made it for him when we first came south." She put the camel in its place in front of Touraine and smiled a smile that looked more like a grimace. "Not me, but Balladaire, the armies. He told me about it later, when he taught me how to play."

Luca said *échecs* in Shālan, and Touraine repeated it. The word tingled in her mouth. Like an intimate whisper. Their Shālan lessons had been on hiatus since the attack, and she found that she missed them.

Slowly, Luca's face softened as she surfaced from the dark mood, and the tension left Touraine's shoulders.

Maybe it was Touraine's own loneliness that let her see the mirror across from her, but suddenly, it was clearer than it had been, even after the ball when they'd talked together for hours—Luca needed a friend. Not an assistant, not guards. Ever since the latest broadside had come out, the cool scholar had bounced between frantic and bitter. It had only gotten worse after Bastien's discovery. Her eyes were bruised with the exhaustion of combing through governor business and history books. If she ever rested, she had no one but Gil. She certainly hadn't come looking for Touraine again.

"And how do you play?" Touraine picked up a square-topped bone tower. It was a near-perfect rendition of the clay-brick houses in the city, down to the tiny ladder running up the side.

Luca pointed to one of her carved black pieces, a tall, singular man. Touraine picked up the corresponding piece on her own side. Instead of a crown, layers of cloth dripped from his head. "Yes. This is the king. Your goal is to capture or kill your enemy's king without any harm coming to your own." Luca stared her down. Her blue-green eyes were red rimmed and bloodshot, a deep line between her dark brows. "He doesn't move well, but you must protect him at all costs. Do you think you can manage that?"

Touraine stared back. Her heartbeat ticked hard in her throat. "I do."

They played—rather, Luca played and Touraine floundered—until the sun set. When Adile brought food, they ate it and wiped their hands on linen napkins before making their next moves. Adile lit the lanterns and closed the deep-red curtains over the windows. No one else disturbed them all day.

Touraine had never been so soundly beaten at anything since her first years in the Balladairan training yard. She learned after the first several games that charging forward with the most powerful pieces wouldn't win shit, so she saw to her defensive tactics. Her greatest success was the last game. Instead of sending all her armies to attack, she barricaded her king in a defensive square of players. It became impractical soon, as Luca slowly winnowed away the makeshift fortress with precision. Somehow, Luca predicted Touraine's moves before she made them, and had traps already in wait.

She gave Touraine no quarter. Not even a little mercy for a beginner. She was hard, harder even than Cantic, who had at least pretended regret when she punished the young Sands for their mistakes. There was nothing like that in Luca.

"You should move your pawns more," Luca said, pointing to Touraine's pale foot soldiers. "Let them guard your king and make trouble so you don't have to spend the more useful pieces."

She threw the comment away as she studied the board, but it made Touraine stutter to a halt. In her mind, Émeline straddled Tibeau's lap, making fun of him while Touraine and Pruett laughed and a cook fire danced happily between them. A brief moment of happiness before the company of pawns went to fight and die for the king in his city. Now Émeline was gone.

"You would make a brilliant general," Touraine said quietly.

Luca startled as she moved her queen several diagonal spaces from Touraine's king. Her cheeks tinged pink, but her look at Touraine was quizzical. "Checkmate."

Touraine swore. "Wait. That last move. What did you do? What did I miss?"

Luca smiled with such pure, wicked, girlish glee that it was Touraine's turn to be startled.

"You should be asking what I did at the beginning. Now. I think I've had enough. Have you?" Luca winced as she pushed herself away from the board. "I feel a little better."

"Better?"

"Better. Now I would like to get up, undress, and lie down."

"All right." Touraine still looked at the end of the game, trying to remember Luca's last moves. It was easier than thinking about pawns.

Luca smiled. "We can have tea again, if you'd like?"

Touraine hesitated, eyes still on the board, her robed king surrounded by two tiny foot soldiers and a watchtower with its ladder. She picked him up and ran her calloused thumb along the smooth, dark wood of his turban.

"The bookseller sent a message. They want to know where you stand. I think they heard about our trip."

"And what of it?" Luca's brief joy faded into touchy irritation. She muttered, "Fine. They're more important now, anylight. If I can't get to the books, it has to be the people. I need to end this. A Qazāli family was murdered in Atyid—did you know that? And later, two of the city's blackcoats were found hacked apart."

Touraine hadn't known that.

"If we don't come to terms with these clandestine little meetings, the next step is war. I can barely hold Cantic off as it is. But I won't sell my empire on the hope of a few magic seeds that never sprout. What do you think? Will the rebels listen?"

Touraine recognized the old folk warning. An itch gathered between Touraine's shoulder blades. She knew what she wanted. And she knew what Luca wanted. Sky above, she was tired of being a pawn. Who was to say she couldn't be a camel knight or stand at the watchtower?

Who was to say she couldn't be the player instead?

Touraine turned the king over in her fingers, running her thumb over the smooth wood.

"It's hard to say, Your Highness." Touraine shrugged. There were too many things she didn't know how to talk about. The magic. The Sands. Her own creeping discontent. "They don't seem..."

"I've already asked you—be frank with me. Would you tiptoe around your soldiers like this?"

Touraine tightened her lips and shook her head tersely.

"Then open your sky-falling mouth. What do you think about the rebels? Is their friendship worth slapping the face of every noble from here to Béson?"

Luca's temper flared like a struck match, and Touraine lit like a cannon fuse. She slammed the king on the board with a satisfying clack.

"If it wouldn't get me hanged, I would slap the face of every noble from here to Béson and back again. It makes me sick to see you court them. You want to stop this rebellion, then give the Qazāli what they want. Free them. Do it and they might even become allies. You don't need the nobles' approval for it. You're the queen."

"Those nobles are *my* people, and if I don't end this rebellion the right way, my uncle won't even give me my throne. Then the Qazāli get nothing. Or did our dear friends tell you they'll help me oust my uncle by force?"

Luca flicked a hand dismissively. As if Touraine couldn't possibly understand the stakes. Touraine understood them all too well.

"*Our* friends? You want their magic, but what have you done for them except finally treat them like humans? They offer advice, and you ignore it so you can chase down their secrets and almost get drowned for your trouble. Is everything yours for the taking? Do you care about anyone but yourself? Guérin almost died for you—I'd bet she wishes she had."

A muscle twitched in Luca's jaw. Good.

"I've changed Qazāl for them," Luca said through gritted teeth. "The children I sponsored have already started schooling. Qazāli are working under better conditions than they've ever had, thanks to me going *against* the nobles. Guérin has the best medical treatment in my considerable power. Because of that, she'll survive."

"Without a leg. Do you know what it's like for a soldier to lose her fucking leg?"

Luca raised her chin and faced Touraine full on. She folded her hands slowly on her cane in front of her. "No. I don't. Tell me."

Touraine had gone too far, and she wanted to go farther still.

"You're trapped in bed until you heal enough to get up again—if you heal at all. You struggle to learn the crutch, the balance of it all. When you feel like you can walk again, you fall flat on your face because you forget a whole sky-falling leg is gone. It doesn't feel like it. It even itches, and you're half-mad with wanting to scratch it. You feel weak, with nothing to stand on. Less than everyone else around you."

Luca raised an angry eyebrow. "I have a certain empathy—"

Touraine shook her head, tears of fury on her eyelashes. Too many of her men and women had lived through this—too many of them had not. She pointed at Luca, pointed at the sky-falling queen of Balladaire. "No. No, you don't. Take off both your legs and look at all you have left." She threw her arms wide. Luca just stared at her. "I said, look!"

Slowly, Luca turned her head marginally, flicked her eyes right, left. Plush carpets and carved wooden tables, upholstered chairs, everything but the servants pretending not to hear the future queen and her pet Qazāli shouting to the rafters.

"You will never have nothing. Not like we have nothing. Not like the Sands have nothing, not like the Qazāli have nothing. Not like a carpenter's daughter in Nowhere, Balladaire, has nothing." *You will never have to sell yourself to live.*

She stopped to swallow away the hitch in her throat. "Guérin lived by the strength of her legs, the speed of her sword arm. You lived by them."

Luca's throat bobbed as she swallowed. Lamplight broke on a streak of tears on her cheek.

"And now she will live by me. She'll have a lifetime pension. She and her family will never want for anything."

"Of course. Nothing but her leg."

Luca sniffed, but Touraine could see her jaw working as her teeth ground. The ice was cracking.

"I just wish I knew...If we had access to Qazāli magic, maybe we could have healed her. Or maybe our own magic could have helped. That's why I'm doing this, Touraine. Don't you understand? It's not just about this city or these rebels. My people have been plagued by disease and war for decades. I would do anything for the power to save them."

Touraine's fists shook as she turned.

What was Touraine willing to do for the Sands, these pawns? What would she give up to keep them on the board a little longer?

Everything.

Behind Touraine, a palm slammed against a table, and a chess piece clattered on the board.

"Touraine." Luca's voice cracked, and Touraine stopped midstep.

Touraine's pulse throbbed somewhere low in her stomach. It made her want to throw up. She turned slowly.

"The magic is real, Luca." Touraine slid her sleeve up her forearm so the silvery brown of the scar shone in the lamplight. "I don't know if it does more than this or how it works. All I know is that I was hurt, and the cut shouldn't have healed as quick as it did." Her only theory was that the girl on the gallows had done it. The tingle as their skin had touched, when Touraine slipped the noose around her neck. The girl's prayer. Could it be as simple as that?

"The problem is," Touraine continued, "I don't trust them. I don't trust the Jackal. She wants a fight."

Luca stared at Touraine in silence, her lower lip caught in her teeth. Her eyes trailed from Touraine's arm to her eyes and back again.

"Say something," Touraine whispered after a full minute of silence.

Luca held Touraine's eyes and drew out the tension a moment longer. Finally, she said, "Tell them...tell them I'll give them one hundred guns. For the magic. I want to know how it works. I want teachers—or healers or what have you. Nothing less." Luca began to right the échecs pieces she had knocked down.

"What?" Touraine stepped forward, unsure she'd understood. "You want to *give* them guns? What about the Jackal? I just said—"

"One hundred guns," Luca repeated. "They get the message that I trust them, but they won't do more than scratch us if they decide to attack. Trust me."

"But—"

"Enough," Luca snarled. "That's my decision."

Touraine froze. Then she snapped to attention, as if the habit were activated by the command in Luca's voice.

"As you command, Your Highness." Touraine bowed. When their eyes met, Luca's lip was trembling. Touraine glared to keep her own angry tears at bay. "How will they get them? They'll want to know details—"

"I don't *have* details yet. Just tell them I will. I need time to figure out the rest. And if that's not enough for them, walk away. I'm done negotiating."

One hundred guns. Pitiful, compared to the thousand Balladairan soldiers garrisoned just outside the city. And yet more than enough to ruin Luca if anyone found out.

Touraine walked into the meeting and dropped a basket of food unceremoniously in front of the Apostate. The Jackal half rose from her sprawl. Malika and Saïd frowned.

The witch straightened. "She's made a decision."

Touraine nodded. She'd tried to shake off the piss-poor mood, but it clung like the smell of shit to a latrine pit, even though she had good news for once. She nodded her chin at the Jackal.

"She says a hundred guns. A hundred and five, more likely, because they're packed in crates of fifteen. That, or we're done here."

The silence held. Dragged.

"One hundred?" the Jackal finally snarled. "Why doesn't she add a handful of couscous and call herself generous?"

"She did." Touraine pointed to the food at her feet. The wicker basket steamed with the fresh grain mixed with vegetables and spices. It would have smelled delicious if her stomach hadn't been knotted up with hurt and anger. "Do you even have a hundred people who can shoot?"

"We have enough who can teach."

The Apostate's raised palm silenced them both. "And if I recall correctly, you were an esteemed lieutenant in the Balladairan army. That should help."

Touraine snorted. Good luck talking her way out of that treason, even with Luca's help. "Where can I teach fifty people to shoot without accidentally hitting some poor shit in the foot?"

The Apostate looked between Saïd and the Jackal. "We can find a place."

"Then a hundred is more than enough. What about Luca's part? She wants people who can teach Balladairans magic and anything you know about Balladaire's old magic." Touraine still couldn't wrap her head around the latter.

As one, the rebels looked to the Apostate. The Brigāni woman smiled with an ironic tilt of her head.

"I'll come to her when we have the guns and I'm certain she hasn't trapped us with them." Steady golden eyes limned with kohl studied her. "We still want to meet her. Personally. Before I tell her anything. We can outline the finer details then."

Touraine snorted. "Good luck."

"You said she wanted to know us. I want to see what kind of person she is. If she won't meet us face-to-face, there's no accord."

"I'll try."

"I can't help but wonder if this is all a scheme of hers. Theirs." Malika's words were philosophical, but her voice echoed retreat. She nodded toward Touraine. "The rebellion itself. If we rebel, they bring more troops. To aim for our throats instead of our heels. Maybe we shouldn't do this." Defeated.

Touraine was suddenly very aware of her breath. It sounded too loud, too quick.

"I see it as more of an assurance. Better to have them and not need them," Saïd said, his voice a reassuring rumble.

"Malika has a point." The Jackal finally deigned to sit up, resting wrist and stump on knees. "Why trust the word of the conqueror's favorite whore?"

Maybe the argument with Luca had frayed Touraine's nerves too much. Left her a bit raw. And maybe it was that the sentiment was too close to what Pruett had said. Too close to the drawing on the broadside. Too close to guilty feelings that snaked across her chest when Luca made her laugh over the governor's records.

"No." Touraine pointed a trembling finger at the woman. "You do not get to put me down for working with her. Can none of you bastards think how sky-falling lonely it must be for me, for us? It's a wonder I haven't fucked my way through her household, just to have someone to talk to." She kicked the cushion she hadn't sat on at the

Jackal. She scowled at the Apostate. "And you would abandon us to it, just as smug and self-righteous. Fuck your...goddamned rebellion. Fuck your guns. If you want them, send someone else, and more pleasure to you. Take a look around. I don't see that you've got too many options, or we wouldn't be having these little talks."

Touraine would not be blamed for feeling lonely.

She stomped out of a room for the second time that night and, for the second time, was called back.

"Mulāzim." The Jackal's voice caught her, scraped her like a bayonet caught in the ribs. It was bitter, but soft enough that Touraine shook her head without turning. The Jackal's boots scraped the floor as she stood.

In Touraine's bones, in her blood, she knew what was coming. She started to laugh. "No. No, no, no, no, no. Not you."

"Look at me."

The Jackal held her scarf in her hand, her head and face bare in the candlelight. Her hair fell in finger-width dreadlocks. Her full lips were twisted with hate.

"Jackal, sit down. You don't have to—"

"Enough, Djasha. Enough with the games. I want my daughter to see me, to know me, so that when she runs back to that woman's bed, she knows exactly what she leaves behind."

The Jackal—Jaghotai—stepped close. They could have hugged in desperate thanks, reached out hands to learn each other's faces. Kissed cheeks, foreheads, all the little bits of love you take for granted when they're common.

"You killed my brother, Touraine. You've made it clear that you want nothing of your own people, so I have nothing to give you. Get us the guns. Bring your princess. Let's see how far this goes."

Touraine didn't remember leaving the hideout. Just that by the time she reached the streets, she was stumbling as if drunk, a wordless pain in her chest that blocked out everything else, making her feel numb.

On the way to the Quartier, her feet took her past the gallows. The ropes were empty tonight and hung limp in the still air. The memory of the hanging cropped up often. Too often. She'd killed plenty of Balladaire's enemies before and never with as much guilt.

Who were her enemies, though? It hadn't mattered to her before. And it wasn't the idea of enemies that troubled her now. It was allies.

Her mother. Who hated her.

Back in the Quartier, the town house was still the deserted battlefield. Only missing the crows. Lanquette stood outside Luca's personal chambers, and Gil sat in the sitting room. The men looked up at her, then went back to their own thoughts. Dark thoughts, by their expressions.

She had the guards' room to herself. In the darkness, she scrubbed her face with her hand. She stopped with her fingers on her eyebrows and chuckled. When was the last time she'd looked at her reflection? Oh—Luca's party. She'd been in that costume, but she'd felt handsome. Proud. Until Rogan.

As quietly as she could, she cracked open the door between her room and Luca's, and listened to the other woman's breathing. Slow, barely audible huffs met her ears. With her memory and her fingers, she found the small hand mirror that Luca kept on the dressing table and carried it back to her room. She lit a lantern and let it burn bright enough to show her image on the glass.

It was hard to tell anything without the Jackal next to her to compare. Memory coupled with desire could play cruel tricks on the eye.

Desire. Was this what she wanted?

Thick eyebrows, like the Jackal's. A scar across Touraine's temple, shallow. Handsome smile, she'd say, with better teeth. They shared brown eyes, but that wasn't saying much in Qazāl.

She rolled her eyes. Stupid. These were the kinds of things Tibeau and Pruett had done when they were kids, not her. She scowled. The reflection contorted, bitter, angry, even ugly in its confusion.

Touraine's breath skipped in her chest. She tried the scowl again, conjuring up all her resentment.

There. That was a familiar face.

The Jackal's daughter.

The creak of Luca's door behind her made Touraine jump.

Luca stood there, pale and sick-looking against the darkness of her room.

"You took my mirror?"

Touraine turned it over on her bed, smothering herself.

When Touraine didn't explain, Luca looked down at her bare feet. Her pale toes splayed across the rug.

"What did the rebels say?" she asked, just before the silence became even more awkward.

"Oh." It didn't seem like what Luca had planned to say. Touraine flipped the mirror over in her hands again. When she saw her face, she saw Jaghotai's disgust. "They said you've a deal."

A week later, Luca got news that made Touraine's stomach sink further.

They were working together in the official governor-general's office on the compound when an aide brought a report from General Cantic.

The aide tipped his cap to Touraine with a smile as she took it. She barely registered the kindness, she felt so leaden.

"From Cantic? I'll take it." Luca held out her hand expectantly.

The camaraderie they'd built over the last months remained chilled over. They still shared quiet moments together during her Shālan lessons, and Luca wasn't stingy with her praise as Touraine progressed, but every moment was taut with the words they'd said and the ones they hadn't. Touraine sought refuge in the role of obedient soldier. *No, obedient* assistant.

She watched Luca from behind that wall of quiet obedience and saw the princess pale. Luca looked at Touraine and back at the paper.

"Touraine, two squads of colonials—" Luca looked away, eyes fixed on a small, desiccated lizard perched on a shelf, as if it had the words she wanted to say.

Touraine already knew she didn't want to hear the rest. She asked anyway. "What about them?"

Luca spoke in a rush. "Cantic sent two squads of colonials from Rose Company to deal with the desert tribes disrupting our supply lines to the inner colonial cities and their compounds. They haven't come back."

A spike of adrenaline helped keep Touraine upright. "Let's go get them, then. Maybe they were taken prisoner."

Luca was already shaking her head. "I know these people. I've been reading Cheminade's books on them, and they don't take prisoners. They're...like beasts. And I don't mean that they're uncivilized. I mean that...they think *they* are animals. They leave their dead like carcasses in the open plains instead of giving them proper burnings."

She stood and limped around her desk, reaching for Touraine's hand. "I'm sorry—"

Touraine pulled her hand back. "My squad, they're still—"

"They're still stationed in the city. "

Touraine hid her face. She was ashamed to feel so relieved. Rose Company was her company. She'd grown up with those Sands. She'd fought beside them. She felt Luca's gentle hand on her shoulder.

"I'm so sorry," the princess whispered.

"Then why not send the blackcoats?" growled Touraine. She backed away from Luca's hand again. "Why send us—why send the conscripts?"

Luca stared blankly at her until understanding clicked.

"Touraine, they're soldiers. It's their job. The general deploys them based on skill and needs."

Touraine knew all about skills and needs and the "sacrifices" that must be made.

"Then why is it always us first? The first to fight, the first to die?"

"What do you want me to do, Touraine?" Luca gestured in the direction of Cantic's office. "Tell Cantic to never let them fight again?"

"That's the problem, Luca." Touraine gestured through the sandstone walls at Cantic's office and toward the city, too. Her eyes burned, and all of Cheminade's old junk blurred. Her voice came out hoarse, barely above a whisper. "It's not a matter of *let*. They never chose this.

They're not getting rewarded for valor with ribbons and raises. We just die, and when we die, we're not even worth the wood to burn us."

Luca made a small sound as if she'd been punched in the belly.

Touraine's faith in Luca's ability to keep the rebels from turning the guns on the Sands dwindled to nothing.

This time, the princess didn't try to touch her again, even though now a part of Touraine wanted the warm touch of sympathy. But the distance between who Luca was and who Touraine could be gaped impossibly wide.

Touraine sniffed, stepped back, and bowed. "May I be excused, Your Highness?"

Luca ran her hand over her messy blond hair. She started to speak twice before finally saying, "Of course. Take as much time as you need."

CHAPTER 22

AN ALLIANCE

The day Luca meant to meet the rebels, she thought she'd die of the heat first. The last two weeks had seen the dry season rise to a peak, and the sun seared like a judging eye over the city.

Or maybe Luca only imagined it, and the heat was the flush of guilt as she diverted one hundred guns away from her military to her military's de facto adversary. Old guns, likely to be jammed or to backfire in the shooter's face, but still. Weapons that could be used against her people. Of all her concessions, this was the most dangerous. Economic changes she could justify, but this was as good as treason.

It was easy, surprisingly easy, to wedge open this crack in her empire. If Cantic had been a traitor to the realm, it could have been done long ago.

No. It was only the baking earth and lack of breeze that kept her sweating in her office on the compound.

She looked over the last of the notes for her first foray into arms dealing. Two separate shipments, in two separate storehouses. Just in case. When the time came, it would look like someone had broken into her personal stores, guided by an unfortunate leak on the merchant's end or an especially enterprising network of spies. Not a queen sabotaging her rule for the chance at foreign magic. *A chance at peace, not power*, she told herself, multiple times a day. And yet her fingers itched for it. The magic. Her triumphant return to Balladaire, leaving a restful colony behind. Her coronation.

Luca would give the instructions to the rebels tonight—if they upheld their end of the bargain and told her how to use the magic.

As she left, she made sure to take all the papers with her. Just in case.

Back in the Quartier, Touraine was helping the porters pack away Guérin's belongings. They were burly Qazāli, sweat staining their Balladairan shirts across the backs and armpits even though Guérin had but a single chest. Guérin's ship would set sail today or tomorrow, depending on the water conditions.

When the porters carried her out on a litter to the medical carriage, the entire household came to see Guérin off. That surprised Luca more than a little. She didn't think the taciturn woman had made so many friends. And that was even more to Touraine's point that night she had railed at Luca.

Touraine was already dressed for the evening's activity, in her black Qazāli garb, the face scarf hanging around her neck. She clasped Guérin's forearm and then gave her a gentle, brief squeeze on the back. Lanquette practically had to bend double to hug her.

Finally, it was Luca's turn, and her mouth was dry. She hadn't planned words for this moment, and of course *thank you* was shamefully inadequate.

Still, it was the only place to start. "Thank you for your tireless service, Guard Guérin."

She reached out and took the older woman's hand in her own. The skin was dry, the calluses still hard. Her lower half was covered by a thin blanket despite the heat. The gaping flatness next to her right leg drew the eye. Luca forced her gaze to the guard's face. Guérin looked up at her from the litter, her chin high and proud.

"Honestly, I cannot thank you enough for a single lifetime, so I'll make sure your children and your children's children know everything you've done for me."

And I'm sorry. She couldn't bring herself to say that with so many others watching.

"My duty is my honor, Your Highness," Guérin said thickly. "It's been a pleasure. Mostly."

Everyone chuckled at that, even Gillett, who had been grumpy all day. The old man was more sentimental than he let on. That, or he still thought Luca was making a mistake about this evening.

By the time Guérin's carriage was rolling out of the Quartier, the sun had set, and it was time for Luca to meet the Qazāli.

When the invitation to a "cultural celebration" had come, it had been easier than Luca had expected to get Gil and Cantic to agree that she should go—though neither of them knew about Luca's true intent. Though Gil was less than enthusiastic, General Cantic was drawn into the idea of Luca rubbing elbows with the Qazāli immediately. With safety precautions—a squad of Balladairan soldiers, a large personal guard—it was the perfect opportunity to gather information. Luca knew she should be disgruntled at how easily her general agreed to dangle her as bait, but she didn't question her luck.

Still, when she and her retinue set out from the Quartier, she counted and re-counted the guards around her.

"You're sure you trust the rebels?" she asked Touraine.

They rode together in the rickshaw the rebels had sent for her, while the soldiers followed on foot. Luca glanced over. Touraine was looking out, across the desert and into the deepness of the night. Since their argument, there had been no shared coffee, no drubbing her up and down an échecs board. Luca had taken to sending her on errands over the last two weeks just so she would leave the house and take her tight-jawed glare with her.

"Yes," Touraine said, without turning. "For this, anyway. They've had plenty of opportunity for worse than they've done. And—" She shook her head.

"What? Please."

Touraine finally met Luca's eyes. "They've been more than fair, all things considered."

"All things considered?"

Touraine raised an eyebrow, frowning. "An occupying army, stolen children."

Luca side-eyed her, then sighed. "Then away we go."

They traveled deeper into that darkness, away from the city, until the great wall of the New Medina was gone and the darkness gave way to flickering fires amid dry, rocky scrubland. The small fires created a circle within which figures moved to the rhythm of beating drums, and around each fire, people sat and laughed and cooked and watched the dancers.

The people stared as Luca and Touraine arrived with a retinue of guards. The soldiers hung back in a disciplined curve around the perimeter. The dancers in the circle stopped moving as they lost their audience.

So many people. Even Touraine was nervous, hand straying to Luca's knife at her hip.

A Brigāni woman wearing loose trousers beneath a knee-length loose shirt met them just within the circle of light. The one Touraine called the Apostate. Or the witch.

"Welcome, Princess Luca. Welcome, Touraine," she said in Shālan, bowing. "I'm Djasha din Aranen."

Another woman swaggered over, wearing a vest that showed one arm thick and muscled and the other ending in a twisted stump at the forearm. There was a sheen of sweat on her forehead even in the cool night, and her long dreadlocks were pulled back. She looked Luca up and down, glaring. This would be the Jackal. She was handsome, in a familiar, rough-edged way—and that scowl—

Luca looked sharply at Touraine, just in time to see an almost identical scowl. By the sky above and earth below. Had Touraine known all this time? There was clearly no love lost between them, but that was too big a secret for Touraine to keep from her. Luca would bring it up later.

"You sure you're not violating the law, Your Highness?" The Jackal sucked her teeth. "This is a holy celebration, you know."

"The law clearly hasn't stopped you."

Djasha stepped between them and cut the Jackal a wry look. "Jag-hotai. A truce. Remember what that means? Peace over all?"

Jaghotai the Jackal rolled her eyes and spun on her heel, waving a hand as if batting away flies. "Yes, yes. I'll leave the diplomacy to the diplomats."

As Djasha led them around the circle of fires, anxiety built in Luca's chest. She couldn't remember the last time she'd enjoyed a celebration. She would have been young—to attend a gathering without wondering who wanted her influence or who was judging her fitness for the throne. Her own party in the Quartier had been no exception. Above all, she hated dances.

She loved music, though.

In Balladaire, stringed instruments provided subtle, elegant back-ground accompaniment. Musicians were to be heard, not seen, and even the sound was not meant to attract attention.

Here, though! The drummers beat their hide-bound instruments and shouted with joy. Their rhythms sounded broken to Luca's ear until she understood their patterns.

And the smells—spices filled the air as people cooked at almost every fire. Luca's stomach growled. People scooped stews out of clay bowls with round bread and ate small pastries with their bare hands.

The dancers, Jaghotai among them, started up again. They jumped over each other, swinging their legs as if they meant to kick one another. Other dancers simply stomped and clapped their hands as they moved around in circles. It looked so disorganized. What were the partner formulae? How did people know who they could dance with, and when? What was appropriate for what song? She was so entranced that she almost forgot why she was there.

Djasha followed Luca's attention. "Do you like to dance, princess?"

"Dancing is not my strength, all things considered, Djasha din." She held up her cane.

However, Djasha's attention was captured by someone else, and a bright smile cracked over her tired face.

They had reached a fire where sat a middle-aged Qazāli woman with deep brown eyes and short, curling spikes of brown hair spread with shocks of white. She was undeniably beautiful. The woman stood as Djasha approached. Where Touraine's physical grace was dangerous, a snake ready to strike, this woman moved like a stream, at peace with its inevitable course.

"This is my wife, Aranen din Djasha." Djasha clasped the other woman close, and Aranen fell into her. The couple stumbled, laughing. It was the strangest, giddiest thing she could have imagined the Brigāni woman doing. This was the witch? The woman Touraine had said to pay attention to?

"Enchanted," Luca said, bowing slightly to the other woman.

If their positions had been reversed, Luca would not have shown Djasha whom she loved. That knowledge was only another weapon to be wielded.

Gillett and Touraine introduced themselves, as well, but Touraine's attention was clearly elsewhere as her knee jiggled in time with the beat. Touraine hadn't acknowledged Jaghotai as her mother at all, but Luca saw where her gaze drifted almost idly.

"Would you like to dance, Touraine?" Aranen asked. She smiled rakishly, and Luca had to calm the warm spike of jealousy in her stomach. "Shāl moves within you."

Touraine only looked once to Luca before allowing the other woman to lead her away. Soon, her soldier was clapping like the others, flicking and waving her hands. She even picked up the cross-step jumps that Luca couldn't even follow with her eyes.

Djasha caught Luca staring at the dancing couple.

Luca's cheeks burned. "What?"

Djasha shrugged. "You want to dance. Why don't you? I'll take my wife back, and you can go dance with Touraine. She can teach you—she learned quick. She moves like it's her life."

"She was a soldier. It is her life. I, on the other hand, am not particularly graceful." She tapped her cane into the ground again.

"You keep waving that thing around like it means something."

"It does. It means dancing is difficult for me. At the very least, I won't manage like everyone out there."

Djasha shook her head. "Perhaps." She pointed to an old man in the crowd. "Elder Ebrahm manages."

Elder Ebrahm moved slowly, shuffling only side to side, within a pace. He kept rhythm with everyone else, and the drummers near him hooted while he clapped.

"I think I know my body better than you do. Why don't you go out, if you're so keen? Or we could discuss the reason I'm here."

The woman's smile flickered like a lantern going dim. "I don't dance, because I haven't been feeling well. My doctor-wife has ordered me to rest. If you won't dance, sit and eat. It's hard to talk peace on an empty stomach."

They sat on wood-and-hide stools, and another Qazāli at the fire held out two bowls of beans and a hunk of bread. Gil sniffed his bowl, then attacked it like a soldier. How did he know it was safe?

Instead of accepting the other bowl, Luca reached into her satchel and pulled out a waxed leather tube. Their months of hard work, distilled into a few sheets of paper. The rebels' copy of the accord.

"Thank you, but—"

Djasha took the bowl from the other Qazāli and put it in Luca's hands, deftly taking the sealed tube and tucking it away. "Eat, Your Highness. We'll have time for this later. And don't worry about poison," she added wryly. "You're too big a prize. Your death would help us a little but hurt us a lot. Besides, you're a guest."

Gil nodded subtly in encouragement, his cheeks full.

Before Luca realized it, her bowl was empty and Touraine was swaggering back, beaming and breathing hard, a cup in her hand. She gulped down the contents, shuddered, and had it refilled.

"What is this stuff?" Touraine asked Djasha.

"That, girl, is Shāl's holy water. It will make you the most honest woman alive. So tell me—where did you put my wife?"

Touraine pointed behind her. Aranen waved from a group of older Qazāli, and Djasha went out to meet her. Despite her smiles, the woman did move as if everything hurt.

Touraine turned to Luca, apologetic. "I'm sorry. I shouldn't be drinking."

"Do as you like. I have my guards tonight."

"Would you like some?" Touraine held the cup out to Luca.

Luca shook her head. She didn't need that kind of honesty right now. She stuck her hands in her pockets to remove temptation.

"What about the dance?" Touraine smiled slyly when Luca hesitated. "The drink might help." Her lingering anger seemed dulled.

Luca was never one for drinking much more than mulled wine. Spirits resulted in a freedom she was unwilling to give herself. Inhibitions were there for a reason.

Then, still holding the cup, Touraine giggled. This broad-shouldered, muscle-bound ex-soldier, who spent most of her time either glowering or bowing at people, had smirked at her future queen, and now she was actually giggling.

Sky above, Luca wanted to do right by that laugh. She wanted Touraine to giggle at her, to smirk and smile and tease her. She hated to want it. She could have fought it, pushed back, snapped Touraine away. Swatted down the cup. That wouldn't get her anything she wanted.

Luca took the cup.

Only the Shālans' god knew what was in that fucking cup, but it burned Luca's nose as she inhaled, then coughed.

Touraine laughed again, mouth wide and open. None of the conscripts looked like that in the compound. Did the freedom come from the liquor or from being with other Qazāli?

Luca closed her eyes and bowed her head over her drink. For a second, she forgot about the magic and the rebellion.

She had been an idiot all this time. Touraine blamed her for everything—not just Guérin, but the Sands who had died protecting Balladairan interests, too. *Luca's* interests. Luca was as culpable as Cantic, as Rogan. Touraine couldn't possibly forgive her, and so Luca could never have more of Touraine than the occasional late-night tea or afternoon échecs game. This drunken giggle, this smile, might be the closest Luca ever got.

She opened her eyes again. Gil's eyes bulged as he shook his head minutely, which she knew translated to *Please don't do this, not even over my steaming corpse*, but she ignored him and tossed the drink down her throat.

Shālan exclamations erupted around her, and laughter as the stinging bitterness made her cheeks suck in. She sputtered like a drowned woman until only a sour aftertaste and a warm sweetness in her belly remained.

Touraine held on to her by the shoulder, a gentle vise. Luca leaned into the safety of the touch.

She smiled up at Touraine. "Let's dance, then."

Touraine took her hand and led her out to the dancing.

Touraine and Aranen both threw an arm under Luca's shoulders, and other dancers linked around them until they became a circle. The drums beat, tak-tak-tak, but in a rhythm that allowed her to shuffle sideways with the others. Her awkward hops fell in time with each beat. She didn't feel as stilted as she did on a ballroom floor. The drummers slowed for her, and a whole melody sprang up around this new beat. And if she started to stumble, Touraine and Aranen took her weight on their shoulders and carried her through the steps. She focused on keeping the weight on her quickly tiring good leg. Finally, the drummers reached their crescendo, and even Luca gave a short yip at the end.

Still, she was grateful when the drummers stopped to sate their hunger and slake their thirst. Her hip caught with the tightening of muscle. Touraine led her back to their fire, where Gil and Djasha sat with Elder Ebrahm. They had been deep in conversation but stopped as she approached. The elder smiled in her direction, his eyes unfocused. He was almost blind.

She let Touraine guide her back onto a stool, and she slumped there, grinning like a fool.

Is it the drink?

Perhaps, but not only. She felt safe. Even though by anyone else's reckoning, she was in an enemy camp.

No sooner did she think that did she feel the slight dimming in her head. A sharp crack and someone's stifled cry. She jumped, and Touraine was in front of her, hand on her knife.

It was only some sparring dancers. One of them had landed a hit. Jaghotai, standing nearby, noticed their defensive reactions and laughed. It was an ugly, barking sound.

"So scared to be among your conquered? Your Highness." Jaghotai tilted her head and approached.

Touraine kept herself between them, and the other guards flanked her. Gil edged closer to Luca, the better to whisk her away.

"And you defend her." Jaghotai sneered as she addressed her daughter for the first time all night. "You really are a faithful hound, all dressed up in her collar. Where is your spine?"

Touraine's palm cracked against her cheek.

The sound rang across the fires, and people hushed to watch. They smelled blood on the air, sizzling in the flames. The peace Luca had thought was so certain developed a brittle texture.

Aranen stepped forward. "Touraine. Jaghotai. This is unnecessary."

"Come out." Jaghotai ignored Aranen and jabbed her thumb to the empty space behind her. "Just a friendly go."

"Be careful," Luca murmured. "I'd hate to have to find a new assistant."

Touraine rolled her neck and shoulders. "No one else would do it."

Luca couldn't tell if that was a joke or not.

The two squared off in the center of the fires.

"No fancy knife?" Jaghotai circled Touraine, barehanded.

Touraine gave a faint, barely perceptible smile. Gone was the exuberant woman who had cajoled Luca into a drink.

Djasha took the role of judge without prompting, as if this were a common occurrence. Space in front of Elder Ebrahm remained clear. Luca wasn't sure how well his eyesight would let him see, but the intended courtesy was obvious.

Djasha clapped once and the fight began.

It was like watching the dancing, only deadlier.

They were both quick, and Luca thought for certain that Touraine would have a clear advantage because of her age, but that wasn't the case. Jaghotai was bulkier, but she was as light on her feet as Touraine. One hit from that powerful arm—a thrill of fear for Touraine jolted up Luca's back.

Such close fighting, so intimate with the body…Luca had never learned that. Her rapier kept enemies at a distance. Touraine and Jaghotai clenched each other in locks before someone got the upper hand and shoved the other away. It stirred Luca's blood even though she hadn't moved a muscle. She barely blinked. Her heart thumped with Touraine's bravado. And what was Touraine to her, again? The governor's assistant? Her companion? Her champion?

Jaghotai got close, pretended to leave Touraine's reach, and then came close again and slammed her elbow into Touraine's gut before twirling away. Luca gasped, held the breath. Touraine doubled over and staggered once before regaining herself. First real contact. It ended the pretense that neither fighter was out for blood.

Touraine struck next, like lightning. When Jaghotai chopped at her, Touraine blocked the attack to the outside with a forearm, bent her knees, and rammed the heel of her fist in the space between Jaghotai's stomach and ribs. That was the end. When Jaghotai bent, Touraine kicked her sharply in the thigh. The other woman crumpled to one knee, clutching her stomach.

Djasha clapped twice and then pointed to Touraine. One person applauded, then maybe three joined.

Touraine strutted toward Luca with her chin high, a smug smile on her lips. Djasha, however, caught Touraine's arm.

"There are three rounds, girl. The victor takes two."

As the edges of Luca's mind still blurred with drink, Touraine walked back into the circle. Gil squeezed Luca's shoulder.

CHAPTER 23

A HOPE IN THE DARK

Touraine squared off in front of Jaghotai again. Sharp inhale through the nose, slow exhale through the mouth. Breathe like the wolf, not the deer. Which instructor had told them this, in Balladaire? Her entire core ached, but she pushed the pain away.

Djasha clapped again. Jaghotai rushed Touraine immediately. Jaghotai spun and kicked, and Touraine batted the leg away with her fist. Another kick. This time, Touraine hopped sideways—but couldn't avoid Jaghotai's second rotation. Her boot clipped Touraine's temple, and Touraine dropped, stunned, to her knees.

Touraine expected someone to call foul, but no one did. Somehow, she had a feeling headshots weren't common in friendly sparring.

Djasha clapped twice and stepped between them. This time, she pointed to Jaghotai.

Touraine blinked the stars from her eyes. Jaghotai's smile was smug. Luca sat on the edge of the hide chair, arms wrapped tight around herself.

Fine. One more time.

"Are you surprised, daughter?" Jaghotai danced around Touraine on her toes.

There was a collective inhale from every person around the fires.

Certainly they couldn't all be surprised. Her uncle had put the pieces together, and Saïd, too. Maybe they never expected Jaghotai to acknowledge the traitor child, as good as a bastard—if they even had that concept here.

Touraine was surprised by many things in this scenario, but the Jackal's fighting skill wasn't one of them. She still remembered the feel of those boots in her gut.

Also not a surprise: the boot didn't feel any better against her head.

The pain in Touraine's torso kept her breaths shallow. She needed to watch out for those sky-falling boots. Balladaire hadn't prepared her for anything like those kicks. The dizzying swirl and shift from one angle of attack to the next—she had been caught off guard. She wouldn't be again.

"When I found out a conscript killed my brother, I swore I'd get revenge," Jaghotai said. Her dancing steps kept her out of reach. "I just didn't expect I'd be *this* unlucky."

Before she finished speaking, she closed the space between them and aimed a kick at Touraine's gut. Touraine spun away from the kick and landed a solid jab in the other woman's kidneys before she widened the space between them again.

"If you're unlucky, I must be sky-falling cursed." Touraine spat. "A mother like you."

Touraine kept circling, waiting, waiting for her opening. The other woman held her arms in a loose cage as she swayed to her own mental rhythm, left elbow protecting her body, her right hand up near her face. Jaghotai was slowing, and a beautiful bruise was already swelling on her face from an earlier hit.

Touraine ducked in, teasing Jaghotai into lashing out with her legs again. This time, the kick came and Touraine was ready. She grabbed the leg, spun Jaghotai off balance, and pounced on her. Somehow, with a deft twist of the hips, Jaghotai pinned Touraine under her instead.

Jaghotai laughed in Touraine's ear. "How long are you going to serve them, Mulāzim?" Her voice was gravelly as Touraine writhed in her grip.

Touraine managed to roll onto her side. The woman's breath was sour with food and drink. Sweat made their skin slick and hard to hold, but Jaghotai still had a fistful of Touraine's shirt.

"She doesn't care about you," Jaghotai hissed in Touraine's ear. "They don't see any of us as people. When she's sucked you hollow, she'll throw you away to rot, and find a new tool."

Past Jaghotai's shoulder, Touraine saw Luca watching from the edge of the circle, her pale hand covering her mouth. Jaghotai was wrong about one thing, at least. Touraine hoped. Luca had *danced* with her.

She wanted Jaghotai to be wrong about the rest, too.

"It's not just Balladaire who doesn't care," Touraine choked out. A quick knee to Jaghotai's crotch gave Touraine just enough space to wrap her legs around the other woman and squeeze her still. "I wouldn't be in this position if it weren't for you."

Jaghotai jerked above her but couldn't escape. She tried to punch, but Touraine locked her arms, too.

"I was a lonely kid," Touraine growled, "crying in the dark of some strangers' ship. Shouldn't *you* have protected me?"

There. There was the bitter truth that lay behind every sharp retort. Touraine didn't care that Jaghotai hadn't stopped Balladaire from taking her. Her life was better this way. She didn't care. She didn't. But if she didn't, why was she yelling it?

Touraine knew only that the words hit Jaghotai where she wanted them to. The other fighter roared and threw herself free of Touraine's hold.

Where the words woke something in Jaghotai, though, they broke something in Touraine, siphoning away her anger, her strength. She countered one, two, three of Jaghotai's strikes only just in time, and as she staggered from the third, the fourth put her on her knees, chest heaving.

Jaghotai looked down on her in contempt. "I would have raised you better than this."

In a rush, the rest of the world seemed to return. Djasha clapped again and pointed to Jaghotai, and the Qazāli cheered for their

champion as if they could dissipate the tension with sheer noise.
Touraine dragged herself to her feet.

Djasha held a cup in front of them, her smile tense.

Touraine stared at it while Jaghotai looked as if she'd been told to
swallow piss.

"Traditionally, you shake the hand of the opponent and share
a drink." Djasha leveled her gold eyes at both of them. She lowered
her voice for their ears alone and said through her still-smiling teeth,
"Now is not the time for petty mother-daughter bickering. You represent two nations trying to make peace, and if you don't fucking act
like it, I will kill you myself in your sleep." Her smile widened.

Touraine couldn't tell whether Djasha was joking, but Jaghotai
dangled her hand in front of Touraine's face.

She took Jaghotai's hand, tempted to twist it until the small bones
popped apart. Then they drank from the same cup. The audience
cheered. Then, her gaze unfocused, Touraine watched Jaghotai saun-
ter away to celebrate with the other dance-fighters.

"Are you all right?" Luca asked, touching her hand gently. Luca's
ring was cool against the heat of her skin.

Touraine struggled to focus on the princess. The ring of fires had
grown hostile. She was too close to Balladaire to be safe here. "Fine.
We should go back."

"I agree." Luca scanned the Qazāli without moving her head. "I am
walking a very tenuous edge of welcome."

"Are you? What did you do?" Touraine's voice was thick and
slurred, even to her own ears.

"Sky above, you really are drunk. By proxy, I took over their
country."

"Oh. Right."

They lingered a little longer, but gloating eyes watched them as they
clung to Djasha and Aranen's fire. Aranen held Djasha in her arms,
and they both smiled and laughed even though Djasha's face looked
drawn. So much joy.

When the knife flashed toward Luca, Touraine was slow. Maybe she was distracted by the two women's happiness; maybe she was just too drunk. Before coming to El-Wast, she'd never fought against assassinations—the Sands got to die in wide, bloody fields.

She jerkily pushed the knife away, but the blade caught Luca's skin before Touraine grabbed the enemy's wrist and tumbled over with them. Luca shouted in pain and the world spun. Sheer luck kept Touraine from getting herself stabbed before she disarmed them and flipped the person onto their back.

A woman looked up at her. No more struggling. She spat full in Touraine's face.

Touraine hauled her up just enough to slam her into the ground. The woman's head bounced once, and Touraine knew it hurt.

Gil had Luca. Safe. Lanquette and the other guards circled them.

"What is this?" Luca waved her forearm, and blood splattered the sand. She held the wound up to Djasha, who also stood. "I thought we were your guests." The cold menace was back in Luca's voice.

"You are." Djasha eyed the woman under Touraine with distaste. "Bring her to me."

Touraine dragged the woman to her feet and over to Djasha before she realized she was following another general's orders. A soldier's instinct beaten deep.

"Yasmine." Djasha said only the woman's name, but the tone of her voice said the rest. Fury. Unforgivable disappointment. Cantic had spoken to Touraine this way before her trial.

Luca broke from her protective circle to stand next to Touraine. Her eyes were as hard as Djasha's. She gestured to her guards. "I want her arrested immediately. Her and anyone working with her."

Touraine was stricken more by Yasmine's face. Anger worked her jaw, tightened it so the tendons showed. A rapid pulse jumped at her throat. Most surprising was the shine of unshed tears.

"We will punish our own criminals," Djasha snapped, without looking at Luca. There was a sense of finality that hushed even Gil's indignation on Luca's behalf.

"Yasmine," Djasha repeated.

Whatever passed between them was brief, but it must have satisfied Djasha's unspoken question.

"I'm sorry, my teacher," Yasmine said in Shālan. Finally, the would-be assassin bowed her head.

Then Djasha pulled a thin knife from her sleeve and stabbed under Yasmine's ribs and into her heart. Crimson leaked from her lips and covered Djasha's hand as she pushed harder to see the job done as quickly as possible.

At the flash of Djasha's blade, Touraine stumbled back into a crouch, belatedly dragging Luca with her. Behind them, steel and wood clattered and the soldiers swore, trying too late to raise their muskets. Lanquette and Gil both had their pistols trained on Djasha the Apostate. It took a long moment before any of them realized what had happened.

When the woman's clutching hands grew limp, Djasha lowered her to the ground. Djasha staggered as she pushed herself up, and Aranen caught her.

"I apologize," Djasha said, bowing her head to Luca. The bloody knife dripped into the sand. Touraine expected Luca to be as stunned as she was, but Luca always had the perfect calm. Unshakable. A wall of control.

Luca stepped out from behind Touraine and nodded at Djasha. "That will do."

That... will do? Suddenly, Touraine wasn't sure whose pawn she was—and which was the more dangerous answer. Cold chilled her stomach. What would happen if either woman found out she planned to break this peace before it began? Maybe it was better not to break it. To hold her tongue and wait for the Sands to take the brunt of it. A small sacrifice.

While Aranen tended to Luca's arm, Touraine scanned for Jaghotai among the rest of the silent Qazāli. She didn't find her.

After Gil had sharp words with the rickshaw driver, the man tossed back a drink and left his friends behind to gather the rickshaw. He helped Luca limp in; the princess barely let her right leg touch the ground.

He looked at Touraine dubiously. "You, too, in?"

"No." She shook her head, and the dizziness made her mind pulse with pain. She grunted.

"Ya, silly, get up there. I can carry. If not, he helps." He pointed to Gil and forced a smile.

Gil didn't smile back. "Get in," he barked.

"Yes, sir." Touraine climbed into the basket next to Luca. Their thighs touched. The adrenaline rush of the assassin and sparring had faded—the fight with Jaghotai already seemed ages ago—and she was drunk. No more tipsiness. No focused invincibility. It was the dark, useless part of the alcohol. A bayonet couldn't pierce the tension between her and Luca. And that had nothing on the tension they left behind them at the Qazāli fires, or a woman's dead body, or the princess's secret bargain that Touraine was regretting yet again.

At the house, Touraine helped Luca down while Gillett paid the driver. The driver nodded soberly after them before pulling his cart back into the night.

"What did you give him?" Luca asked, suspicious and frowning.

"More than enough."

Gil trailed them all the way to the door to Luca's chambers, where he and Luca shared a look Touraine couldn't read. Lanquette took his place outside the door. Touraine recognized the angry, affronted set of his shoulders—too stiff by half. She couldn't bring herself to care.

At the bedroom door, Luca winced. "Would you give me a hand?"

Adile jumped from her sleep just inside the room and rushed over, but Touraine waved her away. "I'll do it," she whispered to the maid.

Touraine helped Luca pull off her outer jacket. Luca's bare neck was smooth, barely kissed by Qazāl's overbearing sun. Touraine's heart beat faster in her chest. Maybe Luca sensed the change. She looked at Touraine skeptically.

"How drunk are you, Lieutenant?" Luca spoke low and very close, but also matter-of-factly.

Touraine wet her lips. "Not very," she lied. The execution had sobered her, as had the long ride, but the room still lurched if she turned too quickly.

"You had several cups and then fought your mother." Luca's brow creased.

Touraine focused on hanging the jacket. "I lost. That's why I don't drink." Jaghotai's words still slid in the back of her mind. *When she's sucked you hollow, she'll throw you away to rot.*

"Then you saved me."

The princess slouched to her good side. Luca's stiff court mask was still up, but Touraine noticed Luca wince as she shifted her weight to pull her inner coat off. Luca smelled like sweat and rose water.

"I'm sorry. I shouldn't have drunk—" Touraine's words fumbled over each other on their way out. The music had made everything vibrate. Dancing with Aranen and Luca. She would do the rest of it all again.

Luca turned around and her mask fell. She watched Touraine with naked apprehension, fear, guilt. "I'm sorry, Touraine. I...know you don't want to be here—"

Touraine couldn't smile at that. "General Cantic made it clear that it was this or nothing. I'm not ready to be nothing."

Only, there was irony in it: now she did want to be here, in this room, with Luca. She shouldn't have. The Sands would never forgive her—Pruett would never forgive her—for enjoying the other woman. And Jaghotai wouldn't, either, for fuck's sake. Not to mention the fragile alliance that had almost ended with a knife in Luca's ribs, the alliance that Touraine was still thinking of ending soon.

And yet there was something in this moment of honesty that Touraine wanted to touch, to hold on to. Sky above knew it probably wouldn't come again.

"Sit down." Touraine pointed toward the bed.

Luca furrowed her forehead but obeyed. Tension eased out of her face in relief. Touraine kicked off her own boots and sat down facing her. Gently, she pulled each of Luca's legs straight, watching her face for discomfort. Then she pulled off the high hose. Luca's face was guarded and suspicious.

She started with the princess's toes on her bad leg, the little muscles in Luca's foot. The tightness pulled her arch into a claw. The skin was clammy. Her mouth fell open in confusion, but a moment later she tilted her head back and sighed.

Still squeezing Luca's foot, Touraine slid her pant leg up enough to reach her calf and began rubbing there. Luca whimpered some at first, eyes closed. The muscles in the leg had knots hard as rock. Beneath the soft, pale hairs was a patchwork of scars as elaborate as her own.

Then Touraine put a hand on Luca's thigh, to warn her. Luca opened her eyes, swallowed, nodded.

"Just—careful, please."

Touraine worked from the crease of Luca's hip down to the knee, squeezing and kneading. Hard muscle-scars ran throughout Luca's entire thigh. At a nod from Luca, she pushed a little harder with her thumbs. A muscle-scar crackled under her hand.

"Fuck!" cried Luca, flinching away.

"I'm sorry—"

"No." Luca gritted her teeth. "It...feels...good, I think." She took a few short breaths before groaning again.

Touraine massaged until she started drowsing off and Luca's breath slowed. She meant to roll away and off the bed, but she was caught by the sight of her hand on Luca's thigh, the cloth of her pale, loose trousers a stark contrast with Touraine's dark skin. Then Luca's hand was on hers, stopping any movement.

"Thank you," Luca said.

She met the solemnity in Luca's face. She swallowed and nodded. She didn't have words. The drive to touch her was like the drive to dance. Natural. Unbidden.

So she leaned over, and the heir to the Balladairan throne ran a finger around the curve of her ear, making Touraine shiver. Her own hand trailing up Luca's leg, across her hip, to rest lightly on Luca's stomach. Touraine could feel the coiled tension beneath her fingers.

And then Luca smiled ruefully and shook her head. "I want you sober or not at all. But—" She covered Touraine's hand with her own again. "Would you...like to stay?" Luca said. Her voice was a little raw. "To sleep."

Luca's hand was soft and warm on top of hers. Touraine brushed her thumb across the other woman's knuckles, surprised at the sharp twinge of disappointment she felt and also surprised at the relief. Luca wasn't like the rest of Balladaire. She wouldn't take and take and take. When she took the throne, she would make Balladaire better, if anyone could. One day.

Touraine let herself entertain that hope while sudden exhaustion dragged her down into the pillows. Or maybe it was their lushness. And Luca settled on her chest.

"What do you want, Touraine?"

The question startled Touraine away from the brink of sleep.

"I don't want to be your servant anymore."

Fuck. Djasha was right. Shāl's holy water. A statement like that couldn't stand alone, though.

"Not Balladaire's. I want to be free. Paid a wage, not an allowance, and free to spend it at my leisure. Free to make my own home somewhere, free to... quit my post. If I wanted to."

Luca went rigid in her arms. "Do you want to quit your post?"

"No—not right now."

The seconds drew out before Luca relaxed again.

"It's done," Luca said. "All of it. We'll draw up your employment papers and discuss wages tomorrow."

"And for the Sands?" Touraine's heart stumbled in her chest.

"That, I can't do. I'm sorry. Not yet." The arm she had draped around Touraine's waist squeezed tightly, and she sounded like she meant it.

Touraine sank back into the too-soft pillows.

Everything she'd ever wanted, and nothing at all at the same time.

CHAPTER 24

CITIZENSHIP

Luca woke up surprisingly warm, her cheek sticky with sweat or saliva or both. She was more contorted than usual, too. It took a long time for her eyes and memory to reveal the cause of all the discomfort. As the curve of Touraine's hip under the blankets solidified, the warmth became suddenly much more pleasant.

Her leg, however, was in agony, and the small knife cut stung and itched. For a moment, she peevishly thought the rebels could have at least healed that. There would be no more sleep today.

The dark, heavy curtains blocked out the day, so she wasn't sure how late they had slept. She felt a pang of guilt for being grateful that the curtains would keep out not only the sun but any chance glances. For the first time, she wished she'd obeyed Gil's advice to stay upstairs. The mysterious broadside artist would have had a fucking festival with this.

In sleep, Touraine's scowl softened, but only just. Even in her sleep, her eyebrows knit and unknit.

I want to be free.

How little Luca knew her, for those words to be such a surprise. There would be time to change that. First, she would fix Touraine's papers. Employment papers, wage contracts—it was all at the compound.

She eased herself out of bed as gingerly as she could—to spare herself pain but also to let Touraine sleep.

Normally, Adile would have entered at the first hint of Luca stirring. The woman had ears like a hound. Her absence now was conspicuous.

"Luca?" Touraine's voice, befuddled with sleep.

Heat in her face again. "I'm here."

Awake, Touraine looked ill. Her eyes were rimmed with dark shadows—one temple was already purplish from where her mother had kicked her. She hunched over her body as if protecting herself.

"Sky above. You need a doctor."

Touraine held up a hand. "No. I'll be fine. I just...don't want to move again. Ever. You're up early."

"Am I? I was going to go to the compound and work on those papers for you today. You can stay here, if you'd like." Luca gestured awkwardly at the bed.

"No." Touraine sat up too quickly and winced. "I'll come with you."

Touraine didn't perk up during the carriage ride. She sat across from Luca, staring out of the small window.

Luca longed to reach across the space and touch her, but she was afraid the other woman was having second thoughts about the night before. She should ask—that was proper—but asking *Do you want me?* opened the door for Touraine to say, *Actually, no.* And right now, that terrified Luca.

So she kept her hands to herself and asked instead, "What's on your mind?"

"The rebels," Touraine answered shortly.

Heat rose in Luca's face. Of course. Everything else hadn't gone away. More was the pity. Still, she didn't understand Touraine's dour look.

"Despite everything that happened, I'm optimistic," Luca said. "Jaghotai seems rather temperamental, but Djasha—I like her." That was an understatement. The Apostate was unflinching, decisive. She never raised her voice, yet the Qazāli followed her lead. She did what needed to be done. Luca wanted that.

Touraine's lips quirked into a shadow of a smile before settling back into a frown.

"Are you sure about this?" she asked Luca.

"About what? An alliance?"

"About the guns." Touraine shifted her shoulders uneasily as she briefly met Luca's eyes. "What if they're lying and they turn on us?"

"As I said before. They would have to be idiots; the Apostate is no idiot. With one hundred guns, we still outnumber them ten to one. It will be fine."

"But if not. It's the Sands who'll have to pay for our gamble." Touraine said it softly, as if speaking to the window.

"I..." Luca tugged at the edges of her jacket. The stiff brocade covered a loose linen Qazāli shirt that went down to Luca's midthigh. She'd chosen the ensemble because it made temperature easy to regulate, but now the carriage felt stifling.

Unflinching. Decisive.

"I've made up my mind, Touraine. We'll go forward as planned." She added tentatively, hoping to offer Touraine something to hold on to, "And after this is over, I'll work on freeing them, too."

The tendons in Touraine's hard jaw bunched, and she nodded once. *I promise*, Luca added mentally.

They arrived at the compound shortly after that. In her office, Luca drew the papers up quickly, surprising herself with how adept she'd become at paperwork since taking on Cheminade's position. While Luca worked, Touraine's attention flicked from the papers to the door.

"You really don't look well, Touraine." Luca set down her pen. "Did she kick something—a rupture inside?"

"I've had worse. Maybe I'll just step out. Some air." She limped slightly as she left.

It was the second set of papers that was more difficult to manage. Papers of citizenship. She'd never had to make those. Nothing codified a Balladairan citizen's rights compared to those of a subject of the Balladairan Empire. A Balladairan citizen was just a citizen. A colonial subject was merely a subject. Maybe she could change that when she took the throne.

For now, all she could do was decree it so. And if it was that easy, maybe she *could* do it for the rest of the Sands. Then, of course, she would have to explain to Cantic why a large section of her troops had the freedom to desert. Luca could recall no precedent for turning so many... foreigners into natural citizens.

Touraine returned just as Luca finished, looking even sicker. "Are you ready to go back to the Quartier?"

Luca put down the rag she'd been wiping her pen with. "Sit down. I'm calling for a medic first."

The medic, however, agreed with Touraine after checking the soldier's eyes and breathing. A concussion didn't constitute "fine" in Luca's eyes, but the medic said she couldn't do anything but tell Touraine to rest.

"No sparring, no stress, sir." The medic eyed Touraine appreciatively, tapping her fingers on her satchel. "Honestly, I'm surprised you're up at all. Still be wallowing in bed if I was you, sir." She turned back to Luca. "Have her watched while she sleeps, Your Highness. That's when the real danger is."

Touraine shrugged when the medic left. "Told you. Not my first day on the field."

Luca intended to order Touraine right to bed and send Adile in with some soup or whatever helped injuries best, but there was a letter waiting for them when they arrived at the town house. A letter scrawled on a ragged piece of paper that looked as if it had been torn from a book. She opened it immediately, right in the foyer.

Touraine raised an eyebrow.

She didn't dare do anything but nod. *The rebels are ready to sign.* She called out to the coachman. "Keep the horses on the carriage!"

The jostling of the carriage made Touraine's head throb. Concussions always made her nauseated, but that wasn't the only reason her stomach was rolling in on itself. Beside her, Luca drummed her fingers excitedly on a knee, probably anticipating victory. Touraine had seen the scribbled note. Djasha and the others thought Luca was trustworthy enough to settle with. To start the long journey toward peace. To trade a few paltry guns for the healing magic that Balladaire had been after for decades.

Luca smiled shyly at her, eyes still crinkled with concern. She leaned her thigh into Touraine's. "I suppose we don't have to wait for me to give you these. Maybe they'll take away some of the sting?"

She handed Touraine two pieces of thick, soft, expensive paper. Touraine felt a lump rise in her throat and couldn't stop her eyes from watering.

"Just like that?" she whispered.

"Yes," Luca said simply.

The first square she unfolded looked almost like a receipt. Touraine followed the description of her position, assistant—not to the governor-general, but to Her Royal Highness Luca Ancier—all the way down to the monthly salary and yearly total at the bottom. Her mouth fell open. Next to her, Luca waited anxiously for her approval.

Touraine unfolded the other paper and skimmed it, too, landing finally on the last line, just above Luca's black wax seal. *I hereby approve the naturalization of Touraine, previously of the Balladairan Colonial Brigade, as an esteemed citizen of Balladaire.*

"Is it all right? I can add a surname if you want to use one. Whatever you like."

Touraine tried to swallow the lump in her throat down. "It's perfect. Thank you."

Earlier that day, while Luca drew up this perfect paperwork in their office on the compound, Touraine had taken the excuse to get some air. Maybe not so much get some air as fight with herself without Luca seeing every expression on her face. Cantic's office was just a door down. Touraine and Luca had come to work here so often, and each time Touraine debated whether to visit the general or not.

Touraine knocked on Cantic's beautiful, forest-themed door.

"Come in," came Cantic's muffled voice.

The general was alone, smoking a cigarette, the air clouded and smelling like smoke. It reminded Touraine of Pruett, and that, in turn, reminded Touraine why she was there. Touraine closed the door behind her.

"Good morning, General. Do you have a moment?"

The older woman's hair was out of its usual tail and hung messily around her shoulders. Cantic raked her empty hand through it before settling her gaze on Touraine. "You sound genteel, but you look like you've taken up pit fighting. What are you doing here?"

Touraine ducked her head, but it couldn't hide the bruising. "Her Highness is seeing to governor's paperwork," she lied.

"I see." Cantic took another drag from her cigarette and didn't look away. She was drawing Touraine out, waiting for her to fall into the silence. It worked.

"Sir, if you had to choose between the good of the empire and your soldiers, how would you?"

Cantic propped her elbows on the desk. Now she was listening.

"That's a complicated question, Touraine," she said in that same smoke-scratched voice Touraine knew from childhood. "When you get to where I am, the only thing that matters is the empire. I can't keep an accounting of individual soldiers. However, you don't get to where I am without your soldiers. Why do you ask?"

And Balladaire would be nowhere without its Sands.

"My old soldiers. We've fought for Qazāl a long time, sir. Our whole lives."

"Well, no, some of that time was spent educating you to a civilized standard." Cantic smiled. "We didn't send you out fighting at ten years old."

Touraine forced herself to smile back, but inside, she felt her resolve crumbling. Never mind. She would take her own citizenship, her own wages, and wait for Luca to give the Sands what they deserved. Those who survived the battles to come—and they would come. Touraine had no doubt that the rebels and their guns would only be the beginning. She wanted to have hope, like Luca did. She wanted peace to be around the corner.

A good leader was supposed to make contingency plans for her soldiers, and yet here she was. Letting them down. For a greater, eventual good.

"Touraine, let me offer you this piece of advice." Cantic stubbed the butt of her cigarette into a tin tray already littered with the corpses of previous smokes. She pushed up her sleeves, revealing age-spotted forearms still ropy with muscle. "You've always been an exceptional conscript. As I said before, I'm glad the princess found a use for you. It would have been a shame to lose your potential so early."

"Yes, sir?"

"You and I understand practical considerations of war. We've lived it. Bled for it. Her Highness is brilliant, but her hopes and ideas have no place here. They belong back home, in La Chaise. You can't plan a campaign based on the 'hope' that an enemy won't shoot you in the back. That's why it's best that the duke regent hold the throne a little longer. We'll get her ready, but I don't want you to fall into her pretty words. People like you and me have to remind people like her the difference between what's important and what's possible."

Touraine felt the blood rush from her face. She had been thinking the same thing. Even though it made her heart sick to think it, Cantic's words made sense. Luca's belief in an easily settled peace after a quick exchange of a few guns for the promise of magic, her assumption that she could control any and all of the consequences from this one deal, made her seem naive at best, arrogant at worst, drunk with self-confidence.

Touraine felt light-headed.

"Thank you, sir. That's good advice, sir." Touraine ducked her head again.

And then Touraine had hesitated, glancing back toward the closed door. Toward the room where Luca had been fervently planning on these hopes and dreams. "Sir?" she'd said. "There's just one more thing."

Clutching the papers—the freedom—Luca had given her as they trundled to the Old Medina to sign a deal with the rebels, Touraine wondered if she had just made a terrible mistake.

Luca would never forgive her if she found out what Touraine had just done. Touraine held the crisp documents tighter and consoled herself with one simple thought: when the rebels found out that Touraine had broken their deal, they wouldn't have the guns to fight back.

The Sands would be safe. For now.

CHAPTER 25

A FAMILY, BROKEN

Luca couldn't hide her triumph as she entered the empty smoking den on the Old Medina side of the Old Medina wall. Almost empty but for a table already set with water pipes and small cups of steaming mint tea. A table tall enough for chairs.

Djasha and Jaghotai already sat around it, along with a man Touraine had called the bookseller. Saïd. Jaghotai had a deep-purple bruise along one cheekbone, but even she exuded the same jovial air of a job well done. Of peace.

Touraine, who still looked ill, was the only one who didn't. At least her presence was a comfort. With a gentle hand at her back, Luca bade her sit before following. Saïd poured them both fresh cups of pale tea, thick with the smell of sugar. He also set new coals on a water pipe before handing the tube to Luca.

She pulled from it. The tobacco was laced with rose, and it couldn't have been sweeter.

"My people have a watch on the warehouses now. They've confirmed your security measures and the contents," Jaghotai said. She dipped her head begrudgingly, long dreadlocks dipping, too. She smoked from her own pipe. "She told the truth."

"So we have a deal?" Luca said from within a cloud of smoke. She pulled out her own copy of the treaty document she'd drawn up.

Jaghotai smoked and jerked her head at Djasha. "Your turn, witch."

The Brigāni slowly turned to look her companion dead in the eyes and held Jaghotai in her gaze for five eternal seconds. A look like that would have made Luca apologize, at the very least. Jaghotai only smirked around the tube at her lips.

"Don't take all day," Jaghotai said. "I want my new toys."

"We have a deal." Djasha pulled out the wax tube Luca had given her last night and uncurled the paper. "We'll send one priest to you when we have the weapons. They'll tell you everything you want to know."

"Very well." Luca pulled out a pen and a small bottle of ink. She laid both contracts out and copied the Apostate's amendment to her own.

When she finished and held the pen out for Djasha to sign, the Brigāni woman's golden eyes were hooded and unreadable. She clutched her robes to her, as if she were cold.

Luca leaned closer, felt herself falling toward the woman, toward a depth she knew was hidden just out of reach. She was a child again, peering over the edge of a boat into the lac de Solange to see what lay in the dark. There was no one here to pull her to safety if she tipped.

"Do you know our history, Your Highness?" Djasha asked finally.

"Of course. All the way back to Empress Djaya at least, but the... curse...on the other city leaves much of that occluded. The Blood and Wheat Treaty, signed by my great-great-great-grandmother after your empress went mad. The Technological Trade Agreement, signed by my great-great-grandfather, that got plumbing and irrigation for you and surgical techniques and vaccinations for us. Then—"

Djasha cocked her head. "And then your father, who dissolved all of it."

Luca's recitation had been rote, as if Djasha were one of her tutors and she were just a child. She was cut off like a child, too.

"And in any case, I'm not talking about your version of our history." Djasha paused. She closed her eyes, as if she were having a fainting spell.

Touraine and Jaghotai startled to their feet a second before the door burst open. Luca couldn't help it—she screamed, ducking under her arms.

It was only Gillett, his face pale in the dim light of the smoking den. The gauzy dyed curtains made the grim lines of his face stand out in green and red and blue.

"Your Highness, we need to leave now. Mesdames, monsieur—" Gil looked meaningfully at the rebel leaders. "See to your people. You're under attack."

"What have you done?" shouted Jaghotai. The Jackal was up and lunging for Luca before Gil's words had sunk in. Touraine tackled the woman in a clatter of low tables and stools, a howl of rage. Gil already had his pistol out, and it was pointed at Djasha.

"Into the carriage, Luca!" he said.

"But, Touraine—"

"Get... the fuck... out!" Touraine said from the ground, restraining the Jackal.

Luca obeyed.

"It wasn't her!" Touraine growled at Jaghotai, holding her down until Luca was safely out the door. More of a whimper, really. Sky-falling fuck, but she hurt. "She didn't plan this attack. It's Cantic."

"Then why the lucky coincidence?" Jaghotai shoved Touraine away.

"I don't know." Touraine heaved herself up and forced herself to meet Jaghotai's eyes, then Saïd's and Djasha's. "This isn't part of her plan."

Touraine hadn't expected Cantic to move so quickly. She had hoped for long enough, at least, to send a message to the rebels. To tell them they'd been compromised, if not by whom.

"I don't have time for your bootlicking shit." Jaghotai ran to the door. Guns fired and people screamed, only getting louder. And yet the streets near the Old Medina wall were emptying quickly, the local silence chilling in comparison.

Jaghotai ducked back in, coming to the same conclusion as Touraine. "Saïd, get Djasha to safety, then grab anyone caught in the cross fire. Take them there, too."

"Take them where?" Touraine asked. "Where's safety?"

Jaghotai frowned at her, her silence accusation enough. Then she shot back out into the chaos. Touraine trailed at a lope.

The storehouse where Luca had ordered the guns stored was on this side of the bridge, in El-Wast proper, down in the heart of the Old Medina. She knew without asking that Jaghotai was running to the heart of the Old Medina. Outside of the slums, it had the highest concentration of Qazāli.

Touraine knew the attack had to be Cantic. What she didn't understand was *why*. All Cantic was supposed to do was send soldiers to get the guns from the warehouse before the Qazāli could get them. She was supposed to contain the violence, not unleash it on the civilians. The guns had nothing to do with the rest of the Qazāli. Her stomach twisted. But now the rebels would blame Luca, and they would never come negotiate again.

The streets thickened with an exodus of civilians in flight the closer they got to the bazaar square. And then she saw the sparkle of sunlight on fixed bayonets, a sight as familiar as the scars on Pruett's back. Heard the pop-pop of musket fire, the soft thwack of the lead balls as they hit dirt and other, more vital places. On one side of the narrow street, a young man sprinted into one building, only to come out of the next—almost unnoticed. Farther down, the silhouette of a climber scaled to the top of a building—to escape across the rooftops? No: a sniper from another rooftop took aim, and the climber fell with a sickeningly stifled cry.

Jaghotai shook her head in answer to a question only she knew, and ducked left, down a side street.

"Where are you going?" Touraine shouted after her.

Jaghotai didn't answer, didn't even turn back.

Touraine looked back down the street. A door slammed shut. A Sand kicked it open. Not someone from her squad, but Touraine recognized him. The Qazāli couldn't wait for someone else to defend them from her mistake.

Then Touraine recognized a figure climbing up a building's outer ladder, a musket on her back. Pruett.

Touraine pushed forward. She sludged through the pulped remains of oranges and peppers and some plucked, raw bird. The smell of crushed food was everywhere.

As she yanked up her hood and its veil, a horse clopped closer. A nearby gunshot made Touraine and the fleeing Qazāli flinch. Ducking, she turned and saw Rogan, his pistol held high, his knees clenched around proud, tall Brigāni horse stock.

And then a fresh wave of Sands was upon them.

Her Sands.

The carriage bumped and jostled as quickly as the coachman could navigate the horses through the narrow roads. Luca looked back through the window, as if she could see her broken peace lying shattered on the road behind them.

"We have to go back for Touraine, Gil. They'll kill her."

The tight lines around Gil's mouth said everything. Touraine was on her own.

"We have to at least see what's happening." Luca reached over for the screen that separated them from the driver.

"Sit down, Luca!" barked Gil. "If you would be the queen, act like one."

Luca froze with her arm outstretched. When was the last time Gil had spoken to her like that? Slowly, she sat back. So be it.

"What do you know about this?" She used the cold scholar's voice, forcing herself into a detachment she didn't feel.

"I was hoping you would tell me." He regarded her with a grim, calculating expression. Part father, part advisor, all tightly checked anger. Or was it fear he held in? For once, she couldn't read the stiffness in posture or the pace of his breath. "I was under the impression negotiations were going well."

"So was I. You said it was Qazāli under attack?"

Gil nodded grimly. He twitched the curtain of the carriage window sharply to peek outside. "Blackcoats and Sands. Cantic isn't happy. What did the rebels do?"

The rebels hadn't done anything. Unless they were planning something and Cantic's own sources had gotten wind of it. Nothing would require this level of force, though. The rebels didn't even have weapons, not yet—no. Cantic couldn't know about the guns. Luca had kept that secret between her and Touraine alone. She hadn't even told Gil.

Perhaps it was time for him to know her dashed hopes in full.

Luca took a deep breath to steel herself. "They made a deal with me. Not just for workers' agreements and land ownership. They wanted guns. I said I would give them some if and only if they gave us magic."

Now she didn't even have the incriminating papers. They were lost in the smoking den for anyone to find and throw at her uncle's feet.

Gil's face was implacable. The concrete of it held no softness at all. "Luca. Luca, my dear, what have you done?"

So quickly, she was a desperate teenager again, trying to lift a sword too heavy for her strength. Mastering Qazāl was outside of her strength. The thought was a thorny vine curled tight around her chest and pricking at the thought that rested always at her core: that ruling Balladaire was also outside of her strength. And if that was true, then who was she?

She willed the cold walls to slam into place. She dug at the resentment she tried to keep buried and let it color her voice, too. Anger was better than this fear that made her want to hide in her rooms and weep. Anything was better than watching her work crumble around her.

"This would have worked, Gil," Luca whispered. She pressed the heels of her palms into her eyes. "Now they'll never trust me again."

"Your father—" He dropped the sentence with a sigh.

Always her father with him. With her, as well. Balladaire had no religion, but she worshipped a dead man whose image she held in her mind, distorted and blurry with time and bolstered with imagination. It wasn't just his image she had distorted and reinforced with her own visions.

Luca looked out the window again. They were in the New Medina, and the streets were almost peaceful, as if the Old Medina wall were a border between two nations. Perhaps it was. It was only almost peaceful, though, because the quiet was a brittle sort—the silence of held breaths and hands clasped over mouths.

She reached for the screen again, daring Gil to stop her. "To the compound, please. Not the Quartier." She closed the screen again and settled back. "I'm going to speak to the general."

Touraine had gotten top marks on the military written tests as a child in Balladaire. She knew the statutes and the drill formations. She'd learned unwritten rules, too, the instincts that kept you alive.

The first of the unwritten rules that she broke was feeling relief as Sands crowded that narrow street. Relief meant you'd let your guard down. But what else were you supposed to feel when the soldiers who'd had your back for years found you with your back against a wall?

And then Tibeau swung at her with his baton. She held her empty hand out.

"Tibeau! It's me, you fucker!" Pulled her scarf down. "There are civilians inside. Help me."

Blackcoats and Sands scattered up and down this street and the next, and finally—finally!—Jaghotai's fighters were cartwheeling in with their flying kicks to defend their own people.

Tibeau pulled back his next blow in confusion. "You're a rebel."

"Not exactly. We can talk later."

"This is treason."

She held his eyes, warm and brown. What she had done was treason, in so, so many ways.

There was a reason Djasha called Cantic the Blood General. What brutal efficiency. She would get the guns back, yes, and any rebels in the nearby districts. And any kid who looked likely to fight back in the next five years. She would terrorize innocent civilians into giving up their neighbors. Touraine knew better than most the bargains you could strike to spare what was dearest to you.

Maybe this would be enough. Cantic would crush the rebellion. Scare the whole colony into submission. Save Touraine's soldiers from one enemy, at least.

And yet here she was, fighting for the other side. *Because it wasn't supposed to happen like this*, she thought. *The civilians were supposed to be safe.* There wasn't supposed to be blood.

"I know," she said.

Tibeau nodded, his grin quick and troubled. "Treason it is."

"Excellent. Let's help."

The city was in chaos now. Young Qazāli had begun fighting back against the blackcoats and the Sands, some of them doing the peculiar kicking dance that Jaghotai had done the night before.

Touraine pointed to a pair of blackcoats dragging a kicking Qazāli man. They stole up behind them, Touraine with her knife and Tibeau with his baton. The thud on the blackcoat's skull made Touraine shudder, even as she knifed her own blackcoat in the ribs.

Then Tibeau seized up, yelling in pain. The choking gurgle of his blood in his mouth was louder than it had any right to be. The blood trickled into the shadow of his beard. So late in the day for him to be unshaven. Maybe he'd had the day off and he hadn't planned on leaving the guardhouse at all.

Touraine hit the new blackcoat in two steps, barreled him to the ground. His bayonet slid from Tibeau's guts, flung Tibeau's blood on her. His blood. Her knife underneath her, between her and the blackcoat, in his guts, now his blood. Tibeau behind her. She didn't look back. She had seen that glassy look too many times before.

Pruett, sprinting out of nowhere to his side, musket held like a quarterstaff in front of her, bayonet bloody. Whose blood?

Blood everywhere.

Touraine lurched over. "Is he—"

"Fuck off." Pruett shouldered her away, but Touraine shoved back and knelt beside him. Stupid to stop without cover, to sit here and wait to get shot in the head, to let him stop—

"Beau." Pruett pushed his hair back from his forehead, cupped his cheek. She flicked his eyelids up.

Pruett pulled his jacket open and swore. A great red slit in his belly. His slick, pale guts slopped over the edge. Split with a smell like shit. Touraine's gorge rose, and she focused back on his face. Sky above, please—

The next unwritten rule she broke was never stop moving. Even if you're hiding, you can't stay in one bunk forever. Someone will find you, catch you, kill you. A soldier dies when she stops. Never stop. Move. Move, Tibeau. Move.

"This is your sky-falling fault, you bastard." Pruett cast a furtive look around while she wrapped his jacket closed. Like it could stop the blood pulsing out of his stomach. It had already drenched their hands.

"No," Touraine said. "The blackcoat—"

Sky above and earth below. She looked up, swaying, suddenly unsteady.

Who should be watching her but Rogan, captain of the Balladairan Colonial Brigade, Rose Company, pistol leveled right at her. She didn't have time to draw a breath before the punch of the musket ball in her chest.

It hurt. Even more than the whips. Pain all over her chest and spreading down to her hip. Even the fabric of her clothes hurt.

She reached for Pruett. "Help me, will you?" she thought she said.

Pruett grabbed her hand. Touraine tried to pull herself steady. Instead, Pruett yanked her forward and slammed a baton into her jaw. Touraine collapsed, her knife clattering away.

She couldn't see anything through the pain. Her ears rang, but she heard Pruett whisper, "That's for Tibeau." Then she jabbed something into Touraine's body right where she'd been shot.

Touraine screamed in multiplied agony, wrenching her already twisted jaw.

"And that is for the fucking princess. Bastard."

And then Touraine felt nothing at all.

"General Cantic, what under the sky above is the meaning of this?"

Luca stormed into the general's office, flinging open the ornate door with all the force of the anger and the blame she had stoked in the carriage.

The room was stifling with the smell of tobacco smoke, and a haze clouded everything. The burst of air from Luca's entrance swirled it in visible eddies.

Cantic stood at the window in a frozen tableau of startled outrage. She had likely been lost in thought, perhaps even thought of the mess she'd brought on Luca's city. She held a cigarette, and her gold left sleeve shone as she held the cigarette halfway to her lips. Half-turned toward the door. Mouth wide to curse the intruder.

And then Cantic wound it all up tight to face Luca with a curt bow.

"What do you mean, Your Highness?" The other woman's voice was hoarse.

For more than two months, Luca had painstakingly built a relationship with the rebels in her colony. For more than two months, she had held hostilities at bay with gifts and an emissary with Qazāli blood. She had come within a hairbreadth of stopping them, maybe for good! And to getting the Shālan magic. This close to not one goal, but two—two! The two things Balladaire needed most from these colonies, and Luca would have been the one to get them. Cantic had ruined it.

"You would rather coat your hands in blood than accept that peace can come without your army. Is that it? Are you afraid you'll become old and obsolete if you're not murdering? Is that why you and Cheminade didn't get along, General?"

The general wasn't wearing her tricorne, and her hair was

pulled back tight in a white-streaked tail. Her dour expression was uncannily similar to the first broadside drawing that Luca had seen. The only thing missing was the ink-as-blood dripping down her fingers.

Cantic pinched out the burning flare of her cigarette with bare fingers.

"Your Highness, I only thought about your safety and that of the citizens. I had information—"

"My safety? You jeopardized my safety! I was in the city, my city, when your soldiers went marauding door-to-door and terrifying my subjects. What if someone had been able to capture me in retaliation?" As Jaghotai would have, if not for Touraine.

Cantic nodded acceptance. "I apologize, Your Highness. That's yet another reason I think it would be prudent if you remained in the Quartier."

"My guards would be enough if they didn't need to protect me in a war zone. Is this how you handled Masridān? The Brigāni? No wonder we have rebels. My father would be ashamed." Or maybe he wouldn't. The truth wasn't the point. She paused for a breath, half weighing the next words before throwing them out, as well. "I'm sure your family would be, too."

"Luca!" shouted Gil, so surprised that he overstepped his public bounds.

Luca waited for the words to have a visible effect on the other woman, but there was nothing. Somehow, she was immune to the worst Luca had to offer, and that added reckless heat to Luca's anger. She took a breath to try something else, but Cantic spoke softly, her voice the hush of waves on sand.

"Perhaps, Your Highness. Perhaps. But never forget—the blood on my hands coats yours as well. Everyone who has ever died at my order has died for the empire. For King Roland. For you. When you sit upon that throne and not before that, I will accept your judgment. Until then, I'm going to hold your colony together, because you don't seem to understand what that takes."

It was so silent that surely all of them had stopped breathing, not just Luca. Surely time had stopped. Surely the world had stopped spinning? Even Gil's lips hung parted beneath his gray mustache.

Cantic moved first. She went to rest her hands upon the desk, which was carved as immaculately as her door. Another forest scene, with rabbits and birds and deer. Easy to see even the leaves of the trees blowing in an unfelt wind. Easier than meeting Cantic's eyes when the general looked up from the desk's surface.

Luca thought of Guérin's daughter, an apprentice carpenter now, in La Chaise. Guérin would be home soon.

"Maybe you're right. I should just soak my hands in it, then." Then, feeling it like the confession of a crime, Luca added, "Like my father." She looked between Cantic and Gil. They stared back at her like statues, unblinking but ever judging, weighing her. Gil at least had a touch of warmth. She turned away from it.

"No, Your Highness." Cantic curled her hands so that her knuckles rested on the table instead. "I wade through the shit and the blood so that you don't have to. So that you can build something better from it. That is what our families wanted."

Luca looked away, to escape the words without lowering her head. Through the window, she saw the bare dirt of the compound.

What good could come from blood and shit? Harvests, of course, with proper seed. What Balladaire was known for. Was it necessary, though? Like this?

Then the general cocked her head. "But, Your Highness—I don't understand. What exactly did you plan to do when Lieuten—when Touraine told you the rebels had guns? Let them keep them? They would have used them on us, maybe even on the civilians to force our hand."

"When Touraine told me—" Luca caught herself in time. In the back of her mind, the scholar in her extrapolated beyond the general's words, finding motives and consequences all before the woman could find the breath to ask the question that the scholar already knew the answer to.

The call of orders and running boots outside of Cantic's office came back in a too-loud rush. She reached unconsciously toward her ears, as if blocking the sound would block the unwanted knowledge. Touraine had told. Touraine was the leak.

"I'm sorry, General. I didn't realize. I suppose that changes everything."

Touraine fluttered into consciousness and immediately wished she could go back under again. So much pain. She groaned.

Pain shattered through her jaw. She wanted to scream, but animal instinct kept her jaw immobile. Dislocated, if not broken entirely. A throaty growl escaped.

Someone was carrying her. She swayed with the rock of a litter. A jostle as they met stairs and then the cool darkness of a building.

"Unghh." Another ripple of pain and the too-loud grind of bone against bone. Broken, then.

"Ya, my teacher, ya, madame—" A man went on in Shālan. Touraine didn't understand the rest. People were speaking Shālan everywhere. She caught only snippets of the most basic—

"Here!"

"No, there!"

More jostling. More groaning. Through the fog in her brain, her nose was attacked by smoke and spices.

"Touraine?" Djasha.

Touraine blinked her sticky eyes open enough to see the Apostate leaning over her. Beyond Djasha, a tall ceiling swirled and made Touraine dizzy enough to close her eyes again. She wished she were dead. Or at least unconscious.

"Touraine, can you hear me?"

Touraine tried to croak, without moving her mouth, "Not...Luca."

"What?" Djasha switched to Shālan and yelled above the noise in the echoing hall.

There was only one place they could be. So many voices speaking over each other, shouting, chanting, praying in Shālan.

"Ya, Aranen!" Djasha's shout made Touraine wince.

Above her, Djasha had a sharp conversation. Touraine recognized a few words—*princess, it's necessary, Shāl*. Aranen's voice came into focus, frustrated and exhausted. Finally—

"Fine, okay. Touraine, we're going to move you one more time. We have—field doctors. They're—"

Touraine opened her eyes enough to see Djasha exchange a long look with her wife. Aranen's eyes were bloodshot and red rimmed.

"Touraine." Aranen put her hand on Touraine's sweaty forehead. "We're going to do surgery. Shāl willing, all will be well."

I don't need false hope, she tried to say, but her jaw—sky-falling fuck! Tibeau! She lurched, climbing the other woman's sleeve to sit up.

Aranen pushed her back down with surprising force—or maybe Touraine was just weak. Her torso was on fire. Her vision spun with dizziness.

"Ti...veau...Ti...veau!" Touraine's jaw wouldn't form his name, no matter how hard she tried. Her face was wet with tears.

More Shālan above her:

"What?"

"I don't know—come on."

Someone held her down as she tried to sit up again. Moved her. Laid her on a stone. Tibeau was lying in the dirt in the street. Cold seeped into her skin. Into her chest.

Aranen took a knife to a makeshift bandage of dirty fabric—no, it was Touraine's own clothing, her fine shirt from Luca thick with blood.

"Don't die on me now, Mulāzim," Aranen grumbled. She slipped between Balladairan and Shālan as she muttered and prepared for the surgery. Touraine couldn't help thinking about Guérin, missing a leg. The guard would never fight again. She flexed her own hands and feet in panic, just to make sure she still could.

"If my scheming wife says we need you, then we need you. But this war...this cruelty!" Aranen's voice broke, and she took a deep breath.

The room was heavy with incense and roasted meat.

The next time Aranen spoke, the quality of her voice had changed. Like a song, joined by a few other voices. Like the woman on the gallows. Then Aranen's fingers plunged into Touraine's wound and sent her back into blackness.

PART 3

REBELS

CHAPTER 26

A DUTY

When Touraine didn't return to the Quartier, Luca went to look for her at the main guardhouse. That other woman met her at the door. Lieutenant Pruett.

When Luca asked for Touraine, she wasn't prepared for the full-body visceral reaction the lieutenant gave, a great flinching, like something taut cut loose.

"Her body wasn't recovered." The lieutenant frowned, as if the news disappointed her. "Is there anything else? Your Highness?"

Luca caught herself on her cane, barely. "Her... body?"

The soldier edged back, warily. Suddenly, she was hesitant. "You didn't know."

"How?"

"She was shot."

"By whom? How do you know?"

Though the lieutenant's mouth spoke the words, Luca could barely comprehend their meaning.

"I saw her fall."

In the silence, Luca's mind conjured up the moment. A carefully aimed shot through the breast, and Touraine lying in the dirt, eyes open.

"Your Highness?"

"Nothing else, Lieutenant. You're dismissed."

Lieutenant Pruett bowed, just barely within propriety, stepped to the side, and stood at attention, staring into the middle distance. Luca wanted to slap her across the face. As she turned, however, Luca noticed the sheen on the other woman's eyes and recognized the tension in her jaw. It was the look of someone trying very hard to keep a neutral face. Luca couldn't help the irrational spike of jealousy—that Touraine should be hers alone to mourn. Stupid and cruel, of course, but then, everything inside her was twisting into something horrible.

"Your Highness." The bitterness in the other woman's voice made Luca slow to turn. The woman's gray-blue eyes clouded over with the kind of rage that would sink ships on the open ocean.

"Yes?"

"Is hers the only body that matters to you?" Lieutenant Pruett's breaking voice was the soft scrape of boots on sand. "Sky above knows we've got plenty more."

Luca gripped her cane until pain flared sharp. The words were ambiguous, but there was insult enough in referencing both a sexual relationship with Touraine and the neglect of her army. She stepped to the woman, raked her up and down with the calculated condescension she'd learned from years protecting herself in the noble court. Took in the crisp uniform, the slight shoulders, the sharp eyes. She stepped closer.

"That bitch abandoned you. If she was half the commander she needed to be, maybe you'd have fewer bodies to scrape off of the sand. She was a traitor, and I gave her a second chance. I will not be that kind again."

She fired her words to hit the woman's vitals, and judging by the lieutenant's bared snarl and clawed hands, she had aimed true. It was only later, after the rage had thawed, that Luca acknowledged the wound she'd given herself. She had trusted Touraine. And Cantic lauded the woman as a hero. It turned her stomach.

And yet she remembered the feeling of Touraine's arms around her at least one hundred heart-stopping times a day.

And at least one hundred times a day, rage tried to start her heart beating again. So far, it had failed.

A gentle knock on Luca's door cut through another nightmare. A variation on the theme she'd been sleeping to since the bazaar.

Smoke, choking the sky lit red—corpse fires. Her father riding into the flames, her mother dancing into them, and now Touraine falling into them. If she was lucky, she woke up then. If she wasn't lucky, the fires leapt from their pyres and devoured the city while she ran too slowly to escape. She would feel the heat on her back, teeth of fire nipping at her heels, until finally, burning, she woke.

She was not lucky last night.

Another knock. She shoved the sweat-soaked sheets aside, repulsed by their damp. Her hair was stringy against her face, and she pulled it up into a hasty bun. A scattering of correspondence she'd neglected for a week fell from her bedside table: a letter from Sabine, a note from Cantic, all of it ignored after opening.

"Come in," she said. Of course, that wasn't what came out. She hadn't spoken to anyone in days. It was a croak, an ugly whisper. She cleared her throat and kept it simple. "What?"

Gil opened the door. He took one look at her and came inside, closing the door behind him. "Luca."

She held a hand up. "Don't." She wanted no sympathy or wisdom or pity. It would only be lemon in the wounds.

He inhaled sharply, gray eyebrows bunched together, but he exhaled without a word. Smart man.

"What did you want?" Luca asked hoarsely as she wrapped up in her robe.

"You have a visitor."

She stopped with the robe half on. "No."

She couldn't. Even sitting upright was a heroic effort too great to bear. The thought of having to face someone else, someone who would want something from her that she couldn't give—a presentable royal, for example—made her want to collapse onto the floor. She held on to her changing screen.

"Luca, it's time to—"

"No, Gil."

"Luca, you have to—"

"I can't!" It came out a growl.

"Luca, it's Paul-Sebastien. He won't leave. He's been standing outside the town house for an hour."

Bastien. The man who shared her passion for research, for Shālan history. A minor noble, but well placed to help her cement important alliances with the other nobles in Qazāl. He knew the Qazāli and the Balladairans, understood the dance between the two factions of the city. He might even be able to help manage his father, the comte. A friend.

You still need them.

She finally met Gil's eyes. Something in her face made him step forward, but she held her hand up again.

"Invite him in," she muttered. "Give him tea, and let him know it will be a while."

Luca wouldn't have said she felt better after having washed and dressed, but she could certainly pretend to be a better version of herself. She had spent so much time trying to look like she wasn't grieving that she was surprised when she walked into her sitting room to see Bastien's splotchy, red-eyed face. His hair was brushed back into a queue, but his jacket looked slept in—or perhaps not slept in at all.

"They took her," he said, standing up from his seat as soon as Luca walked in.

Luca shook her head, searching for solid ground. The first "her" that came to mind was Touraine, because the rebels had taken her body. She blinked the thought away, but it was difficult to dredge up the compassion today to ask Bastien, "Who? Who took whom?"

"The sky-falling rebel bastards have Aliez. They have my sister!" At first, Bastien looked abashed at swearing in front of the princess, but he pushed on. "What are we doing about this?"

"We?" She blinked slowly at him. The edges of her temper crept back up, like bile.

Slowly, he backed himself away from his presumption, sitting back down in his seat and folding his hands across the table.

"Please, Luca. I'm asking as your friend. I'm asking as—as a potential ally. I know you want my father's support in your bid for the throne."

"I'm not making a bid for the throne. It is my throne."

He sat back and laced his fingers together over his lap. "Of course it is, and that's why you're sitting on it now."

Luca glared across the table at him, her fingers pressed against the smooth wood.

"I'm doing the best I can. General Cantic is doing all she can. What else do you want?"

You're lying. You haven't been doing the best at anything but moping like a jilted lover.

"I don't know," he said. The bitter taunt was gone from his voice, replaced with desperation. "You're my queen. I need you to do something."

He laid his bait well.

To ignore it was to ignore everything she'd been trying to prove— to her uncle, to the Balladairans. To herself. The throne was hers, and so was the weight of the crown. Already it threatened to bow her shoulders.

Without Touraine, she'd lost her emissary to the rebels. No one to explain to the rebels that she had nothing to do with the assault on the city. No one to explain to Luca why they had taken Balladairan citizens. Oh, yes. That was in Cantic's note. Aliez must have been one of them.

That was only one front. A general who sees only one battlefront will find herself hamstrung by the end of the war. Was that from *The Rule of Rule*, too? She couldn't remember.

Beau-Sang and the Balladairans in Qazāl represented the other front. And to keep that relationship from decaying any more than it already had—

"Bastien." She put her hand on his. "Bastien? My soldiers will find her. I promise. I'll personally oversee it."

He turned his hand over to squeeze hers. "Thank you, Your Highness." He ducked his head as if to kiss her knuckles but hesitated awkwardly, bumbling. The knot of his throat bobbed with emotion. "My father will be grateful. Aliez is his jewel." He gave a rueful smile.

Of course she was.

"Also... I'm sorry about your soldier." He squeezed her hand again.

She flinched away. His condolences sounded surprisingly sincere. It was an extra twist of the knife that made her lungs hitch, showing her a new depth to this pain, to the crushing loss of something she'd only just realized she had. And he could see it, her nakedness. She slammed down her court mask and nodded curtly. He reached his hand out again for hers but stopped halfway. He bowed instead and allowed himself to be led away.

She stared hard at her hand where he'd held it, the touch echoing. She rubbed her fingers together, as if Bastien's hand had left a tangible film. A stack of letters she'd left unanswered this week waited for her. One of them from Cantic. She called for pen and paper.

"Who are you writing to?" Gil asked, sliding into Bastien's seat.

"Cantic. And Beau-Sang. I'm going to let Cantic disband the Qazāli magistrates."

"You're sure?"

"Yes." *No.* "They can't be trusted. None of them can." The part of her that wanted—hoped—for Qazāli allies rebelled at this. *If they wanted allies, they would behave better.* The part of her that would be queen began to write.

"You don't want to give Beau-Sang too much rope, Luca."

"I know, but I think I need him," Luca told Gil, who sat in

Touraine's chair by the échecs table while Luca paced. The movement hurt her hip, but it was a reassuring sort of pain, like biting one's lips or digging one's fingernails into the palms or bashing one's head into a wall. It distracted her from another, different pain that blossomed when she looked quickly past Gil and he became another person in that chair.

After Bastien's visit a few days ago, Luca had written to Cantic about disbanding the Qazāli magistrates. She just needed to figure out how to replace them. She was governor-general; consolidating power under herself was the obvious choice. Share a little power, though, and you'll have stronger allies. The rebels weren't her allies. Instead of Bastien's tear-streaked face in her mind, she saw his father's, sly under the ruddy blustering.

Before Gil could reply, a blackcoat knocked outside.

"Come in," she called.

"Your Highness." The soldier bowed after he was let in. "This was labeled for you, from the main guardhouse, but I think Guard Captain Gillett should—" The soldier glanced at Gil.

Luca snatched the box. It was plain, with a letter affixed. She opened the letter first.

The paper shook as she read. For some reason, she had been hoping for something good, a gift, even if she didn't deserve one. Anything but a ransom note. It ended with a list of names, and she recognized them from the families whose complaints were scribbled on expensive paper on her desk. Aliez LeRoche's name included.

"Your Highness?" Gil asked.

"They're going to torture one Balladairan for every day we remain in Qazāl." Her voice trembled like the paper.

Gillett crossed the room and grabbed the box away from her. He barely opened the lid before grimacing. The smell of decaying flesh curled through the room and hung like a dead man. Luca retched.

Gil shoved the box back at the soldier, whose eyes darted between her and Gil. "Get rid of that and keep quiet, or I'll put your balls in a box, too."

"Let me see." Luca held out a hand. Gil hesitated. It took one long breath before he proffered it to her. She bit the insides of her cheeks to keep the bile down.

A gray finger, dried brown at the end, a nub of bone sticking out. Blood crusted the grooves in the skin. It curled stiff, beckoning her close. Tufts of fair hair sprouted from the thick knuckles. She exhaled sharply as she handed it back to Gil, trying to blow the stench away from her before she inhaled again. Not Aliez's delicate hand.

"I have to fix this," Luca said numbly after the blackcoat left. She stood in the middle of the room, hand open as if still holding the box. She squinted up at Gil from behind her spectacles and then looked back down at the paper, hoping the words would arrange themselves into a different story.

He looked grim. "You're thinking Beau-Sang again."

"No," she lied quickly. Luca rubbed her forehead with the heel of her palm. There was nothing useful in *The Rule of Rule* on the topic of ransom and the torture of subjects. Nothing useful to her, anyway. If they were valuable, it said, of course they should be rescued—high profile, uniquely skilled, etc. Lower workers, however—expendable.

Was it responsible for her to disagree with that? If complete war was at stake, couldn't she sacrifice a few laborers, even merchants? Aliez was nobility, but her brother was still free.

Beau-Sang had clout in this city. He had clout in La Chaise, as well. He and his son knew El-Wast and its people better than she did.

Luca stabbed her cane into the rug, gouging the ornate diamond-shaped weave. She swallowed.

"Put him in charge and you'll never bring the Qazāli back to your side."

"I know! I know that." She flushed and paced again. "I know you're a sympathizer, Gillett. Sky above and earth below, even I sympathize with them. I've eaten their food; I've danced with them. Only, I made one mistake." She had trusted Touraine. She had wanted her. "Am I supposed to send Balladairans to slaughter for it?"

The old soldier sucked in his cheeks, then puffed them back out.

"You're the queen of Balladaire first, Luca. Even I can't argue with that." Shaking his head, he added, "I didn't expect the rebel council to resort to this method."

"I didn't, either. It's probably the Jackal." Luca dug her cane in again, feeling the satisfying give as the rug's threads split.

Fuck Touraine. This was all her fault. And Luca should have known better.

"I'm not even queen yet. That's part of the problem. If I could do whatever I wanted—"

"May I be frank, Luca?" Gil never interrupted her, and he asked permission only when he was irritated.

"By all means." She braced herself.

"If you were queen and had all the power of the realm to do with this country what you will, would you leave Qazāl?"

Luca scoffed. "That would be impossible. Our commerce is too finely wedded. They depend on us for wood and metalwork, and we depend on their goods to sell in the north."

Gil nodded impatiently. "Yes, but if it were possible, would you?"

Luca frowned down at the carpet. There was so much she still wanted to know. An entire library she hadn't searched. "They have the magic here. We could still find a cure for the Withering."

The plague sounded like a thin excuse, even to her. Her breath escaped in a whistle as she understood Gil's insinuations. If she was unwilling to leave, there would be no peace short of physically crushing the rebellion. Otherwise, the Jackal and the Apostate and everyone else would fight Balladaire, fight her until they had what they wanted or died for it.

She would have to kill them all or scare them so badly they surrendered.

"What do you think my father would have done?"

Gil scrubbed his cheeks. "I'm sure my memory colors him in rose."

As much as he loved the king, Gil wasn't prepared to say her father would have made the right decision. Whatever that meant.

She wanted her throne, and to get it, she needed to end the rebellion.

To do that, she needed power. Maybe it could have come from the Qazāli and their magic, but that would never happen now. So she needed her people's power. The nobles' support. The army's support. And none of them would support her while citizens were held hostage and the princess was a Sand lover.

"I'll send for Beau-Sang," she said, more to herself than Gil.

Gillett scrubbed wearily at the scruffy beard growing on his cheeks. "You're sure?"

"I instated a curfew. I've disbanded the magistrate. There's just the governor-general's position now."

It was time to shift that mantle to someone else so she could wear the one she was meant to.

She turned back to the ransom note. There was a brown stain on the bottom. She threw the letter onto the table and went to a basin to wash her hands.

The comte de Beau-Sang strode into Luca's office—the governor-general's office—as if it were a room in his own home. Luca bristled and sat up straighter. Beau-Sang bowed quickly but carefully within the boundaries of propriety. He spared a sharp glance for Gil and Lan-quette and a more disparaging look at Cheminade's effects covered in their thin layer of dust.

"Your Highness," he said smoothly.

The sandstone walls had come from Beau-Sang's own quarries. Building this compound alone had probably lined his pockets thick with the crown's money. Maybe Luca could promise him more arrangements like that to secure his cooperation.

Luca acknowledged his bow with a nod. She retained some of her court aloofness, but she diminished her casual imperiousness, offering him a slight smile. She didn't need her spectacles to see the smug look on his face, but they made her look more earnest. Cantic appreciated strength and decisiveness; Beau-Sang would be more malleable if he thought Luca was warming up to him.

"I have a proposal for you," she started.

This was her best choice. Without Touraine, she didn't even have an emissary she could trust. Whatever friendship they had kindled with the rebels over the last few months was an illusion. Friends did not send human pieces carved like roast pigs, nor threaten to torture innocents to coerce each other. Of course she had no other option.

"When we spoke at Lord Governor Cheminade's dinner, you had several ideas for the appropriate governance of the peoples here."

"Yes, Your Highness, of course."

"I was overhopeful and thus overlenient on the Qazāli when I arrived." She rubbed her eyes under her glasses.

Her calculations were simple.

She would give Beau-Sang a touch of power that answered to her alone. He would tighten her grip on Qazāl by working with Cantic to root out the rebels, and he would assure the nobles and merchants kept to the new workers' laws (*those* agreements at least, were still right; they would slow the Qazāli's need for rebellion—Luca knew it).

And if necessary—she hoped it wouldn't be necessary—this would lead to support for the throne, *if* her uncle regent refused to cede it. Whether Luca failed or didn't fail in the colony. The throne was hers. The more of the nobility on her side, with their money and regional militia and influence in the cities on and off Balladairan soil, the less likely she and her uncle would come to bloodshed over her rightful position.

It was a small trade.

The correct application of a tool results in its efficiency, avoiding waste.

"I've been looking for a suitable successor to the late Lord Governor Cheminade, and I would like to appoint you."

His reaction was immediate and calculated. First, eyes wide in modest shock before his brows lowered in determination. Luca could have seen his every change of expression with her eyes closed. His courtly mask was so tight that not even a hint of concern or grief for his missing daughter escaped onto his face. If there was any.

"I would be honored, Your Highness, to give the Qazāli a steady guiding hand."

Luca held in a snort. He was overplaying the role; they both knew it. She played hers in turn, nodding and leaning forward warmly. She was gambling, to surrender this power to him, but that was what it meant to be queen. Not always to be strong and rigid—like that, she would snap. To bend, to entice and trap.

Like Touraine made traps.

Like échecs, writ large.

"You would, of course, report directly to me. All orders would come from me. This is governmental, not military."

"Of course, Your Highness."

"I will make the announcement tomorrow in the bazaar, so that they remember the power we have and why we're using it. I'll send a carriage for you."

When he left, Luca held herself stiff, her eager smile brittle.

"Like siccing a rabid dog on the hunt," Gil murmured. "Watch yourself, lest it bite you, too."

Luca frowned. "I know. So stay close in case I need to put him down."

CHAPTER 27

WAKING UP

Touraine stared at the low ceiling, sweaty with nightmare, clenching her blanket and her jaw. Her jaw. She couldn't pry it open. Rest. *Let it rest.* A candle flickered, giving the clay-white walls a blend of yellow and shadow. It wasn't the room she shared with Lanquette. The room next to Luca's. The dyed blanket scratching over her bare skin wasn't hers.

A scar puckered her middle, smooth and shining like brown candle wax that had melted and cooled again. Her stomach lurched. She'd never seen a wound heal like this.

Nearby, people spoke in hushed voices. An earthy, spicy smell wafted to her, and her belly cramped for it. She scanned for her clothing and found the room was full of people-shaped lumps on pallets under thin blankets.

Her clothes weren't there. She found a pair of loose trousers and one of those hooded vests instead and began to dress. There was enough slack in the trousers' drawstring that she had to loop the string around her waist one full go before knotting it. Her only belongings were what had been in her pockets: a dirty handkerchief, a few sovereigns, a letter of writ to Luca's account, and the pass with Luca's seal. She shoved those in her new pockets.

Someone had also retrieved her knife. Touraine traced the leaves on the handle with her thumb. Like Luca, it had grown familiar over the last couple of months. She hesitated. Qazāli weren't allowed to carry weapons in the city. If she had it, she'd draw attention to herself. The wrong kind. She didn't want to leave it behind, though. She buckled it on.

Finally, she twisted to examine herself. A white jolt of pain shot from her waist to her toes. She doubled over, gasping, trying to compress whatever she had stretched too far. Whatever they had done wasn't finished healing.

"Lodgings not to your liking, Mulāzim?"

Aranen stood in the doorway. Touraine gingerly pulled the sleeveless shirt over her head.

"Where am I? How long?"

"The temple. You've been sleeping for almost two weeks."

Two weeks. She scrubbed her head with her hands. The stiff bristles were dry and had started to curl. No wonder she was starving.

"I need to go back," Touraine said. "You shouldn't have brought me here."

"You want to go back to the Balladairans so they can try to kill you again?" Aranen spoke slowly, as if she were talking to a really stupid rock.

Memory came back to Touraine in trickles, so she dammed the flow again. She would be stupider than a whole bag of rocks to go back to that.

How stupid would she have to be to stay with the rebellion she'd betrayed?

"Where's everyone else? Djasha?" *Jaghotai?*

Aranen's face tightened, and she glanced across from Touraine. Another blanket-covered figure. As her eyes adjusted, Touraine recognized Djasha. The woman's cheeks were gaunt, her dark skin pallid, even accounting for the poor lighting.

"Is she—"

"She's fine," Aranen said sharply. "But running around after you is not helping her."

Touraine had actually been wondering if Djasha was contagious. Her face burned.

"Can't you just…" Touraine gestured at her own body.

For a second, the doctor—the *healer*—let worry breach her scowl. "We don't know. I've tried. Whatever I do is temporary before it comes back, sometimes worse than before. Sometimes it's dormant for months. Sometimes weeks."

Touraine had seen Djasha over the last month. Whatever illness this was, it wasn't dormant.

Aranen sniffed sharply. "What are your plans now, Mulāzim? Are you finally with these fools?"

"Am I being held hostage, or can I leave?"

Aranen made a noise of disgust. Touraine didn't blame her. She sounded ungrateful and ungracious in her own ears. She couldn't stay. This was too much.

"This way. Close your eyes."

She dragged Touraine by the wrist until the heat of the sun warmed Touraine's face. A door slammed shut with an echo.

Touraine opened her eyes and was blinded. The sun turned the white domes of the temple into mirrors that radiated light on everything around the massive building. A god might actually be proud of something like that. A god whose magic could keep her alive, pull her back together.

She hadn't meant to sound ungrateful. She didn't want to be dead. If magic is what kept her here, breathing underneath the sun, what did it matter? If she'd been given the choice, she wouldn't have said no. All the same. She was glad she hadn't had to make the choice.

Still, all she had left was the Sands. Maybe. She needed to see Pruett. She needed to apologize. She needed to be with them.

She pulled her hood up. The Grand Temple was in the Old Medina, but the massive fountain in front of it made the area a quiet plaza. At least, there was the illusion of quiet. She could still hear the roll of carts and shouts from vendors on the next streets over. In her head, though, she heard gunshots over it all. She shook her head and reoriented herself toward the guardhouse.

*   *   *

Touraine liked the heat on her bare arms, but the bright light was merciless. That wasn't why she kept her hood pulled low over her forehead, though; the height of the buildings and the narrowness of the streets kept the sun off unless she turned into a square with a miniature bazaar.

No one recognized her as the treacherous Balladairan dog she was. With her rich imitation-Qazāli clothing from Luca bloodstained and ripped beyond repair, there was nothing to mark her as the villain but the knife at her hip.

Already, the city moved on. Like soldiers. This wasn't callousness. It was necessity. You marched on. If you didn't, you were admitting to the enemy that you'd been injured. Wounds had to be licked in private, closed off inside temple walls.

Clothes, shopping, even poets chanting their verses in the streets. Cats wove around her ankles; dogs napped in alleys, tongues lolling. Everything to distract her from the meandering journey. What did she expect from Pruett, anyway? They had always been a team. Pruett cleaned her cuts, and Touraine reloaded Pru's gun (when the Sands were permitted them). Then they docked in Qazāl, and things went wrong one after another. Pruett couldn't have stopped any of that. Throw Luca in the mix and it was doomed.

If she went back to Luca, she would be safe again. She would have her fancy kit back and not have to look for Rogan over her shoulder, unless—until—Luca learned that Touraine had betrayed her. Cantic, though. The general would take her back. Touraine had proven herself loyal to the army, if not the princess herself. That had to count for something in Cantic's eyes.

She slowed as she reached the sector claimed by the Balladairan soldiers. Here, a sharp-boned Qazāli man swept the refuse—human and non—away with palm leaves tied into a bunch. The guardhouse rose innocuously, looking like another yellow-gray clay home—if every home had soldiers posted at its door, on its roof, and at the corners of its street. Any Qazāli passing through did so on the other side of the street.

Rogan would be here, too, or nearby. Horse-fucking bastard. She ducked her head like someone avoiding the glare of the sun and circled around to the alley behind the guardhouse complex.

As Touraine passed the back of the building, still thinking about her approach, she heard a musket click, ready to fire. She spun and crouched, then cringed in pain.

"No Qazāli here. Count of five until I shoot you."

Touraine's cold wash of fear became relief, then fear all over again. Pruett.

She raised her hands slowly, pulled down her hood, and looked up. She kept her hands in the air. The musket barrel held steady on her, and Pruett wouldn't miss from this distance. Touraine swallowed, and her jaw ached in memory.

Five long seconds before Pruett lowered the gun. Touraine couldn't see her expression well, but the silence was telling.

"Stay there." Pruett vanished.

Several minutes later, she reappeared in the alley. "Pull your veil up," she said before jerking Touraine by the arm. Pruett dragged her around several corners until they were in a dead-end, L-shaped alley. No one could see them from the street, and the walls of the buildings around them cooled them with shade.

Pruett pulled Touraine around so that Touraine's back was to the alley's mouth, and then she tore Touraine's veil down again.

For seconds, Pruett blinked at her until finally saying, "What the sky-falling fuck?" Dark shadows marked her eyes, and her cheeks were pink with sun. The lines around her eyes deepened as she squinted, searching for the miracle. "You...I...watched you...Sky a-fucking-bove."

"They did it. The magic. To me." Touraine pulled at the shirt covering her healed torso.

A small bit of sun lanced into the alley to mock Touraine, shining on Pruett's new lieutenant pins, the wheat fronds polished to a gleam.

The alley smelled like stale piss and stale sex. Not quite stale enough, either of them.

"Why did you bring me here?" Touraine gagged.

"No one will come looking for me if they think I went to get laid, but whorehouses are expensive and this alley is almost as private. It's the best we've got right now, so start talking." She rested her head against the wall and looked down her nose at Touraine. "I'd hoped you were dead."

"I'm sorry, Pru."

Pruett looked away. "Killing my best friend's not a shit fucking thing you can apologize for."

"He's my best friend, too. I didn't want him to get hurt. It was an accident." Touraine wanted to put her hand up to Pruett's jaw, like she had countless times before, but she kept it against the wall. "I didn't want to hurt you, either. None of you. You're my soldiers. I was just trying to help—"

"Your soldiers? We were your family, Touraine. And you betrayed us—for who? For the princess? For some sand flea–bitten beggars? What do you know of them? What do they know of you that we don't?"

Flecks of Pruett's spit landed on Touraine's cheek.

"I—"

"Have they seen you bleed? Have they seen you kill anyone? Does she know your voice when you're scared? Could she pick your laugh out of a crowd?"

Touraine sagged under the weight of the accusation. Between Jaghotai and Djasha and Luca . . . it was laughable that any woman could come close to sharing what Touraine had shared with Pruett and the other Sands. No one but a Sand could understand where she came from.

She almost told Pruett about Jaghotai. Almost. What would she have said? *I met my mother. We hate each other. She's tried to kill me. She hates all of us. I don't want her, but she's here. She's real.*

The disgust in the suck of Pruett's cheeks was too strong. Pruett had made no secret of what she felt about her own family, wherever they were, somewhere in the east of the broken Shālan Empire. She'd been sold by her own parents, and she was smart enough to know it, even as a kid. She didn't like Balladaire, but she didn't have high hopes about home like Tibeau did. Touraine understood that much. It wasn't the sort of thing you forgave. Touraine and Jaghotai would probably murder each other if Touraine didn't leave, but at least Jaghotai seemed almost as angry at the Balladairans for taking the Sands as she was that Touraine had come back.

Instead, throat thick, Touraine asked, "How is everyone?" She couldn't ask the real question: *Does everyone hate me?*

"If you gave a ripe shit, you'd never have left."

"I left for you." Desperately, grasping. "I betrayed her and the rebels for you." She had risked her life, an entire city, for them. For Pruett.

The other woman cocked her head sharply. "What do you mean?"

Touraine swallowed and shook her head. To tell the truth would mean confessing that her gamble had cost her Tibeau, as well.

"I'm here now. I am."

"No. What the fuck do you mean?" Pruett yanked her roughly by the shirt.

Touraine looked down at Pruett's fist clutching rough linen. The conviction that had kept her going up to this point had died with Tibeau. All she wanted to do was sink into Pruett's arms like she had three months ago.

"I told Cantic that the rebels had guns," Touraine mumbled. "Luca wanted peace; the rebels wanted peace."

Pruett's eyebrows knit together, and her lip curled in confusion. "What? If they wanted peace, what the sky-falling fuck happened?"

"I sold them out to Cantic." Touraine hung her head. Her throat tightened, and the words were hard to get out. "Luca was going to give them guns, and then...that's what you would have been up against. I couldn't let that happen."

Pruett's hands went slack on Touraine's shirt. Horrified? Surprised? Her wide eyes were bloodshot, supported by sleepless bruises underneath. "You can't be sky-falling serious."

"Why not? You just said it—neither side gives a sky-falling shit about us."

Pruett exhaled sharply through her nose and shook her head. "So I did. Anylight, your princess is just as Balladairan as the rest of them. So the peace probably wasn't going to last."

Touraine didn't like the new, wary way Pruett watched her. "What do you mean?"

"We have the honor of enforcing your lover's new curfew laws."

"They must be Cantic's. Luca loves her grand ideas of noble rule too much." Oh. An accidental slip of intimacy.

Pruett's face darkened. "You don't know her well, then."

"And you do?"

"She announced it herself. Looked none too pleased with your rebel friends. Do they know what you've done?"

Why would Luca be angry with the Qazāli? The Balladairans had started this and Luca knew it. Unless she thought a rebel had leaked the information about the guns. And the rebels... Touraine hoped that they thought Luca was behind the betrayal. If the truth got out, she was dead.

Pruett took her silence with a knowing nod. "Seems like you made a good play. Time for me to get back." She tipped her field cap to Touraine and brushed past.

Touraine's heart pounded in her chest. Her last tether slipped out of her hands. She grabbed frantically for it. "You could have killed me now, if you hated me that much."

"Well, I fucking didn't, did I?" Pruett's voice broke a little before the edge came back. "You sank too low, Tour. If you want to help us, leave us alone. It's hard enough to live with the Balladairans, and it only gets harder when the rebels get bolder. We have to show the officers we aren't sympathizers."

"So come with me. We'll run—"

"You mean desert. And die like Mallorie? Like Tibeau? All of us?"

"Just you and me." Touraine hated herself for even saying the words, but she hated the idea of being alone even more. She finished half-heartedly, her voice cracking: "Steal a couple guns—"

"Stop, Tour. Just stop." Pruett sighed and her body sagged. "Sky above. You almost sound like Beau. Give you one last bit of advice, Lieutenant."

Touraine clung to the way Pruett caressed her old rank with the same wry lilt as before. No, not the same. Not quite.

"Everyone else thinks you're dead. The officers, the princess, the Sands. Keep it that way. Get the fuck out of here."

And then Pruett walked off, hands in her pockets, baton jostling with her hip. She didn't look back at Touraine once.

CHAPTER 28

A LINE IN THE SAND

Pruett was right. As usual.

And it hurt. As usual.

As she bought two big water bags with a whole sovereign, Touraine told herself she wasn't running away. She was free now. She had cut her ties to both Balladaire and Qazāl in one brilliant moment, and she was going to take advantage of that.

Never mind that she'd blown her life apart with canister shot—shredded it into bloody tatters. Never mind that she would never go back to Balladaire, not to thick trees and snow, not to the compounds where she'd grown up.

She hated herself for missing the thunderstorms and the gray stone walls. They hadn't felt like a prison. She hated herself for thinking—hoping, trusting—that Balladaire would reward her one day, that Balladaire was ultimately *fair*. How she had absorbed the cruelties, made excuses for them, thinking if she were just a better soldier, more Balladairan than not...Tibeau had been right the whole time, and now he was dead.

She wanted to scream. She wanted to lie down in the desert and let whatever rabid beasts lived there take what they wanted of her.

Instead, she put one foot in front of the other.

None of her life in Balladaire—none of her life for Balladaire—had been hers. It hadn't really been a life. She could find a life somewhere else.

It was better for her to be dead to Balladaire, and she didn't know a star-blinded shit about the Qazāli. A night of dancing, barely enough of the language to get herself to a toilet.

So she would head south. There were people who lived in the mountains, out of Balladaire's reach and Qazāl's. It was as good a place as any to start over. She bought another scarf on the way out and wrapped it around her face. Better to be safe in anonymity. Hit the southern road and hail a ride with one of the caravans to the next town, where she would stock up on more provisions. For now, all she needed was good boots and old calluses, and she still had both of those.

She left El-Wast through the Mountain Gate, the southernmost gate in the New Medina wall, but as soon as she walked through it, she froze, legs numb from no small terror. She looked back to the city.

No one came after her. *Will this be my life*, she wondered, *always looking over my shoulder?*

No. She was dead.

Even dead, she marveled at the outer wall. The intricate stonework curled in Shālan script. She couldn't understand a word, but she gaped nevertheless before she stepped into the wild desert.

Which wasn't wild desert at all, not exactly. The acres of yellow earth that stretched east from the Balladairan compound were tent slums to the south. She had seen them the night Luca attempted to go to the Cursed City. She wondered how Guérin was recovering. She definitely didn't wonder if Luca thought she was dead, too.

Lean-tos that would collapse—were collapsing—under a stiff wind and proper tents alike were wedged on either side of what Touraine would have called the slums' main road, a winding split that wove through this growth on the city's back. She followed it.

She'd never seen slums in Balladaire. Here, they were like a village. People shouted to each other, faces covered with hoods and veils or scarves against sun and sand. Some of them wrangled children; some laundry. Children raced around her feet with none of the malice they reserved for the blackcoats in the city. A woman pounding a lump of dough on a wooden plank nodded to Touraine as she passed.

Touraine had never lived a domestic life. Never even seen one. So she'd never dreamed of one. Pruett and Tibeau were her only household; training and recovering and fighting, their daily chores.

What she wouldn't give to punch that big man one more time.

She spun around at a yank on her shirt. Three wide-eyed children with knobby bones grinned at her. One boy held another on his shoulders.

The boy riding on his friend's shoulders asked something in Shālan, holding both his hands out in a supplicating gesture, as if he were begging the sky for rain. Which, maybe he was. Touraine recognized the word for *water*, at least.

"Maybe," she answered wryly in Balladairan. She could spare at least a little. And the bags would be lighter.

They didn't even flinch at the language change. The third one changed with her. "We'll carry your bag!"

So she pulled the bag off, and they cheered before taking a drink. The smallest one probably weighed as much as the bag, but he fended her off when she tried to take it back.

They followed her, chattering and singing through the slums, and her entourage of children grew. A child would take a drink from the water boy and skip along beside them. Touraine should have been irritated. She'd spent a lot of money on that water. It would be half gone before she got to the main road.

Instead, she let a little girl grab her by the hand and twirl underneath it, a tiny parody of the dances in the dancing circle.

At the edge of the slums, the desert she was expecting rose out of the scrubland and stretched farther than she could see. The lone road was bordered on either side by scrappy bushes fighting the desert heat to grow, barely more than tufts of grass. Rocks littered the ground randomly, some just knuckle-sized pebbles, others the size of a grown man's torso, and it went on like that, flat and flat and flat until suddenly sharp hills rose up, too far away for Touraine to tell if they were sand dunes or not. Somewhere to her right, in the west, the river continued to wind to the south, but it and the lush mud and farmland it supported were out of sight.

It was just her and the desert.

And the children tagging along.

In the empty stretch of dirt just ahead of them, a group of older children, caught in the awkwardness between soft-cheeked childhood and gangly adolescence, jumped and shouted in imitation of Jaghotai's fighting dance. One girl fought three boys at the same time. Her long braid whipped like an afterthought behind her body.

"Who's that?" she asked the kids, pointing.

The little girl holding on to Touraine's hand answered in Shālan and thumbed her chest with pride. A relative, maybe, an older sister.

Touraine didn't completely understand, but she nodded like she did, and sat down to watch them fight.

The other children sat around her or play-fought, imitating the older ones.

That could have been me.

Here. At home. And she had lost that. The fighting girl, or at least, a girl like her, could have been her child, and that had been taken from her, too. She fought the tears until she couldn't anymore.

"What's wrong?" the water boy asked, still clutching his charge.

"Nothing, nothing."

When the older ones stopped fighting, they walked over to their audience, sweaty and radiant. Touraine had never seen anything so beautiful.

"You're an excellent fighter," she told the girl. She pulled off her last waterskin and handed it to her. As she spoke, she reminded herself of Cantic. Technical compliments and a gift.

The thought didn't please her as much as it would have three months ago.

The girl splashed the water into her mouth and over her face before passing it to her friends. The boy beside her already had a blue bruise opening like a rose on his cheek, but that didn't stop his lop-sided smile. Her heart faltered in her chest.

Touraine had been wrong earlier. You don't find a life. You have to make one, with the people around you and the causes you put your strength into. She'd built a life with the Sands. They had all made the best they could out of a nightmare. But she'd been putting her strength toward other people's causes for so long and deluding herself into thinking that she had her own reasons.

Now she had a chance to choose her own cause.

The older girl walked on her hands while the proud little girl followed her, kicking her short, chubby legs into the sky until she fell over. The older girl came out of her handstand, teasing the small one before grabbing the little girl's legs and holding them up in the air. The little girl's squeals of delight settled the restive aimlessness in Touraine's chest.

The water bag came back to Touraine, and she pushed it away. "Keep it."

Touraine left them, the young children and the old, and took the circuitous route around the slum all the way back to the city. Returning through the Mountain Gate again felt like dipping her head into a cool pool.

She was as free now as she ever would be. She could choose what she fought for. She could choose who she was willing to die for.

When she arrived at the temple, the sky was bright, but the air was already cooling down. Touraine shivered. Then she braced herself and knocked on the smaller, less ornate door.

"You're late—"

Jaghotai's snarling face went blank as she saw Touraine. Blank only for an instant before the snarl came back.

"Why are you here?"

A good question, and after taking the long way around the city to get to it, Touraine had an answer. Still, she lowered her voice.

"I want to join up. Let me talk to Djasha."

Jaghotai shifted to keep the entry blocked. "Why. Are you. Here?"

"Jaghotai."

"They wouldn't take you back."

No. Yes. No. Touraine didn't let the hurt show on her face.

"I'm choosing my own battles now." Focus on that truth, and she could convince them both.

And though she narrowed her eyes, Jaghotai let her in.

As she entered the temple with her wits about her for the first time, Touraine gasped. The floor of the main hall was still littered with the detritus of using the room as an infirmary—scraps of bandages and clothes, fragments of musketry and stone—but that wasn't what stopped Touraine's breath.

The ceiling was made of arching stone and patterned with tiles in shades of blue and green, in white, in gold. Two rows of impossibly delicate marble pillars ran from either side of the main doors to the back of the temple. Sunlight from the windows glinted off the golden caps of the pillars and the shining stones. When a cloud passed and the room sank into shadows, the intricate designs on the ceiling made its height seem unfathomable.

Their boots echoed in the wide, empty hall.

Jaghotai grunted. "Nice, isn't it?"

Touraine snorted.

They followed sharp voices and the smell of fresh bread into an open panel in the wall leading to an almost-secret corridor. If the door were closed, it would be indistinguishable from the rest of the wall if you didn't know to look for it. That must have been why Aranen had covered Touraine's eyes. The corridor must have been for the priests, before the Balladairans banned uncivilized behavior in the city. Jaghotai led her into a small room, where Aranen stood tall and haughty near an oven.

"You're back," Aranen said sourly over her shoulder. "They didn't want you, I suppose?"

Jaghotai snorted. "Exactly what I said. Wants to talk to Djasha."

Aranen's short hair was tousled messily, but she looked a king as she brought the loaves of bread from the oven to the small table. "You're the last thing Djasha needs."

Without a signal, Jaghotai sat at the table and began breaking the thick discs of bread into fluffy quarters while Aranen fetched the last loaves.

Touraine watched in silence. They quartered, then carried the bread away, then came back and carried some more. Though her stomach growled, Touraine kept her hands to herself. They must have been feeding the patients.

They were all part of this system, each with their place. They knew their roles, knew how best to help.

Before Qazāl, Touraine had that. She could make herself useful and have that again. They had saved her, after all. Balladaire had tried to kill her. Would it be like trading one set of masters for another?

Aranen came back with Djasha leaning heavily on her arm.

As Djasha sagged into the chair Aranen led her to, she scanned Touraine up and down before grunting in satisfaction. "Beautiful work, my love. Thank you." She smiled wanly up at her wife, who rolled her eyes and went back to the last of the bread. Aranen didn't see how Djasha's face fell, but Touraine did.

The Qazāli had saved her, but it hadn't been unanimous. Or magnanimous.

A loud squawking echoed through the corridor, followed by Jaghotai's gruff swearing and then a single sharp warning snarl.

"What under the sky above—" Touraine jumped up, ready to fight or flee.

Djasha waved a hand dismissively, a small smile creeping across her face.

A second later, Jaghotai stormed in, muttering. "Bastard. We don't go in desecrating their dung temples to their wild god." She glared at Djasha. "I hope you know what you're doing."

Touraine looked between Jaghotai and Djasha. Hardly a pair so different and yet so inseparable.

"What're you doing?" Touraine asked.

Djasha smiled ruefully. "I'm going to start a war."

"Correction."

A stranger stepped through the door, a very large, very golden cat beside them. They wore pale brown trousers and a loose caftan bound at the forearms by a bracer on one arm and a thick falconer's glove on the other. They wore their scarf differently, too, wrapped in a tight circle around their head except for what draped down to protect their neck from the sun. Their eyes looked unfocused, but their smile was wicked with glee as they scratched their lion between the ears.

"We're going to finish one."

The announcement was postponed by a day. As Luca had expected, Cantic had balked, and Luca had spent the day trotting out legal justifications and explanations for her decisions. More irritating was that Cantic wasn't balking at the solution; she wanted the Qazāli in hand even more than Luca did. She just wanted to hold Beau-Sang's leash. At least the general had stopped mentioning Touraine.

As Luca rode by carriage to the Grand Bazaar, her stomach rebelled. She blamed it on the stuffy cabin. The heat made the air inside feel dense, suffocating. She missed snow. She missed how the snowflakes dusted up against the stone walls of the palace in Balladaire. She missed the brightness searing through her eyelids, burning everything red. The tingle as her toes went numb, the burn as her fingers came back to life after playing outside. Years since she'd done that, but not so long since her last snowfall. *Will I be back in time for winter?*

The most she could expect from Qazāl's seasonal shift was an increase in rain. Spending her days sopping wet or hiding indoors wasn't her idea of pleasure. Then again, anything was preferable to this bone-leaching heat. She just wanted to wear trousers without feeling as if she'd pissed herself with sweat.

Cantic waited on the gallows platform with her usual stern mask hammered out of steel. The wood made a comforting, hollow thunk under Luca's cane.

The colonial conscripts waited in ranks behind the regulars, thick swaths of blackcoats. The sun shone on gold buttons everywhere, but the bayonets, of course, would not be outdone, and sparkled with a vengeance.

A pair of blackcoats escorted Beau-Sang onto the platform as well. Bastien had come, too, but he hung back with the other Balladairan civilians in attendance. Waiting for her.

She traced the cracks of tension that had been cracked wider by the "Battle of the Bazaar," as people had taken to calling it. Qazāli laborers and hawkers grouped together while Balladairan merchants and shoppers clung to each other. Where the borders of each group met, they eyed each other skeptically at best and with outright hostility at worst.

She took a steadying breath and stepped forward. The crowd fell quiet.

With this moment, I make my name.

"Citizens of Balladaire. The Battle of the Bazaar is an unfortunate stain on the relationship between Balladairans and Qazāli. The rebels have capitalized on a divided nation and wish to sow discord where there is none." That part of her speech was inspired by a speech she'd read from another ruler. She couldn't remember quite where or who. She tried to make more spit in her desert mouth.

"The rebels threaten the lives of Qazāli and Balladairan alike. To protect you from this threat—coercion by violence, by blackmail, by any number of things—you need a dedicated governor to replace Lord Governor Cheminade. I have appointed the new governor-general, Casimir LeRoche, comte de Beau-Sang. He will be my hand in the governing of Qazāl with an eye for justice and thus for peace."

She repeated this again in Shālan, the sharp, articulated Shālan of poets and histories she had read with her tutors.

Then Beau-Sang stepped forward, resplendent in his well-tailored coat. He bowed almost to Luca's knees before turning to the assembled.

As soon as she stepped back, her hands began to tremble, and her leg threatened to sink beneath her. She dug her cane into the wood. She wished that she could grab on to Gil for support.

Beau-Sang wooed the Balladairans in the crowd. They cheered or clapped politely by turns. *How does he manage it?*

She answered herself: *A careful chain of power checks and balances, the strategic application of gossip and other useful information to manipulate reputations for his own benefit.* She could quote for herself the scholars of courtly intrigue by rote, and yet applying them in her own life proved difficult.

A gasp rippled through the crowd, followed by the movement of a hundred heads turning. Luca snapped her attention back to the square. Blackcoats dragged two struggling prisoners through the crowd.

That shocked Luca cold. What was going on? Where had he gotten them? She tried to avoid the thought that burned brightest: *Do I know them?*

Luca glanced at Beau-Sang, hiding her confusion and anger with a carefully arched eyebrow. He only nodded. Either Cantic wasn't surprised, or she feigned a better face than Luca would have expected.

Beau-Sang was the picture of grim determination, a father doing what must be done, no matter how distasteful.

"Princess Luca and I want to prove to you that we can deliver upon our promise to end the rebels who terrorize the city. We protect those who are ours."

Luca's cheeks went tight. She tried to keep the surprise off her face. To keep her sudden nausea from showing. As the soldiers dragged the prisoners up to the nooses, the Balladairans began to applaud. To applaud her. She hadn't even done anything.

Yes, she had. She had given Beau-Sang this power, and he had named her so no one—not even she—could pretend she wasn't complicit.

Up close, the blackened swelling of the prisoners' faces distorted any sense of recognition. One, a woman, head half-shaven and fierce, had a scabbing cut across her biceps. The man's face was least recognizable, his lip three times any normal size. They both limped, trousers twisted and barely done up. Luca looked at their feet—*No, look up. They deserve that much.*

Whoever they were, they knew her. The hatred in their eyes was personal.

The blackcoats yanked sacks over their heads and looped them into the nooses. One soldier looked smug and satisfied; the other moved perfunctorily.

Beau-Sang gestured, and the soldiers parted to reveal several Balladairans, unbound now but ragged in triumph. The hostages. Some ran immediately to relatives in the crowd. Aliez ran to Bastien. The rest stood still, fixed on—their savior? Beau-Sang? Or their captors who waited to die?

Beau-Sang's flair for drama embrittled the tension across the square—as if it weren't near to breaking before.

"Princess Luca and I will not let rebels like these divide us. They threaten your lives and livelihoods for desperate, misplaced ideals. We will not let them."

Luca's stomach flipped. This wasn't what she wanted.

Yet there were the Balladairans she wanted to rescue, rescued. There were those responsible for their abduction, arrested. She had thought there would be more time to adjust herself to the tasks at hand.

The rebels swung on their nooses. She was close enough to hear their necks snap, and it made her stomach heave. She clamped her teeth shut.

This was necessary.

CHAPTER 29

THE MANY-LEGGED

B e welcome, Niwai of the Many-Legged. You've come a long way, and the desert is dry," Djasha said formally. Touraine had a feeling she spoke in Balladairan only for Touraine's benefit. "Drink tea with us. Share our bread."

She gestured to a tray with a battered teapot and several glasses too many.

"Thank you. You are more generous than the stories say." A smirk stretched across the stranger's face as they accepted the tea with their bare hand. Their Balladairan was strangely lilted and had the rolling gait of a camel.

Jaghotai bristled. "That's not what you said the last time you and your jackals went goat raiding."

"You can't find our methods so distasteful if you call yourself Jackal." A more wicked, knowing smile. "Oh, don't look like that. My eyes and ears tell me many things. That's why I'm here, isn't it? What exactly is it that you want me and mine to do?" They took the remaining chair and straddled it backward.

Touraine could already tell that Niwai would fit right into the bickering rebellion. The rebels would be lucky to accomplish anything at all.

"How fares the situation in the east, cousin?" Djasha asked. She seemed to ignore their jab. "Have things gotten so bad that you're willing to fight with us now?"

They cocked their head very much like a bird. "The Balladairans are curtailing our herd lands to build settlements and hunting our companion animals for exotic decorations. Have you tried to feed many legs with starving cattle? It's like that from the Middle Desert all the way to Masridān."

"And in what capacity are you here, Niwai? Are you on your own, or do you speak for the Many-Legged?"

They shrugged and looked sideways at Touraine. Those eyes. Where Djasha's eyes were unsettling, a surprising and intense color, Niwai's were unnatural. They seemed to be looking somewhere a world away at all times, and the irises were the deep orange of a desert vulture.

"I'm not a rogue, if that's what you mean. I serve my god as I must. Just like each of you." Their unfocused gaze moved away from Touraine to linger on Djasha, then Aranen.

"I mean accords." Djasha sat up straighter, effort in her face and her voice. "If we strike one with you, will all of the tribes hold it?"

"We are many legs of one beast. We move best when we move in concert."

Jaghotai rolled her eyes. Niwai turned that distant gaze onto her, and Touraine was satisfied at the shiver that passed over the other woman.

"Imagine if you had your own jackal. I think you'd like that."

Jaghotai's disgust was plain on her features. Niwai turned back to Djasha, the only person to meet that unnerving stare without flinching.

"Whatever you want, it will take at the very least a healing trade agreement with all of the Many-Legged."

Aranen sucked in a sharp hiss.

"You asked us for help. I came. Help isn't free."

"Fighting the Balladairans back across the sea helps you, too. We've even enlisted some of the Brigāni nomads. As you said...we would move best if we moved in concert."

"The Brigāni. As in other Brigāni. Not you?" The desert priest cocked their eyebrow.

A terrifying smile spread across Djasha's face, baring her teeth. "As in others like me."

"Now that is interesting. And what about this one?" Niwai turned the full weight of their gaze on Touraine. "According to my eyes and ears, she shouldn't be here."

Jaghotai grunted and muttered, "That's true enough."

Djasha joined Niwai with her own appraising look, but there was a question in it, too. *Why are you here?*

"I fight for Qazāl now." Touraine used her command voice, the steady one that stiffened soldiers' backs. Just wearing that voice made her feel more certain of her steps, even as she walked on this uncertain path.

Four pairs of eyes watched her, and she waited for one of them to tell her she wasn't welcome. Jaghotai, with her clenched fist resting on the table, her mouth shut tight against what she actually thought. Aranen, the exhausted worry lines pulling at the corners of her eyes and lips. Djasha, with a slight smile like a card player who knows she has the winning hand. Niwai, looking at her and beyond her.

"Very well," Niwai said, bowing their head. "It seems we all pray for rain. When do we get started?"

"We're waiting on two more of our council," Djasha said. She slumped back in her seat, which was clearly an ages-old Balladairan castoff that was only a couple months from the woodpile. "Jak. Did they tell you they'd be late?"

Jaghotai rubbed the stump of her left arm absently, frowning with impatience. "No. I've told Malika before—"

"I have a feeling," Niwai said, "that they're at the party in town."

The desert priest's ironic lilt had Touraine and Jaghotai standing, reaching reflexively for weapons.

"What party?" growled Jaghotai.

"There's a woman calling herself the queen regnant. A big man with a big nose. They're standing on the gallows while soldiers...escort?...a small group of Balladairans. Some more are escorting—dragging, really—some Qazāli."

"What?" Jaghotai jumped for the door, forgetting even the lion. It was Djasha's voice that made her stop.

"Jak, you can't do anything without getting strung up yourself."

With Jaghotai's back toward Aranen, Djasha, and the priest, only Touraine could see the flex of anger and helplessness in the woman's face. Touraine knew that feeling.

Jaghotai rounded on the foreign priest. "Can you tell who the Qazāli are?"

Niwai frowned, though their eyes remained out of focus. "A large person. A slightly less large person." They closed their eyes tight and shook their head. "Nothing more than that. I'm sorry for your loss."

The room fell silent, all eyes downcast, but Touraine remembered different deaths, a different war. Soldiers with the magic to inhabit an animal, to become one. She eyed the stranger in front of her. The docile—docile!—lion. The empty falconer's glove. The trancelike stare.

"Sky a-fucking-bove," she swore. "No. No."

She jumped up and backed out of the room, fleeing to the open space of the main temple hall. Not the best place to escape from gods, she supposed, but at least there were no priests or priestesses here.

Luca would have been thrilled in Touraine's place. Not one but two magics—but both of them linked to gods. That wouldn't fit with Balladaire's notions of civilized living at all.

The temple's main hall smelled of incense and stale rugs. There were no ornaments on the walls or the small tables—altars?—throughout the room. They had probably existed before the Balladairans came.

Touraine sat cross-legged on a pouf at the back of the room, looking toward the great doors. The sunset through the slim glass windows dappled the marble floor in shades of gold and rose. Warm. She tried to let the idea of warmth banish the memory of winter nights as one of the Taargens' war prisoners.

"I have a feeling you've met our siblings in the north."

Touraine jumped to her feet again, backing away half-crouched, hands held out in front of her.

The priest from the tribes came on catlike steps, their head cocked.

The lioness trailed their heels, and Touraine checked her exits. She could reach the great doors if she needed to.

At a look from the priest, the lioness found a patch of sunlight and sprawled in it.

Touraine met Niwai's eyes. They looked right at her, the piercing orange iris finally settling into red brown.

"Your siblings."

Niwai sat where Touraine had just been, short, thin fingers like talons interlaced. Their skin was almost as dark as Djasha's instead of Taargen-pale, and Touraine could almost feel her brain trying to minimize her fear by contrasting Niwai with the Taargens. *Surely this one can't be as bad as them.* She lowered her hands.

"We share a god."

Stated so simply, as if it shouldn't twist Touraine's guts into nauseated fear.

"You worship bears. In the desert."

"Faith has no border," they recited, as if from a school primer. And then: "Our connection is with the living creatures of the world. There is no evil in the gifts our god gives us. Are your neighbors not also masters of husbandry?"

"Tell that to my soldiers who had to feed their lives to your 'siblings' so they could—"

She couldn't bring herself to say it even as her mind pulled up the memory. A Taargen changing shape as his bear-fur cloak tightened into him. A roar that coincided with the shriek of a soldier's pain. A guardswoman who had babbled through a laudanum-soaked haze about a boatman with demon eyes. Touraine realized with clarity that the Many-Legged had taken Guérin's leg, too.

And another part of her mind pulled up small, useless facts: the end of the war marked a tentative trade agreement, Taargen livestock, strong and easily bred, for grain and vegetable seeds guaranteed to yield twice the normal harvest.

"There's no act in the world that doesn't require sacrifice," the priest said.

"A sacrifice is given, not taken," Touraine growled back. "What sacrifice will you require from us?"

"That you stop being so squeamish, for starters. I thought you were a soldier."

Touraine could almost feel her hands gripping around their throat. They sighed and stood, and she tensed.

"They used the weapons they had at their disposal. The Balladairans abandoned their god, and that's no fault of ours. They have no right to determine how the rest of us live. We have our own weapons. Are you saying we shouldn't use them?"

"There are guns—" sputtered Touraine.

"If Djasha and Jaghotai had enough guns to win this, I probably wouldn't be here." They added with a grim smirk, "Besides, guns kill people just as dead as magic does. Sometimes less so, and that's another kind of evil entirely."

Everything they said seemed like a philosopher's wind.

Aranen and Jaghotai stepped into the main hall—Aranen suspicious, Jaghotai smug to see Touraine on edge.

"Is everything all right?" the priestess asked. Priestess. Not doctor.

Jaghotai crossed her arms over her chest. "When I called you a dog, I didn't expect you to be such a cowardly one."

Touraine tightened her fists until her pulse throbbed in them. A stupid goad, for puffed-up kids without real experience and sense.

It worked.

She was following them back into the infirmary when the small temple doors swung open.

Malika and Saïd came in, Saïd looking cautiously over his shoulder. Malika's normally composed face was contorted with fear, anger, pain. Anger most of all, Touraine guessed.

In the infirmary, Jaghotai's expression went even darker. "So it's true, then. Who?"

"Maru and Nanti, a young brother and sister." Saïd sighed heavily. "Were the hostages your idea, Jak?"

"What?" Jaghotai asked. Jaghotai turned to Djasha, shaking her head. "No. This wasn't me."

Malika leaned against a wall and let her head tilt back against it. Elegant, even in distress. Djasha stared at Jaghotai with golden eyes narrowed.

"It wasn't me," Jaghotai growled.

They got their marching orders a few days later. Touraine was to go with Niwai.

"No." Touraine snagged Jaghotai by the arm. "I'll come with you instead."

Jaghotai's face was caught between stunned disbelief and a snarl as she looked between Touraine and the fear-tight hand around her biceps. Jaghotai was still angry from the chastisement Djasha had given her over the hostages.

"You'll need support. I'm one of the best fighters—you know this."

Jaghotai shook Touraine's hand off and huffed. "I do know that. That's why I want you with Niwai."

Touraine stepped closer still and spoke in a hushed, definitely not desperate voice. "Is this about me and you? Do you want me to humiliate myself?"

"Mulāzim, I have no idea what you're talking about. As much as you need to get humble, I'm not about to sabotage an entire mission to make you look like even more of a fool. You asked to help. Djasha and I said you could stay. Now you're my tool, and I'm telling you where you'll help."

Touraine's heart swam up to her throat. She looked toward the corner where Niwai and Aranen sat talking about gods while Djasha looked on with a wan smile.

She couldn't do this. She could accept the magic as a tool, even allow that one of *them* would be an ally, as long as she didn't have to deal with it right in front of her. She couldn't help Niwai do it, though. She couldn't watch them use that magic against the Sands. Against Luca.

But Touraine had made her choice when she returned to the Grand Temple and threw her lot in with the rebels. Who was she to tell them what weapons they could or couldn't use? Especially when Balladaire had them so badly outnumbered and outgunned.

Really, though, none of that was the point.

Niwai watched her, their eyes glittering amid dark kohl. They cocked their head at her even as they nodded at what Aranen was saying.

The point was the heat and the sweat pricking at Touraine's skin, the vomit creeping up the back of her throat when she thought not of Niwai but of the Taargens, murdering her soldiers for their magic right in front of her, reaching for her next—

"Please, Jaghotai."

Something in her voice finally caught Jaghotai's attention. Comprehension finally dawned in the other woman's eyes. Her mother's eyes. Had Touraine hit at some maternal instinct to protect her? Sky above, please, yes.

"I'm sorry, Touraine. That's an order. That's how Cantic would say it, sah? We need you there."

Touraine clenched her jaw tight and tried to hold steady enough to glare. Instead, she bolted, to be sick in the temple green.

They stole through the nights like a plague.

The first few nights, Niwai led the way to the Balladairan-owned farms tended by Qazāli farmhands asleep for the night. Fog rolled in off the river, and their feet squelched through plowed fields watered by irrigation ditches fed by the Hadd. With the call of Niwai's god's magic, and clever fingers at gates, goats left their pens, and sheep followed their new shepherd. Chickens flapped, pigeons cooed, and geese honked as they followed overhead. Crows pecked at the grain fields with a voracious hunger, devouring what hadn't already been harvested.

Even in the dark, Touraine could see the ecstasy in Niwai's eyes as they used their magic. It made her shudder, but she followed anyway.

When a young Qazāli goatherd woke and called out in confusion to his charges, Touraine found him and silenced him with a knock to the head. It wouldn't go well for him if people thought he'd shirked his duty, but...

A week later, after Niwai and the Shālans had prayed to their gods and slaughtered the goats, Touraine led a squad of Jaghotai's fighters back through the city. This part was her idea. She knew how to tap the Balladairans' fear, and the Qazāli knew the city. They brought clay jars of goat's and sheep's blood in on silent rickshaws and one by one covered the Balladairan districts, daubing blood on doors, pooling it through the thoroughfares, until it would be impossible for the Balladairans to move without bloodying their feet.

A suitable symbol, Djasha agreed.

Later the next day, one of the watch boys reported, giggling: the shrieks of the Balladairans were like a thousand roosters crowing—all the roosters they no longer had.

CHAPTER 30

A HUNGER

Her city was on the brink of chaos. Food prices were out of hand, and already the Sands and blackcoats alike were stretched thin trying to keep her subjects from thinking too closely of rioting.

Luca hadn't believed it when Beau-Sang came into her command office yelling about vanishing livestock, face red with bluster even as he tried to convince her that he had everything under control.

Now she, Cantic, and Beau-Sang stood in the compound's dim storehouse, hungrily eyeing the bags of grains and beans arrayed on wooden racks that reached up the walls. Cases of salted and smoked meat stretched the length of the building, stacked in orderly rows to one side. Enough food to feed the brigade of soldiers stationed in Qazāl and its auxiliary staff for the season, Luca imagined, but not a hundred thousand civilians.

Mirroring the meat on the other side of the storehouse were crates of muskets and ammunition. Even cannons for field battles. Almost as much weaponry as food. The air smelled like a disturbing combination of cured meat and gunpowder.

"We need the meat we've stored here for the soldiers." Cantic crossed her arms behind her back and glared at Beau-Sang. She still hadn't forgiven Luca for making Beau-Sang the new governor-general.

"Your soldiers aren't even doing their job. Our citizens' lives and livelihoods are at stake while your men and women gamble and our food is stolen by rebels you should be crushing. My connections have found nothing."

"Your *connections*?" Cantic said. "I thought you had a plan. Time for a rougher hand, wasn't it?"

"Please!" snapped Luca. She pressed the bridge of her nose. "General. Lord Governor. This isn't helping. We need a solution. We can blame each other later. And even the rebels can't have caused all of this." She had seen the birds come in. Everyone had. A flock of wild birds had picked the grains clean, no matter how the farmhands shouted or shot them. Abnormal, maybe, but that was only bad luck. Wasn't it? It was a coincidence, but even she couldn't figure out how the rebels could have managed to control wild animals. All of her and Bastien's research pointed to the Shālans having healing magic, nothing else. The Taargens and their bears were up north . . . Could the rebels have allied with the Taargens so quickly? Could *they* do something like this?

"Is it possible that the animals were taken by hyenas or lions?" Cantic turned her back dismissively on Beau-Sang and paced the wide storeroom. "If game is scarce because of the drought, maybe it's emboldened them."

"That many lions? That many hyenas?" Beau-Sang clenched and unclenched his fists. He was the kind of man Luca could imagine liked to strangle things. He probably would have liked to strangle Cantic, but the older woman would have his entrails looped tidily around his own throat before he could get a good grip on her. "They've picked the sky-falling fields clean, woman!"

"Beau-Sang. Watch your tone." Luca stepped between the two before her imaginary vision could come true. "General, I'm inclined to agree with the governor. The birds are one thing. But the livestock . . . especially with the blood . . ."

They all shuddered. One of the Sands had reported it, and Luca insisted on seeing it for herself. She still wished she hadn't. Someone had painted *We pray for rain* in blood across the paving stones. Blood clung stickily to shop doors. The air was thick with the cloying scent of blood spoiling in the heat. She'd retched in the cab. The curtains couldn't keep the stench out. The words were familiar; she'd read that line in the poetry book Touraine had brought, but she couldn't remember enough of it to find another copy and look for clues. If Touraine were alive—no, if Touraine were alive and *hadn't betrayed her*—Luca would have sent her to investigate how the rebels were doing this.

"Your Highness, let me help." Beau-Sang smoothed his shirt over his barrel of a torso. "We've gone over this before. We need to repurpose this energy the Qazāli have. If we put the strongest youth to work in the quarries—"

"Can we stop with the labor camps!" Luca waved her hand toward the room. "These provisions won't last the army a month if we have to feed civilians, too. Balladairan *and* Qazāli. No one knows when the dry season will stop. We can't eat rocks."

Beau-Sang's face went as stony as his quarry, his beady blue eyes watery with anger.

Luca was about to lose the nobles for good. They were already terrified, and if she wasn't careful, they'd be the ones leading the riots. Beau-Sang was meant to have this in hand, but he'd spent most of his time as governor-general trying to sneak in benefits for his own businesses. She glared at him as she swept into the sunlight of the compound.

The frustrating stalemate with Beau-Sang and Cantic drove Luca home to her fighting practice with Gil with more vigor than she'd felt in some time.

After a particularly vigorous lunge, her right leg seized, shooting a brief spasm of pain up her spine—and across her face.

Gil gave her a supporting arm immediately. "Easy, Highness. Easy."

As Luca walked the pain off, the old guard captain asked, "Do you remember when you decided to challenge Sabine de Durfort to a duel?"

"Yes?" She took her position and lunged at him again.

He dodged the blow with a slight twist of his hips. "You couldn't even hold a sword. How did you beat her?"

She stopped and considered him as he held her gaze expectantly. She sensed a test.

"I learned."

"How?"

"I practiced every day."

He smiled. "You did. You were such a determined child. You reminded me—"

"Of my father, I know."

"Of your mother. Étienne was bold in success but even more brilliant after failure." He stepped out of his guard stance and cupped Luca's shoulders. "You and her are so much alike. You worked yourself sick, though. You have room to be a little kinder to yourself."

"Kinder?" Luca laughed in his face. "And who will be kind to me if I fail?"

"All the more reason for you to be. Be patient. Be methodic. If you break yourself now, you'll be too broken to rule."

She held her arms stiffly at her sides as he placed a scratchy kiss upon her forehead.

And what if I already feel broken?

At the edge of the room, the doorman daintily cleared his throat.

"Your Highness. The younger LeRoche is here to see you."

"Without notice?" Luca asked. That wasn't like Bastien, not unless it was an emergency. Like when his sister, Aliez, had been kidnapped. Luca's heart leapt into her throat. She didn't need more trouble. She nodded to the doorman to show him in. "Give me a moment, Gil?"

"Of course." Then he surprised her by wrapping her in a tight hug and whispering, "It will be fine."

He left her in the sitting room they'd been using as a practice room just as Aliez LeRoche stepped inside.

"Good afternoon, Your Highness. Please forgive my interruption."

The warmth from Gil's embrace was sucked very suddenly away. Luca gripped her thin practice sword tightly. She had not forgotten the young woman's mocking voice that day in the bookshop. Months ago, perhaps, but Luca rarely forgot these things.

"Mademoiselle LeRoche. This is unexpected. Is Paul-Sebastien all right?"

Aliez nodded. Her hair was a purer blond than Luca's, golden like wheat under a clear blue sky with none of the soil beneath. Like many of the Balladairans born in Qazāl, she wore the sun on her skin—in her case, as a dense smattering of freckles across the nose and cheeks. She also wore one of Madame Abdelnour's hybrid Balladairan-Qazāli outfits: trousers and a blouse, half-flowing, half-structured.

"I'm here on my own behalf, actually," Aliez said.

Luca waited.

"I want to apologize. For the things I said with Marie Bel-Jadot. About the broadside."

Bel-Jadot. The menagerie girl. *Giraffe.*

"It was cruel of me to go along with her, and cowardly as well."

"Do you know who's making them, these broadsides?" snapped Luca.

Aliez hung her head. A lock of blond hair flopped into her face, and she pushed it back with the same gesture Bastien used. "I'm sorry. If I did, I would tell you in a heart's beat, I swear it."

"What are you here for, then?" Luca pinched the bridge of her nose. She wanted to put the girl outside, with some choice words besides. Something bitter still lodged inside Luca's chest, knowing they had mocked her and she had done nothing. "Do sit. Would you care for tea? Coffee?"

Aliez looked nervously at Adile, who already hovered nearby with a beverage service. "Coffee, please. Thank you." Her hands already twitched and fidgeted like Luca's did when she drank too much of the potent Shālan drink.

Luca took off her fencing glove and stretched out her legs. She had just been warming to it, and the disruption soured her even more.

"Could we speak alone?" Aliez asked softly.

Luca paused, cup halfway to her lips.

"It's very personal," Aliez added.

With Luca's look, Adile bowed over the coffee tray and left the room.

"It's about some of the other broadsides, actually. I've seen them, you understand—everyone has, and I'm not saying this to mock you. I'm just—"

"What's your point, Mademoiselle LeRoche?" Luca said coldly. She held her cup steady and gritted her teeth.

"Hélène is missing."

"Who is that?"

"My...friend. Who I'm fond of. More than fond." She looked down at her coffee cup. Tears caught themselves on her thick blond lashes before jumping into her drink.

Luca tried to imagine why Aliez would bring this problem to her, of all people. The girl was ten years Luca's junior, and they had never passed more than a faux-friendly word to each other.

"Bastien says when he came to you—when I was missing—that you were so helpful. That I was rescued thanks to you."

Heat rushed to Luca's face at the tinge of admiration in the younger woman's tone.

"That's not how it—that wasn't the same thing. I can't help you find one person."

"I know. I know you can't. Only. I hoped." Her hands shook, and her words burst out in a rush: "Because of the broadsides. That you might understand how I felt."

Luca's face burned hotter as Aliez's concern became clear.

"Your friend is Qazāli."

"Yes," Aliez said in a small voice.

"And your father."

Aliez shook her head. "We met in school. He never wanted me to see her. After the first time he saw her, we decided that it would be best if she only visited when he was away. She was too uncivilized, even though we were at the same Balladairan school. Now that I'm back from the rebels, he says Qazāli are too dangerous and I should have learned my lesson." She scowled through her tears. "He's so smug about it. It makes me furious!"

The more that Aliez divulged, the quicker Luca's own heart thrashed against the cage of her chest. It felt as if her secret, half-broken feelings for Touraine were being pulled out of her. She clamped down on them hard with that familiar, comfortable cold.

"What do you expect me to do about it?" Luca asked.

Aliez's face was nothing but hurt, wide-eyed innocence. "Don't you have...people? Who can help you find out things like this?" After a beat, she added, "I suppose that I'm afraid."

"Of?"

She shook her head, and her voice came out a whisper. "I'm afraid he's done something to her. I'm afraid if I ask around for her, I'll find her body instead."

Though Luca didn't let it show, Aliez's words struck a nerve. Her own grief over Touraine's death still felt fresh, despite Touraine's betrayal. Sometimes, she found herself wishing for Touraine just so that she could ask the soldier, *Why?*

"I would rather she left me, decided I was silly and that she didn't want to be bothered with me anymore," Aliez said hoarsely. "Even that would be better."

"I'm sorry, Aliez." Luca's voice cracked, too, though she tried to hide it. "I don't have any ties to the Qazāli side of the city right now. We're all—" *Floundering*, she almost said. She couldn't admit that aloud. "Doing what we can to get the city back upright. It's a difficult time."

She hated how false her words sounded. She hated that this *child* had ridiculed Luca and now had the audacity to ask her for help. She hated that this girl also loved a Qazāli as openly as she dared and now faced the consequences for it. There were always consequences. Threats, broadsides, political losses. If Cheminade had been here, maybe she would have advised Aliez and Luca both.

There was more to this, though, than Luca's own grief. The girl sat there, blue eyes just like her father's, pleading, clinging hopefully to Luca's break in composure.

"Why do you think your father had anything to do with it?" Luca asked.

"Well, that's how we get to the other part. I was—it was before I was kidnapped, before any of that bazaar nonsense took place. He heard me talking to Bastien about her. I could tell he wanted to beat me right then, but I kept my distance. The things he shouted at me, though." Aliez shuddered and looked around the room to make sure they were alone.

Luca clutched her coffee cup, waiting for the girl to arrive at the point and dreading it at the same time. Beau-Sang wasn't beyond reproach. No noble was. Even Luca had done things she wasn't proud of by now.

"He said some things about the old governor-general," Aliez said. "The one who died? And I wondered if…Well, he made it sound as if…" She waited for Luca to complete the thought, but Luca's teeth were clenched tight. Aliez finished in a voice so low that Luca had to lean closer to hear it. "As if he had something to do with it."

"That's quite an accusation," Luca said when she could finally speak.

"It's not an accusation." Aliez looked down again, this time as if she were disappointed with herself. "I don't have any evidence. It just *feels* like it. Call it intuition. I do know my father," she said darkly. "You can look into it if you want to."

Luca took a shuddering breath. Cantic, who hated Beau-Sang and had practically frothed when Luca installed him outside of the military's control, would have to hunt down that evidence. The governor-general that Luca herself had chosen, against Gil's warning. Killing Lord Governor Cheminade would have opened the way to his placement. She didn't want to believe she'd fallen into someone else's elaborate plan, but what if she had?

She certainly felt trapped. With the public announcements and the eyes of the Balladairans, especially the nobles, on her, she felt like she didn't have a choice but to see this through. She couldn't afford to be mistrusted and disregarded right now, not with Qazāl in such a fragile state. Not when she was this close to losing the city already.

"Your Highness?" Aliez twisted her empty cup while she searched Luca's face. It was as if she'd finally remembered whom she was talking to.

"Mademoiselle. Thank you for bringing me your concerns." Luca set her cup on the table with finality and stood, signifying the end of their chat. "I have a lot to consider, you understand." By which Luca meant she was going to swing that damned rapier back and forth until she collapsed and couldn't think about everything crumbling to shit around her.

Aliez followed suit and curtsied prettily, but her face echoed the pain and frustration in Luca's heart. "Thank you for your time, Your Highness."

Adile made to show the young woman out, back into the waiting sunlight, under which all their troubles were bared. Luca looked back at her fencing sword and glove. She could be finished practicing for the day.

"Mademoiselle. Aliez. I find that a walk often cleanses the mind." Luca followed her outside, squinting at the bright sky.

Aliez smothered a giggle with a pale hand. "You've been spending time with Sonçoise de l'Ouest, haven't you?" She smiled ruefully. "I would enjoy the company."

"So would I."

After taking a turn around the Quartier with Aliez, Luca's mind was "cleansed" enough to come to at least one decision. She spent the evening asking herself, *Who is closest to the conflict? Who walks with it through the streets?*

How many times had Touraine told her the Sands were always at the front?

And if the Sands were at the front, they would see the most. Luca knew just whom to send for.

When Lieutenant Pruett arrived at the compound the next morning, Luca tried to put Aliez's revelations about Beau-Sang aside. If he was behind the assassination, to deal with him would take resources she didn't currently have. Luca invited Pruett to take a promenade around the top of the compound walls, with Gil and Lanquette following behind. From that height, the desert scrub stretched toward the south and east until it rose into dunes. Toward the north, they could see the sea, a blue stretch beyond the Quartier.

Luca and the lieutenant walked the rampart with cool cups of avocado juice sweating in their hands. At the first sip, the lieutenant shivered in delight.

"It's good, isn't it?" Luca smiled, as if they weren't both remembering the last words she'd spoken to Pruett at the main guardhouse in the city.

Pruett smiled with closed lips. "Delicious."

Luca waited until they passed the soldiers at the southwestern corner before speaking.

"How are your soldiers finding the situation in the city?" Luca had not gone back since reports of the first hints of discontent had come in. Gil had forbidden it; it wasn't worth the risk. Guérin was too near her memory for her to argue.

Lieutenant Pruett's eyes barely lingered on Luca before casting back out over the wall as if she expected an attack any moment.

"We're holding well enough. Captain Rogan has us on double guard shifts, everyone. With the other guardhouse platoons, we can cover most of the city..." She trailed off.

"Yes?"

"If there's gonna be a riot, Your Highness, it's not coming from the sky-falling Qazāli."

Behind them, Lanquette cleared his throat roughly.

Lieutenant Pruett smirked and took a delicate sip from her juice. "Pardon my language. All I mean is, your Balladairan civs aren't too good at telling the difference between my soldiers and the rebels. Things might get messy if this food business doesn't get sorted soon."

"You are still well fed, aren't you?" Luca looked meaningfully at the other woman. She wanted to let the threat linger. "If you need further provisions, write directly to me."

Pruett raised an eyebrow but nodded. "To what do we owe this kindness?"

Luca smiled tightly. "It's my duty to make sure my soldiers can do their jobs, not a kindness."

"And our job?"

"Do you have any idea who's doing this? What's causing this?"

"Huh. It's just animals, isn't it?" Pruett raised her eyebrows in mock surprise. "Inept Qazāli farmers not keeping hold of their herds, the broadsides said."

"But *if* it isn't," Luca said sharply. "If it isn't, I want to know who and I want to know how." She softened. "I know this must be difficult. I'm asking you to turn on your people."

The lieutenant grunted. "They're not our people, Your Highness. Not anymore. And anyway. It's not food we're hungry for."

"Then what are you hungry for?" Luca asked. "The pay raises weren't enough for you? You seem to be enjoying your new uniform well enough."

The soldier stopped midstep and looked down at herself. The horror blooming across her face like spring tulips set a smile growing on Luca's. The new uniforms weren't quite as well made as Touraine's had been, but they were a far cry from the scrap material their regular uniforms had surely come from.

"You're welcome," Luca said.

Pruett's nostrils flared. "Your Highness." She ducked her head once then looked away, intensely focused on the vista beyond the wall.

And then, inexplicably, Luca felt ashamed. Touraine had accused her of buying away her guilt over Guérin's injury. This wasn't much different. Luca hadn't decided if Touraine was right or not.

"I'm sorry," Luca said. "I know I don't deserve your approval and that I do deserve the things you said before. I'm working to earn your loyalty from now on."

For several steps, Pruett didn't respond, the silence bordering on insulting, but Luca waited.

Behind them, the men's boots scuffed gently. The sun burned

down, so she tilted her tricorne down low over her brow. Lieutenant Pruett kept her face turned so that Luca could see only the other woman's sweat-darkened curls clinging to her neck, and the muscles clenched in her jaw.

"You really don't know?" Pruett's voice was rough with some kind of emotion that didn't make sense.

"Know what?" Gently, gently. Luca didn't want to scare her away from whatever truth—confession—was coming.

Pruett laughed harshly, tinged with a manic edge. "It's Touraine."

The red fury returned faster than Luca thought possible. As her hand gripped her cane so hard the handle bit into her skin, she calculated how much force it would take to tip Pruett over the wall and break her neck. She stopped, and Pruett turned back to her with a wry, bitter expression.

"Understand me. I am your queen. Earning your loyalty does not mean I'm your *mate* to have a joke with."

Lieutenant Pruett snapped to perfectly erect attention and still managed insolence. "Oh, I understand, Your Highness. I'm telling you the truth, or you can hang me like a dog on your little gallows. If it pleases you."

"What do you mean Touraine is behind this? Did she leave a plan to be followed upon her death? Are you saying you're responsible? You, the Sa—the conscripts?"

Pruett quirked her mouth at the casual slip of the pejorative name for the conscripts but enunciated slowly. "No. We're not. Touraine is."

"By which you mean to say, Touraine is alive."

"I do mean to say that, Your Highness. She's working with the rebels."

Luca let herself consider the possibility for a moment. If Touraine was alive—that would mean the woman who had betrayed her was alive. The woman she had begun to...care for...was alive and working even now to undermine her rule.

"When I...visited you at the guardhouse, you said you watched her die yourself."

"That I did. Apparently, I was wrong. She paid me a visit, too."

A pang in the chest, a writhing in the gut. Pain and jealousy twined together like complementary theories from cruel philosophers. If Touraine was truly alive, why hadn't she visited Luca? *She is a traitor. Why would she visit you?*

"And you didn't tell me this." Luca tried to keep the tremble from her voice.

There was proud malice in Pruett's eyes. "You haven't stopped by since your last visit. It's why we call it news, Your Highness. It's new."

Lanquette stepped between them smoothly and looked down at Pruett with cold eyes.

"You're addressing the queen, Lieutenant," he said. His voice was like the whisper of his sword in its scabbard, but his hand was on the butt of his pistol.

"My apologies, sir." Pruett saluted him first and then bowed nearly in half to Luca.

"Thank you for the information, Lieutenant. You're dismissed. When you get back down, go directly to the offices, and fill out a report on this visit from Touraine like you should have done before. I want every detail, no matter how personal." Luca's stomach quailed to think what she might receive. Maybe Pruett would elide those details anyway. No—she'd probably take a perverse pleasure in the description. "I want it delivered to my desk before you return to the guardhouse."

Another salute. "Aye, Your Highness. No detail spared." There was still half a glass of her avocado juice, and she gulped it down indecorously, throat bobbing and glugging. She wiped the last trace of green from the corner of her lips with the back of the hand that held the glass, and then she raised the cup to them all before she swaggered away.

Touraine. Alive.

CHAPTER 31

A WARNING

Two weeks passed in a haze of smoking meat and bleating animals. Slowly, Touraine began to blend in with the other Qazāli. With a scarf wrapped around her head to cover her face, she helped herd the animals deeper into the desert, where the Balladairan patrols were weak and Niwai's Many-Legged would retrieve them. At the temple, she helped Aranen and Djasha make daily meals and ration them out to the Qazāli. Their gambit had cost everyone in the city, not just the Balladairans. The rebels would take care of the Qazāli.

Touraine was in the main hall of the Grand Temple, filling a bowl with couscous and vegetables to hand to a young man with an attractive swoop of dark curls, when someone pounded on the temple's main door.

The boy flinched so hard that he nearly dropped the bowl of food—nearly. His grip on the bowl was as tight as Touraine's grip on her knife.

The knock came again, harder, more insistent.

Aranen frowned, but she remained leaning over the table where they served the food. Her flat palms were pressed hard against the stone, though. Once, it might have been an altar. "There's no meat here. If they ask, it's only charity."

Touraine went to the smaller side door, the one that all the Qazāli came through, and cracked it to scout the danger.

Through the door, she saw a single soldier kicked at the ground in aimless irritation, muttering a stream of curses, all of which mentioned Touraine by name. Aimée was about to slap the ornate knocker on the decorative doors again.

"Psst. Hey."

Aimée spun around, into a fighting crouch. When she saw Touraine at the door, she straightened and walked over, mouth hanging open.

"You sky-falling ugly fuck. You—but you—"

Touraine wanted to say something clever back, but emotions blocked her throat, forcing her quiet.

Aimée kept sputtering. "Pruett said—she named you—when the princess asked who was responsible. I thought it was a shit joke. How—sky a-fucking-bove—"

"You shouldn't be here," Touraine said, her voice low. "If the black-coats catch you here, you're—they'll kill you."

"No, *you* shouldn't be here. I'm on orders for the lieutenant." Aimée meant Pruett. "We're supposed to be hunting for your merry band, but—look, can I just come in?" Aimée craned her neck to look past Touraine's shoulders to see inside the temple.

Touraine had never seen her like this. Eager. Earnest. She'd spoken more than five words without swearing. After Touraine hesitated a second longer, Aimée pushed past her and into the temple. The other woman took two steps before she stopped, gaping at the ceiling with its marble and the glitter of gold and colored stone swirling through intricate geometries. Touraine felt a tender warmth, even as she chuckled. This was what she must have looked like the first time she saw the inside of the temple: mouth slack, head tilted, trying to take it all in.

Ecstatic.

Aimée walked to a nearby pillar and placed her palm flat against it.

"No wonder Beau would never shut up about this place," she murmured. Aimée had been turned into a gleeful child. Touraine couldn't help a small bubble of pride. She shoved Aimée in the shoulder playfully.

"Fine, just invite yourself in."

Aimée's rueful gaze was only half a joke. "You should have invited us, Lieutenant." She spread her arms wide to encompass the vastness of the temple hall. An entire company one hundred soldiers strong could sit for lunch on the marble floor if they moved some of the "unused" altars.

"I mean, look at this place," Aimée continued. "Plenty of room for all of us. Sky above, it smells, though. Like a cross between soup and some rich asshole's powder room." She crinkled her nose.

Touraine nodded at one of the smoking incense bowls. "You get used to it." In a hushed voice, she added, "It's amazing, isn't it?"

Aimée didn't answer at first. Just closed her mouth and peered around, taking in the small crowd of Qazāli on the other side of the temple and their bowls of food, the worn rugs and poufs where a person might sneak in and pray in secret to a forbidden god.

"What's amazing is you, here. How the sky-falling fuck are you alive?" Aimée turned and pushed Touraine in the chest. "I saw you go down. You didn't fucking get up again."

Touraine rubbed the spot, already feeling the possibility of a bruise. She shrugged, uncertain how much to say. She trusted Aimée, but Aimée hadn't joined the rebels, and she didn't know whether to trust her with the secret of the Shālan magic.

"I was never dead. Just a bad shot. The Qazāli still have a few good doctors from before, you know."

With narrow eyes, Aimée scanned Touraine up and down, as if she could see the scars from a cutter's surgery through Touraine's clothing.

"What do you want with us?" Best to change the subject quickly. And to figure out if they should expect more guests soon.

Aimée's scrutiny didn't let up. "Pru's orders. Your pillow friend called her to the compound, looking for answers." She turned the scrutiny on the others in the temple.

Touraine's lips twisted sourly. "My pillow friend. Answers for what?"

"You do know what's been happening in the city, don't you?"

"Let's pretend—for just a second—that I'm supposed to be a corpse. I wouldn't get out much, would I?"

"Maybe not. I'm sure there'd be worms to get you whatever sky-falling news you wanted in your little hidey-grave."

"Say there weren't. What's happening to the Sands?"

"Well, your princess wants to know if we're responsible for it. Barring that, if we know where you are."

Alarm locked Touraine stiff. "If you know—how does the princess even know I'm alive?"

The other woman shrugged, but Touraine could tell Aimée was pissed. "Pru told her. Surprised the sky-falling fuck out of the princess, to hear Pru tell it. Surprised the sky-falling fuck out of me, too. Said you were responsible for the attacks and then laughed like a madman in the princess's face."

"What else did she tell her?" Touraine asked through gritted teeth.

The air felt too thick to breathe. She would have to tell Djasha and Aranen that she'd been compromised. Blackcoats would be on their way. Jaghotai would be insufferable.

"Nothing, I guess." Aimée shoved her hands in her pockets. "Fuck if I know why, but Pru said she didn't know where you were. Then she sent me here to warn you off. She's hunting you and the rebels."

Even though she feigned casualness, Aimée kept seeking Touraine's eyes. Touraine kept trying to shrug the looks away, eyeing everything from a volunteer's worn trousers to the faded fabric of an embroidered cushion.

"I know why," Touraine said wryly. "She may hate me now, but she hates Luca more." Pruett never wanted to rebel against Balladaire outright like Tibeau had, but she had a petty streak. Touraine imagined Pruett was more than happy to hurt Luca with the truth or hamper the hunt for Touraine. The thought that Pruett would rather see Touraine slip the blackcoats' clutches than hang was a small comfort.

Aimée gripped Touraine's arm. "Is there a reason she wouldn't tell the princess where you were?" she asked quietly. "Are you with the rebellion?"

Finally, Touraine looked up. How did Pruett know she'd stayed in Qazāl? Had Touraine been seen, or did Pruett just know she couldn't stay out of trouble?

Whatever Aimée saw in Touraine's face must have pleased her. She nodded once. "How can I help?"

Touraine wanted to lead Aimée over to the Qazāli waiting for their rations. She wanted Aimée to know what she was doing. She wanted some of the Sands to see, to approve. And secretly, selfishly, she hoped Aimée would spread the word and convince the others to join them. She wouldn't admit that she was lonely, but she was surrounded by people who didn't understand where she came from, how she had lived. Even living with Luca had felt less isolating; at least then she had understood the language and expectations.

Instead, she tightened her shoulders and let them fall. Then she shook her head. "There's nothing you can do without risking yourselves. Pruett already told me the Balladairans are breathing down your necks."

Aimée looked hurt. "Some of us want to help. Pruett said you wanted guns, right? I can do that."

"No!" Touraine said sharply. Aimée jerked back.

More gently, Touraine repeated, "No." She put a hand on Aimée's shoulder. "I risked everything to keep you lot safe. If you want to help…could you keep an eye out for the people around here? The blackcoats like to target the Qazāli near the temple. On suspicion of religious practice."

Their eyes met for a long, silent moment, then Aimée gave the ration line one last look.

Aimée shrugged out from under Touraine's hand. "As you like, Lieutenant."

After Aimée left, Touraine swore so loudly that everyone turned in her direction. Sky above. Pruett had hardly done enough to head Luca off. Even if Luca didn't know where Touraine was, she knew that Touraine was alive, and Luca wasn't the type to rest until she sussed out the truth.

The rebels were committed to their path now. They wanted the Balladairans out, and they were willing to sacrifice for it—even the Qazāli who weren't active rebels donated a few extra supplies here or shared information about the blackcoats there. Touraine doubted that Jaghotai and the others would consider any more deals from Luca, but maybe, just maybe, Touraine could try negotiating one more time.

Otherwise, it was going to take a lot more blood before the rebels got the rain they wanted, and the Sands wouldn't be the only unwilling casualties.

In her sleeveless shirt the brown red of a dry scab, Touraine looked like any other Qazāli laborer. There were few enough to recognize her face as she walked from the Old Medina to the Quartier, even if she weren't wearing the common hood and sand veil.

And in her pocket, she had the writ of passage Luca had given her. It was crumpled, and one edge was brown with old blood, but Luca's signature and stamp were clear.

When the trio of blackcoats at the entrance to the Quartier stopped her, she held it out.

A blackcoat with a sergeant's wheat pins took the paper and looked Touraine up and down. She stepped close enough that Touraine could smell her cologne, a heavy, sweet thing that mingled well with her sweat. "Who are you, to have something like this?"

Touraine swallowed and kept her head down. She wasn't sure what Luca had said about her or how things stood between the blackcoats and the Sands right now.

"It's classified, sir. She wanted me to report as soon as I was able."

"Are you a Sand?" The sergeant tipped Touraine's chin up. The other two soldiers flanked her.

Shit.

"Sir. Yes, sir."

"Then where are your pins?"

"I'm—I've been secret, sir."

"Well. Seems to me that we could use some more proof. So how about you go with my boys to see the captain, and we'll see what she thinks. It's a tricky time, you understand. You can't be too careful, especially not with Her Highness's person."

Touraine stepped back reflexively, and a blackcoat behind her moved closer. She couldn't afford to be taken in. There were too many unanswered questions about her position as a not-quite-dead traitor to the queen and informant for the army. A tight spot, all right.

One of the blackcoats locked Touraine's arms behind her and began to frog-march her to the Quartier guardhouse, where she'd be fettered more adequately.

Touraine struggled, but the blackcoat's grip held firm, and the sergeant wasn't moved. "The pass is valid. I have information about the rebellion. The princess will want to see me—"

"I'll want to see whom?"

Touraine hadn't noticed the carriage driving up from the direction of the compound. The disembodied voice came from the open window.

Surrendering to the blackcoat's grip, Touraine called, "Tell them it's me, Your Highness. I have news you'll want to hear."

Touraine held her breath too long waiting for an answer. Finally, Luca leaned forward enough to show her face through the carriage window. Her eyes widened only marginally.

"Escort her to my home, Sergeant."

"You're lucky I was on my way back into the Quartier. They would have taken you to Cantic." Her smile was a cruel quirk of the lips. "You and she are apparently quite close. Only, she's less inclined to consider you a hero now that she knows you're helping starve her city."

Luca's body betrayed her cold insouciance. Her face was pale as a corpse in snow.

At the side of Luca's salon, Guard Captain Gillett stood somberly.

Lanquette's sharply arched eyebrows had jumped up his face when Touraine pulled her veil down. Now he feigned stoicism, too.

"I'm sorry." She stepped forward and surprised herself by kneeling, head bowed.

"You're . . . sorry?" Luca said archly. There was no sign of the woman who had curled into her shoulder. That was fair enough, Touraine supposed, when the woman you lay beside stabbed you in the back.

She dared a glance upward to meet Luca's eyes. Luca approached Touraine like a woman in a trance. Her hands trembled as she grabbed Touraine by the wrists, tugging sharply to urge her to her feet. Touraine's heart pounded in her throat as Luca traced the air above her arms, not daring—or willing?—to touch more of her. Luca's eyes shone.

"I should have you killed."

"I'm a free woman. You drew those papers up for me yourself. Are you going to take them back?"

Luca's voice went low as a whisper, her face scarlet. "How dare you? Have I ever given you reason to doubt my word?"

Touraine wanted to apologize again. She wanted to start over and ask, *How are you?* And yet she was so tired of apologizing to people who didn't care for her and hers. And for better or worse, the Qazāli were slowly becoming hers.

Instead, she said, "How could you put Beau-Sang on a governing seat? You know how he is."

"You were gone. I thought he was the best chance I had to secure the Balladairan hostages. I was right." Luca dropped her hands and balled them into fists. "Hostages that wouldn't have been taken if not for you. Why did you do it, Touraine? We were so close to bloodless peace."

Luca limped back to her seat, and Touraine followed. She took the cup of coffee Luca offered her.

"Innocent people died, Touraine. Civilians, soldiers, your own sky-falling Sands. What was worth all of that?"

Touraine had accounted the price more often than Luca knew. A night hadn't passed without her picturing Tibeau's outstretched hand still clutching his baton, or his blood soaking the knees of her trousers as she knelt by his side. She hated herself enough without Luca's goading.

How many more of them would be dead, though, if the Qazāli had gone against Balladaire with guns? And she still wasn't sure she had made the right choice.

"My family."

"Your family?" Luca said incredulously.

"To be a lieutenant—or a captain or, sky above, a queen—you've got to do the hard math. You've got to protect what's most important."

"You're lecturing me again on how to be a leader? You didn't even do the hard math—how many more people will die if the rebellion doesn't stop?"

"I know. I made a mistake. That's why I'm here now. The rebellion won't stop, Luca. Not until you leave. I know them now. I've been living with Djasha and Aranen since—"

Touraine looked down at her boots, the supple leather shining. "Luca. Tell me the truth. Do you still want peace with Qazāl?"

The question was as much for her own heart as for the Qazāli. She missed playing échecs with Luca here, drinking coffee. She didn't want to believe Pruett was right—that Luca was as Balladairan as the rest of them. Maybe that was partly why Touraine had decided to venture out to the Quartier today. To see her again. To see for herself.

"I did, until they took Balladairans hostage and sent me their sky-falling fingers!" She splayed her own ink-stained fingers.

Touraine frowned. "The hostages weren't the council's idea."

"What about throwing the city into starvation and riots? Terrifying my citizens with—sky above, I hope it was only goats' blood. It's—you're—" Luca struggled to find the right shade of insult. "Barbaric."

"I didn't come here to trade insults," Touraine snarled back. "I wanted to offer you something."

Luca snorted and lowered herself onto her usual chaise. "You did, did you?"

"Something you've been looking for."

The princess's eyes narrowed, and she tilted her head to look just behind Touraine, as if for a hidden package.

Touraine smiled bitterly and tugged up her shirt. Lanquette and Gil were private enough. The shining scar on her belly was small but plain. "The council still has the magic. Can still teach it to you. And it's more powerful than we ever thought. The bullet wreaked havoc on my insides during the Battle of the Bazaar. They said my own shit had poisoned my blood. Common enough on the battlefield. Not common to recover from it."

Luca's eyes flicked across Touraine's body. She licked her lips and looked like she wanted to touch the scar but only tact held her back. "This is what we came here for."

"I was hoping that I could convince you to…make a gesture of faith."

"Excuse me?"

"Get rid of Beau-Sang, and let the council take over. Start making your exit now. Qazāl deserves to be sovereign. Let the Sands do as they choose."

Luca shook her head, chuckling and leaning back in her seat. "Pardon me." She faltered as she stretched her leg. "Let's say Beau-Sang has killed a dozen or so Qazāli a day for the last couple of weeks to discourage their association with the disloyal. The Qazāli civilians will stop abetting the rebellion, which will then gutter out as it starves for food, funds, and fools."

She beckoned for another cup of coffee. She gestured to Touraine, but Touraine shook her head. Luca was playing with her.

"I didn't come here to gawk at the sights, Touraine. My capabilities as a ruler are under scrutiny. If I can't handle the Qazāli situation, my uncle could make a case of incompetence against me and hold the throne even longer.

"Do you know who thinks the Qazāli are barely capable of rational thought? My uncle. Do you know who recommended an 'experimental' education program with a brigade's worth of Shālan children? My uncle. And if I don't keep a foothold here, the likelihood of my uncle surrendering the throne when I return is slim." Luca held her index finger and thumb apart for emphasis. "That means civil war and tens of thousands more dead, and if you don't think they'll try to pull your precious Sands in, too, you're badly mistaken."

Touraine winced at Luca's words. Too much of it rang true.

"If you want to end the bloodshed," Luca finished, "you tell the rebels to stand down and be patient."

The words rang true, but just to a point, and only from one point of view.

"How long do they have to be patient on their own soil?" Touraine countered.

Silent seconds crawled by.

"How many people do you lose to every plague?" Touraine asked. "To accidents and blood poisoning and childbirth? If you brought Qazāli healers willing to work with you—willing to, not forced to..."

Luca's chest hitched, though she tried to hide it with cool disinterest. Touraine heard the catch in her breath.

"What would it be worth, to stop that from happening?"

"Well, if they're willing to trade it, they should have said so several decades ago," Luca snapped. "Maybe none of this would ever have happened."

The dismissive tone of Luca's voice shattered the glass wall Touraine had been using to keep her contradicting feelings apart from each other.

"We aren't your toys or coins to be passed from hand to hand, Luca. If someone prefers not to fuck you, are you disgusting enough to force them anylight?"

Luca's face twisted. After a long moment she said, "Give us a cure to the Withering, and we'll discuss terms. I'm prepared to offer their magistrate, with elected officers this time. They would have their own government while remaining under our protection from other powers in the north. A true protectorate. After I have my throne."

"It's not a cure. It's a skill—you can't just take it like you take their stone or their beads—"

"Then I want a hundred doctors or healers—whomever. I want a cadre to teach us, and then I want my throne. Help taking it, if need be. Then a protectorate."

Touraine shook her head, incredulous. Who was this? What had happened to the dreaming scholar?

The answer was glaringly simple. Luca was Balladairan. She was Balladaire.

Touraine stood. Luca's pale jaw flexed. The hollows of her eyes were skeletal in the dim light of the salon.

"And let them pay you in their own resources for the privilege of your protection?" Touraine scoffed. Her eyes burned and she blinked them clear. "You can't be yourself unless you have a leash in your hand, and there's always got to be someone attached to it."

"Not you," Luca said, voice surprisingly soft.

"No. Not me. Not anymore. And how long until the rest of Qazāl says the same? The rest of Balladaire?"

Touraine let the silence sink between them.

"They don't need your protection. The magic does more than heal. If the rebels come for you, don't look for me to stop them."

"Are you threatening me?" Luca stood and walked slowly around the table, her cane tapping, until Touraine could have leaned over and kissed her.

"No." Touraine dug her fingernails into her palms. Despite everything, the idea of Luca being hurt set her heart racing.

The sharp edge of Luca's voice rested against Touraine's throat. "I'm letting you walk out of here on one condition. Get the rebels in line. I don't want any more bloodshed than you do. The sooner they stop fighting, the sooner I call off my hounds."

"You deserve this fight."

"The civilians, too? The children?"

"You teach the children to spit on us! Crawl out of your books, and open your fucking eyes, Luca. This is real. We are real."

At the whistle of air, Touraine flung her hand up by instinct. Luca's wrist crashed against her forearm, and Touraine whipped her hand over, grabbing Luca's wrist so hard that Luca's pulse pumped against her thumb.

"Boot me to the moon if I'll let another of you women hit me in the face."

"Let go of me." Luca didn't struggle.

"Keep your hands to yourself. I'm not your pet anymore."

"Touraine—" For a moment, something softened her face. Touraine could almost hear her say it: *Come back*. The temptation to surrender and apologize was there. She could tell Luca wanted it. So did she. Just not with this Luca.

The window of apology slammed shut. "I hope their magic is as strong as you say it is," Luca said. "If I were you, I would ask your new friends to hide you well."

Her voice didn't shake, and her blue-green eyes were colder and more uncompromising than frozen earth when you had a whole squad to bury. Her face flushed. They shared the silence and the air between them for three breaths, breaths that shuddered in Touraine's chest. Her heart pounded all the way to her fingertips. She dropped Luca's hand and brushed past Gillett without meeting his eyes.

CHAPTER 32

A FAMILY (REPRISE)

The sun was blazing when Touraine made it back to the Old Medina, and she was fuming. She tried to wipe the evidence of her visit from her face behind the veil as she wove through the almost-familiar streets to Djasha and Aranen's riad. The priestess had finally deemed her wife recovered enough to move, so Djasha and the pack of strays had relocated.

Jaghotai arrived at the same time, carrying a tray of khubza, the thick rounds of bread that Qazāli ate at meals. "Where have you been?" she grunted.

"Nowhere," Touraine grunted back. She reached out to catch one end of the tray, but Jaghotai twisted away and nodded at the door instead.

The sharp smell of pungent vegetables met them immediately, along with the sound of pleasant banter. Saïd the bookseller was there, two books beside him while he cut the vegetables that Aranen threw into a pot already simmering.

Djasha lay in a corner, and Malika padded around her in bare feet and a casual dress—which meant it was still more elegant and sleek than anything in Balladairan high fashion. She held a cup of water for Djasha. A quick smile at Touraine and Jaghotai tugged the scar on her chin.

"She said she was fine." Malika rolled her eyes, but Touraine heard the twist of grief in her voice.

"I lied." Djasha winced as she pushed herself up to take a drink and tried to turn it into a scowl.

"Aranen said rest." Malika pulled the thin blanket up Djasha's stomach.

"I am. We are," Djasha said, teeth gritted. With a start, Touraine noticed the tribal priest's giant cat, its head resting at Djasha's side. Their golden eyes matched. "It just hurts so Shāl-damned much." She shoved the blanket off. "And it's too damned hot in this place."

"Can I bring anything?" Touraine directed the words more to Malika, who looked grimly at their patient, but Djasha answered.

"Both of you. Stop hovering over me like a nest of mosquitoes. Go bother my nurse."

The doctor-priestess snorted from her side of the single room. "It is time you learned how to make a proper Qazāli dinner. Even Niwai is...helping."

The tribal priest was poking at something in the tajine while Jaghotai peered suspiciously over their shoulder.

"Ya, Touraine!" Saïd threw his arms wide, knife included, which made Aranen squawk indignantly before swearing at him.

Touraine greeted him back in her awkward Shālan. Though Luca had been teaching Touraine the stiff scholar's version of the tongue, being surrounded by the rebels' liquid syllables was rubbing off on her. She braved the vegetable knife to kiss the man on both cheeks. Of all of them, he was still the warmest toward her.

"Watch yourself, Saïd," Aranen said. "If you lose your lips—or anything else—I can't promise to heal you." Aranen twirled her own knife through the air, smiling down at her vegetables.

"What? The mulāzim wouldn't hurt me. I gave her the gift of poetry."

They spoke a combination of Shālan and Balladairan, heavy on the Balladairan, that Touraine could sometimes follow. Their nickname for her stayed the same—the lieutenant.

They cooked a small feast in the happy chaos, and Touraine let thoughts of Luca, thoughts of Pruett, and even thoughts of Tibeau fade just a little.

Warmth.

Djasha was right. It was sweltering. Sweat on Saïd's brow, soaking the broad back of his shirt, making patches under Jaghotai's arms. There was more than that, though, and Touraine could feel it between them.

There was something like family here, even if it was the familiarity of desperation, scrounged from necessity and danger. Just like the Sands had become her family.

Touraine and Malika carried the food to the low table, where Aranen helped Djasha sit. The sick woman clung to her wife's arm. Despite their laughter, Djasha's cheeks and eyes were hollow. She'd lost weight. When Touraine first met Djasha months ago, the rebel leader's presence had been forceful, even terrifying. Her rapid decline was even scarier.

"A blessing from Shāl," Aranen said after everyone sat down.

"A blessing from Shāl," the other Shālans murmured. Niwai said their own whispered thanks. Djasha the Apostate said nothing. Touraine stayed quietly self-conscious.

They ate.

Touraine still didn't know if she believed in Shāl. Not like Aranen, with her unshakable faith. Why would a god direct her life to this moment, this side of the rebellion? No adequate weapons, no actual soldiers, and it was a lot harder to dig out an entrenched army than to rout a marching one. This looked like the losing side. It even felt like the losing side.

It didn't feel like the wrong side.

Touraine jostled elbows with Saïd as they raced for the same pieces of bread. The first time, he popped the stolen bread into his mouth and made a show of savoring it. The second time, she grabbed his wrist and squeezed the small bones until he yelped.

"Merciful—shit!" He dropped the bread and wrung out his hand. "Did you see that, Djasha?"

Djasha smirked. "Why do you think we keep her around? We're all very good at what we do."

"So Saïd's a very good...bookseller?" Touraine waved her warm, crusty prize in front of him.

Saïd straightened and pulled his thick shoulders back, cracked his knuckles. "I am."

Despite the games and the warmth, Touraine felt small around them. The same way she felt around Tibeau and Pruett—that people didn't follow her for her sake, but because she had older, smarter, stronger friends. It didn't help that she had betrayed these friends once.

Touraine dunked her bread into her harira, a red soup with small beans and herbs. "Can I ask how you even got into the rebellion?"

"How does anyone?" Malika tore her own bread in half as sharply as she spoke. "It's the only thing that makes sense."

Saïd's face sobered. "Let Djasha tell it. She's the storyteller." He turned a piece of tomato idly in his fingers.

"It's not my place to tell everyone's story," Djasha said softly. She met Touraine's eyes with a golden stare. "I do think it's a good time for you to hear it, though."

Saïd shrugged his massive shoulders. "I was fifteen, maybe. Old enough to push rocks for Beau-Sang. And I had a younger brother. Bastard followed me around all the time, even wanted to come and work. The quarries weren't a place for little boys. Shouldn't have been there myself, but it was tough work. Made me feel strong. And the city being what is was...you have to eat to live," Saïd said.

"So I go to work one day, and Sahir sneaks behind me the whole way. Lucky I caught him before an overseer did. Could have put my foot through his asshole. I shook him till he cried and left. I thought he had made it safely home, but when I got home that night, my mother and father were crying, and Sahir was gone. Him and a shipful of other brats."

His eyes shone when he looked at Touraine. Her blood ran cold, her hand frozen with bread and beans on its way to her mouth.

"I know there were a lot of you. Did you know him? Is he here? He was around ten."

He described his brother, but Touraine wasn't listening. She could already see Tibeau so clearly. The thick black curls that grew out only on campaign and the beard to match. The tiny scar on his chin where Touraine punched him once and caught him with her thumbnail. As a child, as a grown man.

Tibeau was not Sahir. He had been Aziz. But maybe somewhere, another Saïd was telling someone else about his brother; another mother was missing her son. Some of the Sands were missed.

It was only confirmation of yet another way she had failed Tibeau.

"I don't, no." Touraine avoided his eyes and forced the hunk of food into her mouth.

Saïd shrugged. "I figured. I keep hoping I'll meet him. Or can fuck the Balladairans over for taking him."

"I'm sorry," Touraine said. Hollow words to fill the warmth that had filled her, almost suffocated her moments before.

Aranen put a hand on Saïd's shoulder. "I'm in this mess because I fell in love with a fool." She sat behind Djasha now, half casual affection, half support. She kissed Djasha's braids.

Djasha murmured, "And I was the fool."

On their other side, Jaghotai rested her forearms on the table, a hollowed-out crust of bread wrapped around half of a boiled egg in her hand. She stared at no one even though she faced Niwai and their lion.

"What about you?" Touraine prodded. It felt good to strike at something she knew would spark into flames. If not the familial warmth, at least anger was heat.

Jaghotai stuffed the egg and bread into her mouth and left, still chewing. Touraine watched her broad back all the way out of the room, imagined the slope of thick shoulders as her mother walked down the stairs and slammed the door shut. Touraine almost stood, her own legs coiled to chase after. She pictured the empty street she would see when she got outside.

Since she was a kid, Touraine had dreamed of nothing but becoming what Jaghotai and Djasha hated most. A hero of empire who conquered for empire, who killed for empire. She had shown an aptitude for learning the geography, the history, the mathematics of warfare. She would be kidding herself to think there could be anything else in the world for her. What else could she become? Sick with vengeance and cloaked with false peace, like Djasha? Bitter and angry, holding love at a distance, like Jaghotai?

Each path seemed like a different kind of powerlessness, but Touraine didn't know where else she could turn.

Touraine roused herself at Saïd's snore, and she thought for half a second that it was Tibeau's deep ripping breath inside the barracks. Saïd lay warm beside her, and Malika lay on her other side, rank, warm morning breath coming from her mouth.

As far as Touraine knew, Jaghotai hadn't come home that night. She might have had a lover in the city or stayed at her own safe house. Good. Touraine wasn't ready to face her mother by morning light.

She had spent the rest of the night building up a thousand conversations with Jaghotai in her head.

"Are you a rebel because they took me?" Touraine could ask.

"Yes," Jaghotai might say. She might even say, "They took the daughter I loved."

She would also say, "They gave me back one of their tools. A dog, loyal to the wrong hand."

And even in her imagination, no matter what else they said, Jaghotai always told her to go home—not to the temple or Aranen and Djasha's house, but back to the Balladairans. Scorn in dark, kohl-rimmed eyes, the same disappointment twisting wide lips. A few times, though, Touraine dared to paint sadness there. On the off chance, at least, that Jaghotai would miss Touraine if she never came back.

Djasha slept fitfully on her mat in the corner, and the lion slept between her and Niwai. Aranen, however, was gone.

Carefully, Touraine picked her way around the sleeping bodies and out of the riad.

Sunlight bleached the dirt roads, the clay buildings, the temple domes. When she reached the massive temple, she let it drag her gaze all the way up to the topmost spires. It pulled her every time. Wasn't so difficult to believe in Shāl, or any god, when she looked up at something like that. She'd never seen anything like it in Balladaire. Even the royal palace couldn't hold a candle to it.

"You can come in." Aranen stood outside the small side door. Instead of the laborer's vest and trousers, she wore loose-fitting gray pants and a bright red tunic wrapped with a gray-and-yellow patterned sash. It was simple yet elegant.

"Shāl's peace on you," Touraine greeted her in Shālan.

Aranen's eyes lit up. "And Shāl's peace on you." She raised an eyebrow and kept speaking in Shālan. "And how are you this morning?"

Touraine hunted for the words. "I was...more good. Before. Not bad now." She shook her head in frustration. There were so many words she still didn't know, so many things she couldn't express. She spoke in Balladairan instead. "Did Jaghotai come back?"

Aranen made a knowing sound in her throat. "Give her time, Touraine. She will come around."

The doctor-priestess led her into the coolness of the temple, and Touraine sighed in relief. She drank the ladle of water Aranen offered from a pitcher resting on one of the ex-altars between the two rows of marble columns. Then she beckoned Touraine to follow her into the hidden area of the temple.

Over the past weeks, Touraine had realized how deceiving the massive size of the temple was from the outside. A narrow corridor hidden behind clever sliding walls had once been used for the priests to move around the circumference of the temple without disturbing prayers, like servant corridors in a palace. Before the Balladairans came and banned religion, the priests had slept and cooked and doctored patients in the rooms within. As far as Touraine understood, the priests who hadn't abandoned the faith still practiced throughout the city as doctors, sometimes even to wealthy Balladairan patients, but for healing—for injuries that couldn't just be stitched and illnesses that wouldn't pass—faithful Qazāli still came here in secret.

"Have you sat down with her? Just to talk?" Aranen asked.

In the hidden kitchen, a pot waited over the low coals of the stove. At the smell of roasted meat, Touraine's stomach growled.

"About something other than the rebellion," the priestess added. She doled food onto plates, handing Touraine a plate of warm bread and beans. For herself, she took a kebab of meat and tore it off, chunk by chunk, with her teeth.

"Why would I do a stupid thing like that?" Touraine asked.

"She's your mother."

"She tried to kill me."

Aranen paused, shifted a chunk of meat from one cheek to the other thoughtfully. "You know it's more complicated than that."

"Should it be?"

Touraine's voice was bitter, and too petulant for her own liking. Hadn't she claimed that the Sands didn't need to find their blood relatives? Hadn't she sided with Pruett, that perhaps it was best to stay close to what they knew? To what fed them, in the end? Wasn't that why she hadn't told Tibeau about meeting with them?

Something in Touraine's voice made Aranen reach over and squeeze Touraine's arm. "Does Jaghotai have somewhere for you to be?"

"No."

"Good. Come help me."

The priestess loaded a few more bowls of beans and bread onto a tray and shoved them into Touraine's arms. Then she picked up a box of long matches and a box of incense cones with one hand and a candle with the other, and beckoned for Touraine to follow with her head.

Aranen led her down the hallway and a small stairwell. The room they walked into was familiar: it was where Touraine had woken up just a few weeks ago. When her life had turned upside down.

The infirmary was large, as big as the main hall of the temple above it. The ceiling matched the temple above, cold marble with dark veins and mosaic tiles, but the tiles here were dark—brown or black—and white. With the light of the table lanterns, it made the room feel cozy and comfortable instead of grand and expansive. Patients lay on pallets or sat on cushions, depending on their dispositions. Curtains separated certain sections, but enough were pulled back that Touraine saw there weren't very many patients right now. They greeted Aranen and Touraine in Shālan as they entered. Some of them were older, nursing bandaged wounds. A child lay cradled against her mother while the woman sang a gentle song.

Aranen plucked a cone from her box, set it on a beaten metal tray on a small altar near the door, and lit it. The tray looked like it had once been a plate before meeting a spray of musket fire. The scent that wafted up was heavy and burned Touraine's nose.

"Why do the Balladairans let this place stand?" she whispered to the priestess.

Anger laced Aranen's chuckle. "They know they can't get away with anything else."

"Doesn't it just stay here as a bastion for Shālans? It's the biggest in the empire, right? Seems like the Balladairans would want to remove the temptation."

"In the old empire, yes. People came to do pilgrimage here and to study at the university. That empire is broken and her people divided." She gestured above, to the main hall. "They gutted the entire building— except the hidden rooms and the infirmary. Gold, holy artifacts—gone. We bring incense and cushions from home. We do our best."

Touraine followed Aranen with the tray of food from patient to patient as Aranen changed bandages, threw the used ones into a reed basket, and offered reassurances in that mélange of Shālan and Balladairan that was common in the city. Sometimes, Aranen put a hand on them, closed her eyes, and prayed. Sometimes, the patient joined her.

The sheer religiosity of it made her nervous. The whip scars on her back tingled.

One patient, a young man lying flat on his back with a broken arm in a sling, passed out after Aranen whispered with him.

"What happened to him?" Touraine murmured.

"He fell in the quarry. The Balladairan overseer left him for dead." The priestess gently adjusted his legs, tugging them slightly. "Broken back, broken legs. Healing so much damage takes a lot out of a patient. And the healer." Aranen sighed wearily as she pushed herself to her feet and headed to the child and her mother.

Touraine stared grimly into the last two bowls of food. "A long time ago, you told me that Shāl was a just god. What's just about this? Why would a god let all of this happen?" Touraine waved her free hand to encompass all of Qazāl.

Aranen's dark eyebrows lowered over her deep brown eyes. "Shāl is balanced. Technically, that's the Second Tenet."

Balance sounded nice. Something out of reach but worth working toward.

Touraine reached to hand the bowl to the child with a smile, but all thoughts of balance vanished when she realized the kid was covered in patches of rash. She flinched and held back the bowl, afraid to seem afraid, but also afraid of disease. Touraine might not have been Balladairan, but she had grown up with the same healthy fear of the Withering, of any contagion, that every native Balladairan had.

Aranen raised an eyebrow quizzically. "Surely you've already had the laughing pox?"

"Uh," Touraine stammered. The kid was staring at her, wide brown eyes watery and pitiful. "I don't know?"

Aranen chuckled again and took the bowl from Touraine. "It's okay. It's very contagious but mostly harmless. We usually expose children to it on purpose so that they don't get anything worse. Jaghotai will know if you had it or not." The priestess shared a comment in Shālan with the kid's mother, and they laughed together as Touraine's face heated. The mother and child took their bowls with thanks.

By then, the incense had diffused through the hall, no longer cloying and intense but relaxing and sensual. Aranen led Touraine back upstairs through the priests' corridor and into the kitchen. The roasted meat still smelled delicious, even mingled with the incense clinging to their clothing. They sat in the rickety chairs, Aranen with her long legs stretched out.

"Don't look so disappointed," Aranen said to Touraine when she caught the soldier eyeing the kebabs. "I need it for my work. Short supply."

"Your work? You mean healing them. Like you healed me." Touraine held her left forearm out so the thin scar shone. "The girl I—the assassin did this. How does it work, exactly?"

Aranen traced the scar with a sad smile. She considered Touraine carefully before answering.

"Shāl requires flesh to mend flesh. That's what the meat is for. We eat it, we pray, and if Shāl blesses us, we heal."

"Or you use it like Empress Djaya. To destroy. Djasha said—"

"No," Aranen said harshly. "That's forbidden."

Touraine bowed her head in acknowledgment. "Anyone can do it, though?" she asked shyly. "Heal, I mean."

"No. It is and always has been a matter of faith. And training. If you don't know the body, you can't knit it back together properly."

Touraine dragged her eyes from the lamb and picked a stray incense cone up from the table, rolling it between her fingers. She thought of balance again. The balance of a flawless knife. Of standing steady and strong on one leg. Finding your place between two parts.

The cone of incense broke in half, one part a solid chunk. The other half crumbled to a smear of fragrant dust against Touraine's skin. "If I wanted to pray, could you teach me?"

"What?"

Touraine clenched her fist around the broken cone, crushing the other half as she fought her embarrassment.

Aranen took Touraine's hand and opened it, letting the powder fall to the floor. "It's all right. I just thought you would have asked Djasha instead."

Touraine snorted and dusted her hands on her trousers. "She only tells me stories about the old empress." The Apostate, overall, didn't seem to approve of Shāl.

The priestess glowered at Touraine. "What about her? Empress Djaya was a fanatic and a murderer. Don't take her for a model of faith."

"She took on the Balladairans with Shāl's magic."

"If you come to gods seeking power, you'll only find ruin. Has Djasha done something?"

A dark weight on the word *done.*

Touraine looked away, focused on the incense dust under her fingernails. "Did Cantic really kill her family?"

"Yes."

"People say a Brigāni...destroyed Cantic's company after that. Was that Djasha? Did she really?"

"Yes."

"With the magic."

"Yes."

"Is that why she can't do Shāl's magic anymore?"

Aranen looked sharply at her.

Touraine shrugged. "I figured it out. Is it why she's sick, too?"

Aranen rubbed her hands over her knees, almost as if distracted. "When she lost her family, she lost her faith. That's why she's called the Apostate. We don't know if it's why she's sick. Maybe something of Shāl's curse on Djaya lingers, passed on in the blood."

"I'm sorry," Touraine said softly.

"Don't mistake me. Shāl isn't dangerous. Shāl is balanced. Shāl is...so many things. I can't teach them all to you. But Shāl values peace above all. That you should understand."

"I do." In theory. The first thing Djasha and Jaghotai had done was beat her, after all. Touraine gathered that Jaghotai was only marginally more devout than the Apostate. What she didn't understand was what place a god of peace had in war if he wasn't going to end it.

"You need to get out more. Listen less to Djasha's theology lessons. Come here instead."

After a few moments of silence, Touraine couldn't help asking, "What *is* wrong with her?"

The priestess inhaled sharply and closed her eyes. Her exhalation came out with a visible shudder. "Essentially, her body is attacking itself. I can't stop it. I have to help the patients who may actually survive. She and I both know this. I was thinking to stay home with her tomorrow, though." Her hands trembled.

Touraine hesitantly reached out and squeezed them.

"I'm sorry," Aranen said. "You can't possibly..." She looked up, but instead of seeing Touraine, she was looking somewhere else. The frown lines around her mouth were deep, but so were the smile creases in her cheeks. "This is what I do. This is what I have."

Then Aranen snapped herself upright and alert. She pointed at the dirty basket of blankets and scraps of cloth from bandages that she had carried upstairs from the infirmary, and then to the pot on the fire. "Next, we need clean linens, and I've got to prepare the people's lunch." She meant the free food the rebels made sure all the Qazāli could have, even with the food shortages.

Touraine nodded, realizing the pot on the fire held only hot water. Her nose twitched at the familiarity of the grim stains and smells wafting up from the basket. How long since she'd been on campaign against the Taargens? A little more than a year?

"I can handle it," she said.

While Aranen stacked a tray of empty bowls, Touraine poked the coals until the water was boiling again and then dumped in everything that would fit into the pot. She stirred with a long, heavy stick. The methodical stretch and pull of the muscles comforted her, and she lost herself in the quiet camaraderie of their work.

CHAPTER 33

A FAMILY, BROKEN (REPRISE)

Then a heavy knock resounded through the temple. It wasn't loud to the ear, but Touraine felt the vibration through her body. Aranen looked up sharply.

"Expecting someone else?" Touraine asked her.

Aranen frowned. Her eyes were alert, but her shoulders sagged with weariness beyond the day's efforts. "Shālans use the side door."

"Excellent," Touraine grumbled. She pulled the heavy stirring stick from the water, letting it drip onto the ground.

Aranen reached into one of the little kitchen boxes and pulled out a small knife. She tucked it into the gray-and-yellow sash around her waist.

Together, they left the hidden priests' passage for the main hall. Aranen sealed the door behind them and headed briskly to the main doors just as they echoed again with another knock. This time, the sound was like a god clapping in her ears. Maybe that had been the intent of the architect.

"You're still not supposed to be alive," Aranen said as Touraine trailed her. "Stay back. If I need help, I'm sure you'll know."

Touraine nodded, fighting the impulse to say, "Yes, sir." She took her stick and hunkered down behind one of the marble columns, still close enough to hear what happened at the door. She pulled up her hood and covered her face with her scarf.

With a heave, the priestess opened the door.

"Sun shine upon you, sirs." Aranen greeted the visitors in the Balladairan she used only with Balladairans—and Touraine.

"And upon you, I'm sure."

Touraine's stomach was seized with rage and fear the moment she recognized the entitled lilt of a Balladairan accent.

"I'm Captain Rogan. To whom do I have the pleasure of speaking?" His voice oozed insincere charm; the word *pleasure* dripped with condescension. Touraine could see the expression on his face without even peeking around the pillar.

She swore under her breath. In battle, a second could be the difference between life and death. Wait too long to act, and you could lose an advantage. Move too soon, though, and you could lose an entire company. She let Aranen speak, waiting. Her forearms strained as she gripped the stick, and she forced her hand to relax.

"My name is Aranen. I'm not practicing religion here, if that's why you're here."

"Then what is it, exactly, that you use this place for?"

"We feed the hungry, as we can, and we use it as an overflow space for any wounded who need care." Aranen's voice turned sharper as she said, "We've had so many of both, of late."

"And you are a doctor, then?" Rogan asked idly.

"Yes," Aranen said defensively.

"Excellent. Arrest her."

A sudden rush of movement and Aranen's protests rose to a shriek. A soldier cried out in pain, and Touraine remembered Aranen's knife as she dashed out from her hiding spot. *Good.*

They were already dragging Aranen from the temple as Touraine sprinted headlong through it. It went against every instinct she had except the instinct to *hurry.* Sometimes, all you needed was a strong charge to break an enemy.

This wasn't that time.

Touraine managed two solid cracks on one blackcoat with the heavy stick, and he fell. A third hit on a second soldier, and then her element of surprise was gone, and Touraine had to reckon with the eight other blackcoats in front of the temple.

She was ducking before the first pistol fired, running toward the pair holding Aranen between them. Another shot, though, and Touraine jumped back.

Aranen struggled weakly in front of her, lip swollen and bleeding. Touraine dashed for her again, but this time a blackcoat locked an arm around Touraine's neck, yanking her back and off her feet. The stick fell with a clatter and rolled uselessly away.

"Take the witch and go," Rogan snarled. His noble veneer was cracking. If he hadn't recognized her already, Touraine was sure he would soon.

Let go of her! Touraine wanted to scream. She struggled to meet Aranen's eyes as her vision splotched from hopeless tears and lack of air both.

Aranen shook her head and yelled to her in Shālan. "They want me alive. Run. Tell the Jackal."

At first, the Shālan was too quick, but comprehension came. Aranen was a doctor. They wouldn't hurt her, because they wanted what she knew. *The magic.* Luca wouldn't need to make a deal if she could take it by force.

"Shut your mouth." Rogan slapped Aranen across the face. "Get her out of here."

As the other soldiers dragged the priestess across the plaza to a carriage, Rogan approached Touraine with a leisurely bounce in his step. The cold fear flushed out the heat of Touraine's anger and froze her stiff. A smile of smug recognition spread across Rogan's face, a dark eyebrow quirked up. She could see him again, that night, coming at her while she was pinned against the brick wall of the barracks.

No. Not now. Touraine forced herself back into her body. Focused on the heat of the soldier's body behind her. The slick sweat between their forearm and her own neck. The sour smell of old cigarettes on their breath. Her body knew how to fight if she kept her mind out of it. Tibeau had put her into locks like this in their training all the time. The memory was in her muscles.

Touraine went limp in her assailant's arms. Caught off guard by her suddenly falling weight, the blackcoat's grip slackened, and she twisted herself free, then heaved a fist into their gut. She didn't even stay long enough to watch them double over.

She realized too late that her scarf had definitely slipped. Not the biggest problem at the moment. There was nothing but the animal fear in her now. That and the flooding sense of shame as she obeyed the priestess's orders.

She ran.

Touraine arrived at Djasha's house winded and ready to be sick, her heart thundering in her ears. The Brigāni woman was frowning at her before Touraine had enough breath to close the door behind her.

As usual, Jaghotai hovered like a gargoyle on a cushion beside Djasha, arms crossed, but the others—Malika and Saïd, the ones least likely to gut Touraine first and ask questions of her corpse later—were gone. It looked like the two women had been talking.

"What happened?" Jaghotai hopped to her feet immediately, ready for a fight.

Touraine shook her head as she gulped in air.

"Someone's coming," Djasha said.

Touraine shook her head again. She couldn't say it. The truth of it stole her voice more than sprinting from the temple had.

The single room still smelled of last night's food, but the echo of ease and joy was gone. It seemed like the emptiness held danger in its corners.

"I was at the temple," Touraine finally whispered.

Djasha's dark skin went ashen. "Where is my wife?"

Touraine looked anywhere but at the Apostate. Dishes from

someone's breakfast waited on the low table for someone to pick them up. Crumbs or dried sauce still clung to them. She didn't look at Jaghotai at all.

"Touraine. Where. Is. My wife?"

Jaghotai grabbed Touraine by the collar and shook her. A tremor ran from the Jackal's hand up to her mouth. "Answer her," she growled.

Touraine didn't even fight Jaghotai off. "The Balladairans took her."

"Took her but not you?" Jaghotai's wide nostrils flared. "The missing traitor?"

"I tried," Touraine croaked. "I'm sorry. I tried—she told me to go—"

"She saved your sorry life and you left her?" Jaghotai shook her again, and Touraine hunched her shoulders.

"Jak, put her down." Djasha spoke quietly, but her voice was hard as the temple's marble.

"But she—"

"Put her down."

When Jaghotai put her down, Touraine knelt down in front of the Brigāni woman.

"I'm sorry," she said again. "But she said they wanted her alive. And they did, or they would have—"

"Why?"

The whole mad sprint from the temple, this question had run through Touraine's mind. Only one thing made sense.

"The magic," she answered.

"But why *now*?" Jaghotai growled, grinding her stump into her hand.

"I'm sorry, Djasha." Touraine ignored Jaghotai to meet Djasha's gaze instead. Touraine wasn't afraid of Jaghotai. She was afraid of the golden-eyed woman whose face was utterly calm in her grief. That calm steadiness that meant she was beyond the reach of irrational lashing out. Whatever came out of her would be calculated.

"I can't do anything with an apology," Djasha said, disgusted. "We lost half of our priests this morning."

"What?" Touraine asked, startled.

"Malika brought word," Jaghotai said, scowling. "Blackcoats are taking doctors and anyone who's been seen lingering at the temples throughout the city. Half a dozen missing at least."

"They know too much," Djasha said grimly.

"I told you we should never have trusted that bitch," Jaghotai snapped at Djasha.

Djasha closed her eyes, and for a moment, her illness and grief combined to make her seem impossibly fragile.

A new guilt rose. Luca was the only one who knew about the magic. Touraine had gone to Luca, showed her the extent of what the magic could do. She'd only meant to encourage another alliance, not this.

"Let me talk to the princess one more time," Touraine said.

Behind her, Jaghotai scoffed, but Djasha stared Touraine down. "You want to see if she'll make another trade."

It would be impossible to fix every betrayal on her shoulders. Too many of them were contradictory. She wished she could fix them all at once, tie them together like the laces of a boot. This was what it meant to be responsible for a company. Not every choice was a good one; usually good choices didn't even exist. Even so, she had always been honest with her soldiers on the field.

"She said she's willing to make another deal if you are."

"We made that mistake once already," Jaghotai snarled.

Djasha, however, was quiet. Her eyes narrowed minutely. "You've already spoken to her."

Guilty heat flushed Touraine's skin. "I only went to help. I thought if I could end this sooner, it would be better for everyone."

"You what?" roared Jaghotai from behind her. She stormed around to stand over Touraine and Djasha. "You did what?"

Djasha went still on her pallet.

"I told her the truth. I told her the magic is real and you might be willing to send Balladaire healers if she agreed to leave—"

"You invited her to take a bite out of our ass!"

"Touraine, do you know how hard we've worked to keep the extent of Shālan magic a secret?" Djasha asked coldly.

Touraine swallowed. She suddenly remembered, all too clearly, how quickly and efficiently Djasha had stuck her knife in the young woman's ribs at the dancing circles. That was what the rebels did to people who went against council orders.

Jaghotai waved her amputated forearm in Touraine's face. "This. This is how much that secret is worth." The Jackal turned to the Apostate. "Djasha, we're fucked. She's not going to stop until she has it or we use—"

Djasha shook her head, with a sharp nod at Touraine. They didn't trust her anymore. Maybe Jaghotai was right and they never should have. Touraine was nauseated with the shame of it.

"She won't stop," Touraine agreed, with resignation. "But she said if you give her healers and a cease-fire now, she'll turn the colony into a protectorate after she has her throne. It's not the best, but surrender and promise the healers will work with her willingly, and maybe we can get your people back safely." Now that Luca had the healers, the rebels were running out of leverage.

"Fuck her," Jaghotai growled. "Fuck this. What right does she have to our magic? To our god? To our land!" Her voice softened in a way it never had for Touraine. "We'll get Aranen back another way, Djasha."

"Let me at least try," Touraine pleaded.

She shot a glare up at Jaghotai, who loomed over her, arms crossed, her fingers digging into her biceps. Like she was trying to keep herself from flying apart. Or from wrapping her hand around Touraine's throat instead of her collar. Her breath came in heavy puffs, like a bull's.

With a massive grunt, Djasha pushed herself up from the pallet, surprising Touraine and Jaghotai both. She swayed a little but ignored both of their hands when they reached out. Instead, she stepped haltingly over to the kitchen area, which Aranen reigned over so handily. She ran a finger over the lip of a bowl, the handle of a knife.

"I'm not dying without seeing her again, Jak. If not this, something else. Soon."

Djasha didn't see Jaghotai's eyes close in defeat or the dampness on her eyelashes. Her back was turned. She probably didn't hear Jaghotai's voice crack when the fighter whispered, "Fine."

Djasha didn't, but Touraine did.

Touraine stood, stepped gingerly behind Djasha. "If we surrender, she might release some of them."

Djasha's thin, hunched back heaved with the weight of her sigh. The Brigāni woman turned, her golden eyes seeking Jaghotai's across the room. Her fingers played idly over the kitchen knife. Something passed between them that Touraine couldn't read, and Jaghotai nodded, her jaw tight.

"Touraine," Djasha said, "there is no 'we.' The only reason you're not dead now is because I asked my wife to heal you. It would be a waste. Go, and this time, don't come back."

And yet Touraine felt like she had been stabbed, for all she'd expected it, for all she deserved it. She tried to step back, but her legs wouldn't obey. She opened her mouth to plead her case, but nothing came out.

Jaghotai stepped in beside Djasha, and they made a threatening wall.

"Get out."

Touraine backed out of the room on unsteady legs.

The last time Luca had ducked into the cool dark of the compound jail, she'd offered Touraine a choice. She'd never imagined that choice would lead her here. A miscalculation of strategy. She could never have predicted it, in this combination.

Less than a year, and so much had changed.

The jail was louder than she remembered, the stench stronger. The blackcoats had come back with a dozen doctors or suspected priests, or at least Qazāli suspicious enough to warrant questioning. *Each of them is your fault, Touraine. You chose this for them.*

Some of them cursed her from their cells. They clung to the bars, the better to aim their insults in the dim lantern light. The jailer barked back, kicked through the gaps, even if he could understand only half of the disgusting things they said. Some of them ignored her, kneeling with their hands folded in their laps or sitting with their knees pulled up to their chests. Meditating, thinking, praying. To find peace somewhere like this—they had to have some god. Whatever their outer appearance, she knew they hated her deep down, as much as those swearing at her did. They had to. She would, in their place.

Would you do it again?

She was queen. This should be the least she was capable of. So why did it turn her stomach?

She steeled herself before entering the side room where Cantic waited with the woman who would have the answers.

Cantic sat on a stool, looking for all the world as if she were in a commoners' public house. Which, Luca realized, might be as much a mask as her own icy facade. Strangely, it reminded her of Touraine. False casual, always on edge. If Touraine were colder.

Touraine, who was alive. Touraine, who had been healed.

Aranen din Djasha sat across from her, hands in irons behind her back, feet locked together. Bruises lined her face in fresh purple and stale yellow. Her crisp short hair stuck up at all angles as if tousled by sleep.

"Good afternoon, Aranen din Djasha. I'm sorry that the general's soldiers were so rough with you. I hope the military medics were sufficient?"

"Their hands are rougher than necessary, Your Highness." Though the woman spoke to Luca, her eyes never left Cantic. They burned with fascination.

"Do you know the general, Doctor? General, are you two acquainted?"

The deep triangle of lines around the general's mouth deepened as she frowned. She leaned this way and that to get a better angle in the flickering of the lantern light, but she shook her head in the end.

"The general knows my wife, Your Highness."

"Djasha din Aranen, leader of the rebel council?"

"The one. Also called the Brigāni witch by some." The doctor blinked brown eyes slowly at Cantic.

Cantic stiffened at the mention of the Brigāni, like she always did. There were some mistakes that left scars in you no matter how long ago you made them. Was Luca making a similar mistake, or would she look back on this and feel justified?

She was too close not to try.

"Why is she called the witch? Did she have anything to do with Lieutenant Touraine's healing?"

In that fateful court-martial months ago, Touraine mentioned a Brigāni witch, and it was Djasha who had promised magic.

Aranen straightened, the irons around her wrists banging. She met Luca's eyes for the first time. "No. She didn't. I did."

General Cantic barked a laugh, but the dismissal didn't have the same effect when her body went erect. Luca held up a hand. She hadn't told Cantic why she wanted Aranen and the other doctors and rumored priests.

"By 'healed,' Doctor, what do you mean? You plied your trade as a physician?"

"You know that's not what I mean, Your Highness."

Cantic stood so quickly that her stool fell back with a clatter. The muscle in her jaw flexed, and her hands clenched. "Your Highness, we're being baited."

"For someone who was so eager to find the source of Shālan healing magic thirty years ago, you're quite reticent now, General." Aranen sat back in her chair, a small smile playing on her lips. "I'm not here to bait you. Unlike my wife, I'm willing to tell you what you want."

"Why?" Luca asked.

"Because. I am a priestess of Shāl. We practice peace above all." The doctor-priestess shrugged and smirked at the general. "Forgive me. I'm not perfect. If you give us peace... I'll tell you everything."

Luca rolled her pen between her fingers. "And what exactly do you mean by that? Peace?"

"Don't listen to this nonsense, Your Highness." General Cantic had governed herself enough to hold her volume in check, but her voice still strained with anger. "It does us no credit to entertain believers."

"It does you no credit to pretend you never did."

"Balladaire is more civilized than that."

"You were plenty interested in our god when you went hunting down Brigāni tribes. I heard that one of the Brigāni came back for your company."

Cantic had Aranen by the collar before Luca understood what was happening. "Hold your tongue!"

"General!" shouted Luca over the clatter of iron and chair and the grunt of the scuffle. "Release her immediately, then go see to the state of the compound, if you please."

Cantic loosed the priestess, then scrubbed her face with her hand. Something disbelieving showed in her face, and Luca wondered at it. The general had been fighting this fight, or something like it, for at least thirty years. If Luca ended it now, with this conversation, what did that mean for the decades of Cantic's life? Would the soldier feel wasted or relieved?

"Your Highness. You don't know what you're doing with her. You can't trust them."

"Thank you for your concern, General. You're dismissed."

For a moment, nothing in the room moved while Luca and Aranen both waited to see if Cantic would obey. Then, with the curtest of bows, the general made an about-face and left.

After the door closed, Luca sagged back down into her chair. "That was peace over all?"

Aranen's smug look was gone, leaving only a distant, vacant expression. "Some scores are worth settling."

Comprehension finally dawned. "Surely Djasha wasn't the Brigāni who...? It wasn't just a rumor?"

"The Brigāni who tore through Cantic's camp using magic forbidden even by our god?" Aranen smiled. "My wife would never do such a thing."

Luca recalled Djasha that night at the festival. How swiftly she'd pierced her student's body, how ruthlessly, never once looking away from the girl's eyes.

"Forbidden even to you?" Luca asked.

"When I say 'peace,' I mean that I want you to leave. All of you. You. Your soldiers, the entire compound emptied. The merchants gone except by invitation. All land reverted to Qazāl. No Balladairan representation at all unless and until we've courted you for trade."

"And would you?"

"Shāl willing, no. We have others to ally with. Depending on your good behavior, however, all things are possible."

"You sound like a diplomat, not a doctor."

"A priest of Shāl is a mediator. We heal more than bodies."

Luca breathed deeply. The jail was cooler than the surface outside, but her shirt clung to her sweaty back. "I told Touraine this. I cannot simply leave. I will work toward it."

"My wife tried to make a partial peace with you before. Something you would work toward. The next thing we knew..." Aranen shrugged again.

It was all Luca could do not to show her full surprise. "She lied to you, too."

Aranen frowned. "Who?"

"Touraine. She told Cantic. She broke the deal I made. On purpose. To save the Sands."

Luca watched as surprise and pain—and, for just a moment, rage—moved across the woman's face. Then she bowed her head once.

"That's unfortunate. I didn't want to heal her at first. Djasha insisted." Aranen smiled ruefully. "I was beginning to like her."

"What will stop me from torturing the methods out of you?"

"I would say your conscience, but I suppose that's not true, is it?"

Luca ignored the prickle of guilt tensing up her shoulders.

"The magic is easy." She smiled in a way that told Luca it was anything but. "Do you have any fresh meat held over?"

Since the animals had been...vanished...it was difficult at best to find any meat at all at a reasonable price. Some had been requisitioned for officers' meals, though.

"How fresh, exactly?"

Aranen arched an eyebrow. "Fresh enough for you. Bring me a warm meal of it, and I'll show you."

Luca got up and, still watching Aranen from the corner of her eye, poked her head outside the interrogation room. Unsurprisingly, Cantic was still there, fists tight by her sides.

"General. Perfect. The prisoner and I would like some lunch. Have them send us something with meat." She forestalled the general's protests with a raised hand. "It's important." Then she went back inside the room with Aranen and closed the door, without waiting to see if Cantic obeyed.

"So you need meat. What else?" Luca asked the priestess after she sat down.

"After that, it's a simple matter of faith in Shāl and devotion to his tenets." Aranen shrugged and cocked an eyebrow as if to say *What else?* and the links of her fetters clinked with warning.

CHAPTER 34

A MATTER
OF FAITH

A matter of faith, the priestess had said.

After Aranen's demonstration, Luca's mind was full of possibilities. Full of fear and curiosity. Full of hope. The magic *was* simple, or at least, simple enough. The only thing she still struggled with was that sharp little word, *faith*.

When she returned to the Quartier, Luca went straight to her bedroom to contemplate it in private. She sat in one of the comfortable chairs, half reading while she mulled over the question in the back of her mind.

Faith was the purview of the uncivilized. Her father had taught her that, and after he died, her tutors and her uncle. Gods were crutches for the weak willed, they said. Well, she was no stranger to crutches. She smirked to herself. What was one more?

Luca pulled the sleeve of her dressing gown up to look at the small sliver of a scar on the underside of her forearm. Aranen had cut her there. It was smooth under her thumb, as if it had healed years ago. She couldn't see it without thinking of the cut Touraine had shown her on her own forearm, longer and thicker but just as aged.

A gentle knock on the door jerked Luca out of her thoughts. She let her sleeve fall back down, covering it protectively with her other hand.

"It's Gillett," he said.

"Come in," Luca called. She forced her hand away from the scar.

Gillett closed the door behind him and took the chair from Luca's small desk. The chair seemed too small for him, crowding his knees into his chest, but he looked at ease.

Then Luca noticed the fan of lines around Gil's mouth and the wrinkles on his brow.

"Hello, Gil," she said softly. Before Qazāl, they used to meet and speak regularly, even if he wasn't guarding her person himself. Now there was distance between them.

"Luca." His smile brightened his face. "How are you?"

Luca nodded slowly, putting her book on the side table. "I've been better, but I've also been worse. Things aren't going as I expected."

Gil smiled wryly. "That's the trouble with expectations." Then he sobered. "Something is bothering you."

First, Luca shook her head. Then she reconsidered. "What does it mean to have faith in something?"

The guard captain blinked, but he had known Luca since she was an inquisitive child. For certain, this couldn't be the strangest thing she'd ever asked him.

"It's the absence of doubt," he said after only a moment's pause. "I had faith in your father. I have faith in you."

"Did you never doubt my father?"

Gil crossed one leg over the other knee. "It's in our nature to doubt. The key to faith is standing by someone anyway."

The answer of a man who had devoted himself to serving others: first as a soldier, then as a royal guard. It felt too... *unthinking* for Luca. To say she didn't follow others well would have been an understatement.

"What about when he gave you orders you disagreed with?" she asked.

"I followed some of them. I didn't follow others." The sudden grief in the old man's face made Luca's heart catch. The apple of his throat bobbed hard as he swallowed. "I regret some of the things I did on each side. But I don't regret standing by Roland. I never have."

Is that what faith amounted to? Love and devotion? Obedience?

"I see," she said, looking down at her lap.

Gil cleared his throat. "Lanquette said you spent the day at the prison with priests and doctors." Disapproval laced his words.

Luca nodded, but she recognized the lecture coming and turned the subject just slightly. "Gil, what if I lift the ban on religion?"

His gray eyebrows shot up his face. "Why would you do that?" he asked slowly.

She picked her book back up and flicked its pages. "I wondered if it would help change things with the Qazāli. Give them less motivation to rebel."

"I don't know." Gil stroked his mustache, his grief and lecture both seemingly forgotten. "It would be hard to convince Beau-Sang or Cantic that was a good idea. And it wouldn't change how other Balladairans treated believers. Qazāli who want to work with them will still be best served without it, no matter what laws you make."

Luca tugged at the cuff of her dressing gown. "What if I wanted to follow a god?"

Gil grunted as if he'd been punched. "And why...would you do that?"

"Because I'm curious." It was hard for Luca to say the next words aloud even though she had been thinking them all day. "The magic comes from their god. The magic is real. That means the god must be real, too."

Gil's hand floated between his mustache and his short steel-gray hair.

Finally, he clasped both his hands in front of him, resting his elbows on his knees. "I take it you want to learn the magic yourself."

"That would be uncivilized of me," she said bitterly.

"Who did you talk to?"

Luca didn't have to ask what he meant. "Aranen din Djasha."

Gil's face went slack. Enunciating word by slow word, he said, "You kidnapped the wife of the leader of the rebels you're trying to subdue."

"I didn't ask for her specifically, but I did ask for doctors and suspected priests. This is what came up in the nets. It's paid off."

Only now, though, was Luca thinking about Aranen's ironic smile as she said her wife would never use magic to destroy a company of soldiers out of vengeance. She sniffed matter-of-factly. "The priests are valuable hostages. We'll use them to negotiate their surrender."

Gil worked his jaw as he sat back again, tension slipping from his body. "I suppose that might work." He covered his eyes with his hand. "But I thought you wanted to be a new kind of queen? I can't see how this is any different than what your father or even Nicolas would do." His brown eyes flashed with angry heat when he uncovered them again.

"You heard Touraine," Luca snapped. "She wants to give me an ultimatum. I'm giving her one back."

"This is about her, then. You're taking your anger at her out on an entire city?"

Her face warmed with anger and embarrassment both. "No, I'm not. This is about strength, Gil. This is about ending this on my terms."

Touraine had made her choices, and Luca was free to make hers.

He nodded slowly, frowning with distaste without meeting her eyes. He stood. "Your will, Your Highness. As I said, I have faith in you. That means I'll stand by you." He sighed heavily. "But I thought I taught you better than this."

"I'm doing my best, Gil," she said. Luca pressed the heels of her palms against her eyes as if she could avoid Gil's disappointment if she couldn't see it. "I don't have anyone to show me." She looked up and saw his broad back where he'd paused with his hand on the door handle. "I want to be a good queen," she said, her voice a hoarse whisper around the tears in her throat. "I can't do that if I don't have the throne. You know Nicolas will keep it from me if he has any excuse."

Gil spun slowly on his boot heels. The sound was muffled on the thick Shālan carpet. "What does it mean to be a good queen? To show everyone your power? Do you want people to respect you or just obey you? Or do you want them to believe in you?"

Yes. All of it. She wanted all of that. And yet she knew that wasn't the answer Gil wanted her to give, so she kept her mouth shut and buried her eyes in her hands again. She heard the door open and close, and then she was alone.

Touraine had nowhere to go. She wouldn't be a Sand again. Luca wasn't going to take her in again.

So she lurked in alleys in the Old Medina to keep a low profile while she debated whether it was worth it to spend the few sovereigns she had with her on time at a smoking house for a water pipe and a cup of sweet Shālan tea. Even coffee wouldn't be bad. She just needed time to think. There still had to be a way she could help.

In the end, it was her stomach that chose for her. Instead of a smoking house, she headed to the Grand Bazaar. The sky was clear and peaceful. The sun was setting, and the thin clouds were melting into the desert sunset that Touraine was growing to love. Seabirds in the air spiraled in their rounds, looking for food in the bazaar: dropped crusts, discarded fruit too rotten even for cheating someone—or discarded after the cheating had happened.

Fruit and vegetables were almost as expensive as meat, since they were the next best source of food for the Balladairans. The fruit carts were almost empty as Touraine shuffled through to find something to eat and, yes, something she could carry with her when she inevitably joined a caravan.

The phrases she'd learned of market Shālan echoed in her head. A few sovereigns jangled in her pocket. None of the writs from Luca today. If she ran into any trouble, she might be able to say the usual: *The Jackal sends his regards.* It was a sly code to cloak Jaghotai's identity while using the Jackal's reputation. At the thought, Touraine couldn't help but frown behind her mask. She had fucked up. Again.

It was so easy to slip back into the mundane bits of life, even when you knew the world around you could break at any minute. Even though Aranen had been taken, even though a part of her was begging to run to Luca and ask her to free her, another part of

Touraine slipped easily, almost gratefully into chores like haggling over food.

Just like she and the Sands had learned to completely dissociate themselves from the reality of their lives, on campaign or off. They would go mad if all they thought about was the next battle they were marching to. Some of them had. Setting up camp, digging latrines, drinking and fucking and fighting and laughing, it was all part of real life. And if they gave up that, they'd be admitting they had nothing else but the war, and if they believed that, what exactly were they fighting for?

Like everyone else, she pretended to ignore the gallows as she meandered toward the fruit stalls. No bodies hung from the ropes today.

The noise that Touraine had thought was only bickering and haggling in the market became clearer as she approached. The shouting clarified itself. Shouting for apples and oranges in both languages. And the word *thief.* At the center of it, a Balladairan merchant stood in front of a cart heavy with apples. They must have come from Balladairan orchards. Then again...

She didn't notice the kid until he rammed into her gut. One apple fell from his hand and rolled back toward the crowd. He held another clutched tight in a grubby fist. He shook, and his lips trembled, his eyes already shining with tears.

"Steady on, kid," she said. "It's okay. You're okay." Then it dawned on her. This filthy boy hadn't paid half a sovereign for an apple. Definitely not for two. And she wasn't the only one who noticed.

A Balladairan in a well-tailored jacket dragged the boy back and smacked him in the face so hard that the boy fell and dropped the second apple.

"Sir! It's all right. I'll pay for them." She tried to wedge herself between them.

The man in front of her was handsome, with gleaming dark hair and cruel dark eyes. The kind of man used to putting people underneath him. Touraine would have bet her life he was a Droitist.

He swung his backhand at her next. How dare she stand between him and his rightful duty? He would put her in her place, too. She should have let him hit her, or at the very least dodged, but she'd spent enough of the day with her head bowed, and to people who deserved it. Besides, Touraine had always preferred the offensive. One of her weaknesses.

Before she realized it, she'd blocked him with a forearm and shoved him back. He fell to the ground, half-shocked, half-furious. She looked for the boy, hoping to grab him and blend back into the crowd. He was already gone.

In his place, the crowd of Qazāli had grown. "Give us the apples," they chanted. "Give us the apples." It echoed through the bazaar and filled Touraine with sudden, sharp pride.

Then a volley of disciplined Balladairan musketry took out one of the men standing beside her. Another volley, and the crowd scattered. The blackcoats had come to restore order.

Touraine almost crashed into Jaghotai as the other woman was running out of Djasha and Aranen's apartment. The other woman's scarf was wrapped around her face, too.

"What in Shāl's name did you do this time?" Jaghotai asked, eyes wide with fury or fear, Touraine couldn't tell. She noticed that the two emotions tended to coincide in the older woman.

Touraine turned with her, and they loped in the direction of the bazaar. The orange glow of sunset had turned into the burn of torches and lanterns, but instead of being a sign of the cozy revelry of the city in the evening, it sent a forbidding shiver up Touraine's back. Her soldier's instincts screamed against it.

"Food riots finally cracked." Touraine still hadn't found the street boy. "And the Balladairans are taking it out on everyone."

"Everyone?"

"Everyone that's not Balladairan."

"What about the blackcoats?"

"They're 'helping' the Balladairans, obviously."

Jaghotai swore.

"The people know to get to the Grand Temple," Jaghotai said between breaths. She was flagging. Sometimes Touraine forgot that the woman had to be fifty years old or near enough. "They'll be safe there."

"Will they? That's where Rogan found me and Aranen, remember? It's compromised."

"Djasha." Jaghotai stopped abruptly and swore again. "She and Malika went to check on the patients. Meet them there. It's the closest thing to a fortress we have. Our people will go there for instructions if they don't get caught up sooner. I'll see what's to be done in the bazaar. You organize them from the temple."

Touraine blinked in surprise. "You're putting me in charge of your fighters?"

"You're not up to it, Mulāzim?" Jaghotai was ready to run off again, chest rising steadily.

Despite the situation, the other woman was poised with a seemingly unshakable calm. Like Cantic. Like Djasha. Was this something that came with age? Was that why Touraine's stomach still roiled with guilt and anxiety at the prospect of ordering men and women into battle? She tucked those thoughts away. If nothing else, she was good enough at pretending to be calm.

"Aye, aye, Captain." Touraine threw her mother a salute.

Touraine's stomach sank as she came up on the temple. Outside it, a group set to battering the doors down with a low-backed couch. Only a few wore Balladairan blacks. The others looked like civilians, with bellies of comfort and long hair slicked with sweat. Their faces twisted with the effort; they laughed like drinking friends.

The Grand Temple's glass windows had been shattered with projectiles—bullets, rocks, Touraine didn't know. Smoke billowed from them in thick clouds, a black haze above the flames. The night was perfumed with frankincense and sandalwood, as if all the incense in the world had been lit at once, for one great prayer. Enough to appease an entire world of gods. Inside, people were screaming.

"Heave!" A broad woman at the back of the couch called to her friends. Her thick shoulders strained the coat of her uniform across her back and arms. With one arm guiding the couch, she waved the other arm like a flag. That's when Touraine realized they weren't just laughing. They were singing. The Balladairan imperial anthem.

After over twenty years of training and fighting and studying with them, she hadn't managed to prove that she, that Qazāli, were worth more than this. What would it take for Balladaire to see them as more than cheap labor and cannon fodder?

Maybe watching death come for them, wearing her face.

Touraine barreled into the macabre conductor knife-first. She collided with so much force that the woman lifted off the ground and toppled into her neighbor. They all fell in a heap, and the end of the couch slammed near Touraine's face.

The woman beneath her stared up with glassy eyes. The man beneath the woman squirmed under the combined weight. Touraine jumped up and snapped his neck with her boot.

The four Balladairans left gaped in confusion, still dumbly holding their sections of the couch. Two civilians, two blackcoats. Only one civilian had sense enough to flee from the look in Touraine's eyes. She yanked her knife from between the conductor's ribs and flicked it toward the others. They flinched as blood speckled their pale faces, and she leapt before they could coordinate themselves.

Shāl, if you really give a shit about anyone here, let them be safe... Touraine was out of practice on the prayer bit. *I promise I'll do better if I make it out of this alive.*

Her first slash caught one blackcoat on the inner forearm, and his hand flopped uselessly without its tendons. Then the blade was through the man's stomach and up, up into his heart. Then she ducked the blow she knew would come and shot her heel back and up. A satisfying crunch of contact.

One blackcoat left.

The soldier had his rifle back in hand. He lifted it to fire as one of the Qazāli rebels ran up behind him on silent feet. Faster, faster—

The energy in Touraine's legs bunched and coiled, and she sprang backward through the air, like Jaghotai had taught her, one hand grazing the ground. When the world had righted itself, the last soldier was dead, a gash on each side of his throat.

"Thanks, brother," Touraine said in Shālan.

"Mulāzim." The rebel dragged Touraine by the arm, looking over his shoulder. His scarf covered most of his features, but she recognized his green eyes, wide in horror. His cheeks were wet as firelight from the temple danced across his face. His name was Faran, one of the younger rebels, like Malika, who was either below the theoretical "prime age" or not yet born when the Droitists took the Sands for "reeducation."

Touraine coughed as the incense-heavy smoke filled the air. Sky above and earth below. Surely Cantic hadn't ordered this. Luca wouldn't sanction it.

"We have to get them out," Touraine said. She dragged frantically at the heavy couch. "Grab it—help me!"

Smoke crept from the cracks of the main doors. When she ran to the small side door, she had to jerk her hand away from the heat. Whatever the torches had caught burned quick and hot. She let her palm hover in the space, unable to move for several heartbeats.

"They're smart, Mulāzim. They'll take the tunnels." Faran's choked-up voice brought her back to herself. He nodded back to the center of the city. He sniffed. "We should help the Jackal."

Right. Jaghotai had told her to gather her fighters and organize them. She could already see pockets of flame and smoke blossoming in other areas of the city like morbid night flowers. The boy's tears made Touraine feel like the lieutenant again. She grabbed his shoulder, forced him to look at her and not the smoking temple. "No. If there are tunnels, get to them. Help people get out. If you see any more of the Jackal's fighters, take them with you. Evacuate any civilians. They need you. I'll help the Jackal."

It wasn't hard to make the words. She had a lot of practice sweetening the stench of death to come. And the rebel bought the words as easily as any of her soldiers ever did—meaning he barely bought them at all. But it was enough to put his battle fear to work for him instead of against him.

Touraine didn't have high hopes for Jaghotai's rebel fighters against the blackcoats. They were underarmed, with little training and no strategy. Whatever the Jackal said, this was a losing game. She wasn't going to send the boy into the thick of the fighting to die.

And this is the side you chose.

She heard shouts and rounded the corner of the temple. A pair of blackcoats knelt beside the building. A moment later, they jumped up and ran, straight for her. They were surprised to see her, but they had a wild look in their eyes and didn't stop to engage her.

We are fucked.

For a split second, she paused, and the world paused with her. Her instincts screamed for her to follow them, but it took so long to issue the command to her body. She turned. Her legs reached. Then the world moved at normal speed again, with a sound like a thousand cannons fired at once.

A rush of hot air at her back pushed her through the air. Flat on the ground, she watched the high bowls and spires of the temple shudder and sway, like a mirage. Slowly, as if fainting, it collapsed, spraying a shower of dust and chunks of stone.

For a moment, everyone nearby was transfixed, Touraine and the Balladairans all. Then the cloud of dust expanded like a stampede, and the Balladairans fled.

Touraine buried her head and let the cloud pass over her. She tasted blood in her mouth. Blood ran down her face, too, and she felt like she'd been trampled by a horse. She considered lying there and not getting up until it was all over.

Instead, she rolled over to her hands and knees and spat a gob of blood and phlegm and marble grit. The dust hung in the air like fog and was just as hard to see through.

She was here because she was a soldier. A fighter. She didn't know anything else, and she was good at it. Cantic had made sure of that. And Touraine enjoyed it. She could still feel the glee of punching Tibeau for the first time. It would be the death of her, but she'd always expected that. She'd been raised for this, and she had nothing but this, even though she had tried so fucking hard to find something else.

She was needed here. She got back up.

She went to fight with the Jackal for the Qazāli.

Shāl, have mercy on us.

Shāl, have mercy on us, Luca thought, squeezing the handle of her knife in her left hand while blood welled from the new cut on her forearm.

She glanced furtively over her shoulder. She had barricaded herself in her office in the town house, all the way upstairs, just so that she could have privacy. The last thing she wanted was for Gil to walk in and catch her.

The slice Luca had made was just under the cut Aranen had made earlier that day. The blood was a deep wine burgundy in the lamplight, stark against her pale skin. Her dinner of stewed lamb and chickpeas was mostly gone—she'd requested it especially for this. It was a local dish, flavored with dried fruit and warm spices, and the scent lingered.

She squeezed her fist to make the blood come faster and closed her eyes, like Aranen had done. *Shāl, have mercy on us.*

Luca peeked one eye at the small wound. Nothing. Nothing but the sting of the cut and the tickle of blood sliding down her arm toward the crook of her elbow.

She tried again, thinking the words in Shālan, murmuring them under her breath. She tried different combinations of phrases she'd heard Shālans utter automatically or when they thought Balladairans couldn't hear. She even resorted to simply asking Shāl to hear and heal her.

Still, nothing happened.

Luca *had seen* the magic work. She had seen Aranen do it with her own eyes. That was proof enough that Shāl existed, and so Luca no longer doubted. And yet it wasn't enough. Apparently, you couldn't simply ask a god to intercede. You couldn't simply *want* badly for a god to be real, or believe in phenomena created by a god.

The vision of herself on the Balladairan throne, banishing the Withering and healing the people, the greatest queen of an age, died with a frustrated whimper. She snatched up the cloth towel on her desk and wrapped it around her still-bleeding arm, grateful for the way the burn of the cut matched that frustration.

Shāl, she thought petulantly, *at least give me a sign that you're real.*

A resounding boom vibrated through Luca's chest and left her ears ringing.

"Shāl?" she said in a strangled whisper. She cast about sheepishly for some angry deity but saw nothing.

But someone was pounding frantically at the door and shouting.

Luca wound the cloth tighter around her forearm and hid the bloody knife in the drawer.

"What?" she called. "What's happening?"

Gil burst through the door. Was Luca imagining it, or were his eyes rimmed red with tears? The last time she'd seen him like this, she'd been trampled by a horse. Maybe she had struck a nerve with her questions earlier. She hadn't meant to hurt him.

"What?" she asked again.

"The temple, Luca." Gil's voice was thick with horror. "Blackcoats destroyed the Grand Temple."

PART 4
MARTYRS

CHAPTER 35

AN UNEARTHING

The early evening sun shone through a sky streaked with smoke. The Grand Temple was a mountain of cracked marble slabs, pebbles, and dust. Touraine's boots crunched on pulverized glass. She pulled her scarf up to keep from inhaling enough dust to make mud in her lungs. The wreckage smelled like prayers. She wasn't a Shālan, not yet, but she ached for this. She replayed its collapse in her mind, the earth shaking beneath her feet. She imagined the explosion echoing in the corridors. Even buildings along the outside of the courtyard hadn't been safe. Cracks splintered like rivers across their walls; one wall had crumbled.

The Qazāli resistance was just as broken. It seemed like half the city was unaccounted for. On the other side of a chunk of the temple's walls, Malika's face fell as she understood the extent of the Qazāli losses. Until this year, Touraine had never thought it possible to see a heart break. She had been naive. Finally, Malika met Touraine's eyes and held them. Desperately, like a piece of flotsam in the sea.

"Ya! There's someone here!" a person shouted in Shālan.

Touraine jumped at the voice, picking along the heap of rubble. Delicately, to keep from collapsing the rock and killing someone they hadn't found underneath. Quickly, so that this someone wouldn't suffocate. There had been survivors. There had also been corpses.

"Shāl, be gentle," someone prayed as two men shifted rock.

Touraine's fingers were scraped and bleeding, coated white. She and the others—including Sands who had abandoned their uniforms—formed a line to shuttle rocks away from the buried person. Her breath came in anxious, hopeful bursts.

"I have a leg!" the man at the front of the line called.

"Quicker!" she shouted.

They worked harder. Touraine realized she was passing her rocks to Jaghotai. She nodded. Like everyone else, she wore her scarf up for the dust, and like everyone else, her eyes were red rimmed. Dust mingled with the gray hairs in her dreadlocks.

A voice tunneled from the rocks. "Shāl is merciful," it said, over and over.

Touraine gave a relieved laugh as two men pulled up the last massive rock enough for a man to sit up.

"His legs are broken!"

"Carry him!"

"Healers!"

The last was a reflex, and it met a solemn hush. There were no more healers. They were all in Cantic's—in *Luca's* cells.

Another pair of Qazāli pried the man out of his crevice. Onlookers cheered.

Touraine clapped with them, but her mind had already moved on. She went to Jaghotai. "We need to figure out our next position. Attack or retreat, is there somewhere we can set up a defense—"

Jaghotai frowned incredulously. "What is wrong with you?"

Touraine should have known that Jaghotai of all people wouldn't want to work with her. If Djasha had been here instead of Jaghotai, they would have had a plan already. Instead of answering, Touraine circuited the excavated parts of the collapse to the far edge, where a Qazāli woman worked with a Sand. Noé. He always managed to get body duty. He tapped his forehead in solemn salute. He'd been one of the Sands who'd joined the rebels in the chaos the night the Grand Temple fell.

They'd found another body in a black coat, its skull half-flattened. While everyone else looked pointedly up and away, Jaghotai looked over the Balladairan coldly.

Touraine pointed with her head. "Put him with the other dead."

Noé and the woman pulled him out of the wreckage and carried his mangled body to a growing row. Touraine's stomach turned. She wretched, barely able to swallow the vomit, burning, back down her throat. Sky above, she'd gotten soft.

Jaghotai pulled her away, white-dusted fingers gripping Touraine's biceps hard. "Go home."

Touraine pulled away. "It's a bit late for that—"

Jaghotai shook her head wearily and held her palms up. "Not what I meant." She started to walk away from the wreckage, away from the people digging up answers in the shape of flesh.

In a low voice, she continued as they walked. "Half the council is dead. Our temple is in ruins. My city's still smoking. You're not gonna fix this right now—doesn't matter how many orders you give."

Touraine scoffed. "I'm not stupid. We have to prepare."

"Prepare? Ha! If they come for us now or they come for us next week, what will they get?"

Touraine looked over, eyebrows tight in confusion.

"Everything. All of it. Anything they want," Jaghotai said. She stepped closer. Tentatively, she put a hand on Touraine's shoulder. "You've been out here since they brought it down. Take some time. Clean yourself up. It won't make any difference."

Touraine looked down at herself. Her trousers were splattered with blood, pale with stone dust. She put a hand to her sweaty forehead and wiped at the grit.

"Go wash in one of the channels. The crocodiles don't usually wash up so far inland."

The darkness Touraine had been avoiding lurked at the side of her vision, crept at the edges of her limbs, and threatened to weigh her down. She tried to fight it.

"What right do you have—" To care? To give her orders?

"Every right." Jaghotai headed back to the temple, leaving Touraine no dignified choice but to walk away.

Touraine followed her anylight.

"Touraine..." Jaghotai warned.

Touraine kept marching back to the mess she'd made, to something she could do. Jaghotai flung her arm out to catch Touraine in the chest and shoved. Touraine pushed her back and stalked on, back to the rubble.

"Are we really doing this?" barked Touraine over her shoulder. "We've got work to do."

"Touraine—" The other woman tried to grab her in a bear hug, but Touraine spun, breaking the grip with an elbow. She hooked a punch into Jaghotai's jaw.

Jaghotai went sprawling. It took a second before either of them registered what happened. As she rubbed her jaw, Jaghotai's eyes went dark. She bared her teeth, and Touraine saw blood streaking them. Her hand was still clenched in its fist. It hurt to ease her fingers apart.

"I'm...sorry." Touraine clenched and unclenched her fists again, working the fingers loose. She shook her head, trying to clear away that...that darkness that was invading. With Jaghotai still on the ground, she turned on her heel and strode toward the river.

Touraine scooped water onto her face from a tepid little pond made by the irrigation and damming architecture that the Qazāli had learned from Balladaire. The water, trapped during the Hadd's flood season and the rains, normally watered goats. The goats were gone now.

The water dripped onto her aching shoulders and soaked into her scalp. She waded farther in. Maybe if she lay down in it, she could wash away the smell of the smoke. Maybe if she kept her ears stopped up with water, she wouldn't hear the screaming and that infernal imperial anthem anymore.

They had sometimes sung it when they marched, the Sands. Noé leading the verses while they all chimed in, variously out of tune. It was too sore for some of them, though. Instead, they preferred songs like "Jolly Soldier," which were morbid but at least reflected the lives they lived instead of an ideal Balladaire that they would never be a part of.

She hummed as the water tickled her scalp and she splashed a handful on her face.

Welcome, soldier. Welcome, jolly soldier. How can I help you today? Can I take your boots, sir, your army-issued boots, sir? How can I help you today?

The water dripped down her bare neck and drew goose bumps across her skin. The sun was on its way down, and the night was cooling quickly.

The river was lower than usual, people said, and this pool was barely knee high, murky with mud and plants, and too still to be completely fresh. It still smelled better than she did.

She stared at the Cursed City on the other side of the river. With the River Hadd between them, patrolled by the Many-Legged, the border between Qazāl and Briga stretched anywhere from a mile to several. At first, she'd thought it bizarre, the Qazāli leaving a whole city uninhabited because of superstition. Now Touraine knew what magic could do, and she didn't care to test it. Like Djasha had said months ago—superstitions came from somewhere.

Thinking of Djasha gave the darkness another push. It closed tight around her chest and made it difficult to breathe. She took off her shirt, waded into the water, and stopped fighting it.

Djasha, dying. Tibeau, dead. Pruett, who hated her. A sob wrenched out of her, and she turned it into a growl.

Her legs were heavy in the water. She soaked her shirt and used it to scrub herself down. She'd grown so dark in the southern sun, and her wet hair shook out in short dreadlocks and braids. She wasn't the soldier she'd been so sure of months ago.

She laughed at herself, at the irony. She wasn't sky-falling obedient anymore—that was certain. The easy camaraderie of the barracks was so far behind her, it might as well have been a dream. She didn't believe in Balladaire anymore, either. She would never be content on their side. The last hope she'd had died with Luca. Luca would never make Qazāl accept Balladairan rule. It was sovereignty or nothing at all.

And she could see the shape of that sovereignty now. In the distance, on the other side of the Mile-Long Bridge, El-Wast was a sprawl of clay squares like the earth's teeth. The skyline was missing the huge dome of the temple in the Old Medina, but there were smaller domes— smaller temples, shops. Balladairan flags waved at the different city gates, black rectangles that slowly vanished as the sky darkened.

It was easy to imagine the flags not being there at all. It might not come soon, but she could see the shape of that future in the girl she'd met in the slums, back when Touraine thought she could leave this all behind. The girl and her friends, fighting, fighting.

Touraine would keep fighting, and she would die. She could see that, too. It was coming.

It wasn't here yet.

She dragged herself out of the canal, shivering. *This must be what it's like to stand at the edge of a cliff and decide to jump.* From here on, it would be the rush of air, the speeding inevitability coming toward her, water or rocks—eventually she would make contact.

When she got back to the tiny rebel camp embedded in the slum city, she found Jaghotai in her tent.

"Jak?"

"Come in."

Jaghotai was sprawled over a thin blanket laid right on the dirt. It was dark in the tent, but Touraine could make out the darker shadow of the other woman's forearm across her face.

"I'm sorry about earlier," Touraine said. "And thanks."

Jaghotai grunted and rubbed her jaw. "Feel better?"

"No," Touraine laughed, the edge of the dark still there. *Yes.* "I thought about what you said, though. You're wrong. About Balladaire. They're going to come for us, and they're going to come hard. Waiting a week to prepare will mean the difference between saving anyone who isn't fighting and throwing them all on Balladaire's mercy. I know Balladairan mercy. It doesn't last long."

Jaghotai pushed herself up to sitting.

Touraine continued. "They'll threaten you. They're going to come for the children, the way they came for us. The last time that happened, they broke you."

Jaghotai made a noise of protest, but Touraine cut her off with a gesture. The water had washed the fog from her mind. She could see the pieces they needed to move. It was the endgame, and there were few ways to win but a hundred ways to lose. She was done negotiating, done trusting Luca. And unlike Luca, Touraine knew battles. She knew blood and she knew soldiers under fire. She knew what it was to have faith not in power, but in the person fighting beside you. Luca didn't have that.

She could see something else, too. She didn't want Balladairan respect. Not after this. Maybe she had been a dog all this time, but she was ready to bite back.

"Cantic only knew about half of the gun shipment. We can move them in the dark, hide them out here, distribute them. Set people to stockpiling water, hiding it, rationing it. We'll tighten the food rations."

"We have more guns?" Jaghotai whispered slowly, as if saying the fact aloud would make it not true.

Touraine nodded, smiling briefly before sobering. "What about the terms of surrender? If it comes to that?" Which it probably would. She wasn't naive about their odds.

"You mean under what conditions we'll surrender the city?" Jaghotai sucked her teeth and breathed slowly, taking in the empty tent and the movement outside—their people, still buzzing like a kicked hive. She smiled back. "None."

CHAPTER 36

REPARATIONS

W e need to launch an offensive," Beau-Sang said, slamming his fist on the war room's wooden table.

Luca, the governor, and the military's senior officers sat in the planning room where Touraine's court-martial had been held months ago. Today, the table sat in the center of the room again, with all the puffed-up Balladairan dignitaries crowded around it, trying to figure out what to do with the seething city that had imploded almost a week ago.

Colonel Taurvide, still just as thick in his head as he'd been before, agreed vehemently with Beau-Sang. "They're weak. Crush them now and we can crush them for good."

"What do you call burning their homes, looting their shops, and destroying their temple?" snapped Luca. She shot the colonel a dirty look. The general maintained that none of the destruction was under her orders, but it was *her* soldiers—and Taurvide's, but ultimately Cantic's—who had escalated the riots instead of stopping them.

Gil was right. Luca didn't want to be this kind of queen. She wanted power, yes, respect, absolutely—but her stomach turned whenever she thought of the smoking ruins of the Grand Temple's beautiful domes. *The Rule of Rule* said that a feared ruler had all the means to be a great ruler. Yverte would probably agree with Beau-Sang and Taurvide if he were still alive. If Luca didn't get the city in hand, she would never get to be a ruler, great or otherwise. She couldn't help thinking about the two cuts on her arm. The second one was scabbed over, the flesh tender.

"There must be another way," she reiterated.

On Luca's right, Cantic made a frustrated sound low in her throat. "We can't tell who a rebel is by looking at them. They don't wear uniforms, and this isn't an open battlefield. Anyone could be plotting against us."

"So we round them up and make an example," Taurvide said. He knocked on the wood with thick, hairy knuckles. "It worked with my Sands."

"And it worked in the quarries," Beau-Sang added. "It will work now. We'll show them that *anyone* can be punished, so *everyone* must behave. Then they'll police themselves."

Luca shivered at the cruelty, but Beau-Sang had a point. The Qazāli could be frightened out of joining the rebels. A large enough swath of "examples," and Qazāli civilians would fall over themselves to turn in suspicious neighbors, if only to protect themselves. They would be cowed. For now. Eventually, though, they would rise above the fear to fight again, and Luca would still have to live with a massacre on her conscience.

Cantic was deep in thought, or perhaps memory, her brow furrowed. Maybe she was thinking about the massacre at Masridān. Had that started like this, a war room full of desperate soldiers and politicians? After the Battle of the Bazaar, Cantic had said it was her job to bloody her hands so that Luca didn't need to. So that Luca could be the one to build something new out of the blood and shit. Sky above, there was plenty of blood. When would Luca get to grow something?

When you have it under control.

"Lord Governor Beau-Sang and Colonel Taurvide might have the right of it, Your Highness."

"Indeed," Beau-Sang said. "I've been managing these dogs for decades. That is why you appointed me governor, Your Highness. Let me do my duty to the empire." He puffed out his chest and raised his chin.

Still, Luca shook her head. She had spent most of her time in Qazāl *changing* the way Beau-Sang and the other Balladairans were allowed to treat their Qazāli laborers. She had made him governor so that he could be the sting of the whip, but that didn't mean there was no place for the honey.

"No," Luca said finally. "Not yet. General, you say the problem is that anyone can be a rebel. That's because everyone has a reason to rebel right now. The people are hungry, and the *rebels* are feeding them. We need to give them a reason to come to us instead."

Taurvide huffed. "You'd short our own people for these ungrateful—"

"They are also my people," Luca said sharply. "And 'rebellions begin when the status quo fails to provide for its people.'"

"With all due respect, Your Highness," Beau-Sang said, his ruddy cheeks stretched taut in a frown, "quoting Yverte will not get us out of a delicate situation. We all have the experience necessary to handle it."

Beau-Sang opened his arms to include the veteran officers sitting at the table. Taurvide, with his graying beard and his bluster, one hand in a fist, the other ready to rap knuckles on the table again for emphasis. Cantic, her face haggard though her blue eyes were clear and alert, smelling of cigarette smoke and the coffee in front of her. Even Gil was included in this, though Luca's guard captain remained silent. When she met his eyes, though, he nodded and gave an almost imperceptible smile. That was enough to bolster her.

"I don't doubt your experience, any of you. However, I want different results. We try this my way first. If it doesn't work, there will be plenty of time to go murdering my innocent subjects at your leisure."

Taurvide, Beau-Sang, and Cantic all stared at Luca blankly, surprised either by the words or by her vicious sarcasm. This wasn't the cool and collected princess they were used to. Luca stared them down in turn until finally, Cantic nodded.

"That will be expensive, Your Highness, but it could work. We'll begin preparations."

Colonel Taurvide began to object, but Cantic silenced him with a look. "We'll begin preparations, Colonel."

The colonel nodded stiffly, though he shared a dark look with Beau-Sang. The governor, however, calmly bowed his head to Luca and said, "Indeed, Your Highness. We'll see it done."

His acquiescence came almost too easily, and she wondered what machinations were turning behind those small, calculating eyes. Not for the first time, she thought of Aliez's suspicions about her father and Cheminade. But thinking of Aliez made Luca think of Aliez's missing lover, and that made Luca think of Touraine, so she pushed all the thoughts away again.

"Very good," Luca said. She straightened. "I'll have the writ signed and announce the changes to the city afterward. You're dismissed."

Ink dripped from Luca's pen as she hovered over her signature. The ink of her name was still wet, glistening in the low lantern light of her office on the compound later that night. Though Beau-Sang was the governor-general now, she had grown attached to the space.

The writ she had just signed would—if all went as planned in a city where nothing she'd ever done had gone according to plan—save the Qazāli and kill the rebellion in one blow.

She had just—to think the rest of the sentence made her sick to her stomach with guilt, but she made herself finish the thought. She had thought she could win the city back more cheaply. She had thought the rebels would relent when she had the doctors and priests as hostages. There was no better way to say it.

The greatest benefit, more than the soothed populace, was that the proclamation would douse the rebellion's fire before the rebels could stoke the coals of Qazāli anger in the wake of the tragedy.

All the Qazāli who brought proof or notification of dead family, injuries, or damaged property would be given recompense from the hand of the throne itself.

She would be paying a lot. And using soldiers to monitor the claims.

Luca lit her sealing candle and waited for the wax to heat, to make the slow transition from a single cohesive block to disparate drips. Slow. She'd chosen the gold wax this time, and the flames streaked it black.

She'd demanded the reports from Cantic since Gil and the general both agreed that it wasn't safe to have her in the streets. The fires—literal and metaphorical—hadn't been put out. It had been nearly a week since she'd run to the window at the sound of the thunderous explosion. She couldn't see the temple from behind the Quartier walls, but that hadn't stopped her from imagining the slow motion of the domes collapsing on themselves every day since. When she'd left the Quartier, just to see, the night sky had been bright with the burning heart of the city.

Luca pulled her shawl tighter against a shiver. She snapped to and realized the wax puddle was larger than she'd intended. She blew the candle out and stamped her rearing horse into the mess, with the L. A. of her initials in faint relief.

She had also sent a letter to dear Uncle Nicolas before the bastard could get any orders back in this direction. It was going to be hard enough to deal with Cantic in this situation.

Speaking of the wolf... the sharp click of military confidence only one person in the world could have stopped outside of Luca's office door.

"Come in," Luca said.

General Cantic gave her usual salute and curt bow before handing Luca yet another stamped letter. This one was on cheap military stuff, likely scraped over and over again. It crinkled as she held it. The black wax in the corner bore the seal of Balladairan commanding officers, a fist clenching a wheat sheaf and crossed arrows, Cantic's own signature beside it.

Cantic shrugged, hands clasped behind her back, so Luca skimmed it. Then tracked back to the beginning and read more carefully, unable to account for the way her heart lurched in her chest.

"You're executing them? In public?"

Cantic nodded sharply. "You asked earlier to be kept informed of our actions. This is merely a courtesy, Your Highness."

Luca sat back. "I wanted to be informed so we could discuss the best steps. We just discussed how volatile the city is, General. Give it more blood and—"

"You can be informed, Your Highness. Not dictate the military consequences. I already involved you more than I should have once, and that's done us no good."

"Make it private, then, General."

"They tried to defect, Your Highness. I'm making an example of them. It's hard enough to trust the rest of the Sands right now as it is. I'm reminding them of their place."

"That sounds very Droitist of you."

Luca clenched the paper, and it trembled with her. She didn't know if it was sadness or anger or guilt or dread.

Cantic sighed and pointed to the other chair in the room, the one Touraine used to sit in. "May I?"

"As you like."

"Ruling a nation is like being a teacher, Your Highness. The Droitists and the Tailleurists fight back and forth over the minute details, but the core principles are the same. You cannot be the guide and the friend. A teacher, like a king—or queen—needs a firm hand that's willing to cause pain or discomfort even if the student doesn't understand why. They don't need to understand fully; they only need to trust you enough to accept that you have their best interests at heart. With that trust, they'll take any amount of unsavory medicine."

"And executing two Sands for their benefit is unsavory medicine?"

Cantic pulled a face and looked all the more haggard for it. "No, Your Highness. That's discipline."

Luca pushed her decree across the desk.

After Cantic read it, she gave an approving grunt and a nod.

"And that is how you build trust. One must have both. Excellent." One edge of the general's mouth turned up. "You can announce it before the hanging."

Luca opened her mouth, but Cantic preempted her.

"Tomorrow, sunrise. That should give you time to ready one of your speeches."

"I already have a speech. I'm going to announce it today."

Touraine stared at the dark roof of the tent she shared with Jaghotai while the other woman's heavy, steady breaths filled the small space. It put her too much in mind of the cell she'd been left in on the compound before Luca had pulled her out.

Luca, who was already turning their game against them.

Touraine felt nauseated, feverish with frustration, just thinking about the princess.

By the time word of Luca's plan to repay Qazāli for their losses on the burning night reached them, it seemed like half of the slum had already emptied out, racing to collect.

Jaghotai had gone from a foul, if determined, mood to rage in an instant. That sky-falling liquor had to be the only reason the Jackal had even fallen asleep.

Touraine couldn't sleep. All the mistakes she'd made rattled in her head like dice. She wouldn't sleep well until she knew how they'd land. Not until she knew who would have to pay for Qazāl's freedom and how much. Her gut told her she wouldn't like the answer.

It didn't help that she wasn't feeling well today. She thought it was the cloistered air of the tent and staggered up to get some fresh air. A wave of fatigue made her stumble, though, and she caught herself on the tent flap.

"Are you going back to her, too?"

Jaghotai's voice was thick from where she lay on the other side of the tent. It was too dark for Touraine to make out the colors of the blankets or the expression on her mother's face.

"I know you sold us out to Cantic."

Touraine's retort dried in her throat. She hunted the dark for Jaghotai's weapons. Desperation coiled in her stomach, but shame held her still. She felt warm. Too warm.

"What I couldn't figure is...your princess seemed so attached to you. I kept wondering why you never went back to her, kept asking myself if maybe you really were here for us. I don't think so. You could have had anything at her side. Only reason to leave would be if you knew she wouldn't want you there. So why wouldn't she want you there? You'd have to have done something she couldn't forgive."

Jaghotai stood. Touraine stepped back, making it look like reflex, and cracked the tent flap open enough to let in the moonlight. The pale light slashed across Jaghotai's face, showing deep bags beneath her eyes. "She really was trying to make peace. Do you know how many people you've killed?"

Touraine swallowed. "My family was in danger."

"Your family." Jaghotai's chuckle sounded pained.

Touraine's back went rigid in response. Instead of stepping away again, she dug her words in even harder. She said, "More family than you ever were."

Jaghotai snorted. "I had no choice in that. They took you—"

"And I came back. You knew who I was when you broke my ribs with your sky-falling boot. You'd have killed me then if it would have gotten you what you wanted," she snarled.

Jaghotai hesitated. "I wouldn't have."

Touraine laughed, too, incredulous even though she wanted to believe it was the truth so badly that she couldn't help but break that hope for the lie that it was. Otherwise she might cry instead, and she wouldn't give Jaghotai that satisfaction.

"You're saying if it had come down to Djasha and Aranen—or me, some strange enemy—you wouldn't risk my life?"

Jaghotai flinched back into shadow.

Touraine had her beat. She twisted the sharp words tighter. "If you wouldn't, I don't need you as my family anylight."

Touraine would work with her. She could. If the woman kept her space. The closer Jaghotai got, the more panic sent her flailing. This was the closest she could get right now to a concession. She would try—later, when this was all over, if she survived, she would. Touraine crossed her arms over her chest but didn't back any farther away even though her legs felt weak.

"Tell me where the guns are."

"A warehouse on rue de Sarpont, one of those little obnoxious streets in the Puddle District."

Jaghotai sniffed. "First thing I do when I'm rid of your masters is rip down every one of those stupid street signs. Rue de Sarpont, my ass." She sat back down to tug on her boots with the edges worn out. "I'll take a small group now and see what we find before the sun comes up."

"I should come with you. And a couple Sands. You're short on fighters."

"Short on fighters I can trust, sah. Doesn't mean I want to add fighters I don't."

Touraine rolled her eyes. "As you like."

Jaghotai turned to her with a wicked grin. "While we're gone, do something useful, eh? We could use a few new shit ditches."

"Oh, fuck you."

The other woman's loud laughter danced through the night as Jaghotai walked away.

When Touraine fell back into a fitful sleep, she was woken from dreams of incessant digging by an intense rustling of her tent wall and the whimper of a child. She thought it was part of the dream, until a second, more insistent voice joined the whimper.

"Mulāzim!" Touraine recognized the voice of the fighting girl with the braid. Her name was Ghadin, and she lived with her uncle and her grandmother and her little sister. Touraine had spent a little of her time each day roughhousing with the children, because somehow, it made the weight of the rebellion less. But Ghadin was a serious kid, the self-proclaimed leader of the slum children, and she wouldn't wake Touraine up in the middle of the night for nothing.

Touraine rolled to her feet and pulled up the tent flap. The cold air bit at her hot skin, and judging by the thin line of pale blue on the horizon, it was early morning, not the middle of the night. Outside the tent, Ghadin held a small boy's hand and tugged her long braid with a worried expression.

"This kid was looking for you," Ghadin told Touraine as explanation. Like most of the children, she spoke to Touraine in what Touraine was beginning to think of as "Qazāli"—that combination of Shālan and Balladairan. The girl nudged the boy forward gently.

"What?" Touraine asked, gesturing for him to speak.

He flinched when she looked at him, hesitated at her open palm. She recognized that fear. Droitists had gotten to this kid. Sky-falling fuck. She forced her hands down and open instead of making fists to imitate the sudden rock of anger settling in her gut. Fucking Balladaire.

"She said it was important," he said, voice barely squeaking out.

"It's all right, it's all right." Touraine knelt down on one knee to meet his eyes. "What do you need, dear one?" She used the Shālan endearment, and the boy's face relaxed marginally.

"The lieutenant from the guardhouse. She told me to get help."

Touraine's stomach dropped to her bare feet. "The lieutenant. The one with bluish-gray eyes. That lieutenant?"

"Yes. She said look for the mulāzim. Everyone sent me here. To you. I know you."

Pruett. How did she know the name—? Pruett.

"Help for what? What's happening?" She had to stop herself from gripping the boy in her desperation for answers.

"I don't know. I don't know! She didn't say, sir."

"Sky above." She pushed back into the tent, swearing as she fumbled on the rest of her clothes. Her limbs were heavy; her mind was slow and bleary with fever.

There was so much for the rebels to do, still so much to plan. But Pruett needed her. The Sands needed her. Her family needed her.

CHAPTER 37

A REMINDER

The carriage rattled Luca's concentration as she practiced her latest speech. Already, Qazāli civilians were acting on yesterday's declaration of reparations. They queued at the Balladairan bank, waiting to be verified, to have their grief quantified and paid for.

Cantic still insisted on Luca saying something before the hanging to encourage "loyalty and duty."

"Loyalty and duty," Luca muttered to herself.

Beau-Sang, on the bench across from her, nodded.

"Indeed, Your Highness. The most important attributes of a civilized citizen."

"Indeed," she echoed. Loyalty. Its opposite, treachery. So hard to detect sometimes. She sensed no loyalty in Beau-Sang, so she wasn't worried about mistaking him for an ally. On the other hand, she'd been blinded to the treachery in Touraine.

"My family has been most loyal to the Ancier crown, in fact."

Luca raised an eyebrow. "Indeed." She waited.

"I suppose you must think me ham-fisted and vulgar"—he smiled—"but a father with his children's best interests at heart can't help but notice. You've spent time with both of my children of late."

At that moment, the carriage jostled over a rough patch in the street, and Luca used the surprise to cover up the flush of embarrassment that crept up her cheeks.

"To my eye, a match would be beneficial to both of us," the comte said after the road evened out. He adjusted his coat carefully around his broad shoulders. He clung to Balladairan-style clothing despite the heat, and in return, the tight coat and trousers clung to him, and sweat stained the layers of silk and wool even though the morning was still cool to Luca.

"Indeed?" Luca tried not to yawn, and the effort almost cracked her jaw.

Beau-Sang gave Luca a paternal smile, as if it would reflect the depths of his affection for his own children. "I understand what's at stake for you here. You're afraid of failing to crush the rebellion, your uncle calling a trial of competence against you."

Suddenly, Luca felt stripped bare. It wasn't as if Beau-Sang's observations were secret, but one would point them out only if one wanted to do something about them—for better or for worse.

"We have the rebellion well in hand, my lord."

"Of course we do," he said, as if he believed anything but. "However, we're losing control of commerce. It's difficult for your merchants to turn a profit, especially in more expensive industries, like stone." He waited for her to ask for more, but she only stared him down. He continued on his own, "I'll take the prisoners in the quarries. You can keep your high-handed ideals and appease the rebels. The prisoners aren't subject to your new laborers' laws. You marry one of my children, and that wealth comes to you. You lose nothing."

Beau-Sang folded his thick, hairy fingers together on his lap. Though the hour was early, he didn't look bleary at all. Luca, on the other hand, had taken two cups of strong coffee, without even milk to soften the bitter flavor. She was awake, but the heady rush was building in her blood.

Or maybe it was apprehension.

She would be lying to herself if she pretended the idea hadn't occurred to her. Bastien in particular had proven a reliable friend and was easy to talk to. He shared her interest in scholarly pursuits, and there was comfort in huddling over books with someone who understood her.

Circumstances had stopped her, though, not chief of which was a troublemaking turncoat soldier whose face Luca still saw with painful clarity whenever she closed her eyes.

There was also the matter of Aliez's allegations against her father. Luca hadn't had time to look into them yet, but they turned Luca's stomach more than ever. Beau-Sang had been vocal in his praise of the Balladairans after they had razed the Qazāli neighborhoods. He'd even made snide comments about the fall of the temple.

And the reverse of his offer was clear—if she didn't accept the proposal or one in kind, he would endanger her road to the throne, possibly sabotaging Luca's plans to end the rebellion.

Through the carriage window, desert-yellow buildings passed by, grayish in the early morning. They would be at the Grand Bazaar momentarily.

There was no way to guarantee loyalty from anyone except to give them what they wanted and keep up the supply—or hope that no one came along with a better offer. Beau-Sang thought he was holding a knife to her throat and forcing her to empty her pockets, a common thug. At the very least, she could buy herself more time to determine an escape route. Or time to find out the truth Aliez had hinted at.

Luca adjusted her own short coat over her thin Qazāli-style tunic, trying to let the sudden flush of body heat escape. "I'm honored that they would be interested, my lord. Both Paul-Sebastien and Aliez do you a great credit." *More than you deserve.* "I'll be glad to consider this after I've thought about who might make the best companion."

"Very good, Your Highness. Let's speak again next week. That should be enough time."

"I'll send for you when I'm ready," Luca said. She met his gaze and held it until finally he bowed his head.

"Your will, Your Highness."

Luca closed her eyes and leaned back under the guise of sleepiness, though tears pricked at her closed eyelids.

Without Touraine, the way was clear for her to choose a consort. Not that she would ever have gone through with proposing that to Touraine, but it had been...such a nice idea. A gentle what-if that had never occurred to her until the night Touraine had rubbed the ache from her legs. And then the next day, she'd betrayed Luca for the first time.

Even worse than Touraine's betrayal was the sneaking guilt that crept along Luca's shoulders like a roach—that she was no different.

Touraine started toward the guardhouse, thinking to find Pruett there. As Touraine got closer to the center of the city, though, she heard the rapid tap of a Balladairan drummer, waking people up and calling them out.

She and Noé and the few other Sands who had escaped on the burning night followed the sound unerringly to the bazaar. The Grand Bazaar, now more often called the Gallows Bazaar.

Already, a groggy crowd was present. The Qazāli stall owners who hadn't lost their livelihoods—or their lives—in the rioting, early shoppers trying to get the best scraps of food, and Balladairan merchants whose eyes gleamed with an ever-present hunger.

Above, gulls squawked, waiting for their share. They wouldn't get it, though. Desperation had made everyone quicker to snatch at anything—including Luca's handouts.

The drums stopped. And then, from the back of the crowd, Touraine saw Cantic take the gallows stage, followed by Luca, who leaned lightly on her cane. *Her leg must not hurt today.* The thought came automatically, but it vanished as Touraine watched two pairs of blackcoats drag two prisoners up the stairs. Though the prisoners weren't wearing their uniform coats, she could tell they were soldiers by their military-issue boots.

"Closer," Touraine muttered to Noé and the others. She pushed into the crowd and lost sight of the gallows stage.

"Those sky-falling dogfuckers," Noé said, standing on his tiptoes.

Touraine couldn't see. "What? What is it?" The nausea was rising in her again. It was just the press of the crowd and the smell, she told herself. But she was also dizzy with exhaustion. She steadied herself on Noé's shoulder and tried to focus.

"They have—I think—"

"Sky above, who, Noé?"

"Henri and..." He looked down at Touraine, anguish in his eyes as he hesitated. "Aimée."

"Shit." Touraine shoved harder, forcing her way to the stage.

Cantic's harsh voice silenced the crowd. "Citizens of Qazāl, subjects of the Balladairan Empire. The last few weeks in this city have been grim, and I'm not near eloquent enough to address them or the reason we're here today. I present with honor Her Royal Highness Princess Luca Ancier, queen regnant of Balladaire."

Around Touraine, a scattered few clapped, but even the applause was subdued.

And then Luca started to talk, her voice clear and resonant.

"Loyalty is part of the social contract we commit to when we decide to be civilized. As humans gathered into societies—tribes and villages, cities and nations—we committed to each other. We promised to protect our fellows, to honor the promises we give and the exchanges we make."

An elbow to Touraine's jaw as she shoved her way to the front showed Touraine just how minute those exchanges could be. She almost fell to the ground, but Noé reached for her, held her up with concern in his soft brown eyes.

"To betray that trust," Luca continued, "chips away at the stone upon which we build our great cities. Broken promises weaken the bonds between siblings. When parents abandon the child, do their young hearts not break?"

Finally, Touraine arrived at the front of the crowd, close enough to get a full view of those standing on the gallows. She and Noé hung back just enough to be invisible behind a group of Qazāli quarry laborers, as stone-faced as their work. Luca. Cantic, Rogan, and that bastard the comte de Beau-Sang stood just behind her. Cantic and Rogan were cloaked in military impassivity.

Two pairs of blackcoats held Aimée and Henri up by the nooses, Aimée jerking her arms out of their grasps even though her hands were cuffed.

"Luca," Touraine whispered. "What are you doing?"

The princess stood tall and regal, her gaze piercing the crowd. The sunlight sparkled on her spectacles. "If we apply these solemn rules to our most intimate relationships, should we not maintain them in all of our dealings? Merchant to customer, doctor to patient. Subject to crown. Soldier to general."

Touraine looked for the other Sands, but the only soldiers keeping the peace were Balladairan. That meant Balladaire didn't trust the Sands here. Were they being punished for the deserters, like Noé? Or had Aimée tried something on her own and gotten caught?

"Yesterday, I told you how Balladaire will care for and protect all of its subjects and enact justice. Similarly, though it is hard to govern the treacheries of the heart, the government can protect against the treacheries that threaten the society as a whole. False merchants will be fined. False doctors will be arrested. Traitor soldiers will lose their lives.

"After you return home today, think well on the type of person you want to be in this beautiful city. Will you uphold it, or erode its foundations? Thank you."

Luca bowed her head delicately to the assembled crowd, who watched her in a hush. Even Touraine's breath caught in her chest. Finally, she let her focus shift from Luca to the nooses behind all the Balladairans and fully absorb the sight of her friend about to be hung.

Traitor soldiers. Noé's fingers went tight as a battlefield bone cutter's vise on Touraine's arm.

"Sky a-fucking-bove, you assholes! I can escort my sky-falling self, thanks."

Noé's nails dug even deeper. "No," he whispered. Whimpered.

Touraine shook her head. This couldn't—this wasn't—

It didn't matter how eagerly Aimée shoved her head into the noose or how she smirked at her blackcoat guards. She was terrified. Touraine could see it in the performance and the quick flicker of her eyes toward the crowd, maybe looking for a familiar face. Aimée was being made an example of, and she knew it.

No. No. No—"Luca, no!" screamed Touraine as loud as she could. Kept screaming it, even as Noé tried to drag her back, out of sight. Blackcoats were coming for her now, too—

"Luca! Luca, stop them!"

"Lieutenant, we have to go. They're coming—" Noé pulled harder, and she yanked herself free, ran to the gallows until she could see the whites of Aimée's eyes.

Luca saw her, and the cool mask dropped, replaced with a frightened young woman for just a second. She mouthed something, but Touraine didn't wait for it.

Because Aimée's mask dropped, too, and for a second her fear was plain. She held Touraine's gaze. "Lieutenant!" She smiled ruefully, like she did whenever Touraine beat her at a hand of cards.

Then the blackcoats had Touraine by the arms, with an arm around her neck, and she couldn't breathe. Or maybe—or maybe it wasn't them, and maybe it was the sobs choking her—

"Pray for fucking rain!" yelled Aimée. The wooden floor fell from beneath her feet.

CHAPTER 38

A SICKNESS

The rebel Sands dropped with a gagging sound and the smell of voided bowels. That wasn't what made Luca's stomach writhe with barely suppressed nausea. Nor was the disturbing angle of the hanged Sands' necks or the rapidly changing colors of their faces from smooth, wet sand to blotchy purple.

Well, it was in part, but not near as much as her role in it. And her role in it didn't make her as sick as knowing Touraine had seen her do it.

Now Touraine was silent, limp in a dead faint, in the arms of a pair of blackcoats. Luca hoped it was just a faint. More soldiers had formed a protective cordon around the gallows while the civilians were forcibly dispersed. Thankfully, the people left willingly, no matter how or what they muttered. Luca didn't need another city-destroying riot. Was it the sting of Cantic's metaphorical whip that kept them placid, she wondered, or the honey Luca herself had promised?

And there was that phrase again. *We pray for rain*. A natural thing to pray for in the desert. Now it was a rallying cry for the rebellion. She hoped the people would ignore it. The message of the hanging was clear: *joining the rebels will only bring you pain*.

"Release her!" Luca demanded of the blackcoats holding Touraine, as she limped down the stairs.

Luca still hadn't discovered the knack for praying, so she tried hope. The soldier was breathing but pale.

"What did you do to her?" she asked the blackcoats.

"Nothing, Your Highness," one of them said, bowing awkwardly with his half of their burden. "She passed out before we got to her."

Luca pressed a hand to the other woman's face. Too warm, but clammy at the same time. Touraine was ill. "Take her to my carriage."

Instead of obeying, the soldiers looked over Luca's shoulder.

Cantic glared down her nose between Touraine and Luca. "We'll take her to the brig and sort out what's to be done with her later." She wrinkled her nose. "She looks sick."

The blackcoats flinched. One of them dropped the arm he held. The other held on to discipline but only just. Their face went pale under a spate of sun freckles.

"I'll have her seen by a doctor at my home," Luca told Cantic stiffly.

The general's eyes went wide. "I beg your pardon? This soldier is a traitor to the empire. When I released her into your custody, you said her life was forfeit. We should hang her right there, right now." She sniffed with anger. "The last thing she deserves is a doctor."

Luca drew herself up and sniffed back. "With all due respect, General, Touraine isn't a soldier, and her crime was not against you and the military. My business with her is my own."

She rounded on the poor blackcoats, who were looking anxiously between their commanding officer and their future queen, as if they realized they probably shouldn't have been witness to this dispute.

"Take her to my carriage," Luca repeated. "Be gentle with her, and you'll be compensated for your trouble."

With apologetic salutes to the general, they picked Touraine up and started to drag her away. Still, the woman didn't wake. Luca bit her lower lip. What if she didn't wake again?

She turned back to Cantic and smiled her thin court smile, a bare quirk of the corners of her mouth.

"If you please, General," Luca added in a low voice, "I want her to be seen by a particular doctor. You know which one. Have her sent to my town house in the Quartier as soon as possible. Bound, of course."

Cantic's face was splotchy with fury, but she was dutiful. She took in the gallows square, the curious and lingering civilians both Balladairan and Qazāli. The rest of them went back to their routines: running their stalls or shopping, cleaning the streets or transporting goods from the docks to some New Medina merchant's shop. It was strange how eager people were to get back to their normal lives after a death. It was like they *wanted* to forget.

"This is madness," Cantic hissed.

A heavy weight settled in Luca's chest.

"It is madness, General. A very particular madness, and we brought it here."

Aranen arrived that evening with an escort of five blackcoats. Her wrists were raw with the chafing of her iron cuffs. Her hair was stiff with oil and dirt, and her skin grimy with prison filth. Her bright tunic and trousers were stained and stiff as well. She smelled awful.

Adile hesitated when she led Aranen into the town house. "Are you sure, Your Highness?" The servant kept her distance from the priestess.

Luca nodded. "Bring her in." She led the way to her bedroom, where she'd set Touraine up in the bed. She put on her gloves and wrapped a scarf around her face and bid Aranen follow suit.

Aranen raised her eyebrows but complied.

Then they went into the room and closed the door, leaving everyone else outside.

On the bed, Touraine lay propped on the pillows. She had gone from bad to worse over the course of the day. She'd been so hot that Luca had been sure she would die. Then a rash had come from nowhere, covering her like dog spots. Then she'd started vomiting. Luckily, the basin for her sick was empty at the moment.

The priestess made a small sound of surprise.

"A bath and a meal for your help," Luca said simply.

Aranen cocked her eyebrow. "You're not what I expected, Princess. Give me my freedom, and I will help."

"No. Help her, or I send you back and take one of the priests who will."

The priestess's mouth thinned. "I stand corrected," she muttered.

She turned and gave Touraine a cursory glance. Stepped closer to tug her collar down and look at the rash along her neck.

"I'll call for Adile. I had her prepare some food for you. Something with meat, like you said."

Luca didn't tell Aranen that she had tried to do the healing magic herself.

"I'll take the food," Aranen said, straightening. "I can give her a little strength. But she's not in danger. Better to save my strength so you can force me to care for someone who really needs it."

Aranen's smile was as sharp as her words.

Luca looked down at Touraine. Her brown skin was ashen except for the blotchy rashes.

"She'll be fine," the priestess reassured her. "It's just a bad childhood disease. But if you care so much about her…" She gestured around what was clearly once a royal bedroom now turned infirmary room, her brow furrowed. "I know you're not like the old king. You're not like the Blood General. So why are you doing this to us?"

Luca went to stand beside the priestess and next to Touraine's sleeping form. She put a gloved hand on the long curve that was the soldier's shin. There was probably a rash there, too. Luca imagined she could feel the throb of Touraine's fever through the blanket.

The old king. Luca's father.

She met Aranen's dark eyes, not expecting the tenderness she found there. The sorrow, open but unjudging.

Aranen put her bare hand on Luca's glove, the iron a heavy weight on them both.

"You don't have to do this."

Yes, I do. Luca slipped her hand away before Aranen's became too comforting, and held it across her chest. She couldn't afford to doubt now. But what if Aranen was right? What if Gil was right?

"I'll send for Adile," Luca said curtly. "She's already drawn up your bath. Dinner is ready, too. Which would you like first?"

Aranen took a deep breath, but she didn't push Luca any further.

"A bath, Shāl willing."

Luca stroked Touraine's hair. The other woman's forehead was warm still, even through Luca's gloves, and damp with sweat. Even though Aranen said the sickness wasn't fatal, it had been two days. She would have Adile burn the gloves later. Extreme, perhaps, but Luca was afraid of the risk. Luca wore a scarf wrapped around her face, and her breath was hot and cloying beneath it.

She caressed Touraine's cheek and let herself imagine what things might have been like if they had been different people or met at a different time. Before her father grew more aggressive in his desire for Shālan magic, Shālans had visited La Chaise often. She'd known her Shālan tutor had had a Balladairan lover. She smiled as she pictured Touraine in the formal garb of a Qazāli ambassador or council member on a state visit. The line of her shoulders in elegant cloth, as dashing as she had been the night of Luca's ball. And the tender strength of her hands on Luca's leg the night before everything fell apart. Mere months ago, and yet it seemed a lifetime.

With a low mewling that might have been adorable under other circumstances, Touraine woke. Luca yanked her hand back, heat flushing up her cheeks. Not that Touraine would have noticed. Her eyes were still unfocused, and her mumbling was incoherent. More fever dreams. Inexplicable disappointment settled back into Luca's stomach.

"Luca?" Then sharper, alarmed: "Luca, what under—" Touraine fell into a fit of coughing.

"Here." Luca held a cup to Touraine's mouth. The other woman hadn't kept anything down for the last couple of days. The empty sick basin waited on the side of the bed, just in case.

Slowly, the fog in Touraine's eyes cleared. She pushed herself up, then fell back against the pillows, too unsteady.

"Don't move. You're all right. I'm—you're at my house. In the Quartier."

Luca realized her hands were twitching in her lap while Touraine eyed Luca's room suspiciously. She clasped them together and took a breath to steady herself.

"You killed her."

"No, I—" This wasn't how Luca had expected Touraine to start. "I tried to get Cantic to stop. She refused—military discipline is out of my purview until I'm crowned."

Touraine turned away. The tendons in her jaw stood out. So did the ones in her hand where she clenched Luca's plush blankets. Luca put her own hand over Touraine's, expecting the other woman to jerk away.

Touraine didn't. After several long, silent breaths, Touraine turned her hand over and clasped Luca's fingers in hers.

Luca's stomach fluttered like pages of an open book left in a pleasant breeze. It always came to this ache and flutter of her insides, this feeling that things could be *more* right if just this—

They stared at their linked hands, Luca's in her black glove, Touraine's bare and freshly scrubbed.

"Why am I here?" Touraine's voice was hoarse. She still wouldn't meet Luca's eyes.

"Cantic wanted to arrest you, but I took you instead."

"Why?" Touraine finally looked up. Her half-lidded eyes were bruised with sickness. Purple-red splotches crept along her skin, too. Up and down her torso, peeking from beneath the collar of the shirt Luca had dressed her in.

Because I owe you.

Because I wanted to take care of you.

Because I wanted to spite Cantic.

"Are you…in disguise?" Touraine asked before Luca could find the right response.

Luca blushed behind her scarf, suddenly self-conscious. With her other hand, the hand that hadn't touched Touraine, she pulled the scarf down just slightly.

"You're sick. The—doctor says you'll get better, though." Mentioning Aranen would only bring up more questions that Luca couldn't answer.

"So you put me in your room. In your bed." The look Touraine gave her was too much like Cantic's.

"It's quarantine enough. And we'll sterilize everything. We're all taking precautions."

And they were. Every time she left the room, she stripped the robe she was wearing and the gloves and the scarf and left them in a bucket that Adile took away to boil. It was the best they could do, short of leaving Touraine alone in her fever. She didn't want to bring Aranen back and face down that knowing stare.

Luca gripped Touraine's hand tightly. She fought the urge to bring it up to her lips, instead just stroking Touraine's fingers with her thumb.

"The things I said before, Touraine—" She couldn't take them back. She still meant them. She had made the calculations. She was right. And yet there were some things she hadn't calculated for. "I'm so sorry for the temple. Do you think that Djasha would accept funds for its repair?"

Touraine snorted a laugh that turned into dry coughs. "Repair?" she said when she caught her breath. "You haven't been out to see it."

Luca busied herself with a loose thread in her robe. "Gil and Cantic…advise against it."

Touraine leaned back against the pillows. "Of course they do. You've really fucked things up, Luca. I don't know why I hoped for better."

"I hoped you would understand now."

"Who gave the order for her death?"

"Pardon?"

"Who ordered Aimée executed? For what crime?"

"Cantic. Desertion. They caught her trying to escape to join the rebellion."

Touraine closed her eyes and slipped her hand out of Luca's. "I think I'm going to be sick again. Do you mind?"

The dismissal was so abrupt it caught Luca mid-justification, and it made something unpleasant lurch in her chest. Her eyes burned, but she stood calmly.

"Of course." Luca retreated into formality. "Ring the bell when you're finished. Adile will come."

She took off her contaminated clothing, dropping it in the basket for Adile, and left without looking back. She didn't want Touraine to see how much her words had hurt.

When Luca returned the next morning, Touraine was gone.

Touraine stumbled back into the slums, half-conscious. The fever was back. The rashes up her body were itching more than she remembered them itching at Luca's.

That's because you were unconscious, idiot.

A cry went up as the children, serving as both official and unofficial lookouts, saw her.

"Stay back," she rasped at them. "I'm sick." So the children gawked at her and whispered.

"You have the laughing pox," one of the little ones said, happy to be a know-it-all. "Like Hamid last week."

Oh. The children she'd been playing with.

It wasn't long before Jaghotai came up to meet her. Her mother only grunted, but Touraine could see the slouch of relief in her shoulders. "Your man Noé said you'd been taken. He's been a mess. Thought for sure we'd see you strung up the next day." Jaghotai came closer and examined a spot on Touraine's neck. She whispered, "I just thought you'd gone back to your master. Glad to see I was wrong. Was I?"

She pulled back and bared a jackal grin.

"You've got laughing pox," she added. "Makes sense. You didn't have time to catch it as a child before the Balladairans took you." She said it almost wistfully.

"Can I just…go lie down?" Touraine growled the words between gritted teeth. "It was a long walk." Touraine was half a second from passing out, right there in the dirt. Jaghotai grabbed her by the arm to carry some of Touraine's weight and lead her through. Touraine didn't have the energy to jerk away.

"Stop. You'll get sick, too." Her protest was feeble, and they were already walking. Jaghotai shooed people back.

"Nah. I had it when I was a kid."

"Am I going to die?"

"If we all died from it, there wouldn't even be a Qazāl. It's a weird thing." Instead of lapsing into her usual glaring silence, Jaghotai kept up the idle chatter as they walked. Touraine wondered if this meant Jaghotai was becoming…friendly. "I don't really understand it, but Aranen and Djasha do. You get it once, you don't get it again. It also keeps you from getting the death pox." Jaghotai helped Touraine slide back into her old bedroll.

The hand supporting Touraine went suddenly slack, and she slammed into the dirt.

"Sky above, Jak—" Touraine groaned and rolled over. "What's wrong?"

"*We* don't get the death pox," Jaghotai whispered, a hopeful and calculating expression spreading on her face, "because we've already had the laughing pox. We need to talk to Djasha and Niwai. We need that Many-Legged priest's animals again."

CHAPTER 39

A PANIC

Three nights after Touraine slipped out of the town house like a ghost, Luca dreamed, wild with her own fever.

In one dream, on the second night of Luca's sickness, Touraine led her by the hand, smiling, smiling, and behind Touraine, the gallows, and waiting on the gallows, Cantic, an empty noose swaying in her hand. Above them, a mixed flock of birds blotted out the sun. Crows, seagulls, pigeons cooing and screeching and cawing as they passed.

"You don't have to do this," Cantic whispered in her raspy voice as she placed the noose around Luca's neck.

"Your Highness," murmured Lanquette, shaking her awake with his gloved hand. "Princess."

Her eyes fastened on him in the haze of afternoon sunlight. "Something's happened?"

"You cried out." Lanquette averted his eyes and removed his hand. "I thought it best to wake you, Your Highness."

Luca sank back into the pillows, damp with sweat but feeling properly coherent for the first time in a day. She looked her guard in the eye and swelled with sudden gratitude. "Thank you, Lanquette."

Her relief was short lived. The next day, while she recovered her strength with chicken broth and soft grains, a letter came from the compound with a young soldier wearing a scarf around his face. He left the letter and departed without a word.

That told them enough, even without opening the letter. The compound was suffering from some sort of outbreak, too.

Cantic's handwriting was hasty: *Soldiers ill. Rash, vomiting, death. Does not affect Qazāli prisoners. Using them to try to heal the others. Not helping much. Stay away.*

Luca pieced the message together. It seemed like the soldiers had something similar to her and Touraine—except for the death. She was already starting to feel stronger. Was it only a matter of time before it got worse again? Was Touraine dead in the city somewhere? She exhaled sharply, irritated that she even cared.

Cantic was using Aranen and the others to heal the sick soldiers, or at least to help care for them, but there was nothing about how many had succumbed and how many had recovered.

Luca should have asked Aranen more about the sickness. Pride had kept Luca from sending for the priestess when she fell ill herself. Aranen had said Touraine's illness wasn't fatal, so she'd decided to let the disease run its course. Luca had been a fool to trust her.

There was one person she could trust who might know almost as much about Qazāli diseases, though.

"Lanquette?" Luca called. "Could you send a message to Bastien LeRoche? I need him to bring his books."

The next day, Bastien LeRoche arrived at the town house, a satchel on his shoulder and his father's young manservant laden with more books.

When they joined Luca in her upstairs office, he gestured toward Adile, who waited beyond the threshold for any requests, a scarf covering her entire face save her eyes.

"What—oh." The young lord looked Luca up and down. His smile was warm and charming. "You have laughing pox."

"It could be dangerous," Luca said defensively. "Adile will bring you scarves and gloves to protect yourselves, and you should stay back."

Bastien laughed and shook his head. "It's not dangerous. I had it before. It's common here. When I caught it, my father locked me in my room with only water and…" He trailed off. His face held the shadow of latent rage, but there was no sign of it in his voice. "Well, I didn't die, so eventually he let me out again."

Bastien's eyes flicked toward the servant boy, Richard. "You've had it, too, haven't you?"

"Yes, my lord," Richard said softly. Then he bowed over the books to Luca. His slight shoulders were tight with the strain of the heavy books. "Your Highness."

"Here, put those on the desk, please." She gestured to Adile for coffee. Then she sat heavily in her chair.

"If it's not dangerous, Bastien, why did I get a message from General Cantic about a new plague? She said soldiers are dying. Fever, rash, death." She rolled up her sleeve to bare a patch of itchy red skin on her arm. "Why am I not dead yet?"

Bastien shook his head again. "I'm not a doctor, Luca, but this is definitely laughing pox. I don't know what's happening at the barracks, but it's different." He patted the stack of books Richard had just put down. "I take it that's what we're going to look for, then?"

She smiled, and he returned it with his own grin. Sky above, it felt good to be understood.

"Richard, can you read?" Luca asked the boy.

"Yes, Your Highness. I can help." He bowed again.

"No. Take your ease. I have some books you might like downstairs. Fun books. Adventures. Adile will give you lunch and tea, whatever you need."

Richard looked uncertainly between Luca and Bastien. When Bastien nodded, a hesitant smile curved the corners of the boy's mouth.

After Adile led the boy down to Luca's reading corner, Luca and Bastien got to work. It also felt good to do what she was best at.

They spent the afternoon picking through their collective texts, looking for records of a disease like the one at the compound, how it spread, and any known medicines. Luca didn't know what it meant that the Qazāli prisoners weren't helping much—did it mean that the healing magic was ineffective or that the prisoners were uncooperative or that there were just too many sick for the priests to cure?

Bastien hunched over the desk, tracing the lines of text with his fingertips, nose barely a handbreadth away from the page. That same lock of blond hair flopped over his hand, and he flicked it back without breaking his concentration.

She hadn't told him what she had learned from Aranen. It felt like a betrayal of their friendship, since he had helped her in her research before and was helping her now. She suspected her desire to keep it secret was partly because she had failed. She hadn't been able to *do* the magic, and she didn't want him to think her weaker for it.

"Aha!" Bastien bolted upright, startling Luca out of her thoughts.

"What? What!"

He smiled sheepishly. "Sorry. It's nothing, but I'm just—it seems like—here, he writes about sick people being connected. We know that already, contagious. But it also talks about sick people being connected to dirty animals. The city is full of rats, obviously. And then there are all the sky-falling cats and mangy dogs in the Old Medina. Maybe the soldiers were careless."

He kept talking, but Luca was no longer listening. The flocks of birds that had swept down on the crops. The farm animals that had vanished without a trace, as if they'd simply *walked away*. What if it wasn't just animals thrown out of their habits by the delayed rainy season?

Would the Taargens be so bold as to risk a practically brand-new peace treaty? She closed her eyes to better remember the wording on the treaty. Though the Taargens weren't allowed to take up arms or "perform acts of aggression" on Balladairan territories and subjects, it wasn't spelled out explicitly that they couldn't interfere with the colonies' food supplies using…animals.

She opened her eyes again. Bastien was staring at her, waiting for an explanation. Her eyes fell, however, on the small snake skull on her desk. Luca had taken it from the governor-general's office on the compound. It had been one of Cheminade's, like all the trinkets in the command office.

The late governor had said the lion pelt in her house was a gift from the wild tribes that roamed the desert. *Call themselves the Many-Legged, for the animals they worship.*

"Sky above," Luca swore, jumping up and grabbing the snake skull. "Shit. Shit shit shit." A wave of dizziness knocked her back into her seat. "It's not the Taargens."

"Luca?"

The call was echoed from the other side of the door as Gil knocked on it.

"Come in. It's all right," she said to both men. Only it wasn't all right. "Gil? We need to see Cantic."

Gil and Bastien looked at each other quizzically.

"We're under attack. The rebels are using the animals."

"Your Highness, I heard you were sick. Why are you here?" Cantic met Luca at the door to the administration building. The scarf around the general's face was black and gold, her blue eyes fierce above it.

I am sick, Luca thought. She drew herself up and planted her feet. *I am also a queen.* "This is the rebels, General. We're under attack."

Around them, the compound's clean orderliness had vanished. It was everything she'd been afraid of. Bodies burning on the plague fires beyond the walls. Plumes of smoke sent her back in time, to Balladaire and the Withering Death. To her parents' funeral and the pillars of smoke that had loomed in every direction beyond the walls of La Chaise.

Only here, instead of withering into husks in their beds...

The sick bay overflowed, and blackcoats vomited and moaned outside the building. The healthy ones rushed about the compound, spare shirts or handkerchiefs or even arms over their mouths. They were bees in a kicked hive.

"It's a plague, Your Highness—"

Luca pushed past Cantic, careful not to touch her. Just in case. Careful not to show the remnants of her own body's weakness.

Cantic followed Luca into the general's office, past that beautiful doe door.

"Where are the Qazāli healers?" Luca asked for Cantic's ears only.

The general looked askance. "I pressed them as hard as I could. They went unconscious. Some of them haven't woken back up." She shrugged, frustrated in her helplessness. Luca knew exactly how she felt.

Luca swore. "I thought they'd be able to stop the worst of it. This is an attack, General. I think the rebels allied with the Many-Legged tribes."

Cantic sneered with distaste. "Those jackalfuckers in the desert?"

Luca grunted, surprised at the general's break in decorum. "I think they're like the Taargens."

The general froze. "How do you mean?"

"They have some sort of link with the animals. Paul-Sebastien LeRoche and I were doing research. Animals can pass diseases to people. It all makes sense, all the way back to the animals vanishing from their farms, the birds destroying the crops. This is planned, Cantic. Something is happening." Touraine. Djasha. Touraine knew tactics. And Djasha...

Had Djasha been the one to take down Cantic's company, back when Cantic was a captain? She would know how weak the military was under plague fear. So would Touraine. They would be idiots not to press an advantage.

"How weak is the compound?" Luca asked.

"It's not—"

"How weak, General? How many soldiers are down?"

Cantic leaned over her desk on flat palms and closed her eyes. She shook her head. And her shoulders shook, and her hands trembled on the desk. She said something, but in such a low whisper that Luca didn't hear it.

"What did you say?"

"I said, it's my fault. In four days, I've lost a third of my soldiers. A full fourth of them dead—the rest are just on their way, and it's my fault, Your Highness."

Four days ago. Touraine had snuck away seven days ago.

"What do you mean?"

"That Brigāni bitch planned this. It's vengeance. I know it. She's doing it again."

Luca stilled, worried that Cantic was having a mental breakdown. "Doing what, General?"

The tightly coiled tension left Cantic's shoulders. She faced Luca, eyes bleak above the mask. "The stories are real, Your Highness."

"Your attack on the Brigāni tribe is a matter of state record. You were moved to the education division to teach the Sands. I know the story." Luca tried to speak soothingly. She needed the general whole and ready.

Cantic shook her head. "If only." She twisted the thick grief ring on her right middle finger for a quiet moment before she continued. "That witch destroyed my entire company. After the...incident...I rode off to—mourn my family. I came back to carnage you can't imagine, Your Highness. Only one of my soldiers survived, and it broke him so badly that he ran away to find the southern monks. For all I know, he died in the snow, raving mad."

Luca searched Cantic's eyes for anything less than lucidity, and the calm grief she found there frightened her even more than madness. "If it's real, why haven't they used this magic on us before?"

Cantic gave a helpless shrug. "I don't know, Your Highness. My only guess is that they can't. Or they're preparing to. I've been afraid of this since Lord Regent Ancier sent me down here."

Luca pinched her temples. She didn't know how to fight that kind of magic.

Cantic rubbed her own forehead. "But if they attack us, they risk getting sick themselves."

"You have their healers in your custody. Have you asked them?"

Luca was practically yelling and had to pause to catch her breath. "Get answers."

Cantic scowled. "I'm not going to torture the only people who can help my soldiers, Your Highness." Then, surprisingly, her voice went solemn and thick. "On the subject of the doctors. You should know... I promised Aranen din Djasha that if we captured her wife, we would let her see her again. She says the bitch is dying."

For a second, Luca lost her breath. "You promised her...what?" she stammered. "Why? Did she give you something else? Something good?"

"For healing my soldiers." Cantic sighed. "You've never given your life to someone, only to learn they've been ripped away from you forever. People think I'm ruthless. A monster. But even I know that some things are just right, Your Highness. And some things aren't. I don't regret anything I've ever done for the benefit of your father or your uncle. Even the statesmen in Masridān. All sky-falling one hundred sixty-one of them, Your Highness. It secured the eastern reaches of your empire, so it was worth it." The older woman stared Luca down, as if she were willing Luca to understand. Like she wanted someone to hear her and tell her what she had done was justified. "But when I lost Berst...our children...I made a mistake, that night with the Brigāni. That wasn't for Balladaire. That was for me. And I regret it."

Luca's heart lurched down to her stomach. She had felt something like that when she thought Touraine had died. She and Touraine had never been married, had maybe never even loved each other, but there had been rage in her heart, and if she could have killed the ones she deemed responsible, maybe...

That didn't matter, of course. She already knew who she would give her life to: her citizens came first.

"Whatever you need to do to fortify the compound, do it. We have other bases in Qazāl. Send for reinforcements. Where's Beau-Sang?" snapped Luca.

The general snapped back, "The rich coward you picked to run this city is buying the first free berth out of it."

They stared at each other, mouths hanging open at Cantic's words, and perhaps even at the way she'd said them. Even Gil's eyes went wide.

"He's doing what?" Luca said, her voice small.

Cantic scrubbed her hand over her eyes above her black face scarf. "He's fleeing the city, Your Highness. He was packing up his town house in the Quartier this morning."

"How do you know?"

Cantic shared a look with Gil. "I've had him watched." She twisted her grief rings around, around. Luca almost reached for her own rings.

"Watched." Luca looked between the general and her most trusted advisor, who had clearly known about this but hadn't seen fit to tell her. "Watched."

"You said you wanted to be careful with him," Gil said softly. "A leash?"

"I didn't mean have it done behind my back," Luca snapped. If Gil could do this behind her back, how could she trust his opinion of Cantic?

"Your Highness, I—did you even read the letters I sent you after the skirmish in the bazaar?" the general said.

It was hard to think back to that cloud of overwrought pain and anger. She had glanced at Cantic's letters; most of them were updates on missing persons from the battle, and all of that was to be expected. And then came the hostage letter and accompanying finger, and then Beau-Sang as governor-general.

"Of course I did. They didn't say anything about him."

The deep lines in Cantic's face deepened. "There was something strange about the missing people and how quickly he found these so-called hostages. And the culprits."

It would take a particular kind of gruesomeness for a Balladairan to cut off another Balladairan's finger just to get himself a place in the government. A kind of gruesomeness that sounded less and less far-fetched when taken with Aliez's own fears about her father. Luca hadn't even had a chance to check on the girl.

"You think he orchestrated the hostage taking."

Cantic nodded.

"Do you think…" Sadness rose in Luca's heart, not for herself but for a young woman whose father had had her abducted and held for a very different kind of ransom. "Do you think he had anything to do with Cheminade's death?"

"I don't doubt he's capable of it, Your Highness. I'm only saying that I never found the proof."

"Then why aren't we sky-falling arresting him?" cried Luca. "Let's go. Bring a squad of whatever soldiers look healthiest."

When they arrived at the comte de Beau-Sang's town house, Richard the servant boy was carrying a small wooden box out of the house while two Qazāli men carried out trunks and loaded them into a large carriage. The boy froze midstep when he saw Luca, his eyes wide like he'd been caught doing something he shouldn't.

"Beau-Sang!" Luca called. She turned to the boy while the grown men looked between her and the house. "Richard, will you take me to the comte, please?"

"Yes, Your Highness." He bowed over the box he still held. It was a dark wood inlaid with stylized pearl lilies, perhaps a jewelry box. He scurried away without even placing it into the carriage with the trunks. Luca and Cantic followed.

Not everything in the house had been packed, but enough of the Balladairan touches—the painted forests and stags and chevaliers—were gone that the place felt hollowed out. The sudden emptiness made the sitting room feel less like a museum of Balladaire and more like an ancient tomb.

"Your Highness?"

Luca turned to see Aliez halfway down the stairs, a surprised look on her face. She did not look like she was preparing to leave. She wore tight Balladairan trousers under a bright green Qazāli tunic; her hair was in a careless bun, and her feet were bare. She seemed smaller than Luca remembered, and Luca wished she had better news for the girl.

"We've come for your father," Luca said softly. "Is Bastien here?"

The young woman inhaled sharply, then padded down the stairs to join them. "He's out."

"You aren't trying to run, too?" Luca murmured.

Aliez scowled up at Luca. "Qazāl is my home, Your Highness." Then she added in a hesitant whisper, "Did you find her?"

Luca shook her head, not because she didn't know but because her suspicions were too horrid to drop in Aliez's lap so suddenly. The girl's restraint was admirable; she only bowed her head in solemn acceptance, as if she'd let the flame of hope die out some time ago.

"You should go back upstairs," Luca said.

"No. I want to see this."

Beau-Sang was in his office, loading his papers and books into watertight boxes himself. Richard announced them, even though the Comte stopped as soon as they walked in.

Casimir LeRoche de Beau-Sang smiled, as if the two most powerful people in the colony hadn't just walked into his office with Balladairan soldiers at their back.

"Your Highness." He bowed. "General. To what do I owe the pleasure of your company?"

"Sky above, Beau-Sang, you're the governor-general," Cantic shouted, pushing into the room. "You're supposed to be running the colony, not cowering in your study!"

"It's a dangerous time. I would be willing to submit the city to temporary martial law." He shrugged his broad shoulders and turned back to his desk.

"Martial law means I can shut down every ship in port."

"And watch the Balladairans riot again? I'm sure the Qazāli would love that." Beau-Sang turned his smile on Luca. "How deep do the crown's coffers go? Deep enough for another round of reparations?"

Luca ignored the barb. "You're not leaving, Beau-Sang. I'm stripping you of your post, and you're under arrest."

The comte chuckled. "Arrest? On what grounds?"

"Dereliction of duty, for a start."

"A jury will find I've performed my post admirably. Unlike you." His grin vanished, and he looked Luca directly in the eye. "I brought them to heel, and at every turn, you squandered it. If your uncle wants to conduct a trial of competence, you'll be found wanting."

Their audience rustled behind Luca, and she felt the pressure of their uncertainty. Beau-Sang knew Luca's insecurities and how to capitalize on them. Then she felt a warmth behind her. Gil stood just behind her, and his presence lent her strength. His nod was slight, and she remembered his words the day she'd tried to use Aranen's magic.

Faith is the absence of doubt. I have faith in you. She wasn't alone. He would stand by her in this.

Luca stepped over to Beau-Sang's desk and peered into the half-full box. Their arms brushed as she plucked up a paper nonchalantly and pretended to read it. Then she spoke calmly, to show his threats had no effect, even as a part of her screamed that he was right, that she needed him. She needed that steadiness to maintain her bluff.

"We have other suspicions." Luca let her gaze drift to Aliez, who waited at the threshold with Richard and Gil. She murmured for the comte's ears alone, "You want the best for your daughter, but she suspects you. The general and I have evidence enough to have you hanged for murder. Either way, you're leaving this house with me. Whether you do it with your last shreds of dignity intact is up to you."

Beau-Sang threw his head back and laughed, his shoulders shaking. Luca stepped back to avoid being jostled. He was the kind of man who thrived on control of the bodies around him. She wouldn't give him the satisfaction of so much as a shove.

"I'm glad you're so thrilled," Luca said. "General, we're done here. Bring in your men."

Cantic nodded and signaled for the blackcoats to come in with their irons.

Beau-Sang smiled broadly the whole time. "You don't have enough to convict me for murder, Princess."

"Two young Qazāli have been reported missing. You hanged them the day you took office."

The comte's eyes widened just enough that Luca knew it was true even though he scoffed. "Those Qazāli were hanged for kidnapping Balladairans. They were rebels."

Across the room, Aliez's hands covered her mouth in horror. Luca grimaced. She wished Aliez had stayed back.

"Rebels or not," Luca said, with all the certainty she didn't feel, "they didn't commit the crime you executed them for. You did."

They all watched her now, silent, hanging on her next word. It was a thrill she'd never felt before, this frisson of power. They were hers and she was queen, and for once, every part of her was aligned.

Cantic's blackcoats arrived, and she directed them wordlessly. Aliez and Richard made space for them, both looking rudderless. Gil stood just off to the side, one hand on his pistol and one hand on his sword, which he was wearing for the first time in months.

Beau-Sang growled as the soldiers cuffed him. "Your uncle will learn what you've done," he snarled at Luca, face purpling with fury. "You'll never touch that throne! You are a disgrace."

Luca flinched, but she said nothing as they dragged him away, only stood among his belongings as if they were now hers. She kept her jaw hard and steadied her trembling leg with her cane as one by one, the room emptied.

By the time Luca made it outside, Cantic and Aliez were watching Beau-Sang's carriage roll to the compound. Cantic stood beside her horse.

"I wonder how many civilians know what's happening." The general looked askance at Beau-Sang's daughter beside her, as if gauging the girl's capacity for gossip.

Now that Beau-Sang was gone, Luca felt as if she were slowly deflating. This was only the beginning. "If the illness hits the city or the Quartier, we'll have chaos."

*   *   *

It did hit the city.

The first case was a merchant whose brother was a soldier. Or maybe the merchant gambled with soldiers or sold to soldiers—the facts were unclear, and rumor carried the day. The important part was that the entire family took sick, and the merchant died on the third day, covered in a blistering rash.

The chaos was immediate.

As the illness spread from merchant to customer to child to child to parent, Luca could practically hear the wail of terror rise up from the city.

Because of her choices, everything was crumbling around her. Even the city she was supposed to stabilize as proof that she could steer an empire.

Where El-Wast had seemed lifeless and hollow following the burning night, reports said it was now a corpse infested with maggots. The harbor was overrun, civilians storming every seaworthy vessel. Luca could see the picture in her mind. Balladairans shoving forward, waving money and sheaves of paper, shouting their names and affiliations and influences. Whatever would help them escape.

CHAPTER 40

A SACRIFICE

In the weeks since the Grand Temple fell, the ranks of the slums had swollen. The displaced Qazāli crowded around the edges of the tent "quartier," huddled against the elements with nothing but heavy blankets and the dung fires to stave off the desert night's chill.

Though the children roamed freely, occupying themselves with mischief, the adults and some of the older children, like Ghadin, moved through the camp on edge. They knew that something was coming, even if they didn't know what.

Only Touraine, Jaghotai, and the other rebels knew the edge of the cliff they overlooked while the Qazāli death pox ravaged the Balladairans. Only they knew how far they had to fall if they took one false step.

The night Touraine and the others were to attack the compound, they held a feast for everyone. Another circle of fires, another night of dancing and music, and the luxuriously average meal of dried goat meat, beans, and stringy vegetables shared thinly among the slum dwellers. The fires fought back the night, casting the walls of the New Medina in gold as if it were sunset. The worn Shālan script seemed to come alive in the flickering of the firelight. In a way, it was alive; the dancers cast shadows on the wall, which danced in turn.

Touraine tried to pull her head back to the celebration. She sat around a fire with Noé and the few other Sands who turned coat the night the temple fell. Their silence was familiar and comfortable. The noise was not, though she was glad the Qazāli had some joy to scrape out of the ashes Balladaire had made of their city.

She thought again of walking away, but it was only idle now. This celebration was as much for her as for the civilians who'd spent the last weeks mired in fear and grief. It was to celebrate Niwai's rats and dogs and the ingenuity of decimating the enemy with what they feared most, and to celebrate that Balladairan fear. And it was to atone for the deaths of Qazāli caught in the cross fire of the disease, those who hadn't caught the laughing pox as children. It was one last night of life for Touraine and Jaghotai and all the fighters who would likely die for Qazāl later that night.

And to prepare Djasha to become another kind of death plague, one that would sweep through the darkness and tear the last remnants of the Balladairan army to shreds. If Shāl would hear her prayer for power.

This was the decision Jaghotai and the others had come to while Touraine was gone. A good thing, too. She would never have agreed.

And yet...

How far would you have gone, if you could have saved Aimée and Tibeau?

From across the circle, Djasha caught Touraine's eye, then stood and left the circle of light. Touraine left Noé and the others at her fire and followed. One by one, the rebel council slipped away.

The darkness swallowed them up. Above them, the millions of stars scattered like shrapnel across the blackness. On the edge of the desert, away from the desperate joy, Touraine and the rebel council and their foreign priest gathered in a circle around the dead body of a blackcoat. Jaghotai helped Djasha to kneel over the dead woman. Niwai's head was cocked to the side, their vulture perched on their thick glove.

Then the Apostate began to pray.

Jaghotai, Saïd, and Malika were silhouetted against the darkness by their lanterns. The flames carved their faces into sharp-cheeked masks. They looked more like Touraine felt. Queasy. Uncertain. Not for exactly the same reasons, but Touraine appreciated that much.

She was still grappling with what they were about to do here, and what that meant for later that night. She had never forgotten Djasha's threat after she and Jaghotai had taken her. To use Touraine's own blood against her. She hadn't forgotten the Taargens stealing her soldiers for their own rituals. And she definitely hadn't forgotten the lesson that was beaten into her—or out of her—in Cantic's training: Uncivilized. Uncivilized. Uncivilized.

Touraine's stomach clenched but held steady as Djasha made her first cuts along the body.

No one else had to be here, Djasha had said. And yet here they were, all of them. What did that say about the rest of them? Not Niwai, who had made their own sacrifices to appease their god—but the rest of them? The Qazāli had cut themselves off from the Brigāni sect of Shāl because of this exact use of magic. Because of the Emperor Djaya and her bloody use of Shāl's gift.

The magic wasn't a corruption itself, Djasha had explained to Touraine when the plan was decided. Every god had two sides, like a coin, and each gift had a price. Knitting and unknitting—which required animal flesh and human flesh respectively, the life's blood. Other gods governed elsewhere, just as costly. Farming and plague. Hunting and husbandry. Wisdom and madness. Empress Djaya had reached too far, forgetting Shāl's One Tenet. That was all.

"Aren't you worried about reaching too far?" Touraine had asked Djasha before, in Jaghotai's tent.

"I've reached this far before." Djasha had grimaced. "Shāl's mercy be upon me as I deserve."

Her tone of voice had made it clear what mercy she thought she deserved: none.

"I thought you couldn't do Shāl's magic anymore?"

The Brigāni woman had sniffed hard, fiddling with the golden ring in her right nostril. "I couldn't. I lost my faith in Shāl when he took my family from me. I lost my magic. I found a new god with the monks, and then I lost that one, too. And yet here I am."

"The Apostate."

The older woman's golden eyes had flashed as she grinned a jackal's grin. "We'll see."

A desert wind made Touraine pull her borrowed robe tighter in the darkness far from the bright celebrations. She knew what her fascination said about her.

Despite everything, a part of her wanted this.

As Djasha cut, she prayed. Jaghotai prayed. Malika and Saïd prayed. Even Niwai closed their eyes and murmured in their own language.

Touraine watched.

Even in prayer, Jaghotai didn't relax fully. She did soften. Anger turned solemn. Touraine could tell that it was no idler an exercise than training, though. It comforted Jaghotai, as much as the Jackal could be comforted.

Touraine had gone so long without comfort. The people she'd trusted to do that before were dead or in prison. And sky above did she need something.

Djasha's prayer rose to a pitch as she cut out the blackcoat's heart and raised it to her lips. The sharp coppery tang of blood filled Touraine's nose and coated her tongue, even though she kept her mouth clenched tight against rising nausea.

A thrumming in the air tingled over Touraine's skin and through her chest, like lightning striking too close and the clap of thunder that follows.

Touraine knelt.

The compound wasn't home.

It had never been home, but it reminded her of home. The layout of the desert compound was a yellowed mirror of the compound in Balladaire, but tonight, in the dark, she could almost pretend they were the same.

Touraine crouched on the walkway of the compound's southern wall, where the soldiers on guard duty patrolled the perimeter. Djasha had climbed up first and unraveled the patrolling soldier's heart. The silent death unnerved Touraine more than watching a soldier blown apart by cannons. Then Djasha crouched beside Touraine, eyes glowing golden, even without the stars. It was bizarre to see the once ex-priest with so much strength.

"I can't maintain this for long," Djasha murmured as if she could read Touraine's thoughts. Perhaps, Touraine thought with a start, the other woman could.

While the others climbed up the ladders and onto the ramparts in their dark clothes and veils, Touraine surveyed the place that was not her home and yet held her heart in its fist. To her left, the gate in the west wall facing the medinas. A bare dirt road ran from the gate and split the compound neatly into north and south: the infirmary in the northwest corner, where even now Touraine wretchedly hoped Balladairan soldiers were dying and the Sands were not; the brig in the northeast corner, where Touraine had spent more than enough time and where Djasha would rescue Aranen; between the infirmary and the brig, the administrative building, where she had been court-martialed, where Cantic gave orders and Luca wrote laws and Touraine had tried desperately to find a place in it all. The compound had never seemed so huge from the ground. The height of the wall also gave Touraine the perspective to see how badly she'd failed and how badly Balladaire had failed her.

Every time she was here, she felt helpless. Always at the mercy of some Balladairan or another, hanging from their whims. Not tonight. Tonight, she came of her own will. She didn't want mercy. She wanted them to burn.

There were six more buildings on the southern side of the compound, closest to Touraine and her mixed company of rebels. Two barracks faced each other in the southwest corner, and another two faced each other in the southeast corner. In the middle, the canteen faced the administrative building, and the supply stores sat squat behind the canteen. The remaining Sands were probably under guard in one of the barracks; the rest were garrisoned by the Balladairan soldiers.

The compound was noisy, and despite the order of the tents, she had a feeling that the well-oiled army of Balladaire was gunky with fear and sickness. The figures running circuits from barracks to tents to mess hall seemed manic, not efficient.

On either side of Touraine, the leaders of the rebellion crouched: Djasha, with her golden eyes, frail body, and the force of a god in her veins, and Jaghotai, raw strength and over thirty years of just rage begging for an outlet.

"You sure you don't want to stay up here?" Touraine asked them. "We'll need you to get out."

"I'll end this with my bare hands or die trying," growled Jaghotai.

No less than Touraine expected.

Djasha nodded solemnly, her eyes locked on the jail where her wife waited.

They took each other in one last time. The moment seemed to stretch, until Jaghotai held out her forearm. Touraine clasped it.

"We pray for rain," Touraine said.

"No." Jaghotai squeezed Touraine's arm tightly. "Be the rain."

The rebels descended on the compound like a summer storm.

The attack went wrong from the very beginning.

Jaghotai surged down the wall with a platoon of her best remaining fighters, aiming for the western barracks to surprise the soldiers in their beds. The rifles would be least useful there, in the close quarters. Above them, looping around the wall they had cleared of sentries, some Sands who had joined the rebels waited with Touraine's treasonous guns to give Jaghotai cover. As the alarm cry went up, Saïd and his group snuck east with Djasha to the jail under cover of chaos.

Touraine led her group up the middle, to the supply stores where the Balladairans kept spare munitions as well as blankets and uniforms. She and her new soldiers crept through the shadows, and all around her, the darkness seemed alive with danger. Which it was. Her lungs swelled with the heady buzz of doing what she was meant to do.

Two of her makeshift soldiers took out the two guards at the supply door. Easily done—they were confused at the alarm and groggy with sleep or illness. The guards hadn't fully registered that the compound was under attack until it was too late.

Touraine and Noé slipped into the building, leaving a handful of their soldiers outside to guard their backs. Something was wrong. There was no clerk, but that didn't set her senses off. She sniffed.

"Sir, there's no powder," Noé said in a low voice.

"Down!" she hissed. She signaled at the rest of them, but they were slow to react.

In the close quarters, the gunshots sounded like thunder, and smoke clouded the dark room, ruining the little night vision Touraine had. She ducked low and ran. She and Noé scrambled together for the door. She tripped over soft, solid lumps as she wove a snake's path back to the exit.

She gulped fresh air when she was outside and dived immediately to the side. The rebels she'd left were wide-eyed in the dark, holding their knives and the muskets Touraine had kept from Cantic.

"A trap," she said raggedly. "Don't go in. Don't show them your back."

She dragged Noé aside. "We need to get to the barracks. The other Sands—"

He nodded, his narrow face solemn in the dark. He turned to go, but before she even let go of his shirt—the hooded shirts the Qazāli wore, not the standard-issue conscript coat—they paused at an all-too-familiar sound.

Balladairan marching drums, keeping a sharp cadence.

"The alarm," Noé said, maybe in denial. He tried to shrug her off and see to his mission, but Touraine held fast.

She shook her head. "Alarm's been set off." It had been for ages, though the attack couldn't have been on longer than ten, fifteen minutes even. This sounded too far away, from the south. "The Balladairan reinforcements are here."

Sky-falling fuck.

Noé's eyes widened.

"Come on," Touraine said. Noé turned tail and sprinted to the southernmost barracks in the southeastern corner, quiet as a fox in a den of gunfire and death screams, and Touraine bolted for its neighbor. Freeing the Sands was their only hope of getting out of this compound alive.

She sent another rebel after Noé and took a second to assess the rest of their little company. Jaghotai raising a holy devastation through the west of the compound. There was no sign of Djasha and the prisoners.

Touraine took out the only Balladairan in front of her barracks building before he could level his musket and fix his aim. Blood gurgled from his belly and across his eyes as he screamed. Touraine hadn't quite gotten the hang of using the long knife instead of her baton, and it showed. She got the important parts, though: poke them hard, hit with the sharp side, and be fast.

But when she opened the door to the barracks, there was no one there. Just rows and rows of empty double bunks. At a loss, she stepped in farther, even going so far as to kneel and scan under the beds. The room was dark enough to hide in, but it was quiet as death.

Outside was another case. She listened and watched as Sands and rebels died. She had planned for this. She'd looked as many moves ahead as she could, and she was exploiting every piece, every weapon she had.

The jail was across from her, on the other side of the packed dirt road from the empty barracks. She didn't know how many of the rescue squad had managed to get into the jail, but as she watched, prisoners burst from the door, Saïd at the fore with an injured arm, dragging one woman on his good shoulder.

It wasn't Aranen or Djasha.

A sound like a sudden rainstorm made Touraine duck low. A shadow passed over the sky. A massive flock of seagulls blotted out the stars, flying toward the eastern wall. Toward Shāl's Road, where the Balladairan reinforcements were coming from. Beneath the flapping of their wings, other sounds got sharper: gunshots farther away, outside the walls, and the yelp and snarl and bark of hyenas. The roar of a lioness.

Touraine let herself smile.

In a kinder world, she could wait for the Many-Legged to break through. Or she could look for Luca, ask her one last time to stop this. There was no time for either.

She skirted the chaos of her rebels meeting musket balls to her left, their knives and batons against Balladairan bayonets. To her right, empty training fields, the practice dummies like leering enemies in the dark. In the noise of the night, she was one lone and silent shadow slipping easily across the street and into the jail.

The jailer was dead, clearly the first casualty inside. He'd been taken with expert knife work: a stab through the ribs followed by a slice across the throat to leave him sprawled across the short entry corridor. His blood was already sticky under Touraine's boots.

Along with blood, the place smelled like sickness. Not the clean, disciplined Balladairan prison smell she had taken for granted. Her stomach turned, and she thought about running the other way, back under the sky, but even the open air wasn't safe today. She didn't let herself think long on how many Sands weren't immune to the death pox.

"Aranen!" Touraine called. "Aranen, are you here?"

She grabbed the jailer's lamp and held it high enough to illuminate the sandstone cells as she turned into the jail's main corridor. Their metal gates were flung open like welcoming arms. The Sands weren't here, either. She passed cell after cell, afraid each time she looked that she would find the dead bodies of people she knew.

Where are you, you witch? Where are you, Pru?

Touraine spun around at the heavy rush of boots at the entrance. The clink and clatter of belts and muskets. A hoarse voice swearing in Balladairan, saying, "Clear it. Anyone not in a cell dies."

Maybe two of them, probably three. They hadn't seen her yet. She had the element of surprise. She took a deep breath, gripped her long knife tighter, and sprinted around the corner. *Poke them hard. Cut with the sharp side. Fast, fast, fast.*

She hit the closest blackcoat point-first in the stomach. The blade swooped under the barrel of the blackcoat's musket and disappeared. It came out through the soldier's back. Touraine barreled through. Her momentum pinned a second blackcoat against the wall while the first one bled out between them. She anticipated the blow from the third blackcoat behind her and ducked. Her blood-coated knife came with her. The third assailant's musket butt hit the first blackcoat's corpse in the face, while Touraine slid her blade into his side. He fell to the ground.

Touraine turned back to the second blackcoat. The woman had lost her human shield, slumped in a heap at her feet. She held her side, where Touraine's knife had nicked her through the first blackcoat's body. Her other hand hung slack around a musket, fixed bayonet gleaming in the shadows.

"Please," she whispered. Her lip trembled. Her dark eyes were wet with terror or pain.

And Touraine hesitated. This blackcoat wasn't an officer. She hadn't given the order to kill anyone outside a cell. But she was a part of this, and she had never stopped it. She was Balladaire's pawn.

So were you.

"Get out," Touraine growled in disgust that was half directed at herself. "And don't come back."

The blackcoat nodded and started to run.

"Leave the gun," Touraine barked.

The other woman dropped the musket and fled into the night. Touraine got back to her search but kept her ears open for more visitors.

She found Djasha and Aranen embracing in the last cell at the end of the corridor. Tears streaked the women's faces in the brig's lamplight. Relief weakened Touraine's knees.

"Ya, Mulāzim." Aranen pulled away from Djasha and wiped the Brigāni woman's tears away with a thumb. Aranen's usually short-clipped hair was a thicket of overgrown weeds. Her voice sounded sick and hoarse.

"We're breaking you out, if you haven't noticed," Touraine said. She would find Pruett and the rest somewhere else. Maybe Jaghotai had already freed them. She let herself hope. She couldn't bear the alternative. "Let's go."

The two older women shared a glance. "Can you make it, love?" Aranen said softly.

Only then did Touraine see how much Djasha leaned on her wife. "I can make it far enough."

Outside, shots still popped in the air, but they were slower and one-sided.

Her back ached under the contortion of supporting Djasha and carrying the dead blackcoats' muskets, but they couldn't stop.

"Go ahead," Touraine huffed. She pointed straight ahead. "The southern wall, southeast corner. I'm going to help Jaghotai."

Aranen nodded.

Around them, her soldiers—no, not her soldiers, Jaghotai's soldiers, the rebels and a handful of Sands—were dying. The growls and cries of animals outside the walls had died down, but the number of blackcoats in the compound seemed just as thick as before. She wasn't sure she had anything under control.

Djasha hadn't moved. Her feet were planted as she stared down the wide dirt road that led to the gate. The blackcoats had formed a line two rows deep and were taking turns shooting at the rebels, who used the barracks and supply building as cover. Touraine and Aranen could both see, in the flash of musket fire and torchlight, who had caught the Apostate's attention. Cantic's golden sleeve was a flag in the night.

Standing behind the line and barking orders was the Blood General. She was like a matchstick in the dark, her thin figure a dark silhouette, her blond-white hair and its flying strands like a flare. The cords of her neck bulged as she shouted to fire, load, change weapons, over and over. Firing on Touraine's people. She understood the struggle on Djasha's face.

"No." Aranen tugged Djasha's wrist, the word already broken with loss as she said it. "Djasha, come with me. Please."

Djasha took a dazed step toward Cantic anyway. Touraine threw her arm in front of Djasha to stop her, and the Brigāni woman wrapped her hand around Touraine's forearm. Touraine almost screamed at the burn of the woman's touch. She jerked her arm away.

Djasha turned back to Aranen and gripped Aranen's arms with both hands, as if her touch wasn't fire.

They spoke in Shālan too rapid for Touraine to follow, but the plaintive look on both of their faces told Touraine enough.

Then Aranen whispered, tear choked, "You're going to die."

Djasha's smile was haggard in the shadow. "I will either way. But I can finish this. Go." She pointed the same way Touraine had, forward, to the southern wall where the rebels might still be waiting for more prisoners, the injured, and the coming retreat.

"No. Together." Aranen squeezed Djasha's hand hard.

They were resolute. Touraine understood. Cantic had broken their lives. She had broken Touraine's life, too, in a way, even as she had built it. They all had some kind of unfinished business with the Blood General.

"I take it you still have Shāl's magic?" Touraine asked, holding up her burned wrist.

"I have enough."

"Then you come at her from this way. I'll loop behind that building"—Touraine pointed to the administrative building—"and come at her from the gate side. Attack when she's busy with me. Take these." She unslung the muskets. They felt cumbersome to her now. She moved better without them.

The two priestesses nodded, and Touraine took off. She ran through the empty darkness between the north wall of the compound and the jail, the command building, and the infirmary, with the noise of Cantic's line to her left. Occasionally, a wild shot from the rebels pinged the ground near her, but nothing hit flesh. She slipped through the alley between the infirmary and the command building. It was already stacked with corpses, but they were too orderly to be anything but plague deaths the soldiers hadn't taken to the fires yet.

Touraine looked back down the road, to her left, where Djasha and Aranen were waiting for her.

Cantic's back was to her right. She was flanked by a junior officer on each side, their pistols in hand, their swords on their belts. One of them was speaking to an aide, and Touraine waited for them to finish, for the officer's attention to return to the battle. Her long knife was both slick with fear sweat and sticky with blood. As the aide ran off to relay their message, Touraine finally stepped out.

The noise that had been muffled a moment ago now hit Touraine with full force. Cantic's voice was raw and ragged as she shouted orders. The yelling was interspersed with gunfire and cries of pain. They were all so busy with the fight in front of them that Touraine stabbed the junior officer to Cantic's right before anyone realized an enemy had gotten behind their lines. She stabbed the one on the left clumsily, trying to hurry as Cantic turned. The young officer staggered back, almost taking Touraine's knife with him.

"General." Touraine straightened in the middle of the street, holding her long knife en garde.

The general's open coat fluttered in the night's gentle wind. She looked at her two guards, one dying, the other hunched over, trying to get a grip on his pistol. She held out a hand to stop him.

"Lieutenant," Cantic growled. She barked at the young officer, "Take over the line. Keep the sky-falling dogs pinned." Then she turned to Touraine, drawing her officer's sword.

Touraine told herself that she was not afraid to die. She told herself that she didn't care if she died now or thirty years from now. That she didn't care if she never saw Pruett or Jaghotai or even Luca ever again. Each thought was a lie, but she acted as if she believed it. She looked up at the night sky above the compound and inhaled deeply. The dust of the desert had a distinct smell, and Touraine caught it even in the stench of battle.

Hurry, Djasha. Then she focused on the moment—and the steel—in front of her.

Another rumor the Sands had spread in their bunks long ago: Cantic had been the best sword fighter of her age, second only to the princess's guard captain. Touraine hoped that particular snatch of gossip, at least, was stretched.

"I'm sorry things will end this way, General."

Touraine tested Cantic's defenses with a jab of her long knife. She didn't have to win. She just had to buy Djasha time.

With your life?

Djasha was the reason Touraine was still alive, despite everything. She had saved Touraine's life and given her a place to belong. She'd shown Touraine mercy when she could have destroyed Touraine with the flick of a wrist. This was the least Touraine could do.

Cantic lazily parried Touraine's blade to the side.

"You've lost your mind, Lieutenant." Cantic stepped closer, her sword pointed toward the dirt. "Tell me they have some magic hold on you."

"No." *Draw this out.* She settled her weight on her back leg, coiling her power there. "More like they cleared my eyes, sir." But Touraine wasn't good with words. She wasn't like Luca, stabbing cleverly at just the right weak spots. Touraine's best weapon had always been her body.

She sprang at Cantic, knife aiming for the older woman's chest. She ducked under the expected parry, twisting under and away like Jaghotai's fighting dancers. She skipped back in again.

But Cantic had nearly fifty years of experience. If Touraine's dancing was unexpected, her face didn't show it. She blocked Touraine's strike with a subtle twist of her wrist, and her steady, icy eyes never left Touraine's. She pivoted, and her counterstrike came deceptively heavily for Touraine's head.

Touraine ducked again, felt the whip of air above her head. Fear almost turned her knees to water. As she lost her balance, she tucked, rolled, and sprang back to her feet. Close to Cantic's line of soldiers, who were still firing at the buildings on the south side of the compound. Touraine hoped Jaghotai had called a retreat by now, but the Jackal wouldn't leave until everyone was accounted for, dead or alive.

From the corner of her eye, she saw one of Cantic's blackcoats notice Touraine and the general fighting. He turned the musket he had just loaded on Touraine instead. Her blood ran cold. She remembered other musket fire, other pain, ripping through her and spilling her out in the street.

With the blackcoats to her right and Cantic to her left, Touraine was still facing where Djasha should have been coming from. The woman was sick and flagging, she knew, but if Djasha didn't show up and do her unknitting, her distraction was going to die.

Then Cantic held up her empty hand. "Hold your fire," Cantic barked at the blackcoats. "We'll take her surrender."

The few other blackcoats who had turned now hesitated. Cantic held her empty palm out to Touraine now, ready to take the hilt of her knife.

"Fuck off." Touraine hawked a gob of spit at the general's gleaming boots. The blackcoats surged forward, but Cantic held her hand up to stop them again.

"This isn't like you, Lieutenant." Cantic approached warily, like she would a rabid dog that needed putting down. Despite their quick clash, she wasn't even breathing hard. "Don't forget, I know you. I fed you, taught you, cared for you. Surrender."

Touraine blinked rapidly to keep her vision clear. All it would take was one signal from Cantic, and the blackcoats would fill her with lead. But Cantic wouldn't do that. She had always liked her students to admit their wrongs before she let them go.

Balladaire, land of honey and whips. That poisonous combination of fear and hope had kept the Sands in line for ages. Had kept *Touraine* in line for ages. Every moment of her life had been spent dodging the pain of punishment and striving for a reward from Cantic or someone like her. Including Luca. Until recently.

Since Tibeau died, since she woke up from what *should have been* her own death, Touraine had made her own choices. She was her own sword, pointed where she willed. She submitted to Djasha and even to Jaghotai because in the end, they were right. The rebellion was right. And they respected her, however begrudgingly at first.

Be the rain.

She deserved to place her own steps, and the Qazāli deserved to govern themselves. And she believed in the bonds she'd made. The bonds of the family she'd built.

"Sorry, sir. Not surrendering." Touraine ran at Cantic with the knife again.

This time, when she got close, she let Cantic focus on the incoming blade and aimed a kick at the general's knee. Cantic pivoted away at the last minute, off balance for the first time, and Touraine's blade sliced across the general's rib cage, beneath the open coat.

Cantic hissed in pain, but that was all the time she took to acknowledge the hit. Touraine scrambled to get out of the way of the master's flashing blade and was lashed by the tip. No time for fancy flips. Cantic pushed Touraine back on her heels. Each parry was desperate, each kick was frantic. Wisps of Cantic's hair stuck to her forehead with sweat. Blood glued her shirt to her torso. Sweat trailed down Touraine's own brow, too, despite the desert cold, and it stung in a dozen fresh cuts. A drop clung just above her eye, threatening to blind her with salt. And there, just there, was a shadow that was too deep to be just a shadow, creeping from behind the command building.

When the end came, Touraine didn't see it arrive.

Faster than Touraine thought Cantic could move, the general thrust her blade at Touraine's face, closing the gap with her feet at the same time. Touraine's training fled. She bent back, pulling her head away from the thrust as she raised her own knife to parry the blade clumsily away. Only, the blade was already gone.

It bit into Touraine's ankle, severing the tendon. She crashed to the ground immediately, crying out as pain shot from her toes to her hip. She felt, more than heard, Cantic's boots crunch in the dirt as the general approached her. Touraine saw the boots first, gleaming in the darkness, and then the blade of the officer's sword, wet with her own blood.

She propped herself up on her palms. Her knife. She crawled for it, dragging her bad leg behind her. Better to die with a blade in her hand.

She looked up at General Cantic from the ground.

"Surrender, Lieutenant."

Touraine wondered if she was imagining the regret in the general's voice. She focused on that voice, though, and on the aged face it came from, because there, coming from the shadows to Cantic's right—Touraine didn't dare look and give Djasha and Aranen away.

"Maybe you should surrender, General," Touraine said, holding her old mentor's eyes. She smiled. "And Shāl's mercy be on you."

A cry rang out as Djasha jumped forward in one last burst of energy. Djasha's battle cry or a blackcoat's warning or even Touraine's accidental whimper—Touraine would never know. It was lost in the flash of Djasha's pale palm in the dark, there and gone, like the shimmer of a fish belly. It flopped like a fish to the ground after Cantic severed it, almost faster than Touraine's eye could follow. And faster still, the sword sliced across the Apostate's throat in a spray of blood.

Aranen, who had been behind Djasha—so close and yet as helpless as Touraine—wailed as she rushed to her wife's side, pressing her hand uselessly against the flow of Djasha's lifeblood.

Moonlight glinted on the general's bloody sword as she raised it high for another killing blow, and Touraine surged up from the ground on her good leg. She channeled anguish into rage to mask the pain in her cut tendon, and she screamed wordlessly, knife high. Cantic turned to parry the sloppy strike, and the force of it rang all the way into Touraine's shoulder. It almost sent her sprawling again, but the blade of her knife was the only thing between Cantic's sword and Aranen's neck.

Then she heard a familiar voice calling her name.

"Lieutenant Touraine! Where are you?" Rogan's singsong voice echoed across the sudden lull in fire as the soldiers on both sides realized their commanders were fighting. Touraine wheeled around so she could get Rogan and Cantic both in her sights.

In one hand, Rogan waved a pistol against the sky. In his other, he held an iron chain connected to manacles on Pruett's wrists.

No.

Touraine looked down at Aranen cradling her dead wife. Djasha's braids were dull now, and her skin sagged where illness had taken its toll. The vibrant power that had been there just moments before was leaking out with the blood that covered Aranen's hands. Aranen, hunched over in her grief, bloody hands pressed to her mouth, then bloody lips pressed to Djasha's brow.

Somewhere, Jaghotai was—Touraine hoped—giving the order to retreat.

"Call them off," Rogan said. He aimed his pistol at Pruett's head. Difficult target to miss. "Arms above your head, on your knees. Call them off."

Touraine's shoulders slumped.

"I can't call them off," she said. "I don't command them."

"That's horseshit," he spat.

He half cocked his pistol, and the metal scrape was the loudest thing Touraine had ever heard.

"Stop!" she cried out. She fell to her knees and put her hands above her head.

"Order your men into the street," Rogan barked. "Make them drop their weapons."

"Tour, don't you fucking dare," Pruett said. "I swear on my mother's name—"

Touraine fought back tears and a helpless laugh. "Fuck that. You hate your mother." Then, wrecking her throat, she screamed as loud as she could, "It's over! Drop your weapons!" She said it in Shālan, too, for good measure.

The scattered musket fire stopped. Slowly, rebels peered around corners to see who had given the order, still deciding whether to obey or not. She cast around, looking for the rebel she most wanted. Where was Jaghotai? Jaghotai could call a retreat and save what there was left to save. Touraine would go down with the Sands and Djasha and Aranen. Jaghotai was stronger. Harder. She had nothing but Qazāl. *Let us burn.* Jaghotai deserved to survive the night. Then, one day, she would pray for rain again.

In the rebels' moment of confusion, the blackcoats were on them, beating the weapons out of their hands, cuffing them, dropping them to the ground any way they could. Someone shot at her, the musket ball pocking the earth at her side, and she flinched more out of reflex than any desire to live. It would be over soon, though, she had no doubt. Rogan's face was too smug. Two blackcoats pulled Touraine to her feet. Two more pulled Aranen away from Djasha's body.

Touraine had promised to fight for Qazāl's freedom. She had promised to be theirs, and she had kept that promise. She was ready to give her life for that promise.

Not the Sands' lives. Not Pruett's. She couldn't do this math. This was the line she couldn't cross. The Sands were her first family, and she belonged to them, despite everything between them in the last year.

Pruett stood across from her, her eyes screwed shut. Sky above. *It isn't supposed to happen like this.* The last of the rebels emerged in a trickle, hands over their heads in surrender, muskets trained on their backs. Finally, Touraine spotted Jaghotai, who held both arms high. A battlefield bandage on her long arm was already soaked through with blood. She let a blackcoat cuff her hand to a long chain that linked the rebel prisoners. The soldier kicked her in the back of the knees to drop her to the ground, in line with the others.

"Jaghotai!" Touraine didn't move toward her, but the blackcoats wrenched her arms back anyway. A blow to the head left Touraine dazed.

"Easy, Lieutenant." Rogan called Touraine's attention back to Pruett. To the pistol at Pruett's head. He cocked the pistol all the way.

Before Touraine could scream, Rogan turned the pistol onto her. The strike of the flint on steel hissed through the night air. Pain ripped through Touraine's calf, and she fell back to the ground.

"You sky-falling bastard," she growled as the man's smile spread across his face.

They had lost.

The next punch came to her temple.

CHAPTER 41

TO UNKNIT

When Gil at last permitted Luca to step outside, the compound, which had become a battlefield, was quiet. The shots she'd heard firing outside her window had ceased, and Cantic had given the all clear. The fighters' shouts had died. The prisoners—except for Touraine—were cuffed and held under guard at the far end of the compound. Balladairan soldiers dragged the dead outside the compound to be carted away and the wounded to lie outside the already overflowing sick bay. Beyond the yellow walls, the plague fires still burned; the orange glow lit the sky. As if the world had broken and the sun with it, setting on the wrong side of the sky.

Their plan had worked, but at a cost.

It smelled like blood. It wasn't coppery, like it tasted in your mouth. It was thick and heavy, mingled with voided bowels to make a stench like a thick fog that she had to push through to get to the jail.

Beneath the horror of the sight of a soldier's guts spilling from her black coat or a rebel face half blown apart by a bullet, Luca felt a disturbing thrill of relief. She had never wanted to be so vulnerable, so close to death herself—but here she was, and she had survived. She was alive, if only because she'd hid under her table in the governor's office with a caustic Beau-Sang. The comte had spent the entire attack threatening her with her uncle's reaction. As if Luca needed him to remind her of what was at stake. She'd almost thrown him out to die in the cross fire.

Luca pushed into the jail, ignoring the on-duty soldier's protests.

"Please, Your Highness, the general—"

She half turned and said over her shoulder, "Shut. Your mouth. And wait outside."

He shut his mouth. He closed the door and waited outside. It was easy to be a villain when she felt like one inside. She was hurting herself, too, and she had to give them both one last chance to save each other.

The first time she'd met Touraine in this jail, she hadn't been attached to anything here. Curious about the Sands, even more curious about the handsome soldier who'd saved her from assassins and been abducted by the rebels. The gloom had been harmless and temporary. Now a desperate tug drew her to the cell where Rogan had dumped Touraine, and the darkness pressed her on all sides, threatening to trap her.

"Touraine?" Luca whispered. Any louder, and she didn't trust her voice to stay true. She had hoped for confidence, something Touraine would have faith in. Something Touraine would not doubt.

A laugh, sharp and disbelieving. "Your Highness."

So it was back to titles, then.

"I came to check on you. To make sure...Rogan didn't hurt you."

"Hurt me?" Touraine's voice flared with the crackling rage of fire on a new log. "He threatened my old soldiers so I would hand him my new ones. And I gave them to him." Luca heard the waver of tears, too.

"The Sands were never in danger. I would never have let him hurt them. I just needed you to believe it; I needed you to stop. If it were me, you would have known I was bluffing—"

"Stop talking. You're not making this better. You used them against me."

Luca finally gathered the courage to step closer and let the narrow stream of lantern light illuminate Touraine's sharpened cheekbones, her grief-hollowed eyes. She was half-naked, and the smell of piss wafted over.

"What happened?" Luca asked sharply. "What did he do?"

"Just let me out. You've done it before."

"There are guards posted outside. You're not my prisoner."

"But I was *yours*."

The words, and the plaintive truth in them, cut her. Made her want to undo the last year entirely and fashion them so that she had another choice. She imagined them at a ball in Balladaire, dancing together, with Touraine in a fabulous suit with the right to a pistol at her hip.

"Cantic already let you go once; she won't do it again. Not after all of this. She's brittle iron—she doesn't bend. She'll break first. You know that better than I do."

"Then why are you here?"

Luca swallowed the nerves climbing up her throat like worms.

"If you recant, confess, I can keep you alive longer. A pardon from execution. You'd come to Balladaire a prisoner, but I could get you out between here and there. I'll find a way. I can't get you out of anywhere if you're dead."

"Why? You lied to me. You said you'd help us."

"I have never lied to you." The words fell softly, like the last clinging leaves before winter.

"Then what has all of this been?"

"Not a lie."

"Then why are we here?" Touraine slammed the bars of the cell with her palm. The sound rang through the empty jail. "No, I know. I know. Your precious throne."

A cold anger settled in her stomach at the judgment in Touraine's voice. Touraine had ruined Luca's first peaceful attempts to end the rebellion for a handful of soldiers, and she dared judge her for selfishness?

"I am my throne. You stupid, stupid woman. I was born to this, raised for it, and I have fought for it this year harder than I have ever fought for anything. There is more at stake here than who I want to fuck, and I have made sacrifices because of that."

Touraine's shoulder, holding her up as they danced in the circle of Qazāli. The brief moment of skin against skin in her bedroom after.

The anger and shame and arousal that washed over her the first time Touraine called her out for her pretensions.

With her head against the stone, Touraine sighed. "I've made sacrifices, too." She limped back from the cell door and lowered herself gingerly. "For the soldiers who follow me and the people who welcomed me as I am and not for how they think I'll be useful. Though I can't say I'm sure who's who."

"I'm not doing this so you'll be useful to me."

"I know. If you thought I'd be useful, I'd be free by now."

It stung worse than a slap.

"When I'm in power," Luca said, "I can make this better. Even Cantic will answer to me when I'm crowned."

"Executing a traitor and stopping the rebellion will help you get there. They'll know you're strong, efficient, and willing to do what's necessary."

"Touraine, please—"

"I hope your rule is so magnificent that this was worth it."

There was no spite in the other woman's voice, no sarcasm, only calm certainty. She could hear the unspoken words, too: *I hope you think about this moment every day you sit on that throne.*

Luca looked away. Her magnificent domain, the jail, sandstone and clay, the piss and shit of prisoners Touraine had freed. Just outside, more prisoners and the dead. Beyond that, other compounds in Qazāl, throughout the whole empire, perhaps only a breath away from catastrophe like this. She and Cantic had seen a chance, and they'd taken it. The rebels were crushed. Their gamble had paid off. Hadn't it?

"You aren't the only one who's grown here, Your Highness. If you won't compromise yourself, why should I? Why should the Qazāli wait on your mercy, wait for you to have your crown? This is their home."

"Not yours?"

Touraine tilted her head up to look at Luca. Luca shifted the lantern to better see the disdain, but there was none. She wished there were. She wished there were anything to make her feel like Touraine would fight for her life. Luca saw only a torso full of bruises, bones jutting where they shouldn't, bloody wounds wrapped in bloodier clothing. Touraine needed medical attention.

"I don't think I'll live long enough for it to be." The soldier leaned back against the wall, her right leg stretched out, her left knee pulled against her bare chest.

"Please. Think about it."

Touraine pursed her lips. She tapped at her knee with one hand. The other hand was palm up, eerily still against her other thigh.

"If you can pardon me, can you pardon them, my soldiers, the rebels?"

She'd known that would come, and she knew her answer, as well. "No. That many proven enemies—no."

"Then it's probably best not to spare even one."

"Touraine, you're not—I'm not—"

"Please, Your Highness. I'd like to pray alone."

Pray? Since when does she pray? She waited, stunned into silence, before she realized she'd been dismissed. Rejected and dismissed. Touraine always did have that tendency, of dismantling Luca and making her want more at the same time.

"Then I'll see you tomorrow. I hope your god answers your prayers." *And talks sense into you where I could not.* If that was how the gods worked.

Luca wanted to jump into the cell with that idiot woman and hold her, to stand between her and Rogan and Cantic, but she turned and started up the corridor.

"Wait! Luca!" Touraine's voice sounded so small now. "When I'm gone, do me one favor. Give Djasha a proper funeral."

The thickness in Luca's throat kept her silent as she left.

After Luca left, Touraine did try to pray. She whispered the small, easy-to-remember prayer that Aranen had taught her. She hummed the song she had always hummed. She did everything she could not to think about Luca's offer.

"Fuck you," Touraine said. The words bounced back at her.

If Luca cared for her, Touraine wouldn't be waiting to die here. Luca was smart; she was calculating. If she couldn't find a way to keep Touraine alive, it was because she didn't want it badly enough.

Luca had made an offer, though. All Touraine had to do was watch the rebels—her soldiers—die while she walked away, in chains but alive.

She wasn't in the position to do much other than die standing or surrender. Something in her shoulder was broken badly enough that she couldn't raise her right arm. She'd stanched the bleeding in her calf with cloth from her own trousers. Her other ankle, her other knee would barely hold her weight. She couldn't fight back, and no one was there to fight for her.

It wasn't that death was so hard to grapple with. Every battle she'd fought in had been possible death. It was always a roll of the dice, a chance of the cards. This time, she had been unlucky.

Still, she had meant every word she had said to Luca. For the first time, she had faced death for a reason of her choosing. She would die for Djasha's vengeance. She would die for Aranen's temple. She would die for young Ghadin and her friends. She would die here, because she chose to. She couldn't ask for more than that.

Touraine barely registered losing consciousness—no one could call the pain-addled visions of her death "sleeping"—before Rogan's voice woke her again.

"Good morning, Lieutenant. It's a beautiful day to die, don't you think?"

"Fuck you."

"I'm not interested, thank you. We have an appointment to keep."

"I'm not interested, thank you."

His pistol clicked and was echoed by a chorus of cocked muskets. "You can die down here if you'd like. I don't think that suits you."

She hated to prove him right.

Climbing to her feet and walking out of the cell helped her inventory her pain yet again. Shoulder, ankle, calf, knee, shoulder, ankle, calf, knee. A litany of injuries that distanced her from what waited.

In the brig corridor, more men yanked her arms behind her and tied them so tight her wrist bones creaked and something in her shoulder popped again, forcing out a grunt of pain. Rogan smiled. She spat on his boots—*Stop smiling, you bastard*—but he only grinned wider, his blue eyes crinkling.

Then he punched her in the side of the head, and light winked in her eyes as she staggered and fell. The brig spun.

"Make sure you get the two women she was with," he told his men without looking away from her. "When we're done, we'll display the bodies in the bazaar."

Tears burned her eyes. He wanted a reaction from her, clear as day. It was hard to know he was telling the truth and not react. She could only hope Luca would do that one thing for her. The other rebels would hang, covered in crows that pecked at the softest bits of them. They would begin to reek in the sun.

An audience waited for her in the middle of the road that split the compound. Blackcoats, some of them sick or wounded but able to stand. Balladairan civilians who worked on the compound. Civilians who didn't, who wanted the protection of the walls, who couldn't afford to flee the pox.

The compound was such a strange, hybrid place. Governed by Balladairan ideas of might and cleverness but still at the mercy of the natural laws of Qazāl—it was made of heat and dust and sand and clay. It would never be Balladaire, no matter how much wood they shipped in or stone they demanded from the quarries.

Two rows of bound figures waited in front of the crowd, some in Qazāli clothing, some still wearing the black Sands' coats. She counted nineteen. Not all of the Sands, not all of the rebels. Jaghotai was there, a musket trained on her. Aranen stood in the line of prisoners, too, staring at Cantic. Other bodies littered the compound. No one would come back for them, not after such a disaster. Not soon enough, anylight.

Any last thoughts of escape dissolved. If she fought Rogan off and somehow ran to safety, the others would have no hope.

Rogan studied her, and she willed her face into a mask like Luca's. Emotionless. Unflappable.

Luca was nowhere in sight. Anger straightened Touraine's back, and she said coolly, "Firing squad, then."

"Yes. First." He sidled closer to her. His presence rose goose bumps on her naked torso. "They won't kill you, though. Not immediately. I will shoot you myself in a noble coup de grâce." He leaned closer, the heat of his lips on her ear. "I'm going to put you down like a dog."

She stilled the shiver of fear, tried to cool the heat of her racing heart. She only had to look at the men and women she had led into this mess. It quenched everything inside her but a seed of resolve.

Rogan pushed her in front of a squad of riflemen. With the onlookers on her right and the other prisoners on her left, the space behind her was empty for missed shots. Aranen met her gaze steadily, her eyes red rimmed and glassy.

You could still run. Let Luca save you.

You are choosing this.

Aranen prayed with her eyes closed. Touraine looked up at the sky instead. Sky above.

Cantic stepped close to Touraine and spoke in a voice audible only to her. "I know the princess offered you another chance, Lieutenant. You're sure this is how you want to spend it?"

Not counting last night, it was the first time they had spoken since Touraine had leaked half of the gun stash to the general. The months in Qazāl had taken a toll on both of them. Cantic's blue eyes were bloodshot, the skin around them tight. A scarf hung low on her chin. It seemed like years ago that Touraine wanted to be just like this woman. Part of her still wanted that. From the very beginning, Cantic had represented respect and power. When Cantic was the Sands' instructor, back in Balladaire, people listened when she spoke. They had obeyed her. Touraine had obeyed her, hoping she would learn enough to follow in Cantic's footsteps.

"Did they make you do this? Tell us," Cantic hissed.

"I'm choosing this," Touraine said aloud.

Instead of becoming like Cantic, Touraine had learned enough to know that the general, too, wanted to mold her into something perfect. And perfect, to Cantic, to Beau-Sang and the lord regent, Duke Nicolas Ancier, meant not Qazāli, not any kind of Shālan. It meant Balladairan born and bred, and she would never be that, so she would never be completely worthy.

Touraine stood up straighter. She didn't need to be worthy to them.

General Cantic shook her head, like she still couldn't believe what had become of her protégé. A turncoat.

"Touraine. Ex-lieutenant of the Balladairan Colonial Brigade. Aide to Princess Luca." Cantic's voice was cold with disappointment. "You've been charged with desertion and treason. How do you plead?"

Touraine couldn't see Luca, which meant she wasn't there. She didn't know if that made her feel better or worse, didn't know if seeing Luca's face would strengthen her or break her. It was better this way.

"I didn't desert. I was made a free citizen by writ of Her Highness Luca Ancier."

Cantic's frown lines deepened. "And the charge of treason?"

"Guilty."

The general nodded to Rogan.

Five musket pans sparked powder.

Time yawned. Bullets hit her in the chest. Lung, hip. Shoulder, stomach, ankle, calf, knee—her knees gave out; her body danced. The acrid metal taste of her own blood in her mouth before it tickled down her chin. She swallowed. Coughed. Swallowed the blood back down.

Jaghotai yelled from her spot in the prisoners' line, and a soldier cracked her in the base of the skull with a musket butt in response.

Rogan approached Touraine in blurry slow motion. His own pistol cocked and pressed against her forehead. The sulfur of gunpowder. The smell of home.

For one overwhelming moment, she thought she could hear the heartbeats of everyone around her. Rapid or slow or stuttering still.

She had made her choice.

* * *

It was dawn.

Luca was due outside any minute now. As the princess, it was her right to witness sedition against her rule punished. Instead, she waited just inside the door of the command building, hand hovering over the door handle. Everyone else who wanted to witness the end of the rebellion was out there. The staff, the soldiers who were able, the civilians bitter enough or frightened enough to be awake at this hour.

Any minute now.

Any minute now, they would haul Touraine out of her cell, stand her up against the wall, and shoot her like a rabid dog. Luca could already imagine her dead. The blood in a pool beneath her body. It wouldn't spread. The thirsty earth would drink her up.

A moan wrenched out of her.

Any minute now, she would push the door open. She would walk out and take her place beside Cantic, who would ask her if she had any testimony to offer. Luca would watch Touraine shake her head, and then watch her die.

Or, if there was a kind god at all in the world—*Are you so desperate that you would pray to it, if it would grant you this thing?*—Touraine would say she was mistaken. That she had moved in misguided judgment, that she would serve penance however the crown saw fit. Luca would pardon her, and they would figure out what came next together.

A volley of coordinated shots made her hand spasm over the door handle.

No.

Luca sprinted with a foal's tangle on rubbery legs. Fifty yards in front of her, Touraine swayed on her knees. Her naked chest ran crimson and dark with blood. Captain Rogan stood with his pistol pressed against her forehead.

"Stop!"

Everyone watched Luca as she ran, awkward and in pain. They didn't matter. She crashed before she even reached Touraine, sprawling into the dust on her knees. Her subjects, noble and military and laborer, watched her crawl through the dirt to the conspirator's side.

Touraine was such a bloody mess. Her eyelids fluttered as she wavered, somehow holding herself upright.

"Where...the sky-falling fu—" She didn't finish the sentence, choking on her own blood.

Luca swallowed and pushed the pistol wide before scooping Touraine to her chest.

"You have no say in military justice, Your Highness," Cantic hissed. As if she could not wait for it to be over. *Are you as ashamed as I am?* Cantic nodded at Rogan. "Finish this."

"I said, stop." Luca stared down the barrel of the gun and into Rogan's eyes. That this horse-faced bastard should be the one to end Touraine was beyond cruel. And anylight: "All she has done, she has done for me."

Cantic hesitated. Her mouth half-open to form what words? A flicker of sorrow broke through the mask of stony command.

Touraine's blood leaked warm against Luca's pale linen shirt, blending in with the black embroidery. So warm. Too warm. Like the glow of a fire in a winter hearth.

"Sacrifices," Touraine choked out. "Must be...made."

"Touraine?"

Before the flash and the sound of a skull shattering, Touraine's eyes glowed golden.

Luca thought her heart had stopped as everything froze around her, but it hadn't. Everyone, including her, had forgotten how to breathe. The air was still; the audience was silent. Touraine, too, lay still in her arms. Utterly still.

She did not believe her eyes, which told her that Rogan's head had broken open, not Touraine's.

Then, like a wave crashing from its zenith, the entire crowd recoiled in revulsion and panic, and Luca flinched with them, spattered in gore.

The firing squad held their spent weapons, blinking in surprise. Only Cantic pulled her pistol, but there was no place to aim.

Fast, faster than anyone could reckon in their confusion, Aranen the priestess, somehow unbound from the ropes that held her, crossed the few paces separating her and the general. Aranen's eyes glowed golden, her hands and mouth were smeared with blood, and she reached to brush a palm over Cantic's cheek.

Luca didn't have time to cry out, but the general's reflexes were well honed.

Cantic pulled the trigger with the barrel of her gun against Aranen's belly. The priestess barely flinched, a slight recoil of force. She never lost contact with Cantic's skin.

Bile rose in Luca's stomach. The general's skin turned grayish and drained, while her eyes rolled into the back of her head. Blood pooled in her eyes until her eyelids overflowed; it leaked from her mouth, nose, and ears.

The brief panic halted in the face of pure shock.

In that interval of horror, Luca laid Touraine down, resting the woman's head in the dirt as gently as she could. Touraine stared at the sky, but Luca saw her eyelids flutter. Golden irises in bloodshot eyes. The relief in her heart didn't last. If Touraine died right now, Luca would hate herself forever. On the other hand, if Aranen wiped out the compound—or worse, the remaining Balladairans in the city—there would be no living with that.

She stood, good and bad leg weak and trembling, and walked to Aranen. The priestess stared at Cantic's corpse, then at her own hands. Luca held herself as straight as she could. She looked nothing like royalty, in a blood-soaked shirt and plain trousers. She probably smelled like sick, like everything else in this sky-falling compound. The broadside artists would have fun with this moment if she survived it.

"Please don't hurt anyone." She lowered her head. She didn't deserve to ask it of Aranen, of any Qazāli, but she would try.

Aranen turned to her. Her eyes had turned the dull gold of an antique. Then she made to pass Luca, and Luca flinched. Another musket fired and hit Aranen in the shoulder. Blood blossomed and spread through the dirty cloth, but as Luca watched, the wound slowly closed.

Sky above and earth below. Luca's mouth worked soundlessly until she found her voice.

"Stop!" She threw her arm out to stave off another attack.

Aranen brushed past her, but she only walked to Touraine.

Half of the audience had already fled, to barracks or for the Quartier or the city proper—wherever they could convince themselves was safe. *Nowhere. Nowhere is safe*, Luca thought.

Many of those remaining were blackcoats. She met their grim or frightened gazes with her own, whatever good the solidarity would do. "Lay down your weapons. No matter what happens, the Qazāli go free today. Rebels. Conscripts. They are not to be harmed today or any day after. We're leaving.

"Have mercy on us, Aranen." Luca spoke to Aranen's back, in Shālan. The priestess was consumed with Touraine's body, running her hands along the woman's torso and legs.

"You have cost me everything," Aranen finally said.

Luca wanted to say that it wasn't her, but Aranen didn't deserve such weakness. "I know. I'm sorry."

Aranen stood and fixed her eyes on Luca again, and Luca knew without doubt that the priestess was not the one appraising her. Every petty thought, every insecurity, every moment of cruelty was exposed. She wanted to throw herself to the ground.

The priestess stepped toward her, hand outstretched, and Luca shrank back. Cantic's dead body was barely two paces away.

Where does a queen's life weigh in the balance of her kingdom?

Aranen pressed a hand against her cheek. Luca leaned into it, eyes closed. She yielded.

Heat, or maybe light, or maybe none of that but *something* rolled through Luca's body. It coiled inside her chest, sliding between her lungs, slipping into the gaps of her intestines. It itched, a fierce tingling that made her want to rip herself apart. It shot up and down her legs, bouncing, heedless of the pain it caused her. At her heart, it felt like a caress, like a fist wrapped around her life, thinking to squeeze.

Balladaire has lost. I've lost us.

And then Aranen broke contact. Luca sagged to her knees, gasping for air. She'd been spared. Touraine's eyes were closed, her chest rising and falling steadily.

"Thank you." She rested her forehead on the ground at Aranen's feet before she could push herself back up again.

To everyone else—her people, the Sands, the rebels—she said in Balladairan, "Citizens, my countrymen. Gather yourselves. It's long past time for us to go home."

CHAPTER 42

THE RAIN (AND YET ANOTHER BROADSIDE)

Luca still hated public speaking. Her stomach flipped over and over as she dressed. She eyed her uncle's letter on the bedside table as she buttoned her shirt.

Bastien was waiting for her. He didn't fault her for his father's arrest, and he'd helped her manage affairs since the surrender. What day had it been? She would have to count back later—the day the Balladairan Empire cracked would be important for the history books. And her name next to it.

She'd sent a note to Aranen every day to see if Touraine had woken up. And every day the response had been the same. *No.* Luca wanted to delay the speech until she knew whether Touraine would stand by her side, but the city was growing restless. And even though she didn't plan to leave Qazāl until she knew Touraine's fate one way or another, the citizens of Qazāl needed to know she wasn't their ruler anymore.

She checked herself once more in the mirror. She wasn't sure she liked the gaunt woman staring back at her. That woman barely looked human, let alone like a queen. She'd finally stopped losing her meals, but food didn't appeal to her.

You're worrying too much, Gil told her repeatedly. What was too much worry, exactly?

She tossed and turned through the night. She spent the days planning how to take her own empire apart. How to let it crumble while doing the least damage.

Bastien helped her slide her arms into a light jacket cut in the Balladairan style, and then they left, Lanquette on her heels, Gil and Bastien by her side. The carriage clattered over the dirt and stones. She winced and held her head when it jostled too much.

Bastien put a hand on her knee to steady her, or perhaps to comfort her. She twitched her leg away, and he drew back. They had had... a moment in the weeks after that day. With all the work to do and Touraine on her mind, she hadn't been able to concentrate. She'd embraced the distraction.

"You don't hate me for destroying your country?" Luca asked Bastien.

He smiled. Such a gentle man. "Technically, Qazāl is my home country."

She snorted. "It won't be for long."

His eyes went soft and sad. "I know. I'm prepared to leave, but I'll wait... until you do."

Luca stiffened and looked back out the window to watch the gates as they passed through them, the worn Shālan words illegible.

"And your sister?" she asked.

"She'll stay, I think. Aliez has always gotten on well with the Qazāli. And I think she wants to see to our father's justice."

"Ah." Luca hadn't been upset to find an excuse to hand the comte over for Qazāl to determine his fate, but she had worried how Bastien would take it. When she told him, he had held silent for a moment before sniffing and saying "Good riddance" and nothing else.

Luca's headache intensified when she arrived at the bazaar and the crowd stretched in front of her. Qazāli filled the square, likely from all over the country. Word had spread, as she'd intended—the Balladairan surrender.

Uncle Nicolas didn't know the extent of what Luca planned to do today. His last letter said to hold. Do nothing drastic. It also mentioned the fate of the Balladairans who'd fled on ships in the initial wave back to Balladaire.

Thanks to your mismanagement of the colonies and your fraternization with the Qazāli—including your indiscretions with the soldier, don't think I was never informed—we had to sink all incoming Balladairan ships for quarantine measures.

So many of her people, even the healthy ones. Dead.

Uncle Nicolas had also included yet another broadside, apparently all the rage: her, kneeling with her forehead on the ground before a darker person in a Qazāli robe, clearly meant to be Aranen. *Do you see this filth?* he had written. News had already spread back to La Chaise. Splendid.

Lanquette helped her out of the carriage, and she walked up the gallows.

Several Balladairans bunched together in the crowd. The ones too poor or unlucky—lucky, rather—to miss the first wave of escape. She could tell them from pale Qazāli because of their frightened faces, like rabbits walking into a wolf den.

Luca tightened her hand on her cane and straightened.

"Peace on you all," she said in Shālan, and then in Balladairan, "Peace. Too long have we struggled against each other. Though I cannot take responsibility for every decision, I am the rightful ruler of Balladaire, and I take responsibility for all that was done in my name, in my family's name. All that I benefited and continue to benefit from. I apologize."

She had worked out some of the speech details with Bastien. She would have preferred to work them out with Touraine. Touraine knew these people. She'd fought with them. She would know the right things to say. But she was unconscious somewhere. Luca scanned the crowd for Aranen or any of the rebels. Saïd, or even that wickedly sharp Malika. She flinched as something wet landed on her nose.

"I ask your forbearance while I remain a little while longer. Some of my citizens took ill, and we must wait until they make a full recovery until we will be welcomed back home. Anyone not adhering to this armistice, anyone not treating Qazāli with the utmost respect due to another sovereign people, may be brought to my attention. I…"

She faltered. There was so much more to say, and nothing that she could say in public. Her heart slid into her throat, but she fought through it.

"Both nations have lost too many good people, too many children and parents, friends and lovers. I have learned that your god says, 'Peace above all.' So let it be."

A smattering of applause. Less than she'd hoped for, more than she had any right to expect.

The ripple of a gasp that went through the crowd and another drop on her nose were Luca's only warning. An instant later, as she walked toward the carriage, the sky opened up. She was soaked to the skin before Bastien could get the carriage door open. She pushed her sopping hair off her face and looked at Bastien's forlorn expression as he dangled his bedraggled cuffs. For the first time in a long, long while, she laughed.

CHAPTER 43

WAKING UP (REPRISE)

This time, Touraine woke up in a tent. She recognized the tightness in her body—recovering injuries. And the bone-weary exhaustion that hounded her after Aranen had healed her the first time.

"Good morning," someone beside her said in Shālan.

Touraine was too tired to jump in surprise. She rolled her head just enough to see Aranen sitting next to her pallet. The thin woman looked awful. Half-starved and haunted. Her nose was red; her lips chapped. Her knees clasped to her chest, she looked like an overgrown grasshopper. With golden eyes.

"And to you," Touraine said, automatically responding in Shālan.

Aranen's dry lips cracked as she smiled. She put a hand to Touraine's forehead. "You remember the language."

"I don't know." Touraine switched to Balladairan, struggling to piece her Shālan together. "I could sleep forever."

Aranen answered in Balladairan with a pained smile. "You almost did. And after I healed you, you were sleeping for a month. I've been keeping you...It's hard to explain."

Touraine's memories were fuzzy. She remembered her body begging to die, not much more than that.

"What did you do?"

Aranen's lips and jaw tightened, and her eyes shone. "I would rather not speak of it."

Touraine realized what she must have done, and her heart broke for the priestess.

"Who—why—" The questions came out even though she knew it was kinder to silence them. Djasha's slit throat.

"Djasha gave her life to kill that bitch. I wasn't going to let her sacrifice go to waste. If I could have slit my own wrists, I would have."

The merciless steel of Aranen's voice left Touraine stunned and terrified. "Was that . . . all?"

"No. You . . . did the same thing. To the man who was going to shoot you." She met Touraine's gaze tenderly and put a hand over Touraine's. "Are you a believer, then?"

Touraine wasn't ready to answer that question.

"Is Pruett alive? She's a Sand. Gray-blue eyes, dirty mouth?" Her tongue still felt thick, but she had to know.

"Your friend the sniper." Aranen scowled. "She's been teaching some of the kids to shoot chicken skulls from rooftops."

Pruett was alive. Touraine tried to grin but turned into her pillow as sobs of relief overwhelmed her. Aranen put a hand on her shoulder.

"I have to tell you. I've only been waiting to say goodbye. And thank you. You risked everything to save me. Djasha loved you."

Djasha. "Where—"

"We've burned her, as we do. We have that in common with Balladaire." She looked at the floor.

Touraine blinked away her own tears to study the other woman. She looked a skip away from death. "You want us to burn you, too."

Aranen looked away. "Yes."

"But . . ." Touraine was struggling to put the thoughts together, but one thing was clear. "We need you."

The priestess shook her head. "I can't. I can't anymore."

It was a few days before Touraine could walk much farther than the tent.

Jaghotai woke her early in the morning with a brusque shake.

"Come with me. There's something I want to show you."

They walked through the slums, toward the south, away from the city. Away from the compound, which was slowly emptying like a leaking water canteen.

They walked in silence for a long time, the wind whipping through their scarves and making their clothes billow around them.

"Are we going to let Aranen die?"

"We?" Jaghotai shook her head. "I can't make her want to live."

And she had tried. Touraine had heard them. Jaghotai begging for Aranen to help her put the city together. To train more priests and priestesses, to teach doctors. Begging not to be left alone.

Jaghotai sighed. "We used to build monuments to honor those who fell in great tragedies. Before Balladaire."

She pointed to the stones growing out of the dry earth like flowers. "When the Balladairans started taking the Lost Ones, their parents took stones from the quarry and dropped them out here."

Touraine stopped. There were hundreds of stones, some small as her fist, others so big it would have taken two Tibeau-sized men to carry them.

"Is there a stone for me?" she asked Jaghotai quietly.

The whip of cloth was the only response for at least a minute. They passed through the field of jagged stones—marble, sandstone, even smoothed river rocks. And then Jaghotai stopped abruptly.

Touraine followed the intense focus of the other woman—*Say it, you coward; your mother, she is your mother*—the intense focus of her mother Jaghotai's eyes.

"That?" Touraine pointed. A long brown stone, four hands wide and a whole palm thick. Heavy to carry so far.

Jaghotai sniffed, though as far as Touraine could tell, her mother's eyes were dry. "Harder than carrying you for nine months to get that fucker out here. And that was before the arm." Her voice was rougher than usual. She waved the stump of her forearm.

Touraine smiled, just barely, and they kept walking. She never thought she would mark the occasion, the first time her mother ever said, "I love you."

Another gust of wind made her blink rapidly to keep the moisture in her eyes.

After word got out that Touraine was awake and walking, she had a stream of visitors.

The day after Jaghotai showed Touraine her stone, her mother ducked into the tent with an irritated expression.

"Someone's here to see you," she said with a snort.

Touraine sighed as she pushed herself upright. "Let her in."

Jaghotai stepped out and Luca stepped in, Gil at her side. The daylight streamed in, showing Luca's tanned skin and the sun-bleached blond of her hair.

Luca gasped when she saw Touraine. "Your...eyes."

Touraine had almost forgotten. "Side effect of the other magic." She started to look down, but then she realized she didn't have the energy to be ashamed or self-conscious. She didn't give a sky-falling shit if Luca or any other Balladairan thought she was uncivilized. "I thought you'd gone back."

"I couldn't. They refused to let the first ships come close enough to dock. They fired on them as a warning, and...of course, symptoms turned up." She shook her head with bitterness. "Cantic managed to get a military ship back home before any of the passenger ships. She told them of the outbreak. Loyal, despite everything. I owe her my kingdom."

Mention of loyalty lit a spark of anger in Touraine's own chest, but weariness squashed it immediately.

"I go back to Balladaire soon." She cleared her throat. "I don't know if they told you? We're pulling out. I don't have full authority, but I'll be fighting for it as soon as I get back. I'll make it official—" She stopped herself and looked down at her boots.

Touraine didn't let her try to say it, to ask, because she knew if she let Luca ask, if she heard it from Luca's lips, it would be that much harder to say no.

"I can't come with you."

Luca bowed her head slightly. "I thought so. May I ask why?" There was no frostiness in her voice, but politeness covered the hurt. Touraine knew what she was really asking. *Is it me you don't want?*

Touraine raised her eyebrows at Gil, who looked to Luca for instructions. The princess nodded, he left, and Touraine stood.

Gil let the tent flap close behind him to give them a moment's privacy, and they were cast in darkness. Only a sliver of light remained to slice between them.

"I never thanked you for taking care of me when I got sick." Luca had given Touraine everything—sacrificed her own bed, her own clothes, risked her entire household for Touraine. The night Touraine snuck away like a thief, she'd wanted nothing more than to stay there and get better and then let Luca crawl into bed beside her.

She couldn't have that then, and she couldn't have that now. She wanted to touch Luca in reassurance. To hold her hand for just a second. That felt like too much of an empty promise.

"It was nothing." Luca's voice hid a blush.

"I started a mess in this country." This country that should have been her home. She wanted to see who she could be here, instead.

"You didn't—"

"I helped. And so did you. I want to see it fixed. The other Sands and I—we're going to do what we can."

"I see." Luca bit her lip. Then she held out her arm for a soldier's clasp. Surprised, Touraine took it weakly. Luca squeezed until Touraine was forced to strengthen her grip. "Thank you for everything, Touraine."

Touraine couldn't quite loosen her fingers, though. Her resolution was coming undone with the feel of Luca's pulse under her fingertips. Luca's fingers on her skin. Would it be so bad if she just—?

With her other hand, Touraine pulled Luca's head closer and kissed her. She smelled like rose water and sweat and ink and tasted like coffee. Touraine was breathless when they finally pulled away.

Luca looked stunned, even though one hand was still warm against Touraine's waist.

"And you're—"

"Staying."

The sun was shining, and there were joyous rain clouds on the horizon the day the Qazāli tore the gallows down.

As the last Balladairan ship filled with soldiers, and the princess left with her household, Qazāli and Brigāni and Sands alike took turns with the axes.

They hacked and cheered and sang and drank and ate and celebrated as the rain came down.

EPILOGUE

TO KNIT

Touraine sat on the rooftop that used to be Djasha and Aranen's, and watched the rain change the city. The streets were always, always, always yellow-orange muck. Touraine had stopped wearing her boots, because it was easier to wear sandals, or no shoes at all, and rinse her feet off. The city was full of people, almost claustrophobic compared to the fear-spawned emptiness of half a year earlier. Farmers and nomads and the homeless all sought shelter or dry land in the city at the top of the hill. The city wasn't especially dry, but the river hadn't swallowed it whole. Qazāl's flatlands—and Briga's on the other side—had drowned.

The river raced to devour it all, like a soldier to her rations between long marches. Touraine smiled ruefully, remembering marches with Pruett and Tibeau at her side. Before she was promoted and could order them around. Before they came here.

Someone cleared their throat behind her. Touraine recognized Pruett's rattle of phlegm. Touraine gestured to the spot on the edge of the roof next to her. Pruett's hair was slicked to her forehead, only just starting to dry. She still kept it soldier short. She looked even more dour than usual, which was saying something. Touraine hadn't seen her smile much since the Balladairans pulled out of Qazāl. Only barely when Touraine had woken from her coma.

It was possible that Pruett just didn't want to smile around Touraine.

That would have been more than fair. Tibeau was dead because of her. Touraine had cast Pruett aside for a Balladairan princess, and when Touraine cast the princess aside, she hadn't come back for Pruett.

They had tried each other again once in the last few months. Several cups of Shāl's holy water between the two of them and they fell into each other like a tongue in the groove. Even excellent craftsmanship wears under enough strain, without maintenance. They got far enough, but the touches were wrong. They fell into awkward silence after. Since then, though, the relationship had warmed. A little. It was as if knowing what they couldn't be made it easier to learn to be friends again.

At least, that's what Touraine had thought.

Pruett didn't sit. She brandished a folded letter with a black wax seal of a rearing horse. Touraine's heart leapt. She tore it open immediately. Her eagerness hurt Pruett. And yet she couldn't stop herself. The most she could do was unfold the letter more carefully. As if she hadn't been praying to Shāl and any other god for a letter from Luca. Touraine hadn't expected to miss her so much. Hadn't expected to miss her at all.

She read the first lines. The letter was exactly the kind of letter that Touraine didn't want to read in front of Pruett. She refolded it without reading any more.

"Is it bad news?" Pruett asked. The note of hope in her voice made Touraine smile. It was how Pruett had spoken to her before all of this. A strain that hadn't been there before, but the same jabs.

Touraine shook her head and peered off to the river. If she looked closely, she could imagine it had stolen a farmer's tools or a lady's basket. It was wide and hungry enough to take much more than that.

Pruett sighed and sat cross-legged just behind her, away from the edge of the roof. "She still wants you to go back."

Touraine hadn't gotten that far in the letter, but the trajectory… *Dear Touraine, I don't deserve anything of you. Not as a soldier, not as a woman.*

"Will you write back this time?"

Touraine shrugged. "How's your Shālan?"

Pruett swore in Shālan, her stormy eyes unimpressed.

"That doesn't mean bad," Touraine said. "It means a thousand—"

"I know. It's just going that fucking well. I'll be fine if you leave, though. I'll pick it up just like we picked up Balladairan." She paused to pick at her Qazāli-style trousers. "I knew it once before, didn't I?" It sounded like she was trying to convince herself.

"I missed you lot so much when she took me. I thought I'd get something out of it. Something for you, something for me. I made that mistake once. I'm sorry."

She imagined what the rest of the letter would say. The cold was wonderful; the nobles weren't behaving. She needed Touraine. Always that sense of need, and Touraine flocked to it. She loved it when her soldiers needed her, too. They didn't now. Some of the Sands had even found family.

Touraine wondered if it was worth it to them. Some of them had romanticized the idea and were disappointed now. She was one of them, disappointed not so much about her family but about the idea of a free Qazāl.

It had been a headache from moment to waking moment. Even her sleep was tormented by nightmares of Djasha's corpse urging her to rebuild the city this way, to keep this man out of power, to keep that woman away from money. She was used to nightmares, but it was too much. Jaghotai and Malika looked as haggard as Touraine felt. Touraine had had to reevaluate her judgments of Jaghotai in the months after the Rain Rebellion, as people called it now.

The council was small, with Jaghotai and Aranen at the head, though Aranen still spent most of her time in a dark room, weeping. Saïd was happy to advise but kept himself bunkered in his bookshop. Committees struggled to manage various aspects—infrastructure, filling the vacant housing, calculating what wealth, if any, the city still had.

"I can't leave until we have a system in place."

Pruett snorted. "You'll be here forever."

"Anything will be better than letting the Balladairans stay."

It was such an obvious lie that Pruett didn't bother taking it apart.

The sky opened up suddenly, as it had done every day for—the count reached three weeks again since the last dry span. They ran back inside, Touraine stuffing the letter into her shirt to keep it dry.

The rooms still held Djasha's things. Aranen wouldn't move any of it, throw anything out. Sometimes, she still cried when she cooked, and Jaghotai did, too. Even their bed was in the same corner. As much as the three rebel women had made Touraine feel at home, it wasn't her home.

She jumped when Pruett put a hand on her shoulder. "When you see her again, ask her what she thinks. Maybe she can help us."

If anyone knew how to put a country together, it would be Luca.

"She has her own country to run."

Pruett squeezed Touraine's shoulder. "Just say goodbye to me this time."

Pruett's touch lingered even after she was long gone. Touraine watched the rain as it fell. Gentle, constant, inevitable, its soft patter soothing.

Finally, Touraine turned to Luca's letter.

TELL THE WORLD THIS BOOK WAS		
GOOD	BAD	SO-SO

The story continues in...

Book Two of Magic of the Lost

ACKNOWLEDGMENTS

To the professionals who have gone above and beyond making this book happen: Mary C. Moore, my agent; Brit Hvide and Jenni Hill, my US and UK editors respectively. Thanks also to Nadia El-Fassi for the advice, Angeline Rodriguez for the wrangling. To Janice Lee for showing me the glory that is a wonderful copy editor and for making a wiki. To Lauren Panepinto for designing That Cover, and Tommy Arnold for making THAT COVER—you both brought Touraine to life in a way I never imagined possible. Thanks also to the numerous people working hard behind the scenes who I haven't met yet.

Thank you to my earliest readers: Julie, David, Yume, and especially Cairo, the first and bravest, and A.E., who did it over and over again and fielded many desperate crises of the soul.

Thank you to the teachers who taught me about the concepts, histories, languages, and cultures that shaped this novel: Samira Sayeh, Maryemma Graham, Stephanie Scurto, Giselle Anatol, Marta Caminero-Santangelo, Elizabeth Eslami, Saïd Hannouchi, Nour and Ashley (Nourshley), Azzedine, Aïcha, and Abdelaziz. And thank you to the teachers who told me to keep going: Mary Klayder and Darren Canady.

To the mentors who steered this novel closer and closer to the goal: Lara Elena Donnelly, Samrat Upadhyay, De Witt Kilgore, and Bob Bledsoe.

To Coach Bennett, whose guided runs helped me drag myself to the starting line again and again. This is about running, and this is not about running.

To the institutions and homes that made my research and travel possible: Qalam wa Lawh, Marouane, and Khadijah in Morocco; Young and Happy Hostel and Simon in Paris; Sylvia and Octavia and Shakespeare and Company, all who gave me a home and hospitality while I wrote and did research (especially David who let me wreak havoc reshelving the science fiction and fantasy section); and L'Institut du Monde Arabe.

Thank you to my cohort at Indiana, who read chapters of this over and over, especially Bix and Joe, who fed me in all ways. To Romayne, for being so unfailingly kind, always. To Black Planet and the pub and the Blind Taste Testers plus Jess for the writing dates and more. To Kelsey, who always believed this book would exist from the very beginning.

To my mother, Rachel, who wrote before me, and my grandmother Dorothy, who remembers lineages like a bard. To my father, Cedric, and stepmother, Cindy, and my grandparents Becky and Frank, who taught me to work hard and play hard. To my grandparents Darsie and Clarence, who first taught me the joy of travel.

To Sara and Jovita, who were home and heart throughout this process.

And finally, to you, the reader. *Be the rain.*

extras

orbit

meet the author

Photo Credit: Jovita McCleod

C. L. CLARK graduated from Indiana University's creative writing MFA program and was a 2012 Lambda Literary Fellow. She's been a personal trainer, an English teacher, and an editor, and is some combination thereof as she travels the world. When she's not writing or working, she's learning languages, doing P90something, or reading about war and (post)colonial history. Her short fiction has appeared in *Beneath Ceaseless Skies*, *FIYAH*, and *Uncanny*, and on *PodCastle*, where she is currently a coeditor. You can follow her on Twitter: @c_l_clark.

Find out more about C. L. Clark and other Orbit authors by registering for the free monthly newsletter at orbitbooks.net.

if you enjoyed

THE UNBROKEN

look out for

THE JASMINE THRONE

Book One of The Burning Kingdoms

by

Tasha Suri

Set in a world inspired by historical India, The Jasmine Throne *begins a sweeping new epic fantasy trilogy in which a captive princess and a servant in possession of forbidden magic become unlikely allies—and eventually, much more than allies—on a dark journey to save their empire.*

Imprisoned by her tyrannical brother, Malini spends her days in isolation in the Hirana: an ancient temple that was once the

495

source of the powerful, magical deathless waters—but is now little more than a decaying ruin.

Priya is a maidservant, one among several who make the treacherous journey to the top of the Hirana every night to clean Malini's chambers. She is happy to be an anonymous drudge, so long as it keeps anyone from guessing the dangerous secret she hides.

But when Malini accidentally bears witness to Priya's true nature, their destinies become irrevocably tangled. One is a vengeful princess seeking to claim a throne. The other is a priestess seeking to find her family. Together, they will change the fate of an empire.

PROLOGUE

CHANDRA

In the court of the imperial mahal, the pyre was being built.

The fragrance of the gardens drifted in through the high windows—sweet roses, and even sweeter imperial needle-flower, pale and fragile, growing in such thick profusion that it poured in through the lattice, its white petals unfurled against the sandstone walls. The priests flung petals on the pyre, murmuring prayers as the servants carried in wood and arranged it carefully, applying camphor and ghee, scattering drops of perfumed oil.

On his throne, Emperor Chandra murmured along with his priests. In his hands, he held a string of prayer stones, each an acorn seeded with the name of a mother of flame: Divyanshi, Ahamara,

Nanvishi, Suhana, Meenakshi. As he recited, his courtiers—the kings of Parijatdvipa's city-states, their princely sons, their bravest warriors—recited along with him. Only the king of Alor and his brood of nameless sons were notably, pointedly, silent.

Emperor Chandra's sister was brought into the court.

Her ladies-in-waiting stood on either side of her. To her left, a nameless princess of Alor, commonly referred to only as Alori; to her right, a high-blooded lady, Narina, daughter of a notable mathematician from Srugna and a highborn Parijati mother. The ladies-in-waiting wore red, bloody and bridal. In their hair, they wore crowns of kindling, bound with thread to mimic stars. As they entered the room, the watching men bowed, pressing their faces to the floor, their palms flat on the marble. The women had been dressed with reverence, marked with blessed water, prayed over for a day and a night until dawn had touched the sky. They were as holy as women could be.

Chandra did not bow his head. He watched his sister.

She wore no crown. Her hair was loose—tangled, trailing across her shoulders. He had sent maids to prepare her, but she had denied them all, gnashing her teeth and weeping. He had sent her a sari of crimson, embroidered in the finest Dwarali gold, scented with needle-flower and perfume. She had refused it, choosing instead to wear palest mourning white. He had ordered the cooks to lace her food with opium, but she had refused to eat. She had not been blessed. She stood in the court, her head unadorned and her hair wild, like a living curse.

His sister was a fool and a petulant child. They would not be here, he reminded himself, if she had not proven herself thoroughly unwomanly. If she had not tried to ruin it all.

The head priest kissed the nameless princess upon the forehead. He did the same to Lady Narina. When he reached for Chandra's sister, she flinched, turning her cheek.

The priest stepped back. His gaze—and his voice—were tranquil.

"You may rise," he said. "Rise, and become mothers of flame."

His sister took her ladies' hands. She clasped them tight. They stood, the three of them, for a long moment, simply holding one another. Then his sister released them.

The ladies walked to the pyre and rose to its zenith. They kneeled.

His sister remained where she was. She stood with her head raised. A breeze blew needle-flower into her hair—white upon deepest black.

"Princess Malini," said the head priest. "You may rise."

She shook her head wordlessly.

Rise, Chandra thought. *I have been more merciful than you deserve, and we both know it.*

Rise, sister.

"It is your choice," the priest said. "We will not compel you. Will you forsake immortality, or will you rise?"

The offer was a straightforward one. But she did not move. She shook her head once more. She was weeping, silently, her face otherwise devoid of feeling.

The priest nodded.

"Then we begin," he said.

Chandra stood. The prayer stones clinked as he released them. Of course it had come to this.

He stepped down from his throne. He crossed the court, before a sea of bowing men. He took his sister by the shoulders, ever so gentle.

"Do not be afraid," he told her. "You are proving your purity. You are saving your name. Your honor. Now. *Rise.*"

One of the priests had lit a torch. The scent of burning and camphor filled the court. The priests began to sing, a low song that filled the air, swelled within it. They would not wait for his sister.

But there was still time. The pyre had not yet been lit.

As his sister shook her head once more, he grasped her by the skull, raising her face up.

He did not hold her tight. He did not harm her. He was not a monster.

"Remember," he said, voice low, drowned out by the sonorous song, "that you have brought this upon yourself. Remember that you have betrayed your family and denied your name. If you do not rise... sister, remember that you have chosen to ruin yourself, and I have done all in my power to help you. Remember that."

The priest touched his torch to the pyre. The wood, slowly, began to burn.

Firelight reflected in her eyes. She looked at him with a face like a mirror: blank of feeling, reflecting nothing back at him but their shared dark eyes and serious brows. Their shared blood and shared bone.

"My brother," she said. "I will not forget."

CHAPTER ONE

PRIYA

Someone important must have been killed in the night.

Priya was sure of it the minute she heard the thud of hooves on the road behind her. She stepped to the roadside as a group of guards clad in Parijati white and gold raced past her on their horses, their sabers clinking against their embossed belts.

She drew her pallu over her face—partly because they would expect such a gesture of respect from a common woman, and partly to avoid the risk that one of them would recognize her—and watched them through the gap between her fingers and the cloth.

When they were out of sight, she didn't run. But she did start walking very, very fast. The sky was already transforming from milky gray to the pearly blue of dawn, and she still had a long way to go.

The Old Bazaar was on the outskirts of the city. It was far enough from the regent's mahal that Priya had a vague hope it wouldn't have been shut yet. And today, she was lucky. As she arrived, breathless, sweat dampening the back of her blouse, she could see that the streets were still seething with people: parents tugging along small children; traders carrying large sacks of flour or rice on their heads; gaunt beggars, skirting the edges of the market with their alms bowls in hand; and women like Priya, plain ordinary women in even plainer saris, stubbornly shoving their way through the crowd in search of stalls with fresh vegetables and reasonable prices.

If anything, there seemed to be even *more* people at the bazaar than usual—and there was a distinct sour note of panic in the air. News of the patrols had clearly passed from household to household with its usual speed.

People were afraid.

Three months ago, an important Parijati merchant had been murdered in his bed, his throat slit, his body dumped in front of the temple of the mothers of flame just before the dawn prayers. For an entire two weeks after that, the regent's men had patrolled the streets on foot and on horseback, beating or arresting Ahiranyi suspected of rebellious activity and destroying any market stalls that had tried to remain open in defiance of the regent's strict orders.

The Parijatdvipan merchants had refused to supply Hirana-prastha with rice and grain in the weeks that followed. Ahiranyi had starved.

Now it looked as though it was happening again. It was natural for people to remember and fear; remember, and scramble to buy what supplies they could before the markets were forcibly closed once more.

Priya wondered who had been murdered this time, listening for any names as she dove into the mass of people, toward the green banner on staves in the distance that marked the apothecary's stall. She passed tables groaning under stacks of vegetables and sweet fruit, bolts of silky cloth and gracefully carved idols of the yaksa for family shrines, vats of golden oil and clarified butter. Even in the faint early-morning light, the market was vibrant with color and noise.

The press of people grew more painful.

She was nearly to the stall, caught in a sea of heaving, sweating bodies, when a man behind her cursed and pushed her out of the way. He shoved her hard with his full body weight, his palm heavy on her arm, unbalancing her entirely. Three people around her were knocked back. In the sudden release of pressure, she tumbled down onto the ground, feet skidding in the wet soil.

The bazaar was open to the air, and the dirt had been churned into a froth by feet and carts and the night's monsoon rainfall. She felt the wetness seep in through her sari, from hem to thigh, soaking through draped cotton to the petticoat underneath. The man who had shoved her stumbled into her; if she hadn't snatched her calf swiftly back, the pressure of his boot on her leg would have been agonizing. He glanced down at her—blank, dismissive, a faint sneer to his mouth—and looked away again.

Her mind went quiet.

In the silence, a single voice whispered, *You could make him regret that.*

There were gaps in Priya's childhood memories, spaces big enough to stick a fist through. But whenever pain was inflicted on her—the humiliation of a blow, a man's careless shove, a fellow servant's cruel laughter—she felt the knowledge of how to cause equal suffering unfurl in her mind. Ghostly whispers, in her brother's patient voice.

This is how you pinch a nerve hard enough to break a handhold. This is how you snap a bone. This is how you gouge an eye. Watch carefully, Priya. Just like this.

This is how you stab someone through the heart.

She carried a knife at her waist. It was a very good knife, practical, with a plain sheath and hilt, and she kept its edge finely honed for kitchen work. With nothing but her little knife and a careful slide of her finger and thumb, she could leave the insides of anything—vegetables, unskinned meat, fruits newly harvested from the regent's orchard—swiftly bared, the outer rind a smooth, coiled husk in her palm.

She looked back up at the man and carefully let the thought of her knife drift away. She unclenched her trembling fingers.

You're lucky, she thought, *that I am not what I was raised to be.*

The crowd behind her and in front of her was growing thicker. Priya couldn't even see the green banner of the apothecary's stall any longer. She rocked back on the balls of her feet, then rose swiftly. Without looking at the man again, she angled herself and slipped between two strangers in front of her, putting her small stature to good use and shoving her way to the front of the throng. A judicious application of her elbows and knees and some wriggling finally brought her near enough to the stall to see the apothecary's face, puckered with sweat and irritation.

The stall was a mess, vials turned on their sides, clay pots upended. The apothecary was packing away his wares as fast as he could. Behind her, around her, she could hear the rumbling noise of the crowd grow more tense.

"Please," she said loudly. "Uncle, *please*. If you've got any beads of sacred wood to spare, I'll buy them from you."

A stranger to her left snorted audibly. "You think he's got any left? Brother, if you do, I'll pay double whatever she offers."

"My grandmother's sick," a girl shouted, three people deep behind them. "So if you could help me out, uncle—"

Priya felt the wood of the stall begin to peel beneath the hard pressure of her nails.

"Please," she said, her voice pitched low to cut across the din.

But the apothecary's attention was raised toward the back of the crowd. Priya didn't have to turn her own head to know he'd caught sight of the white and gold uniforms of the regent's men, finally here to close the bazaar.

"I'm closed up," he shouted out. "There's nothing more for any of you. Get lost!" He slammed his hand down, then shoved the last of his wares away with a shake of his head.

The crowd began to disperse slowly. A few people stayed, still pleading for the apothecary's aid, but Priya didn't join them. She knew she would get nothing here.

She turned and threaded her way back out of the crowd, stopping only to buy a small bag of kachoris from a tired-eyed vendor. Her sodden petticoat stuck heavily to her legs. She plucked the cloth, pulling it from her thighs, and strode in the opposite direction of the soldiers.

On the farthest edge of the market, where the last of the stalls and well-trod ground met the main road leading to open farmland and scattered villages beyond, was a dumping ground.

The locals had built a brick wall around it, but that did nothing to contain the stench of it. Food sellers threw their stale oil and decayed produce here, and sometimes discarded any cooked food that couldn't be sold.

When Priya had been much younger she'd known this place well. She'd known exactly the nausea and euphoria that finding something near rotten but *edible* could send spiraling through a starving body. Even now, her stomach lurched strangely at the sight of the heap, the familiar, thick stench of it rising around her.

Today, there were six figures huddled against its walls in the meager shade. Five young boys and a girl of about fifteen—older than the rest.

Knowledge was shared between the children who lived alone in the city, the ones who drifted from market to market, sleeping on the verandas of kinder households. They whispered to each other the best spots for begging for alms or collecting scraps. They passed word of which stallholders would give them food out of pity, and which would beat them with a stick sooner than offer even an ounce of charity.

They told each other about Priya, too.

If you go to the Old Bazaar on the first morning after rest day, a maid will come and give you sacred wood, if you need it. She won't ask you for coin or favors. She'll just help. No, she really will. She won't ask for anything at all.

The girl looked up at Priya. Her left eyelid was speckled with faint motes of green, like algae on still water. She wore a thread around her throat, a single bead of wood strung upon it.

"Soldiers are out," the girl said by way of greeting. A few of the boys shifted restlessly, looking over her shoulder at the tumult of the market. Some wore shawls to hide the rot on their necks and arms—the veins of green, the budding of new roots under skin.

"They are. All over the city," Priya agreed.

"Did a merchant get his head chopped off again?"

Priya shook her head. "I know as much as you do."

The girl looked from Priya's face down to Priya's muddied sari, her hands empty apart from the sack of kachoris. There was a question in her gaze.

"I couldn't get any beads today," Priya confirmed. She watched the girl's expression crumple, though she valiantly tried to control it. Sympathy would do her no good, so Priya offered the pastries out instead. "You should go now. You don't want to get caught by the guards."

The children snatched the kachoris up, a few muttering their thanks, and scattered. The girl rubbed the bead at her throat with her knuckles as she went. Priya knew it would be cold under her hand—empty of magic.

If the girl didn't get hold of more sacred wood soon, then the next time Priya saw her, the left side of her face would likely be as green-dusted as her eyelid.

You can't save them all, she reminded herself. *You're no one. This is all you can do. This, and no more.*

Priya turned to leave—and saw that one boy had hung back, waiting patiently for her to notice him. He was the kind of small that suggested malnourishment; his bones too sharp, his head too large for a body that hadn't yet grown to match it. He had his shawl over his hair, but she could still see his dark curls, and the deep green leaves growing between them. He'd wrapped his hands up in cloth.

"Do you really have nothing, ma'am?" he asked hesitantly.

"Really," Priya said. "If I had any sacred wood, I'd have given it to you."

"I thought maybe you lied," he said. "I thought, maybe you haven't got enough for more than one person, and you didn't want to make anyone feel bad. But there's only me now. So you can help me."

"I really am sorry," Priya said. She could hear yelling and footsteps echoing from the market, the crash of wood as stalls were closed up.

The boy looked like he was mustering up his courage. And sure enough, after a moment, he squared his shoulders and said, "If you can't get me any sacred wood, then can you get me a job?"

She blinked at him, surprised.

"I—I'm just a maidservant," she said. "I'm sorry, little brother, but—"

"You must work in a nice house, if you can help strays like us," he said quickly. "A big house with money to spare. Maybe your masters need a boy who works hard and doesn't make much trouble? That could be me."

"Most households won't take a boy who has the rot, no matter how hardworking he is," she pointed out gently, trying to lessen the blow of her words.

"I know," he said. His jaw was set, stubborn. "But I'm still asking."

Smart boy. She couldn't blame him for taking the chance. She was clearly soft enough to spend her own coin on sacred wood to help the rot-riven. Why wouldn't he push her for more?

"I'll do anything anyone needs me to do," he insisted. "Ma'am, I can clean latrines. I can cut wood. I can work land. My family is—they were—farmers. I'm not afraid of hard work."

"You haven't got anyone?" she asked. "None of the others look out for you?" She gestured in the vague direction the other children had vanished.

"I'm alone," he said simply. Then: *"Please."*

A few people drifted past them, carefully skirting the boy. His wrapped hands, the shawl over his head—both revealed his rot-riven status just as well as anything they hid would have.

"Call me Priya," she said. "Not ma'am."

"Priya," he repeated obediently.

"You say you can work," she said. She looked at his hands. "How bad are they?"

"Not that bad."

"Show me," she said. "Give me your wrist."

"You don't mind touching me?" he asked. There was a slight waver of hesitation in his voice.

"Rot can't pass between people," she said. "Unless I pluck one of those leaves from your hair and eat it, I think I'll be fine."

That brought a smile to his face. There for a blink, like a flash of sun through parting clouds, then gone. He deftly unwrapped one of his hands. She took hold of his wrist and raised it up to the light.

There was a little bud, growing up under the skin.

It was pressing against the flesh of his fingertip, his finger a too-small shell for the thing trying to unfurl. She looked at the tracery of green visible through the thin skin at the back of his hand, the fine lace of it. The bud had deep roots.

She swallowed. Ah. Deep roots, deep rot. If he already had leaves in his hair, green spidering through his blood, she couldn't imagine that he had long left.

"Come with me," she said, and tugged him by the wrist, making him follow her. She walked along the road, eventually joining the flow of the crowd leaving the market behind.

"Where are we going?" he asked. He didn't try to pull away from her.

507

"I'm going to get you some sacred wood," she said determinedly, putting all thoughts of murders and soldiers and the work she needed to do out of her mind. She released him and strode ahead. He ran to keep up with her, dragging his dirty shawl tight around his thin frame. "And after that, we'll see what to do with you."

The grandest of the city's pleasure houses lined the edges of the river. It was early enough in the day that they were utterly quiet, their pink lanterns unlit. But they would be busy later. The brothels were always left well alone by the regent's men. Even in the height of the last boiling summer, before the monsoon had cracked the heat in two, when the rebel sympathizers had been singing anti-imperialist songs and a noble lord's chariot had been cornered and burned on the street directly outside his own haveli—the brothels had kept their lamps lit.

Too many of the pleasure houses belonged to highborn nobles for the regent to close them. Too many were patronized by visiting merchants and nobility from Parijatdvipa's other city-states—a source of income no one seemed to want to do without.

To the rest of Parijatdvipa, Ahiranya was a den of vice, good for pleasure and little else. It carried its bitter history, its status as the losing side of an ancient war, like a yoke. They called it a backward place, rife with political violence, and, in more recent years, with the rot: the strange disease that twisted plants and crops and infected the men and women who worked the fields and forests with flowers that sprouted through the skin and leaves that pushed through their eyes. As the rot grew, other sources of income in Ahiranya had dwindled. And unrest had surged and swelled until Priya feared it too would crack, with all the fury of a storm.

As Priya and the boy walked on, the pleasure houses grew less grand. Soon, there were no pleasure houses at all. Around her were cramped homes, small shops. Ahead of her lay the edge of the forest. Even in the morning light, it was shadowed, the trees a silent barrier of green.

Priya had never met anyone born and raised outside Ahiranya who was not disturbed by the quiet of the forest. She'd known maids raised in Alor or even neighboring Srugna who avoided the place entirely. "There should be noise," they'd mutter. "Birdsong. Or insects. It isn't natural."

But the heavy quiet was comforting to Priya. She was Ahiranyi to the bone. She liked the silence of it, broken only by the scuff of her own feet against the ground.

"Wait for me here," she told the boy. "I won't be long."

He nodded without saying a word. He was staring out at the forest when she left him, a faint breeze rustling the leaves of his hair.

Priya slipped down a narrow street where the ground was uneven with hidden tree roots, the dirt rising and falling in mounds beneath her feet. Ahead of her was a single dwelling. Beneath its pillared veranda crouched an older man.

He raised his head as she approached. At first he seemed to look right through her, as though he'd been expecting someone else entirely. Then his gaze focused. His eyes narrowed in recognition.

"You," he said.

"Gautam." She tilted her head in a gesture of respect. "How are you?"

"Busy," he said shortly. "Why are you here?"

"I need sacred wood. Just one bead."

"Should have gone to the bazaar, then," he said evenly. "I've supplied plenty of apothecaries. They can deal with you."

509

"I tried the Old Bazaar. No one has anything."

"If they don't, why do you think I will?"

Oh, come on now, she thought, irritated. But she said nothing. She waited until his nostrils flared as he huffed and rose up from the veranda, turning to the beaded curtain of the doorway. Tucked in the back of his tunic was a heavy hand sickle.

"Fine. Come in, then. The sooner we do this, the sooner you leave."

She drew the purse from her blouse before climbing up the steps and entering after him.

He led her to his workroom and bid her to stand by the table at its center. Cloth sacks lined the corners of the room. Small stoppered bottles—innumerable salves and tinctures and herbs harvested from the forest itself—sat in tidy rows on shelves. The air smelled of earth and damp.

He took her entire purse from her, opened the drawstring and adjusted its weight in his palm. Then he clucked, tongue against teeth, and dropped it onto the table.

"This isn't enough."

"You—of course it's enough," Priya said. "That's all the money I have."

"That doesn't magically make it enough."

"That's what it cost me at the bazaar last time—"

"But you couldn't get anything at the bazaar," said Gautam. "And had you been able to, he would have charged you more. Supply is low, demand is high." He frowned at her sourly. "You think it's easy harvesting sacred wood?"

"Not at all," Priya said. *Be pleasant*, she reminded herself. *You need his help.*

"Last month I sent in four woodcutters. They came out after two days, thinking they'd been in there *two hours*. Between—that," he said, gesturing in the direction of the forest, "and the regent flinging his thugs all over the fucking city for who knows what reason, you think it's easy work?"

"No," Priya said. "I'm sorry."

But he wasn't done quite yet.

"I'm still waiting for the men I sent this week to come back," he went on. His fingers were tapping on the table's surface—a fast, irritated rhythm. "Who knows when that will be? I have plenty of reason to get the best price for the supplies I have. So I'll have a proper payment from you, girl, or you'll get nothing."

Before he could continue, she lifted her hand. She had a few bracelets on her wrists. Two were good-quality metal. She slipped them off, placing them on the table before him, alongside the purse.

"The money and these," she said. "That's all I have."

She thought he'd refuse her, just out of spite. But instead, he scooped up the bangles and the coin and pocketed them.

"That'll do. Now watch," he said. "I'll show you a trick."

He threw a cloth package down on the table. It was tied with a rope. He drew it open with one swift tug, letting the cloth fall to the sides.

Priya flinched back.

Inside lay the severed branch of a young tree. The bark had split, pale wood opening up into a red-brown wound. The sap that oozed from its surface was the color and consistency of blood.

"This came from the path leading to the grove my men usually harvest," he said. "They wanted to show me why they couldn't fulfill the regular quota. Rot as far as the eye could see, they told me." His own eyes were hooded. "You can look closer if you want."

"No, thank you," Priya said tightly.

"Sure?"

"You should burn it," she said. She was doing her best not to breathe the scent of it in too deeply. It had a stench like meat.

He snorted. "It has its uses." He walked away from her, rooting through his shelves. After a moment, he returned with another cloth-wrapped item, this one only as large as a fingertip. He unwrapped it, careful to keep from touching what it held. Priya could feel the heat rising from the wood within: a strange, pulsing warmth that rolled off of its surface with the steadiness of a sunbeam.

Sacred wood.

She watched as Gautam held the shard close to the rot-struck branch, as the lesion on the branch paled, the redness fading. The stench of it eased a little, and Priya breathed gratefully.

"There," he said. "Now you know it is fresh. You'll get plenty of use from it."

"Thank you. That was a useful demonstration." She tried not to let her impatience show. What did he want—awe? Tears of gratitude? She had no time for any of it. "You should still burn the branch. If you touch it by mistake…"

"I know how to handle the rot. I send men into the forest every day," he said dismissively. "And what do you do? Sweep floors? I don't need your advice."

He thrust the shard of sacred wood out to her. "Take this. And leave."

She bit her tongue and held out her hand, the long end of her sari carefully drawn over her palm. She rewrapped the sliver of wood up carefully, once, twice, tightening the fabric, tying it off with a neat knot. Gautam watched her.

"Whoever you're buying this for, the rot is still going to kill them," he said, when she was done. "This branch will die even if I wrap it in a whole shell of sacred wood. It will just die slower. My professional opinion for you, at no extra cost." He threw the cloth back over the infected branch with one careless flick of his fingers. "So don't come back here and waste your money again. I'll show you out."

He shepherded her to the door. She pushed through the beaded curtain, greedily inhaling the clean air, untainted by the smell of decay.

At the edge of the veranda there was a shrine alcove carved into the wall. Inside it were three idols sculpted from plain wood, with lustrous black eyes and hair of vines. Before them were three tiny clay lamps lit with cloth wicks set in pools of oil. Sacred numbers.

She remembered how perfectly she'd once been able to fit her whole body into that alcove. She'd slept in it one night, curled up tight. She'd been as small as the orphan boy, once.

"Do you still let beggars shelter on your veranda when it rains?" Priya asked, turning to look at Gautam where he stood, barring the entryway.

"Beggars are bad for business," he said. "And the ones I see these days don't have brothers I owe favors to. Are you leaving or not?"

Just the threat of pain can break someone. She briefly met Gautam's eyes. Something impatient and malicious lurked there. *A knife, used right, never has to draw blood.*

But ah, Priya didn't have it in her to even threaten this old bully. She stepped back.

What a big void there was, between the knowledge within her and the person she appeared to be, bowing her head in respect to a petty man who still saw her as a street beggar who'd risen too far, and hated her for it.

"Thank you, Gautam," she said. "I'll try not to trouble you again."

She'd have to carve the wood herself. She couldn't give the shard as it was to the boy. A whole shard of sacred wood held against skin—it would burn. But better that it burn her. She had no gloves, so she would have to work carefully, with her little knife and a piece of cloth to hold the worst of the pain at bay. Even now, she could feel the heat of the shard against her skin, soaking through the fabric that bound it.

The boy was waiting where she'd left him. He looked even smaller in the shadow of the forest, even more alone. He turned to watch her as she approached, his eyes wary, and a touch uncertain, as if he hadn't been sure of her return.

Her heart twisted a little. Meeting Gautam had brought her closer to the bones of her past than she'd been in a long, long time. She felt the tug of her frayed memories like a physical ache.

Her brother. Pain. The smell of smoke.

Don't look, Pri. Don't look. Just show me the way.

Show me—

No. There was no point remembering that.

It was only sensible, she told herself, to help him. She didn't want the image of him, standing before her, to haunt her. She didn't want to remember a starving child, abandoned and alone, roots growing through his hands, and think, *I left him to die. He asked me for help, and I left him.*

"You're in luck," she said lightly. "I work in the regent's mahal. And his wife has a very gentle heart, when it comes to orphans. I should know. She took me in. She'll let you work for her if I ask nicely. I'm sure of it."

His eyes went wide, so much hope in his face that it was almost painful to look at him. So Priya made a point of looking away. The sky was bright, the air overly warm. She needed to get back.

"What's your name?" she asked.

"Rukh," he said. "My name is Rukh."

if you enjoyed
THE UNBROKEN

look out for

SON OF THE STORM

Book One of The Nameless Republic

by

Suyi Davies Okungbowa

The first book in a major new epic fantasy series, set in a world inspired by the empires of precolonial West Africa.

In the thriving city of Bassa, Danso is a clever but disillusioned scholar who longs for a life beyond the rigid family and political obligations expected of the city's elite. A way out presents itself when Lilong, a skin-changing warrior, shows up wounded in his barn. She comes from the Nameless Islands, which, according to

Bassa lore, don't exist—and neither should the mythical magic of ibor she wields.

Now swept into a conspiracy far beyond his understanding, Danso will set out on a journey with Lilong that reveals histories violently suppressed and magic only found in lore.

CHAPTER ONE

DANSO

The rumours broke slowly but spread fast, like bushfire from a raincloud. Bassa's central market sparked and sizzled, as word jumped from lip to ear, lip to ear, speculating. The people responded minimally at first: a shift of the shoulders, a retying of wrappers. Then murmurs rose, until they matured into a buzzing that swept through the city, swinging from stranger to stranger and stall to stall, everyone opening conversation with whispers of *Is it true? Has the Soke Pass really been shut down?*

Danso waded through the clumps of gossipers, sweating, cursing his decision to go through the central market rather than the mainway. He darted between throngs of oblivious citizens huddled around vendors and spilling into the pathway.

"Leave way, leave way," he called, irritated, as he shouldered through bodies. He crouched, wriggling his lean frame underneath a large table that reeked of pepper seeds and landfowl shit. The ground, paved with baked earth, was not supposed to be wet, since harmattan season was soon to begin. But some fool had dumped water in the wrong place, and red mud eventually found a way into Danso's sandals. Someone else had abandoned a huge stack of yam sacks right in the middle of the pathway and gone off to do moons knew what, so that Danso was forced to clamber over yet another obstacle. He found a large brown stain on his wrappers thereafter. He wiped at the spot with his elbow, but the stain only spread.

Great. Now not only was he going to be the late jali novitiate, he was going to be the dirty one, too.

If only he could've ridden a kwaga through the market, Danso thought. But markets were foot traffic only, so even though jalis or their novitiates barely ever moved on foot, he had to in this instance. On this day, when he needed to get to the centre of town as quickly as possible while raising zero eyebrows, he needed to brave the shortest path from home to city square, which meant going through Bassa's most motley crowd. This was the price he had to pay for missing the city crier's call three whole times, therefore setting himself up for yet another late arrival at a mandatory event—in this case, a Great Dome announcement.

Missing this impromptu meeting would be his third infraction, which could mean expulsion from the university. He'd already been given two strikes: first, for repeatedly arguing with Elder Jalis and trying to prove his superior intelligence; then more recently, for being caught poring over a restricted manuscript that was supposed to be for only two sets of eyes: emperors, back when Bassa still had them, and the archivist scholars who didn't even get to read them except while scribing. At this rate, all they needed was a reason to send him away. Expulsion would definitely lose him favour with Esheme, and if anything happened to their intendedship as a result, he could consider his life in this city officially over. He would end up exactly like his daa—a disgraced outcast—and Habba would die first before that happened.

The end of the market pathway came within sight. Danso burst out into mainway one, the smack middle of Bassa's thirty mainways that criss-crossed one another and split the city perpendicular to the Soke mountains. The midday sun shone brighter here. Though shoddy, the market's thatch roofing had saved him from some of the tropical sun, and now out of it, the humid heat came down on him unbearably. He shaded his eyes.

In the distance, the capital square stood at the end of the mainway. The Great Dome nestled prettily in its centre, against a backdrop of Bassai rounded-corner mudbrick architecture, like a god surrounded by its worshipers. Behind it, the Soke mountains stuck their raggedy heads so high into the clouds that they could be seen from every spot in Bassa, hunching protectively over the mainland's shining crown.

What took his attention, though, was the crowd in the mainway, leading up to the Great Dome. The wide street was packed full of mainlanders, from where Danso stood to the gates of the courtyard in the distance. The only times he'd seen this much of a gathering was when, every once in a while, troublemakers who called themselves the Coalition for New Bassa staged protests that mostly ended in pockets of riots and skirmishes with Bassai civic guards. This, however, seemed quite nonviolent, but that did nothing for the air of tension that permeated the crowd.

The civic guards at the gates weren't letting anyone in, obviously—only the ruling councils; government officials and ward leaders; members of select guilds, like the jali guild he belonged to; and civic guards themselves were allowed into the city centre. It was these select people who then took whatever news was disseminated to their various wards. Only during a mooncrossing festival were regular citizens allowed into the courtyard.

Danso watched the crowd for a while to make a quick decision. The thrumming vibe was clearly one of anger, perplexity, and anxiety. He spotted a few people wailing and rolling in the dusty red earth, calling the names of their loved ones—those stuck outside of the Pass, he surmised from their cries. Since First Ward was the largest commercial ward in Bassa, businesses at the sides of the mainway were hubbubs of hissed conversation, questions circulating under breaths. Danso caught some of the whispers, squeaky with tension: *The drawbridges over the moats? Rolled up. The border gates? Sealed, iron barriers driven into the earth. Only a ten-person team of earthworkers and ironworkers can open it.* The pace of their speech was frantic, fast, faster, everyone wondering what was true and what wasn't.

Danso cut back into a side street that opened up from the walls along the mainway, then cut into the corridors between private yards. Up here in First Ward, the corridors were clean, the ground was of polished earth, and beggars and rats did not populate here as they did in the outer wards. Yet they were still dark and largely unlit, so that Danso had to squint and sometimes reach out to feel before him. Navigation, however, wasn't a problem. This wasn't his first dance in the mazy corridors of Bassa, and this wasn't the first time he was taking a shortcut to the Great Dome.

Some househands passed by him on their way to errands, blending into the poor light, their red immigrant anklets clacking as they went. These narrow walkways built into the spaces between courtyards were natural terrain for their caste— Yelekute, the lower of Bassa's two indentured immigrant castes. The nation didn't really fancy anything undesirable showing up in all the important places, including the low-brown complexion that, among other things, easily signified desert-landers. The more desired high-brown Potokin were the chosen desertlanders allowed on the mainways, but only in company of their employers.

Ordinarily, they wouldn't pay him much attention. It wasn't a rare sight to spot people of other castes dallying in one back-yard escapade or another. But today, hurrying past and drip-ping sweat, they glanced at Danso as he went, taking in his yellow-and-maroon tie-and-dye wrappers and the fat, single plait of hair in the middle of his head, the two signs that indi-cated he was a jali novitiate at the university. They considered his complexion—not dark enough to be wearing that dress in the first place; hair not curled tightly enough to be pure mainlander—and concluded, *decided*, that he was not Bassai enough.

This assessment they carried out in a heartbeat, but Danso was so used to seeing the whole process happen on people's faces that he knew what they were doing even before they did. And as always, then came the next part, where they tried to put two and two together to decide what caste he belonged to. Their confused faces told the story of his life. His clothes and hair plait said *jali novitiate*, that he was a scholar-historian enrolled at the University of Bassa, and therefore had to be an Idu, the only caste allowed to attend said university. But his too-light complexion said *Shashi caste*, said he was of a poi-soned union between a mainlander and an outlander and that even if the moons intervened, he would always be a disgrace to the mainland, an outcast who didn't even deserve to stand there and exist.

Perhaps it was this confusion that led the households to go past him without offering the requisite greeting for Idu caste members. Danso snickered to himself. If belonging to both the highest and lowest castes in the land at the same time taught one anything, it was that when people had to choose where to place a person, they would always choose a spot beneath them.

He went past more househands who offered the same response, but he paid little heed, spatially mapping out where he could emerge closest to the city square. He finally found the exit he was looking for. Glad to be away from the darkness, he veered into the nearest street and followed the crowd back to the mainway.

The city square had five iron pedestrian gates, all guarded. To his luck, Danso emerged just close to one, manned by four typical civic guards: tall, snarling, and bloodshot-eyed. He made for it gleefully and pushed to go in.

The nearest civic guard held the gate firmly and frowned down at Danso.

"Where you think you're going?" he asked.

"The announcement," Danso said. "Obviously."

The civic guard eyed Danso over, his chest rising and falling, his low-black skin shiny with sweat in the afternoon heat. Civic guards were Emuru, the lower of the pure mainlander caste, but they still wielded a lot of power. As the caste directly below the Idu, they could be brutal if given the space, especially if they believed one belonged to any of the castes below them.

"And you're going as what?"

Danso lifted an eyebrow. "Excuse me?"

The guard looked at him again, then shoved Danso hard, so hard that he almost fell back into the group of people standing there.

"Ah!" Danso said. "Are you okay?"

"Get away. This resemble place for ruffians?" His Mainland Common was so poor he might have been better off speaking Mainland Pidgin, but that was the curse of working within proximity of so many Idu: speaking Mainland Pidgin around them was almost as good as a crime. Here in the inner wards, High Bassai was accepted, Mainland Common was tolerated, and Mainland Pidgin was punished.

"Look," Danso said. "Can you not see I'm a jali novi—"

"I cannot see anything," the guard said, waving him away. "How can you be novitiate? I mean, look at you."

Danso looked over himself and suddenly realised what the man meant. His tie-and-dye wrappers didn't, in fact, look like they belonged to any respectable jali novitiate. Not only had he forgotten to give them to Zaq to wash after guild class the day before, the market run had only made them worse. His feet were dusty and unwashed, his arms, and probably face, were crackled, dry, and smeared with harmattan dust. One of his sandal straps had pulled off. He ran a hand over his head and sighed. Experience should have taught him by now that his sparser hair, much of it inherited from his maternal Ajabo-islander side, never stayed long in the Bassai plait, which was designed for hair that curled tighter naturally. Running around without a firm new plait had produced the unintended results: half of it had come undone, which made him look unprepared, disrespectful, and not at all like any jali anyone knew.

And of course, there had been no time to take a bath, and he had not put on any sort of decent facepaint either. He'd also arrived without a kwaga. What manner of jali novitiate *walked* to an impromptu announcement such as this, and without a Second in tow for that matter?

He should really have listened for the city crier's ring.

"Okay, wait, listen," Danso said, desperate. "I was late. So I took the corridors. But I'm really a jali novitiate."

"I will close my eye," the civic guard said. "Before I open it, I no want to see you here."

"But I'm supposed to be here." Danso's voice was suddenly squeaky, guilty. "I *have* to go in there."

"Rubbish," the man spat. "You even steal that cloth or what?"

Danso's words got stuck in his throat, panic suddenly gripping him. Not because this civic guard was an idiot—oh, no, just he wait until Danso reported him—but because so many things were going to go wrong if he didn't get in there immediately.

First, there was Esheme, waiting for him in there. He could already imagine her fuming, her lips set, frown stuck in place. It was unheard of for intendeds to attend any capital square gathering alone, and it was worse that they were both novitiates—he of the scholar-historians, she of the counsel guild of mainland law. His absence would be easily noticed. She had probably already sat through most of the meeting craning her neck to glance at the entrance, hoping he would come in and ensure she didn't have to suffer that embarrassment. He imagined Nem, her maa, and how she would cast him the same dissatisfied look as when she sometimes told Esheme, *You're really too good for that boy*. If there was anything his daa hated, it was disappointing someone as influential as Nem in any way. He might be of guild age, but his daa would readily come for him with a guava stick just for that, and his triplet uncles would be like a choir behind him going *ehen, ehen, yes, teach him well, Habba*.

His DaaHabba name wouldn't save him this time. He could be prevented from taking guild finals, and his whole life—and that of his family—could be ruined.

"I will tell you one last time," the civic guard said, taking a step toward Danso so that he could almost smell the dirt of the man's loincloth. "If you no leave here now, I will arrest you for trying to be novitiate."

He was so tall that his chest armour was right in Danso's face, the branded official emblem of the Nation of Great Bassa—the five ragged peaks of the Soke mountains with a warrior atop each, holding a spear and runku—staring back at him.

He really couldn't leave. He'd be over, done. So instead, Danso did the first thing that came to mind. He tried to slip past the civic guard.

It was almost as if the civic guard had expected it, as if it was behaviour he'd seen often. He didn't even move his body. He just stretched out a massive arm and caught Danso's clothes. He swung him around, and Danso crumbled into a heap at the man's feet.

The other guards laughed, as did the small group of people by the gate, but the civic guard wasn't done. He feinted, like he was about to lunge and hit Danso. Danso flinched, anticipatory, protecting his head. Everyone laughed even louder, boisterous.

"Ei Shashi," another civic guard said, "You miss yo way? Is over there." He pointed west, toward Whudasha, toward the coast and the bight and the seas beyond them, and everyone laughed at the joke.

Every peal was another sting in Danso's chest as the word pricked him all over his body. *Shashi. Shashi. Shashi.*

It shouldn't have gotten to him. Not on this day, at least. Danso had been Shashi all his life, one of an almost non-existent pinch in Bassa. He was the first Shashi to make it into a top guild since the Second Great War. Unlike every other Shashi sequestered away in Whudasha, he was allowed to sit side by side with other Idu, walk the nation's roads, go to its university, have a Second for himself, and even be joined to one of its citizens. But every day he was always reminded, in case he had forgotten, of what he really was—never enough. Almost there, but never complete. That lump should have been easy to get past his throat by now.

And yet, something hot and prideful rose in his chest at this laughter, and he picked himself up, slowly.

As the leader turned away, Danso aimed his words at the man, like arrows.

"Calling me Shashi," Danso said, "yet you *want* to be me. But you will always be less than bastards in this city. You can never be better than me."

What happened next was difficult for Danso to explain. First, the civic guard turned. Then he moved his hand to his waist where his runku, the large wooden club with a blob at one end, hung. He unclipped its buckle with a click, then moved so fast that Danso had no time to react.

There was a shout. Something hit Danso in the head. There was light, and then there was darkness.

Danso awoke to a face peering at his. It was large, and he could see faint traces left by poorly healed scars. A pain beat in his temple, and it took him a while for the face to come into full focus.

Oboda. Esheme's Second.

The big man stood up, silent. Oboda was a bulky man with just as mountainous a presence. Even his shadow took up space, so much so that it shaded Danso from the sunlight. The coral pieces embedded into his neck, in a way no Second Danso knew ever had, glinted. He didn't even wear a migrant anklet or anything else that announced that he was an immigrant. The only signifier was his complexion: just dark enough as a desertlander to be acceptably close to the Bassai Ideal's yardstick—the complexion of the humus, that which gave life to everything and made it thrive. Being high-brown while possessing the build and skills of a desert warrior put him squarely in the higher Potokin caste. Oboda, as a result, was allowed freedoms many immigrants weren't, so he ended up being not quite Esheme's or Nem's Second, but something more complex, something that didn't yet have a name.

Danso blinked some more. The capital square behind Oboda was filled, but now with a new crowd, this one pouring out of the sectioned entryway arches of the Great Dome and heading for their parked travelwagons, kept ready by various households and stablehands. Wrappers of various colours dotted the scene before him, each council or guild representing themselves properly. He could already map out those of the Elders of the merchantry guild in their green-and-gold combinations, and Elders of other guilds in orange, blue, bark, violet, crimson. There were even a few from the university within sight, scholars and jalis alike, in their white robes.

Danso shrunk into Oboda's shadow, obscuring himself. It would be a disaster for them to see him like this. It would be a disaster for *anyone* to see him so. *But then*, he thought, *if Oboda is here, that means Esheme . . .*

"Danso," a woman's voice said.

Oh moons!

Delicately, Esheme gathered her clothes in the crook of one arm and picked her way toward him. She was dressed in tie-and-dye wrappers just like his, but hers were of different colours—violet dappled in orange, the uniform for counsel novitiates of mainland law—and a far cry from his: hers were washed and dipped in starch so that they shone and didn't even flicker in the breeze.

As she came forward, the people who were starting to gather to watch the scene gazed at her with wide-eyed appreciation.

Esheme was able to do that, elicit responses from everything and everyone by simply *being*. She knew exactly how to play to eyes, knew what to do to evoke the exact reactions she wanted from people. She did so now, swaying just the right amount yet keeping a regal posture so that she was both desirable and fearsome at once. The three plaited arches on her head gleamed in the afternoon sun, the deep-yellow cheto dye massaged into it illuminating her head. Her high-black complexion, dark and pure in the most desirable Bassai way, shone with superior fragrant shea oils. She had her gaze squarely on Danso's face so that he couldn't look at her, but had to look down.

She arrived where he sat, took one sweeping look at the civic guards and said, "What happened here?"

"I was trying to attend the announcement and this one"— Danso pointed at the nearby offending civic guard—"hit me with his runku."

She didn't respond to him, not even with a glance. She just kept staring at the civic guards. The three behind the errant civic guard stepped away, leaving him in front.

"I no hit anybody, oh," the man said, his pitch rising. "The crowd had scatter, and somebody hit him with their elbow—"

Esheme silenced him with a sharp finger in the air. "Speak wisely, guard. You have this one chance."

The man gulped, suddenly looking like he couldn't make words.

"Sorry," he said, going to ground immediately, prostrating. "Sorry, please. No send me back. No send me back."

The other civic guards joined their comrade in solidarity, all prostrating on the ground before Esheme. She turned away from them, leaned in and examined Danso's head and clothes with light touches, like one would a child who had fallen and hurt themselves.

"Who did this to him?"

"Sorry, maa," the civic guards kept saying, offering no explanation. "Sorry, maa."

Oboda moved then, swiftly, light on his feet for someone so big. He reached over with one arm, pulled the errant guard by his loincloth and yanked him over the low gate. The man came sprawling. His loincloth gave way, and he scrambled to cover his privates. The gathering crowd, always happy to feast their eyes and ears on unsanctioned justice, snickered.

"Beg," Oboda growled. The way he said it, it was really *Beg for your life*, but he was a man of too few words to use the whole sentence. However, the rest of the sentence was not lost on anyone standing there, the civic guard included. He hustled to his knees and put his forehead on the ground, close to Esheme's sandals. Even the crowd stepped back a foot or two.

Danso flinched. Surely this had gone past the territory of fairness, had it not? This was the point where he was supposed to jump in and prevent things from escalating, to explain that no, the man might not have hit him at all, that he was actually likelier to have fallen in the scramble. But then what good reason would he have for missing this meeting? Plus, with Esheme, silence *always* had a lower chance of backfiring than speaking up did.

He kept his lips tight together and looked down. *Why throw good food away?* as his daa would always say.

"You don't know what you have brought on yourself," Esheme said to the guard quietly, then turned away. As she did, Oboda put his hand on his waist and unclipped his own runku, but Esheme laid a hand gently on his.

"Let's go," she said to no one in particular and walked off. Oboda clipped his runku back, gave the civic guards one last long look of death, and pulled Danso up with one arm as if flicking a copper piece. Danso dusted off his shins while Oboda silently handed him a cloth to wipe his face. The civic guard stayed bowed, shaking, too scared to rise.

Danso hurried off to join Esheme in the exiting crowd, spotting her greeting a couple of councilhands. He stood far off from her for a moment, and she ignored him for as long as she could, until she turned and wordlessly walked over to him, adjusted his wrappers, re-knotted them at the shoulder, then led him by the arm.

"Let's do this," she said.

orbit

Follow us:

f /orbitbooksUS

/orbitbooks

/orbitbooks

Join our mailing list
to receive alerts on our
latest releases and deals.

orbitbooks.net

Enter our monthly
giveaway for the chance
to win some epic prizes.

orbitloot.com